THE SHARPE
COMPANION

By Bernard Cornwell

The Sharpe novels
(in chronological order)

SHARPE'S TIGER
Richard Sharpe and the Siege of Seringapatam (1799)

SHARPE'S TRIUMPH
Richard Sharpe and the Battle of Assaye (1803)

SHARPE'S FORTRESS
Richard Sharpe and the Siege of Gawilghur (1803)

SHARPE'S TRAFALGAR
Richard Sharpe and the Battle of Trafalgar (1805)

SHARPE'S RIFLES
Richard Sharpe and the French Invasion of Galicia (1809)

SHARPE'S EAGLE
Richard Sharpe and the Talavera Campaign (1809)

SHARPE'S GOLD
Richard Sharpe and the Destruction of Almeida (1810)

SHARPE'S BATTLE
Richard Sharpe and the Battle of Fuentes de Oñoro (1811)

SHARPE'S COMPANY
Richard Sharpe and the Siege of Badajoz (1812)

SHARPE'S SWORD
Richard Sharpe and the Salamanca Campaign (1812)

SHARPE'S ENEMY
Richard Sharpe and the Defence of Portugal (1812)

SHARPE'S HONOUR
Richard Sharpe and the Vitoria Campaign (1813)

SHARPE'S REGIMENT
Richard Sharpe and the Invasion of France (1813)

SHARPE'S SIEGE
Richard Sharpe and the Winter Campaign (1814)

SHARPE'S REVENGE
Richard Sharpe and the Peace of 1814

SHARPE'S WATERLOO
Richard Sharpe and the Waterloo Campaign (1815)

SHARPE'S DEVIL
Richard Sharpe and the Emperor (1820–21)

The Starbuck Chronicles

REBEL

COPPERHEAD

BATTLE FLAG

THE BLOODY GROUND

STONEHENGE: A NOVEL OF 2000 BC

By Mark Adkin

THE SHARPE
COMPANION

A detailed historical and military guide
to Bernard Cornwell's bestselling
series of Sharpe novels

MARK ADKIN

HarperCollins*Publishers*

HarperCollins*Publishers*
77–85 Fulham Palace Road,
Hammersmith, London W6 8JB

www.**fire**and**water**.com

Published by HarperCollins*Publishers* 2000
1 3 5 7 9 8 6 4 2

First published in Great Britain by
HarperCollins*Publishers* 1998

ISBN 0 00 257158 7

Drawings by Ken Lewis

Set in Postscript Linotype Minion

Printed and bound in Great Britain by
Caledonian International Book Manufacturing Ltd, Glasgow

Contents

List of Plates

The Duke of Wellington (*National Portrait Gallery*)
Napoleon Bonaparte (*V & A Picture Library*)
The assault on the breach at Seringapatam (*Hulton Getty*)
A modern view of the 'dungeons' of the Sultan Battery (*Bernard Cornwell*)
Tippoo's famous working model of a tiger (*Hulton Getty*)
The principal Peninsular War generals
Some of the British, French and Prussian weapons used at Waterloo (© *Pitkin Unichrome by Newberry Smith Photography*)
French dragoons ambushed in the streets of Madrid (*Hulton Getty*)
The Battle of Vimiero (*Peter Newark's Historical Pictures*)
Tom Plunkett of the 95th Foot (*Peter Newark's Military Pictures*)
The seminary and cathedral at Santiago de Compostela (*Hulton Getty*)
The Battle of Talavera (*Hulton Getty*)
The Portuguese town of Torres Vedras (*Hulton Getty*)
The Battle of Fuentes de Onoro (*Mary Evans Picture Library*)
The bridge in Fuentes de Onoro (from *Wellington in the Peninsula* © Jac Weller, 1962. *Reproduced courtesey of Greenhill Books*)

The assault on the 'Great Breach' at Ciudad Rodrigo (*Hulton Getty*)
The Forlorn Hope of the 4th Division (*Mary Evans Picture Library*)
The escalade of the walls at Badajoz (*Peter Newark's Military Pictures*)
The bridge and cathedral at Salamanca (*Hulton Getty*)
Inside the Irish College at Salamanca today (© *Richard Rutherford-Moore, Midas Battlefield Tours*)
The Battle of Vitoria (*Hulton Getty*)
British cavalry get in amongst the French baggage carts (*Mary Evans Picture Library*)
The crush of carriages struggling to leave Vitoria (*Peter Newark's Military Pictures*)
King George IV when Prince of Wales (*British Museum*)
A cartoon of the period showing the Duke of York (*National Army Museum*)
'Slender Billy', the Prince of Orange, later King William II of Holland (*V & A Picture Library*)

List of Maps, Sketches and Diagrams

MAPS

SKETCHES

DIAGRAMS

Abbreviations Used in Text

The Sharpe Books (in historical chronological order)

ST	Sharpe's Tiger
STr	Sharpe's Triumph
SR	Sharpe's Rifles
SE	Sharpe's Eagle
SG	Sharpe's Gold
SB	Sharpe's Battle
SC	Sharpe's Company
SS	Sharpe's Sword
SEn	Sharpe's Enemy
SH	Sharpe's Honour
SRegt	Sharpe's Regiment
SSge	Sharpe's Siege
SRev	Sharpe's Revenge
SW	Sharpe's Waterloo
SD	Sharpe's Devil

Symbols used on Maps

	British	Portuguese	Spanish	French
Infantry				
Company				
Battalion				
Regiment				
Brigade				
Division				
Cavalry				
Squadron				
Regiment				
Brigade				
Division				
Artillery				
Battery				
Others				
Fortresss				
Town				
Sharpe				

Foreword

I had long considered writing a companion book to the Sharpe series, a book that would describe his army and the battles he endured, but with the indolence that comes naturally to authors, I never did. Now I am glad, for I could never have produced a book so authoritative and comprehensive as this one which Mark Adkin has written.

This, then, is the real story of Sharpe and his army. In truth, that army needs no make-believe heroes, for it was a most astonishing force that achieved extraordinary things beneath the greatest general Britain, and arguably the world, has ever produced. It was my early interest in Wellington that prompted a lifelong fascination with his men and led to the creation of Sharpe, a man of whom Wellington would have roundly disapproved. He did not like officers who had come up from the ranks ('they always take to drink'), and he was suspicious of men who sought fame through heroic action, preferring those steady officers who did their duty stoically, fought efficiently and brought their men safe out of battle's dangers. Wellington is the supreme technician of war, understanding only too well that for lack of a nail a kingdom can be lost. His public face was cool, even cold, he had no small talk for those outside his circle of intimates, and his wit was dry (to Queen Victoria, who wondered how to rid the Crystal Palace of sparrows trapped inside its vast glass roof, 'try sparrow hawks, Ma'am'). He was deeply suspicious of emotional displays; when a regiment cheered his belated arrival onto a battlefield he told their commander to quieten them, for men who cheered him one day could jeer him the next. He liked propriety, order, common sense and he hated waste, disorder and unnecessary flummery. He fought in a plain civilian coat, while Nelson, with whom he is often compared, died smothered with diamonds and stars.

Usually, when the two are compared, Nelson is deemed the more attractive man, for history's greatest admiral had the common touch, knew how to talk to sailors, understood how to manipulate their emotions and was not afraid to show his own. Yet Wellington too provoked loyalty, even affection. More folk lined the streets of London to watch his cortege pass than stood to watch Princess Diana's and if that comparison is a little unfair, it still reminds us that Wellington, though he shunned adulation nevertheless received it. He did it, like Nelson, by winning victories and he did it, too, by his care for his men. Wellington detested unnecessary casualties. In time, I think, he abhorred war itself, recognising its necessity, but hating its cruelties, which is why, when he waged war, he took infinite pains to mitigate its horrors. Nor was he unemotional. He was moved to tears by the pitiless cruelty of a field after battle, but the tears were shed in private.

Which is why it often seems to me that Sharpe would have been much better suited as one of the Emperor's men. Napoleon did not care about casualties ('what are a million men to me?') but he cared about renown and the glory of war, and it was glorious, even if the plumes and pennants did end up in blood-stained mud. Napoleon loved upstarts, gutter fighters like André Masséna, the 'wharf rat' from Nice who became a Marshal of the Empire, Duke of Rivoli and Prince of Essling. Sharpe is precisely the kind of soldier the Emperor wanted and promoted and doubtless Sharpe, if he had been French, would have risen faster and higher, but he would have lost in the end because he would have had to face an apparently cold technician who wore no braid on his coat but won battles anyway.

I have dwelt on Wellington because he is the other hero of the Sharpe books; remote from Sharpe, of course, but always there, a reluctant patron whose genius Sharpe recognises. In 1803, at the battle of Assaye, Wellington (then Sir Arthur Wellesley) was unhorsed and, in the chaos and dust of that Indian battlefield, he was very nearly killed. No one knows precisely what happened because, typically, Wellington never spoke of the incident, but his reticence offers an opening to the historical novelist and so I have Sharpe handily nearby to save the general's life. That happy circumstance ties the two together until Waterloo, indeed, beyond, and though the relationship is ever prickly, it seems to work.

So the Sharpe novels allow a fictional hero to dog Wellington's footsteps, which means I have a duty to be as accurate as possible in my depiction of the Indian campaigns, the Peninsular War and the Waterloo Campaign. It is a duty I do not always fulfil. There are, regrettably, errors in the books and some readers are kind enough to point them out to me. Thus, in a fit of absentmindedness, I claimed the 12th Regiment of the Foot was from Kent and received a chiding, but gentle, letter from the Royal Anglian Regiment telling me what I should already have known, that the 12th came from Suffolk. There are plenty of other such errors, and some will be revealed in the pages that follow, so I will make a defence here, even if it is a paltry defence. I am not a historian but a storyteller. If you want to know what really happened at Salamanca or at Quatre Bras or in the breaches of Gawilghur, you should read a historian's account. But if you want a story, with villains and heroes, hopes and fears and with what life so rarely provides, a resolution, then you will do well to read a novelist. Which does not spare me the duty of getting things right, but I fear that in the throes of storytelling some details get ignored. My fault. Other errors are deliberate. No British soldier got through the breaches at Badajoz and so formidable were the French defences and the obstacles placed in those breaches that even in daylight, after the city's fall, the paths through the wall were reckoned insurmountable. Yet the drama of Badajoz was at its starkest in those awful breaches and so Sharpe, who is burdened with the responsibility of being a hero, had to get through.

Heroes live impossible lives. No riflemen served in the ranks of a redcoat regiment, yet Sharpe and his men do, for otherwise they could not take part in some of the great dramas of those years, and no regiment was so exposed to continual danger as the fictional South Essex. Sharpe and his unit hop from brigade to brigade and division to division, in a most unlikely manner, all so that they can be manoeuvred into maximum danger. The result, I hope, is a picture of Wellington's career from a fictional angle; picaresque, over-the-top, but I trust, exciting, and if it persuades some readers to find out for themselves what really happened by reading the works of historians, then that is a bonus. This book is a splendid place to start, for it takes us behind Sharpe's fictional exploits to the real world of the redcoats in India, Portugal, Spain and France. That world was harsh, uncomfortable and frequently lethal, but the achievements of that army make for a compelling and inspiring story. Mark Adkin explains it all marvellously. Read on.

BERNARD CORNWELL
Chatham, Massachusetts

INTRODUCTION

What is The Sharpe Companion?

FIRSTLY, WHAT IT IS NOT: it is not a rehash or summary of the Sharpe books, neither is it an abbreviated military history of the Peninsular War. It is a book which aims to be a companion, a friend, to every Sharpe enthusiast. It guides, explains and helps to understand what Sharpe achieved in his twenty-two years as a soldier. To rise from private to major (discounting his four weeks on the staff as a lieutenant-colonel in a Dutch regiment during the Waterloo campaign) was outstanding – but not unique. Serving almost continually in the field for the six years of the Peninsular War made him one of the most experienced infantry officers of his day, but dozens of men received (eventually, if they lived long enough) more clasps to their campaign medal.

Sharpe is a fascinating hero; his exploits are bewildering in their variety and bloody in their execution, but they are not impossible. In writing this book, I have dissected the battles he fought in, pored over maps to plot his movements and locate the places he visited. Only once was I unable to relate his activities to actual events: in May 1813, when Major Sharpe was commanding a wing of the *S. Essex* and must have been on the Agueda River rather than the Tormes near Salamanca. Apart from this, it was always feasible to position even fictional places on the map where they would have been. It was often possible to put dates, even times, to his doings with considerable confidence. As I progressed, my admiration grew for Sharpe's creator, Bernard Cornwell. He succeeded brilliantly and accurately in interweaving fictional adventures with historical fact. This *Companion* shows you how.

The book can be used in a variety of ways. It can be read with equal enjoyment and value either before or after reading a Sharpe book. If before, it will surely whet the reader's appetite for his adventures; if after, it will provide an understanding of the significance, in military terms, of what he did or achieved. It may also encourage the reader to dig more deeply into the immensely exciting world of Napoleonic military history. *The Sharpe Companion* can be read from cover to cover, or dipped into at will; chapters can be read out of sequence, or it can be used as a work of reference for explanation or elaboration. It is about 80 per cent fact and 20 per cent fiction. So that the reader can tell one from the other, *fictional people and places have their names in italics*, with the exception of Sharpe himself. Each Sharpe book has a chapter (with the same title) in the *Companion*. Boxes, marginal notes, maps, sketches and diagrams supplement the main text, and there is a comprehensive glossary.

The first two chapters concentrate on Sharpe and the regiments in which he served. Chapter 1 is a potted biography of his life: his background, boyhood and military career. It is elaborated by comments, and some sifting of detail, to provide the reader with useful information on Sharpe's activities in all those years at war – for example, how many men he killed, how many times he was wounded, what medals he won. Chapter 2 looks at the British army of the early nineteenth century, in particular infantry regiments and battalions. An understanding of how the *S. Essex* was organised, officered, and drilled increases the enjoyment of its exploits. A basic knowledge of the weapons it used and faced or of the tactics of the day make it easier to appreciate why the battalion failed so miserably at *Valdelacasa* but triumphed at Talavera. Because Sharpe was a light infantryman by temperament and training, was so proud of his time in the 95th Rifles (although all of it was spent in the non-combatant appointment of quartermaster) and because he always wore his tattered dark green jacket, Chapter 2 includes a quick look at that Regiment.

The later chapters start with a quick synopsis of what the

corresponding Sharpe book contained. A hint of what he did, what battles he participated in, and an indication of what was happening in the war at the time. This serves to remind those who may have forgotten what the story was about or to give those who have not read it enough understanding of events. The main text of the *Companion* explains the background to Sharpe's activities in the context of the campaign, describes their significance and introduces real people who influenced Sharpe directly or indirectly. In other words, it superimposes Sharpe's fictional undertakings on what was really happening. Where a major battle takes place, the *Companion* gives an insight into the opposing commanders' plans and problems, highlights of the main events and shows how Sharpe and the *S. Essex* participated.

The boxes and marginal notes are often anecdotal, and are intended to add flavour to the meal. Frequently (but not always), they are related to something, or somebody, in the Sharpe book. For example, in Chapter 3 (*Sharpe's Tiger*) we know he is flogged. This is of considerable interest, but it would unbalance the chapter to go into great detail or repeat what happened in the book. Two boxes on flogging are therefore included. One elaborates on the number of lashes awarded, and discusses whether Sharpe's commanding officer exceeded his authority in imposing 2000. The other describes a case where a real soldier received and survived 700 lashes. In Chapter 15 (*Sharpe's Waterloo*), although not specifically linked to Sharpe, there is a box on Napoleon's carriage and how it was equipped as a mobile headquarters. There is also a marginal note on an officer named Clark Kennedy, who fought at Waterloo and whose descendant was my company commander at Sandhurst. Both are asides perhaps, but contribute to the interest of the story.

Since this book was first published in 1998 some of Sharpe's earlier exploits in India during the Second Mahratta War, which started in 1803, have been revealed in more detail. We now know exactly why Wellesley, as he then was, gave Sharpe a commission in the 74th Foot. *Sharpe's Triumph* sees Sergeant Sharpe, still of the 33rd Foot but detached on special duties, at the storming of the fortress town of Ahmednuggur. About six weeks later, in September 1803, the fortunes of war place Sharpe alongside Wellesley as his orderly at the Battle of Assaye – a battle Wellington always considered his finest victory, even over Waterloo. Although this book does not have a separate chapter on *Sharpe's Triumph* the statistics of his killings and wounds have been incorporated into Chapter 1, as have brief details of his exploits.

Similarly, Ensign Sharpe's adventures in *Sharpe's Fortress* have only the briefest of mentions. In this book Sharpe participates in the battle of Argaum (November 1803) and the attack on the virtually unassailable fortress at Gawilghur two weeks later. This was the end of the campaign and of Sharpe's active soldiering in India. However, his adventures in 1805 have recently been revealed in *Sharpe's Trafalgar* and there is every reason to hope that more of his earlier career will be described in further publications.

I make no apologies for the number of maps included. It is frustrating, if not impossible, to follow military events without the aid of a map. Sharpe's movements, marches, skirmishes and battles are illustrated in them, and nearly all chapters have at least two. The first is a campaign map which shows Sharpe's movements and route (sometimes a fictional location) superimposed on what was happening in the campaign. All of his activities are highlighted with an 'S'. The second is a battle map which depicts the fighting and how Sharpe and the S. Essex participated. For Waterloo, however, I have used a panoramic sketch instead. For the sieges of Ciudad Rodrigo and Badajoz (Chapter 8) there are, in addition to maps, sketches which represent Sharpe's view of these cities from the siege lines.

Finally, there is the glossary, where abbreviations have been used extensively to save space. The glossary gives, quickly and accessibly, additional information on a person, place, event or military term. It includes virtually all the characters featured in the books or the *Companion* (fictional and factual). In some cases only a line is needed, while in others, such as the entries for *Sergeant Harper* or *Sergeant Hakeswill*, a fairly full biography is required. All the entries covering fictional personalities also indicate the book(s) in which they feature.

Of considerable assistance in compiling this book were the worknotes, technical guidelines and historical characterisations written by Richard 'Rifleman' Moore (Military & Technical Adviser, Sharpe Film Ltd. 1991–97) used in the making of Sharpe, the television series. I much appreciate his generosity.

I want to express my sincere thanks to Bernard Cornwell for being so supportive, encouraging, and complimentary. I am considerably in his debt for the help he has given and, crucially, for his initial agreement to my taking on the task. I hope the *Companion* does justice to his splendid creation – Richard Sharpe. The many months I have spent marching and fighting alongside Sharpe have been a stimulating experience, and writing this book has been rewarding and enjoyable. My hope is that every time a Sharpe enthusiast now picks up, or considers picking up, one of Bernard's splendid books he or she will also reach for the *Companion*.

1

⚜

Sharpe

GENERAL

Richard Sharpe was an exceptional soldier, even by the standards of his day. At forty-two years of age, he had personally killed sixty-five men, mostly in close-quarter combat. These are confirmed kills, where there is no doubt that his opponent died at the time. It is possible only to guess the butcher's bill for his entire career. On countless occasions in battles, sieges, skirmishes large and small, Sharpe hacked, slashed and bayoneted his adversaries, and many must have succumbed later to the wounds he inflicted. They are impossible to count. He also shot his enemies, although his heavy cavalry sword was the weapon with which he did the real damage (forty of the sixty-five known kills). His total tally cannot have been far short of a hundred before he finally hung his sword over the fireplace of his Normandy farm. Few weapons have had so bloody a history.

Not all his victims were killed in battle. He shot two prisoners in cold blood (*SB* – see Abbreviations used in text and glossary, p. 275), murdered a fellow officer (*SE*), killed four civilians, including a priest (the latter in *SB*), shot a fellow officer at his request (*SS*), finished off the execution of his bitter enemy *Sergeant Hakeswill* (*SEn*), slit the throat of four men (one when he was only fifteen), hacked three to death with an axe (*SS*) and drowned another (*SB*). Sharpe could be merciless, could kill for revenge, and he fought dirty – to win.

He was a big man, but not huge in the way *Sergeant Patrick Harper* was huge. He was 6 feet 1 inch tall, and weighed about twelve stone. This was bone and muscle, not a hint of flab. In this he was typical of virtually every infantry soldier in the Peninsula with more than a few months' active service. Their hardness, toughness and fitness far surpassed the soldiers of any modern army, with the possible exception of special forces. At thirty-seven, in the summer of 1814, Sharpe, though still hard and healthy, had a severely battered body. In addition to years of being beaten and bruised as part of life on campaign, he had been wounded twelve times (twice seriously), received 202 strokes of the cat, and been tortured. His left cheek was scarred by a deep cut, the top of his left ear had been shot away and his scalp was furrowed by a bullet (ironically, the latter two inflicted by *Lucille*, the woman who would eventually be his third wife). His back was a mass of welts and weals from the lash, while his shoulders, legs, arms, hands and stomach all bore the indelible marks of bullet or blade. Stripped, an observer must have wondered how he was still alive.

Sharpe saw his first action (Boxtel), fired his first musket in anger, felt the tension and adrenaline rush of battle at 17, having been a soldier for just 17 months. His last action was in Chile (Valdivia) when he was 42. For the best part of 25 years, from boyhood to middle age, he was at war. He fought in Holland, India, Portugal, Spain, France, Belgium and Chile. For six years, from 1808 to 1814, he was almost continually in action, serving throughout the Peninsular War from Rolica, the first battle, to Toulouse, the last. If all his campaigns are included, Sharpe participated in 31 battles, sieges, attacks on forts or major skirmishes (24 actual and 7 fictional), including one at sea.

Towards the end of his life, his unique status as a veteran of the Indian and Napoleonic Wars was recognised with medals. Apart from the Waterloo Medal, issued in 1816 to all who were present at Ligny, Quatre Bras or Waterloo, he received no other medal until 1848 – when he was over 70. In that year the British government issued the Military General Service Medal, 1793–1814. It had no less than 29 bars (clasps). Of these 21 were for battles or sieges in the Peninsular War, and Sharpe was one of over 25,000 ageing applicants. He was awarded 12 bars, which, surprisingly, was not the highest

Peninsular War commissioning

DURING THE PENINSULAR WAR the requirement for young officers was one thousand a year. This high wastage rate was due (in order of importance) to death or disablement from disease or enemy action, retirement, resignation or disciplinary proceedings. Replacements came via purchase (20 per cent), the militia (20 per cent), the ranks (5 per cent), 'volunteers' or probationers, who served as privates while awaiting a free vacancy (5 per cent). The remaining replacements were educated men who had a suitable recommendation – but they did not pay if the vacancy was due to death or active service or a regiment was expanded, for example. In 1814 there were 10,600 officers on full pay, exclusive of foreign or veteran units. Sharpe was one of about 500 who had come up from the ranks, and there were only two other majors like him. Acting rank was universal and the temporary nature of his promotions up to major were commonplace. He was by no means unique in securing a commission through gallantry, although Wellington in later years expressed reservations about ex-ranker officers, '. . . their origins would come out, and you could never perfectly trust them [mainly with regard to drink].' Examples other than Sharpe were Sergeant Newman (43rd) for rallying stragglers during the retreat to Corunna; Sergeant Masterman (2/87th) for capturing an Eagle at Barossa and the three NCOs of the Light Division battalions decimated at Bussaco. The most exceptional contemporary example was John Shipp in India, who was twice commissioned from the ranks, the first time for leading a storming party at Bhurtpoor, and the second (after 'selling out' due to bad debts and re-enlisting) for single combat with a Nepalese chief in the 1st Goorkha War (1815).

number. Two received 15 and 11 got 14 bars. Sharpe had missed battles such as Sahagun, Bussaco, Barossa, Albuera, Nive and Orthez, all of which merited a bar. He was fortunate to be given the Corunna bar as neither he nor the 2/95th was present at the battle, although he had participated in the earlier part of the campaign and famous retreat. He also received the bar Pyrenees. He had to wait another three years for recognition of his Indian service. In 1851 the government decided to allow surviving soldiers to wear the Seringapatam Medal, 1799 (East India Company soldiers had worn it since 1816), and the 'new' Army of India Medal, 1793–1840. Sharpe received bars for Assaye, Arguam and Gawilghur, and his set

Battles, sieges and other actions

SHARPE PARTICIPATED in thirty-one actions:

Actual battles
- Boxtel, 15 September 1794 as Pte. 33rd.
- Mallavelly, 27 March 1799 as Pte. 33rd.
- Assaye, 23 September 1803 as Sgt. 33rd.
- Arguam, 29 November 1803 as Ensign 74th.
- Rolica, 17 August 1808 as 2/Lt. QM 95th.
- Vimiero, 21 August 1808 as 2/Lt. QM 95th.
- Oporto, 12 May 1809 as Lt. 95th.
- Talavera, 27 July 1809 as Capt. *S. Essex*
- Fuertes de Onoro, 3 May 1811 as Capt. *S. Essex.*
- Salamanca, 22 July 1812 as Capt. *S. Essex.*
- García Hernandez, 23 July 1812 as Capt. *S. Essex.*
- Vitória, 21 June 1813 as Maj. *S. Essex.*
- Nivelle, 10 November 1814 as Maj. *PWOV.*
- Toulouse, 10 April 1814 on staff as brigade major.
- Quatre Bras, 16 June 1815 as Lt-Col. (staff).
- Waterloo, 18 June 1815 as Lt-Col. (staff).

Fictional actions
- *Attack on* Santiago, 28 January 1809 as Lt. 95th.

- *Action at Valdelacasa*, 10 July 1909 as Lt. *S. Essex.*
- *Defence of Ft San Isidro*, 28 April 1811 as Capt. *S. Essex.*
- *Action at Adrados*, December 1812 as Capt. *S. Essex.*
- *Defence of* Teste de Buch, February 1814 as Maj. *PWOV.*
- *Action near* Naples, August 1814 as 'deserter'.
- *Sea action*, 1 January 1820 as civilian.

Actual sieges
- Seringapatam, April 1799 as Pte. 33rd.
- Ahmednuggur, 11 August 1803 as Sgt. 33rd.
- Gawilghur, 15 December 1803 as Ensign 74th.
- Almeida, 26 August 1810 as Capt. *S. Essex.*
- Ciudad Rodrigo, January 1812 as Capt. *S. Essex.*
- Badajoz, March/April 1812 as Capt. *S. Essex.*
- Ft Caytano, 23 June 1812 as Capt. *S. Essex.*
- Ft Inglés, Chile, 3 February 1820 as civilian.

of four medals would fetch an astronomical price today. Sadly, he was never able to wear any on his uniform, and it is doubtful if he had occasion to wear all four before his death. But they surely had pride of place for a few years with his old sword, over the fireplace.

Sharpe's main weakness was a pretty face. As a young man

he preferred his women lithe, hard and passionate, but his taste seemed to soften with advancing years. Eleven women are known to have featured in his life, three of whom he married. His first wife, *Teresa Morena*, whom he married in April 1812, gave him a daughter – *Antonia*, who was conceived from a fleeting liaison during the siege of Almeida. A mere two months after the marriage he was unfaithful to *Teresa*

Sharpe's women

SHARPE IS KNOWN to have bedded eleven women, had three wives and three children. They were, in chronological order:

1 *Maggie Joyce*: In London between 1789 and 1792. He remained fond of and grateful to her throughout her life, and entrusted her with the sale of the jewels he picked up at Vitória.

2 A Yorkshire girl called *Elsie* (1793). The killing of the innkeeper was connected with her.

3 *Mary Bickerstaff*: In India (*ST*); Anglo–Indian former wife of a deceased sergeant.

4 *Simone Joubert*. In India (*STr*). Wife of a French mercenary captain.

5 *Louisa Parker*: Met her in Galicia in 1809 (*SR*). She married *Major Blas Vivar* and commissioned Sharpe to find him after his disappearance in Chile in 1819 (*SD*).

6 *Josefina Lacosta*: Portuguese woman with a husband in Brazil. Met in 1809. Was raped by fellow officers, one of whom Sharpe murdered (*SE*). Became mistress of *Colonel Farthingdale* (*SEn*).

7 *Teresa Morena*: Guerilla leader whom he married in April 1812. She conceived his daughter, *Antonia*, in Almeida fortress in August 1810. Murdered by *Hakeswill* in December 1812.

8 *Hélène Leroux (La Marquesa de Casares el Grande y Melida Sabada)*: The sister of *Colonel Philippe Leroux* (whom Sharpe killed at García Hernandez), who had married a Spanish nobleman but was spying for the French. Sharpe, not knowing her background, had an affair with her in Salamanca in summer 1812 (*SS*).

9 *Anne, Dowager Countess Camoynes*: Brief encounter in London in the summer of 1813. (*SRegt*).

10 *Jane Gibbons*: Neice of *Sir Henry Simmerson*, first commanding officer of *S. Essex*. Sharpe married her in 1813 but she was unfaithful and appropriated much of Sharpe's wealth (*SRegt*, *SRev*).

11 *Lucille Castineau née Lassan*: Frenchwoman who became Sharpe's partner in 1814. He married her after *Jane's* death in 1844. Two children, *Patrick* and *Dominique* (*SRev*, *SD*).

with *Hélène Leroux*, the sister of a French colonel he was shortly to kill (SS). Nevertheless, Sharpe was consumed with hatred when ex-*Sergeant Hakeswill* murdered *Teresa* at Christmas 1812, and took absolute pleasure in finishing off the execution of *Hakeswill* two weeks later. *Antonia* was brought up by his wife's relatives near the Portuguese border and Sharpe never had contact with her again.

His second marriage to *Jane Gibbons* in late 1813 did not last long either. She was unfaithful to Sharpe with a cavalry officer and appropriated most of the money he 'found' after the victory at Vitória. Sharpe disowned her but refused to contemplate divorce. In May 1812, he met the widow *Lucille Castineau*, née *Lassan*, a Frenchwoman with a large farm in Normandy, in unpromising circumstances: she shot and seriously wounded him on their first meeting. The relationship which developed later lasted the rest of their lives. After Waterloo they settled down to farming her land about forty miles west of Caen, and *Lucille* bore him two children. Their son, *Patrick* (named after Sharpe's lifelong friend *Sergeant Harper*), was born in March 1815, and eventually entered the French army. Sharpe lived long enough to see his son (who took his mother's family name of *Lassan*) command the 1st Chasseurs d'Afrique in the Crimean War (perhaps fortunately for Sharpe's sensibilities the French and British were allies against the Russians). *Patrick* had been promoted *général de brigade* just before Sharpe died. Their daughter, *Dominique*, was born in June 1817, but apart from her marriage to a Frenchman nothing is known of her.

Sharpe's third marriage was to *Lucille* after *Jane*'s death in England in 1844. They had 16 years left before Sharpe, who became increasingly frail during the last few years of his life, died aged 83 in 1860. He was buried, with his sword (but not his medals) on his Normandy estate close to the village of *Seléglise*. *Patrick* inherited his medals but their whereabouts today are unknown.

BOYHOOD (1777–93)

Sharpe was born on 23 June 1777, in a house near Howick Place, Westminster, London. It forms a junction with Artillery Row about halfway between Victoria underground station and the Metropolitan Police headquarters at New Scotland Yard. His mother, as Sharpe freely admitted, was a whore. She died in the Gordon Riots of 1780 when young *Richard* was barely three. He was placed in a foundling home in Brewhouse Lane (which still exists a few hundred metres west of Wapping underground station in London's docklands), where he had a grim childhood. For nine years he worked (slaved would better describe it) at picking oakum, unpicking hemp and washing monstrous mountains of laundry. He was pale and puny, but although he looked sickly his preparation for army life was unsurpassed. Sharpe lived hard; he understood hunger and knew pain; scrounging, lying and fending for himself with fists or feet became his only means of survival.

In 1789, when he was twelve, he was sold to a chimney-sweep, but, ducking and weaving, he disappeared into the maze of sordid slums, brothels and taverns that made up St Giles Rookery (see Map 30). There he ended up in the arms of *Maggie Joyce*, a prostitute who ran a gin-house in Goslitt Yard. She became a mother, and later his first lover; she also taught him to live on his wits. Burglary became his speciality, but in later years he was strangely proud of the fact that he was never a pickpocket. He did, however, indulge in some 'peter laying', which involved cutting portmanteaus (leather suitcases) off the back of moving carriages. It required considerable agility, and not a little courage. Sharpe developed a deep and genuine affection for *Maggie*. He returned to see her in July 1813 (*SRegt*), and entrusted her with selling the jewellery he had picked up after the Battle of Vitória.

At fifteen, he was tall if somewhat skinny, and seemed destined for a life of crime in London which could easily have been short and squalid, ending on the gallows or coughing up his lungs with consumption. However, he intervened with a wooden stool when he found *Maggie* being beaten by one of her drunken male visitors, and pounded the man's head to a pulp. As the victim had been a notorious gang leader, Sharpe had to leave London. He fled to Yorkshire, where he got work in a coaching tavern. Within six months he had killed again – this time his employer. The reason for their fight was a Yorkshire lass called *Elsie* to whom Sharpe and his employer had both taken more than a passing fancy. Luckily, the innkeeper, a powerful man, picked the quarrel when he was besotted with his own beer. Nevertheless, there was a brutish struggle during which the boy's fingers were badly cut when he wrested a knife from his employer's grasp. Sharpe slashed his throat and left him to bleed to death in the back yard of the inn.

Wanted for two killings and still only fifteen, Sharpe sought refuge in the army. Ironically, he was recruited by the evil NCO, *Sergeant Hakeswill*, who was to become his implacable enemy in the years ahead. He joined the 33rd Foot (1st West Riding) which later became The Duke of Wellington's Regiment. The Regiment was well known at the time as the 'Havercakes' – derived from recruiting sergeants (including *Hakeswill*) enticing recruits with an oatcake on the ends of their bayonets. It was 16 April 1793 and Sharpe was two months short of his sixteenth birthday, but a glib tongue and his height got him through the perfunctory medical.

HOLLAND AND INDIA (1793–1805)

Within days of Sharpe's enlistment, an officer arrived in the Regiment who would rise to be the commander-in-chief in the Peninsula, defeat Napoleon at Waterloo and, ultimately, become prime minister of Britain. He would also shape Sharpe's entire career. Major Arthur Wesley's (the family name was changed to Wellesley in 1798) commission into the 33rd Foot was dated 30 April 1793. It was his sixth regiment in as many years, and within five months he was its commanding officer – through purchase. He was only eight years older than Sharpe. Within ten months he took his new Regiment (and Sharpe) to the Netherlands to fight the revolutionary French. At a small town called Boxtel, on 15 September 1794, Sharpe participated in a rearguard action in which the handling of the 33rd by Lieutenant-Colonel Wesley was the only redeeming feature. As a callow youth in the Light Company, he felt the sting of burning powder on his cheek when he fired his musket, saw blood on the grass, heard the screams of the wounded and the sobs of the dying. He had started to become a soldier.

The 33rd, with Private Sharpe, sailed for India in 1796, arriving at Fort William, Calcutta, in February the following year. He had not joined the army out of choice but out of necessity; he resented and resisted authority, and reacted strongly against discipline – particularly the mindless discipline of the military. To start with in India, he was a bitter, disgruntled soldier, who considered desertion. Part of the problem was his senior NCO, the inevitable *Sergeant Hakeswill*, who was instrumental in getting Sharpe sentenced to 2000 lashes (*ST*). Had the sentence been completed, he would have died but intervention by Colonel Wellesley, on the orders of General Harris, halted the punishment after 202 strokes. Sharpe avoided the continuation by volunteering for a special mission in Seringapatam with the promise of sergeant's stripes if he succeeded. The upshot was promotion to sergeant on 5 May 1799, at the exceptionally young age of twenty-one.

Sharpe saw in his new rank a much brighter future, but not in the 33rd, where many resented his promotion. *Hakeswill* was still scheming against him, so he wanted a fresh start in a regiment which had not flogged him, where he was judged on his merits not his past. He sought and obtained an interview with his new commanding officer, Lieutenant-Colonel Gore. Although sympathetic, Gore was only able to offer two options: either Sharpe waited, perhaps many months, for a ship to England and a depot job, or he could

SHARPE'S REGIMENTAL SERVICE

Discounting the short Waterloo campaign and his time spent in Chile in 1820–1, Sharpe served 21 years in the British army (1793–1814) in 4 regiments: 33rd Foot (1st West Riding) – 10½ years as a private, corporal, private and sergeant (virtually all his service was on detached duties); 74th Foot (Highland) – 2 years as an ensign; 95th Rifles – 3½ years as an ensign (QM) and lieutenant (QM); S. Essex (PWOV) – 5 years as lieutenant, captain and major.

take the vacant post of armourer sergeant at the Seringapatam armoury (*ST*). Sharpe had no wish to leave India, so he accepted the second offer – tedious, well away from any excitement, but not necessarily long term, and it would keep him from constant clashes with *Captain Morris* and *Hakeswill*. So, while the 33rd patrolled the dusty roads of Mysore for the next four years, Sharpe stagnated, counting cartridges and oiling muskets. Then, in mid-1803, Sharpe got the break he wanted when he was selected for another special mission with *Colonel Hector McCandless*, the East India Company head of intelligence for southern and western India. Sharpe was delighted. Unknown to him, when he left the battalion of the 33rd Foot in August 1799, he was never to serve with it again.

PIGTAILS (QUEUES)

Pigtails had been reduced to eight inches in 1804, but abolished only in 1808. The news was greeted with wild enthusiasm. The 28th Foot (Gloucestershires) had them cut off on board ship and ceremoniously thrown into the sea with three cheers. Sharpe wore one as a soldier in India and earlier. He would surely have agreed they were an abomination. 'The hair required to be soaped, floured and frizzed, in order to be tortured into an uncouth shape, which gave the man acute pain, and robbed him of the power of turning his head easily unless he brought his body round with it.'

Sergeant Sharpe was with Major-General Wellesley's force during the Mahratta War in 1803. On 11 August Wellesley attacked the fort of Ahmednuggur. Here Sharpe had his first experience of the difficulties of escalading a defended wall with too few ladders. But it was six weeks later, at Assaye, that the event occurred which changed his life. At the battle on 23 September 1803, at which Wellesley defeated a huge Mahratta army of nearly 50,000 with a mere 7000 men, Sharpe was Wellesley's mounted orderly and using a heavy cavalry sword for the first time. He killed five enemy soldiers with this cumbersome weapon while almost single-handedly defending his general after his horse had been spiked in a mêlée. For this act, he received a battlefield commission – he was twenty-six years old.

As an ensign he could not return to the 33rd. It was a rule, virtually set in concrete, that a former NCO, on being commissioned, could not continue to serve in his Regiment. A transfer was in the interests of the officer and of his men. Jumping the gulf between other rank and officer was hard enough without the added complications, embarrassment, and difficulties of remaining with his former comrades. It was regarded as bad for discipline. So Sharpe was commissioned into the 1/74th (Highlanders, ultimately the

Highland Light Infantry). Although officially a Highland Regiment, the 74th wore trousers at that time so Sharpe was spared the necessity of getting used to wearing a kilt. He was posted to the Light Company. He was to remain a light infantryman at heart, if not in reality, for the remainder of his career.

Sharpe fought with the 1/74th at Argaum on 29 November 1803, and again at the taking of the Gawilghur fort almost three weeks later. However, 1804 was a frustrating year for him: for weeks at a time he was sick with a recurring fever and vomiting. The climate, poor food, the ineffectual medical treatment (which included bleeding) and his own pig-headed determination to keep going when he was ill, drained him. At the end of the year, gaunt and weak, he was ordered home. The first available boat sailed in early 1805 (his Regiment remained in India for another two years); he arrived in England in March and went on sick leave – a seriously dissatisfied man.

By June he was restored to health and desperate for active employment. He had heard that a 2nd battalion of the 95th Rifles had been formed at Canterbury in May. Everybody

---

Sharpe's wounds

DISCOUNTING MINOR INJURIES, flogging, torture, beatings-up, etc. Sharpe received twelve wounds. He almost died after being shot in the stomach by *Colonel Leroux* and almost lost an arm when shot by *Lucille Castineau*. His wounds were:

1 Lance wound in side near Seringapatam, India – April 1799.
2 In head by musket shot at *Chaselgaon* – August 1803.
3 In left shoulder by *tulwar* (sword) at Battle of Assaye – September 1803.
4 Deep gash in left cheek at Battle of Arguam – November 1803.
5 In thigh by bayonet at Battle of Talavera – July 1809.
6 In shoulder by ricochet – August 1810.
7 In right thigh (deliberately) by *El Catolico*'s rapier – August 1810.
8 Shot in leg by *Sgt Hakeswill* at Badajoz – April 1812.
9 Pistol-shot in stomach by *Colonel Leroux* in Salamanca – June 1812.
10 In left thigh at Teste de Buch – February 1814.
11 Shot with horse pistol in arm, ear and scalp by *Lucille Castineau* – May 1814.

THE COST OF
PURCHASE

After Vitória, Sharpe
had acquired
considerable wealth,
but at no other time
was he in a position to
purchase promotion
(even then he showed
no inclination to do
so). The prices were
fixed at Horse Guards,
the most expensive
being in the
Household Cavalry,
then the Foot Guards,
the Cavalry and
finally, the least
expensive, the Infantry
of the Line. During
the Peninsular War,
the official rates were:
lieutenant, £550;
captain, £1500; major,
£2600; lieutenant-
colonel, £3500.

had heard of the Experimental Corps of Riflemen raised five years earlier. They were light infantrymen who fought as skirmishers, always at the forefront in battle, which greatly enhanced the chances of promotion for impoverished junior officers. Perfect for Ensign Sharpe, or so he thought. He travelled to their new barracks near Ashford, Kent, and obtained an interview with the commanding officer of the 2/95th, Lieutenant-Colonel Hamlet Wade. Was there a vacancy? Could an exchange be arranged? Sharpe made out a strong case: twelve years in the army, experience as a senior NCO, commissioned on the battlefield for gallantry, and service as a light company officer. Wade was impressed. His battalion had several subaltern vacancies and one young 2nd lieutenant (as ensigns were called in the 95th) who was deeply in debt. A spell in India away from his creditors, where he could live on his pay and even save, might be the answer. What Wade did not tell Sharpe was that he also desperately needed a quartermaster. In July, by way of a slightly belated twenty-eighth birthday present, Wade arranged the exchange. Sharpe became a 2nd lieutenant in the 2/95th.

Lieutenant-Colonel Hamlet Wade, 2/95th

ALTHOUGH WADE HAD MADE him Quartermaster, Sharpe developed a high opinion of this officer's professionalism, particularly his marksmanship. Wade and a Private named Smeaton used to hold a target for each other at 150 yards, firing with the Baker rifle. During an inspection Lord Chatham asked to see some rifle practice and expressed some anxiety regarding the safety of those marking. Wade replied, 'There is no danger', and, calling on Smeaton to hold a target, he fired and hit it. Lord Chatham was horrified. Wade persisted, 'Oh, but we all do it', and

took the target himself, ran out, and confidently received the soldier's fire.

Wade, a dashing Irishman, saw action at Copenhagen, in 1807, and was again Sharpe's commanding officer for about ten days in December 1808, at the start of the Corunna retreat. He fought at Flushing in 1809, arriving back in the Peninsula in the summer of 1811. To his great regret he had to relinquish command of the 2/95th two months before Waterloo. He was awarded a gold medal for his services in the Peninsula, later made a colonel and CB. He died in 1821.

Sharpe's promotions

To CORPORAL, briefly, during his early service in the 33rd Foot.

To Corporal (for a few days), in a French unit serving Tippoo Sultan inside Seringapatam in April 1799.

To Sergeant, 5 May 1799 – for services at Siege of Seringapatam.

To Ensign, 25 September 1803 – for saving Wellington's life at Battle of Assaye.

To Lieutenant, 22 August 1808 – due to casualties at Obidos, Rolica and Vimeiro.

To Captain, 12 July 1809 – for actions in skirmish at *Valdelacasa*.

To Major, 14 November 1812 – by Prince Regent for actions at Badajoz and García Hernandez.

To Lieutenant-Colonel (in Dutch Army), May 1815 – by Wellington for service on staff of Prince of Orange in Waterloo campaign.

PORTUGAL, SPAIN, BELGIUM AND CHILE (1805–20)

On reporting for duty Sharpe was made Quartermaster. He was devastated and felt cheated, but from Wade's point of view he had the ideal background. His other rank service meant he knew the army 'system', understood all the old-soldier tricks, and would make a consummate scrounger; he could read and write (taught by his officer while both were imprisoned by the Tippoo Sultan in 1799) and thus could manage the books. His new duties kept him in England when five companies went to Germany in October 1805, and again in the summer of the following year when three companies sailed for South America. The three years from 1805 were a major low point in Sharpe's career. He missed active service opportunities, could not afford to buy promotion and he could not relinquish the dull, tedious duties of Quartermaster. Additionally, he was cold-shouldered by some (but not all) of his brother officers, who considered his lack of manners, money, education and social graces made him a second-class officer, for whom his dead-end job was entirely appropriate.

Immediately he disembarked in Mondego Bay in Portugal

BREECHES AND GAITERS

1808 was a good year for soldiers' comfort. As well as the abolition of pigtails, breeches and gaiters were replaced by trousers. The gaiters which buttoned up to the knee were particularly loathed: it took twelve minutes to button them properly, and more if they were wet. Such a chore in the field became intolerable, and men tended not to take them off for long periods at a time. This led to itching, sores which would not heal, dirt getting in, and an unfit soldier.

Sharpe's uniform

HE WORE his dark green, short 95th jacket throughout the Peninsular War and Waterloo campaign no matter which unit he served with. It became unrecognisably tattered, stained and patched, but it was a talisman which brought him luck. Initially the jacket was decorated with sixty-six white metal (surprisingly, not silver) buttons in three vertical rows from shoulder to waist. Few were left by 1815. There were black braid twists between each row, and the jacket had black velvet collar and cuffs (facings). His black belt, worn over the left shoulder, had a small pouch at the rear and a silver lion's head, chain and whistle at the front. Sharpe wore a light infantry, tasselled, crimson officer's sash around his waist (normally the only way he could be recognised as an officer) on top of which was a black leather, S-buckled sword belt. The rest of the 95th officer's uniform was modelled on that of the light cavalry. However, after *Sergeant Harper* killed the Imperial Guard chasseur, *Colonel de l'Eclin*, in early 1809, Sharpe took his overalls (trousers) and boots. These overalls were green, with red stripes and had the inner legs reinforced with leather. The boots were black, covered the calf and, most importantly, were waterproof. They lasted six years. He seldom wore the tapered, peakless shako with the folding flap at the front which had a central, green feather plume and buglehorn badge. He preferred a soft, flat type forage cap or no headgear at all.

on 1 August 1808, his fortunes changed. Within days the battalion was under fire and Lieutenant Bunbury became the first British death of the Peninsular War. At Rolica, on 17 August, Lieutenants Hill and Cochrane were wounded; four days later, at Vimiero, Hill was hit again and three more lieutenants became casualties. The following day Major Travers secured Sharpe's promotion into Bunbury's vacancy. It was a start, although he had to continue his Quartermaster duties until he became separated from the battalion on 31 December at the start of the retreats to Vigo and Corunna (*SR*).

The remainder of Sharpe's career is well documented. His ultimate ambition – to be appointed to the permanent command of a battalion – was never likely to be fulfilled. He had the leadership ability and the battlefield experience, and he

Sharpe's sword

A 95TH OFFICER'S SWORD was a curved, light cavalry sabre which Sharpe rejected in favour of the straight-bladed, heavy cavalry sword, 1796 pattern, the same type he was forced to use when saving Wellesley's life at Assaye in 1803. This was a cumbersome, ill-balanced broadsword, thirty-five inches long, which was supposed to be wielded from the advantage of a horse's height. Although Sharpe was tall, the sling had to be adjusted to prevent the weapon tripping him when walking or running. They were crudely and cheaply made in Birmingham, with each metal scabbard stamped 'Warranted Never to Fail' – a guarantee Sharpe would have disputed; his blade broke in the fight with *Colonel Leroux* in the Irish College in Salamanca in July 1812.

Leroux's weapon was a Kligenthal, a sword of such good design and strength that the French army retained it for another hundred years. *Sergeant Harper* procured another heavy weapon for Sharpe and modified it to suit the officer's requirements. He carried this blade for the rest of his service, and it was eventually buried with him. Even when he killed *Leroux* and took the famous Kligenthal, he soon tossed it into the Tormes River, preferring his friend's gift. Sharpe invariably used it as a bludgeon rather than for swordplay; he went to great lengths to ensure it was honed properly before battle, although for slashing the light cavalry sabre was an infinitely better weapon. Its blade was broad and heavily curved, with the weight and balance giving it tremendous cutting power – able to slice off a head or limb. Nevertheless, the heavier weapon seemed to suit Sharpe's strength and temperament, judging by the kills he made with it.

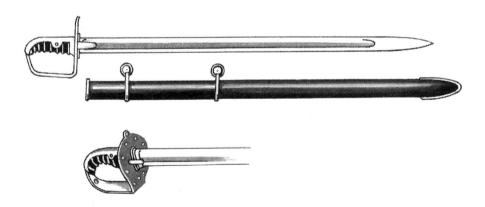

Sharpe's Sword

Sharpe's rifle

SHARPE HAD BEEN a soldier for ten years before he was commissioned, and had spent much of the time marching with a musket or as an armourer sergeant at Seringapatam. He could perform all the musketry firing drills to perfection and, within the severe limitations of the weapon, was an excellent shot. Starting with a loaded musket he could get off five shots in a minute – the normal rate being two. When he joined the 95th as an officer, he made it his business to become equally proficient with the Baker rifle, and continued to carry a rifle, which meant it was difficult to distinguish him from ordinary soldiers – at times an advantage.

Designed by Ezekiel Baker, the rifle had a 30-inch barrel with 7 grooves to spin the ball for greater accuracy, with a calibre varying from 0.615 to 0.70. A reasonable shot could hit a man at 200 yards under battle conditions. Trials at 100 and 200 yards with 36 and 24 shots respectively produced 100 per cent hits. It was an excellent weapon for sniping at officers or gunners: something Sharpe drummed into his men. The shortness of the barrel allowed for loading in the prone position, which was a great boon for skirmishers. Unlike most muskets, its barrel was 'browned' rather than polished, for concealment. Its main drawback was the slowness of loading (two shots a minute) due to the need to force the ball, wrapped in a patch for a tight fit, down the grooves. Initially a mallet was provided to do this because, when first issued, the rifle balls were made from cavalry carbine moulds which had virtually the same bore as the barrel, so there was no windage due to the overtight fit. Each rifleman carried a small tool bag, new flints and patches as well as his cartridges, balls and powder. A 24-inch sword bayonet was provided (Sharpe had his own sword instead) and the word of command in Rifle Regiments to this day is 'Fix swords' rather than 'Fix bayonets'. Some 30,000 Bakers were produced from 1800–15 and were eventually issued to allied units such as the Portuguese Cacadores as well as British Rifle Regiments.

knew soldiers far better than most officers. He did not, however, have the right establishment background. The system of promotion to higher rank was hopelessly loaded against him. If he had made substantive lieutenant-colonel, he would have been eligible, purely on seniority, for general officer rank. To the authorities of his day this was virtually unthinkable. That he rose to major was exceptional (only a handful of other ranks achieved this), and Sharpe realised it.

He had a number of consolation prizes as both captain

SHARPE 17

Sharpe's medals and awards

HE WAS AWARDED the Waterloo Medal (in 1816), the Military General Service Medal 1793–1814 (in 1848), the Seringapatam Medal, 1799 (in 1851) and the Army of India Medal 1799–1826 (in 1851). His 12 bars (clasps) to the MGSM were (using the original spelling) Roleia, Vimiera, Corunna, Talavera, Fuentes d'Onor, Ciudad Rodrigo, Badajoz, Salamanca, Vittória, Pyrenees, Nivelle and Toulouse. Wellesley presented him with an engraved telescope after Assaye and he received a presentation sword from the Patriotic Fund for capturing an Eagle at Talavera. Many men got more bars to their medal. James Talbot of the 45th Foot (Nottinghamshire) and Daniel Loochstadt of the KGL and 60th Rifles both received 15. Of those with 14 bars, only two were officers. Perhaps the most extraordinary was the Hardy family of three brothers in the 7th Foot (Royal Fusiliers) who between them amassed 40. Sergeant John 14, Corporal Peter 13, and Private James 13. Those medals would be beyond price today.

and major. He commanded the Light Company of the *S. Essex* from July 1809, and took them into battle at Talavera, Fuentes de Onoro, Ciudad Rodrigo, for part of the action at Badajoz and at Salamanca. He was given several independent roles where he had to use his initiative and fight his own battles. Examples were his hunt for gold around *Casetejada* in 1810 (*SG*), the defence of *Fort San Isidro* (*SB*), and the bitter fighting against deserters and the French at *Adrados* at Christmas 1812 (*SEn*). As a major he took command of his battalion (*S. Essex*) after *Lieutenant-Colonel Leroy* had been killed at Vitória (*SH*), and again from the incapacitated commander of *The Prince of Wales' Own Volunteers (S. Essex)* at the height of the action at the Nivelle (*SRegt*). He was also in command of the ground forces for the special operation at Teste de Buch in early 1814 (*SSge*). On two occasions the army had made him rich: when he shot the Tippoo Sultan in 1799 (*ST*) and stripped his corpse of priceless jewels; and in 1813, when he took a sizeable slice of the loot lying around after the French defeat at Vitória.

Interestingly, as he got older, Sharpe became less enamoured of war. The recklessness of youth gave way to the

Sharpe's Military Service Medal 1793–1814

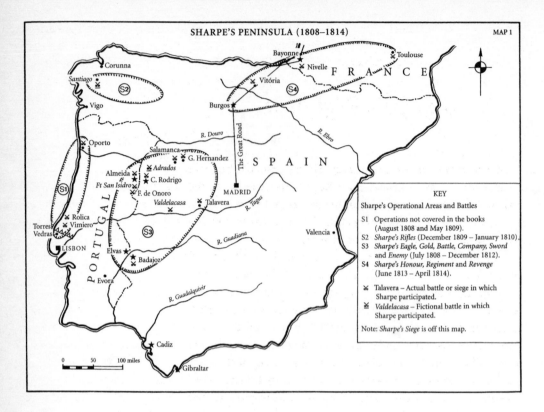

SHARPE'S PENINSULA (1808–1814)   MAP 1

Corunna

Santiago
S2
Vigo

Bayonne
Toulouse
Nivelle   F R A N C E
Vitória
S4
Burgos

R. Douro   The Great Road   R. Ebro

S P A I N

Oporto
Salamanca
G. Hernandez
Almeida   Adrados
Ft San Isidro   C. Rodrigo
F. de Onoro
Valdelacasa   Talavera
R. Tagus

MADRID

Valencia

Rolica
Torres   Vimiero
Vedras
S3
LISBON   Elvas
Badajoz
R. Guadiana

P O R T U G A L

Evora

R. Guadalquivir

Cadiz

Gibraltar

0   50   100 miles

KEY

Sharpe's Operational Areas and Battles

S1   Operations not covered in the books
     (August 1808 and May 1809).
S2   *Sharpe's Rifles* (December 1809 – January 1810).
S3   *Sharpe's Eagle, Gold, Battle, Company, Sword*
     and *Enemy* (July 1808 – December 1812).
S4   *Sharpe's Honour, Regiment* and *Revenge*
     (June 1813 – April 1814).

✗   Talavera – Actual battle or siege in which
    Sharpe participated.
✗   *Valdelacasa* – Fictional battle in which
    Sharpe participated.

Note: *Sharpe's Siege* is off this map.

acknowledgement of fear, the realisation of mortality, and a longing for peace. This was particularly apparent at the last (unnecessary) Battle of Toulouse in April 1814. Like thousands of his comrades, he wanted the war to end, he wanted to go home. Only reluctantly did he take up his sword for Waterloo, and there was much soul-searching before he agreed to the final military adventure in Chile in 1819. He was middle-aged, enjoyed farming, loved *Lucille* and his children – in short, he had a lot to lose. But fate was kind: by then he had lived only half his life.

2

Sharpe's Regiments

THE BRITISH INFANTRY which Sharpe joined while still under sixteen, was organised into Regiments of Foot. By the end of 1809 there were 103, numbered strictly in accordance with seniority: the date of formation. The most senior infantry Regiment of the Line (discounting Guards Regiments) was the 1st of Foot (Royal Scots), the most junior the 103rd Foot (raised as a garrison battalion). Most, but not all, had a territorial title, but recruiting was not confined to those counties. Sharpe served in four such regiments – the 33rd, 74th, 95th and the *S. Essex*. This would have been the 102nd Foot but it was never given an official number possibly due to its militia origins, the fact that it lost a Colour within two months of arrival in the Peninsula, spent much time under strength as a battalion of detachments and was disbanded after only nine years. The regiment that received the number 102 was the New South Wales Regiment.

Unlike the French or most European armies, a British infantry regiment was not a tactical formation. It was an administrative unit which never took the field. It raised battalions, usually two, sometimes only one, rarely three or more; the battalion was the regiment's tactical unit on the battlefield. In 1809 the British army had 179 Line battalions, of which only 28 were in the Peninsula. The great majority were at home (70), the remainder being scattered worldwide: West Indies (27), East Indies (23), Sicily and Malta (14), and the others in Canada, Cape of Good Hope, New South Wales, Gibraltar and Madeira. That some regiments (the *S. Essex* being one of 37) had only one battalion was purely accidental. At the breakdown of the Peace or Amiens in 1803 virtually all regiments had only one battalion but, because such a huge

S. ESSEX
COMMANDING
OFFICERS

*Lt-Col. Sir Henry
Simmerson* – sent
home in disgrace, July
1809.
*Lt-Col. Hon. William
Lawford* – seriously
wounded at Ciudad
Rodrigo, January 1812.
*Lt-Col. Brian
Windham* – killed on
Salamanca bridge,
June 1812.
Lt-Col. Thomas Leroy
– killed at Vitória, June
1813.
*Lt-Col. Bartholomew
Girdwood* – had mental
breakdown at the
Nivelle, November
1813.
Lt-Col. Joseph Ford –
relieved of command
after breakdown at
Waterloo, June 1815.

expansion was needed, over fifty of those stationed at home were ordered to raise second battalions. Those overseas, far from recruiting grounds, were not so instructed and remained single-battalion regiments, although some did later raise another battalion. A regiment was referred to by its number; if it had more than one battalion, the number preceded the regimental number – thus the 1/44th was the 1st Battalion of the 44th Regiment of Foot. The regiment Sharpe first joined, the 33rd, was a single-battalion regiment and did not need a number to distinguish it from sister units.

As the system developed it became common practice for the 1st Battalion to have right of preference for active service, with the 2nd Battalion remaining at home, primarily to furnish drafts to keep its senior partner up to strength. It was exceptional to have both battalions of the same regiment in the Peninsula together. When this did occur, and both lost men to sickness and as casualties, it was invariably the fate of the 2nd to discharge its fit men into the 1st, and for the rump (a handful of officers, sergeants and unfit or time-expired soldiers) to go home.

All battalions in the Peninsula, with the possible exception of those of the Guards, had to struggle to remain in being, to maintain a strength that made them viable as a fighting unit. With single-battalion regiments like the *S. Essex*, the struggle was usually acute and prolonged. There was a stigma attached to battalions of detachments or provisional battalions (two weak ones that had amalgamated). Any unit falling below 400 men had lost over 60 per cent of its full establishment and was seldom viable for anything other than guard or escort duties or providing fatigue parties on the lines of communication.

1809 was the year the *S. Essex* arrived in Portugal. At that time the infantry of the British army consisted of 3 Regiments of Foot Guards (7 battalions), 103 Regiments of the Line, 10 battalions of the King's German Legion, 8 West India Regiments, 8 Veteran battalions and 10 other colonial or foreign units. A battalion was a lieutenant-colonel's

S. ESSEX CORPORAL JUST ARRIVED
IN PENINSULA – JUNE 1809

Eagle in chains badge adopted by S. Essex after the capture of the French Eagle at Talavera in 1809. It was worn on the shako, the crossbelt plate and featured on the Colours.

Hated leather stock. Despite Sharpe using them for target practice, they were still in use in 1813.

Knapsack (not visible). Black painted canvas on wooden frame called the 'Trotter' knapsack after its manufacturer. Wretchedly uncomfortable.

Greatcoat rolled on top of knapsack.

Wings on shoulders denote Gren. Coy. Useful in preventing shoulder straps slipping off.

2 chevrons denoting cpl.

2 white crossbelts, one for bayonet, the other for cartridge box. These, with the knapsack breast strap, greatly restricted breathing when climbing or running.

Box holding 60 cartridges. Also often contained pocket for spare flints and tools. The 'picker' and wire brush for cleaning touchhole and priming pan normally on chain on crossbelt for ease of use.

Brown Bess musket (India pattern with 39-inch long barrel). Smoothbore, flintlock, max. effective range 80 yds. Calibre .76 with .71 ball giving plenty of 'windage' for loading.

Black felt, stovepipe shako with brass plate. Had peak and chin-strap. Despite oilskin cover it quickly lost its shape. 'Distorted by rain and sunshine as well as having served as pillows and nightcaps, our caps had assumed the most monstrous and grotesque shapes.' As the French wore a distinctive bell-topped shako it was easy to recognise friend from foe at a distance. For this reason, Wellington was opposed to its replacement in 1813.

White tuft denotes Gren. Coy.

Short hair, the dreadful powdered queues having been abolished a year earlier.

Yellow facings, cuffs and collars.

Red jacket with brass buttons and Regtl. white lace.

Barrel-shaped canteen (waterbottle) holding 3 pints.

Haversack, usually for rations.

Socket bayonet with 17-inch triangular sectioned blade. Difficult to load when bayonet fixed.

Loose-fitting, comfortable blue/grey trousers had replaced the hated white breeches and long, tightly buttoned gaiters.

Shoes (boots) came in different sizes but one fitting, the same for left and right feet. Worn on each foot on alternate days the equalise wear. Hobnailed, but inevitably wore out and would be replaced with anything available. Initially, spare pair in knapsack.

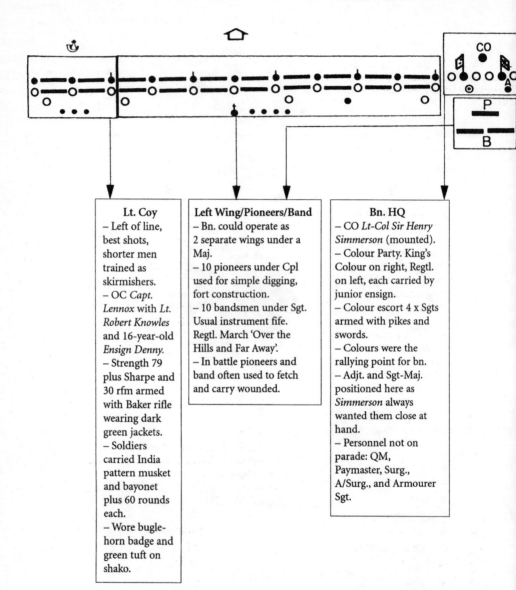

Lt. Coy
– Left of line, best shots, shorter men trained as skirmishers.
– OC *Capt. Lennox* with *Lt. Robert Knowles* and 16-year-old *Ensign Denny*.
– Strength 79 plus Sharpe and 30 rfm armed with Baker rifle wearing dark green jackets.
– Soldiers carried India pattern musket and bayonet plus 60 rounds each.
– Wore bugle-horn badge and green tuft on shako.

Left Wing/Pioneers/Band
– Bn. could operate as 2 separate wings under a Maj.
– 10 pioneers under Cpl used for simple digging, fort construction.
– 10 bandsmen under Sgt. Usual instrument fife. Regtl. March 'Over the Hills and Far Away'.
– In battle pioneers and band often used to fetch and carry wounded.

Bn. HQ
– CO *Lt-Col Sir Henry Simmerson* (mounted).
– Colour Party. King's Colour on right, Regtl. on left, each carried by junior ensign.
– Colour escort 4 x Sgts armed with pikes and swords.
– Colours were the rallying point for bn.
– Adjt. and Sgt-Maj. positioned here as *Simmerson* always wanted them close at hand.
– Personnel not on parade: QM, Paymaster, Surg., A/Surg., and Armourer Sgt.

PLASENCIA (10 JULY 1809)

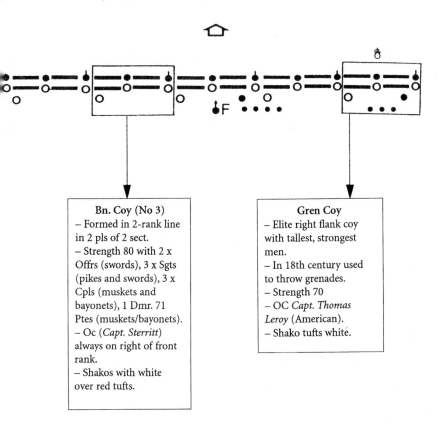

Bn. Coy (No 3)
– Formed in 2-rank line in 2 pls of 2 sect.
– Strength 80 with 2 x Offrs (swords), 3 x Sgts (pikes and swords), 3 x Cpls (muskets and bayonets), 1 Dmr. 71 Ptes (muskets/bayonets).
– Oc (*Capt. Sterritt*) always on right of front rank.
– Shakos with white over red tufts.

Gren Coy
– Elite right flank coy with tallest, strongest men.
– In 18th century used to throw grenades.
– Strength 70
– OC *Capt. Thomas Leroy* (American).
– Shako tufts white.

Key

CO	CO: *Lt-Col Simmerson*
	Maj. (*F Maj. Forrest* 21C)
	Capt.
	Subaltern
A	Adjt.
	Sgt-Maj. (RSM)
O	Sgt.
•	Dmr.
P	Pioneers
B	Band

General Notes
– Bn. paraded at Plasencia to greet Spanish Bn. prior to *Valdelacasa* operation.
– In 2-rank line bn. covered about 250 yds. On parade 870 out of 875 all ranks fit for duty.

Parade state:

Offrs x 34
Sgt-Maj. x 1
Sgts x 41
Cpls x 39
Pnrs x 10
Band x 10
Dmrs x 10
Ptes x 730

command. The establishment allowed for two majors, ten captains and thirty subalterns plus an adjutant, paymaster, quartermaster, surgeon (possibly with an assistant). Seldom, if ever, did a battalion start out with its full complement of officers. DIAGRAM 1 gives details of the *S. Essex*'s internal organisation and how *Simmerson* paraded it in line. Every unit was divided into ten companies. The two 'flank' companies shared the best men in the battalion. The Grenadier Company, with most of the tallest and strongest soldiers, always formed on the right flank of the battalion. The Light Company which was composed of the smaller, more agile men picked for their marksmanship, paraded on the left flank. The remaining companies, numbered from 1 to 8, were the 'battalion' or 'centre' companies. At full strength, the unit would muster around 1000 rank and file plus officers, sergeants and musicians.

In the Peninsular War infantry units served in a particular brigade or division. But it was not until a month after the arrival of the *S. Essex* that the army finally adopted a divisional system. Prior to this Wellesley had a brigade as his highest formation, usually commanded by a major-general and consisting of two or three battalions. The Oporto campaign had been fought with eight such formations, reinforced by Portuguese battalions. A division was a lieutenant-general's command and was, eventually, an army in miniature with permanently attached staff officers, commissariat (supply) staff, independent light infantry companies (from the 5/60th Rifles) and, in 1812, artillery batteries. A crucial and highly successful innovation was the inclusion of a five-battalion Portuguese brigade with the two British brigades. They became Anglo-Portuguese divisions approximately 5800 strong, with around 3500 British and 2300 Portuguese troops in each. Only occasionally did Wellington group two or more divisions together as corps under a senior general, such as Hill, for a semi-independent role. For the French, the corps was a permanent feature of their organisation.

Wellington ultimately created eight infantry divisions numbered 1 to 7 plus the famous Light Division, which was

S. Essex
Infantryman (Sergeant)

formed in the spring of 1810 by adding two Portuguese Cacadores battalions to Crauford's Light Brigade (1/43rd, 1/52nd
and 1/95th). With a strength of about 4000, it was smaller
than the ordinary infantry division but quickly became the
army's élite formation. In its role of screening, it had to cover
a front of up to fifty miles. It did for the entire army what
a light company did for a battalion: kept the enemy at arm's
length, delayed his advance, inflicted casualties and prevented
him from gaining information. Sharpe would dearly have
loved to serve in it. As it was, the S. Essex served in the 2nd,
3rd, 4th and 5th Divisions in the Peninsula and again in the
3rd at Waterloo. Only once, at the Battle of the Nivelle, did
they briefly form part of the Light Division alongside the 1st
and 2nd 95th.

There were two indispensable technical skills for infantry
soldiers to master for success on a Peninsula (or any Napoleonic) battlefield – drill and musketry. Without the drill, a
battalion was an armed mob of individuals: no organised
movement or tactical manoeuvring was possible. Without
the musketry, the enemy could not be killed. Close order
drill filled the life of British infantrymen from the moment
they enlisted. Week after week, month after month, companies and battalions drilled on the parade ground and in the
field. They had to wheel and turn, march and counter-march,
advance and retire, form lines, columns and squares. The
soldiers had to understand, and instantly react to, the shouted
orders of their NCOs and officers or the beat of a drum.
Every man, every NCO, every officer (including the commanding officer) had to learn his drill book. Regulations were
published setting out the movements in which all units had to
be trained; they were commonly referred to as the 'Nineteen
Movements'. Unfortunately for the S. Essex, foot drill and
dress regulations were the sole military interests of their first
commander. When the battalion marched, dust-coated and
sweat-stained, into Plasencia that burning July day in 1809,
they knew their drill and their dress was immaculate, but
they could not shoot. Despite his efforts, Sharpe could not
change this state of affairs in a few hours.

ORDENANZA

The Portuguese
equivalent of the
British Home Guard
of WWII. The
Portuguese levée en
masse produced a vast
body of men – the
Ordenanza – (in May
1810, 329,000) for local
defence. These
part-time civil guards
carried blunderbusses,
pikes and pruning
knives, wore no
uniform, and were
incapable of
maintaining
themselves on a
battlefield. They were
useful as guards,
skirmishers and
sometimes snipers to
pick off stragglers.
They were also an
excellent source of
information on
enemy activities.
Wellington failed to
persuade Masséna that
because they were
called up under
Portuguese law in
times of emergency
they should be treated
as regular or militia
troops. Masséna
refused to recognise
their status, so any
caught were executed
– a policy which
French stragglers who
fell into the hands of
the Ordenanza often
regretted.

MUSKET AND RIFLE – A COMPARISON

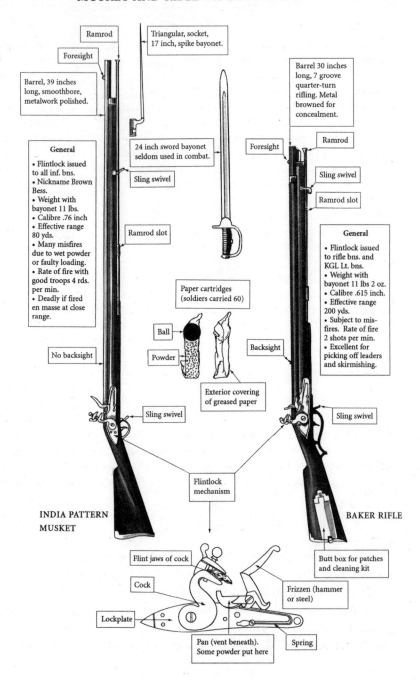

Ramrod

Foresight

Triangular, socket, 17 inch, spike bayonet.

Barrel 30 inches long, 7 groove quarter-turn rifling. Metal browned for concealment.

Barrel, 39 inches long, smoothbore, metalwork polished.

Foresight

Ramrod

24 inch sword bayonet seldom used in combat.

Sling swivel

Sling swivel

Ramrod slot

General

• Flintlock issued to all inf. bns.
• Nickname Brown Bess.
• Weight with bayonet 11 lbs.
• Calibre .76 inch
• Effective range 80 yds.
• Many misfires due to wet powder or faulty loading.
• Rate of fire with good troops 4 rds. per min.
• Deadly if fired en masse at close range.

Ramrod slot

General

• Flintlock issued to rifle bns. and KGL Lt. bns.
• Weight with bayonet 11 lbs 2 oz.
• Calibre .615 inch.
• Effective range 200 yds.
• Subject to misfires. Rate of fire 2 shots per min.
• Excellent for picking off leaders and skirmishing.

Paper cartridges (soldiers carried 60)

Ball

Powder

Backsight

No backsight

Exterior covering of greased paper

Sling swivel

Sling swivel

Flintlock mechanism

INDIA PATTERN MUSKET

BAKER RIFLE

Butt box for patches and cleaning kit

Flint jaws of cock

Cock

Frizzen (hammer or steel)

Lockplate

Pan (vent beneath). Some powder put here

Spring

Musket-loading procedure

ALL MUSKETS, rifles and carbines of all nations were muzzle-loading. They fired a spherical lead ball of varying sizes according to the calibre of the weapon. The French musket ball was fractionally smaller than the British so it could, in an emergency, be used in the Brown Bess, whereas the reverse was not possible. The British ball weighed about an ounce and could inflict horrible injuries at close range when the ball flattened slightly on impact, smashing bones, ripping huge holes in muscles, causing massive bleeding and shock. A 'spent' ball could sometimes bruise, as both Wellington and Napoleon would testify. Cartridges, already made up with powder and ball wrapped in greased paper, were carried in a flapped leather pouch with a slotted wooden interior, each slot containing a cartridge.

To load, the soldier held his musket forward horizontally in his left hand, took a cartridge from his pouch with his right and bit the bullet end off the cartridge, retaining the bullet in his mouth. This was an unpleasant procedure resulting in blackened lips, gritty teeth, and the taste of gunpowder and grease. He then pulled back the cock (hammer) one notch to the 'half-cock' position. If the trigger was pulled at this stage nothing would (supposedly) happen – although the expression 'going off at half-cock' should be remembered. The frizzen was pushed in the direction of the muzzle, opening the priming pan. A small amount of powder was poured from the opened cartridge into the pan and the frizzen moved into the vertical position, thus sealing the powder. The musket butt was then grounded and the remaining powder poured down the barrel and the ball dropped (or spat) down it. The iron ramrod was taken from its channel underneath the barrel, reversed, and with the bulbous end the soldier rammed the empty paper cartridge down the barrel (awkward with a fixed bayonet). This compacted the 'wad', ball and powder firmly at the bottom of the barrel; the ramrod was replaced. The musket was returned to the horizontal, the cock pulled back another notch to 'full-cock' which made the trigger operational, the musket raised and fired. The cock flew forward, the flint struck the serrated frizzen, the sparks lit the powder in the pan and the flash travelled down the vent and exploded the powder under the ball.

Shooting the smooth-bore, India pattern, Brown Bess musket (*see p. 26*) was also down to drills. Even a good shot would miss a man three times out of four at one hundred yards. What was required of the grenadier and battalion companies in particular was mass firing in controlled volleys and speedy reloading. The *S. Essex* could not shoot quickly

Musket-firing – the problems

THE FIRST SHOT fired by any soldier in battle was invariably the most accurate and reliable, because his weapon was clean and the loading procedures had been meticulously followed. Thereafter, the more he fired the more inaccurate his shooting, the more unreliable his musket, and the greater the problems.

● Misfires (which occurred on average once every nine shots) due to damp powder (firing in heavy rain was impossible); the flint did not spark; there was a 'flash in the pan', but it failed to ignite the powder in the barrel; a strong wind blew the powder from the pan when loading; a 'hang-fire' (when the trigger was pulled nothing happened for a second or two as the powder burned too slowly, and the musket fired as you began to look for the problem); the savage recoil got worse as the barrel fouled with prolonged firing;

your face was peppered with grains of half-burnt powder from the pan every time you fired; ramming became increasingly difficult as fouling in the barrel accumulated; and, most important of all, dense clouds of white smoke often obscured the target – firing was blind after the first volley.

● Human error, as distinct from technical problems, was a major factor as fear and fatigue increased. Panic induced mistakes in loading, such as firing away the ramrod which had been left in the barrel, or forgetting the musket was loaded and so loading again – the result was often a burst barrel, eardrums or head. Men under intense pressure sometimes put the ball down the barrel before the powder, which meant it would not fire until they had extracted the ball – a fiddling, time-consuming process.

enough. There were eleven separate drill movements required by the manual to fire a shot. The soldiers (many ex-militiamen) knew the movements and the sequence, but their loading was stiff and slow, the NCOs insisting on smartness and moving together so that they looked pleasing to the eye. The company was therefore lucky to get off two shots a minute, and it was seldom much use firing even volleys at an enemy over one hundred yards away. If you fired at that range and it took thirty seconds to reload, the enemy would be thrusting his bayonet into your belly before you could fire again. There were ways of getting over this basic problem such as firing by platoons (half companies), firing by alternate ranks, waiting until the attackers were much closer – or a combination of these things. But, other things being equal, soldiers who could load and fire four times a minute were likely to beat an enemy who could only do so twice.

There was another critical factor in the equation. The French musket was not noticeably inferior to the British, the French soldier was not necessarily a worse shot, yet nine times out of ten two attacking Frenchmen were seen off by one defender. Historians have discussed endlessly the merits of the British line in generating more firepower than the assaulting column. A key factor has often been forgotten: morale. It was seldom worthwhile to open musketry fire above one hundred yards. Much better to wait in silence with muskets shouldered, let the enemy see the long, solid line and anticipate how deadly the fire would be. Let them feel fear. In one such advance, a voice from the ranks called, 'For what we are about to receive, Lord make us truly thankful.' Then, at thirty yards, let fly one long, devastating volley which rolled from end to end of the line and back again, followed by a wildly yelling bayonet charge. Tactics like this took a lot of guts to withstand. That the columns were rolled to

FIRING RAMRODS

The French also fired off ramrods by mistake, sometimes with fatal results. In 1808, at Valladolid, General Malher was exercising recruits with blank cartridges and made the mistake of getting in front of them; he was transfixed by one of eighteen shot away. In 1804, at Leghorn, the 5th Ligne doing a similar exercise fired off a ramrod that killed a civilian spectator. An inspection revealed the culprit but luckily for him the victim was found to be a notorious brigand taking the day off.

Musket accuracy

THE HEAVY BULLET, considerable 'windage' (gap between the ball and side of the barrel) led to low muzzle velocity which meant short range, inconsistent and inaccurate shooting, particularly by individuals firing deliberately at selected targets. A Colonel Hanger, writing in 1814, said '. . . [the musket ball] will strike a figure of a man at 80 yards – it may even be at 100, but a soldier must be very unfortunate indeed who shall be wounded by a common musket at 150 yards provided his antagonist aims at him; and as to firing at a man at 200 . . . you may as well fire at the moon . . .'

During the heavy fighting at Talavera, in which Sharpe and the *S. Essex* were engaged, Major-General Hughes (in his book *Firepower*) calculated that only three or four musket shots per hundred fired actually hit somebody. Another authority (R. Henegan who was in charge of the field train) calculated that at the Battle of Vitória 3.675 million balls had been fired, causing around 8000 casualties – one hit per 459 shots.

95th RIFLEMAN ON CAMPAIGN – SUMMER 1809

(Rflm. Hagman who fought with Sharpe throughout the war but was killed at the Battle of Waterloo)

Usual issue black felt 'stovepipe' shako, with white metal buglehorn badge. Shako sometimes useful as an aiming rest when firing prone. When shako eventually fell to pieces, a soft, woollen forage cap, similar to a beret, was often worn.

Green cockade indicating marksman (normally black) with green woollen tuft above,

Green shako cord, riflemen being the only troops to have shako cord.

Hair long and heavy beard indicating this rifleman participating in long, hard campaign.

Rolled greatcoat on top of knapsack.

This rflm. has served with Sharpe for some time and been allowed to discard his stock. The 95th were still wearing them in 1813.

Black leather belts and accoutrements.

24-inch, brass handled sword bayonet more commonly used for chopping wood than against an enemy.

The uncomfortable 'Trotter' knapsack has been replaced with a soft calfskin one taken from a Frenchman.

Short, dark green (rudimentary camouflage) jacket with 3 rows of 9 white metal buttons but no lace. Black facings.

Single white armband indicates a 'chosen man' who commanded a squad if the NCO was absent. The original L/Cpl.

General issue 'Italian' style, barrel-shaped, wooden waterbottle.

Powderhorn containing fine, loose powder for careful (but slower) loading for maximum accuracy.

Common cloth haversack containing rations such as salted beef/pork and hardtack biscuit-bread.

Cartridge pouch on single crossbelt with made up cartidges for more rapid loading.

Waist pouch containing loose balls and patches for wrapping round balls prior to loading to ensure a tight fit in the barrel grooves.

Baker rifle. Flintlock, 30-inch long, grooved barrel. Effective range 200 yds. .615 calibre. Barrel 'browned' as distinct from polished. Weight 11 lb 2 ozs. Its greater accuracy was essential for skirmishing and picking off leaders, but rate of fire only 2 shots per min.

Brass covered 'butt box' containing rifle tools/cleaning kit.

Typical veteran's trousers – old, torn, patched and shrunk.

95th Rifleman on Campaign
Summer 1809

ruin so often was, perhaps, as much due to superior morale at the crucial moment as getting more bullets from more muskets. The *S. Essex* at *Valdelacasa* had witnessed a shaky Spanish battalion in square, facing cavalry, open fire at 200 yards and then collapse when the horsemen were upon them before they could reload.

Although every battalion had one light company of skirmishers they were armed, like their comrades in the battalion companies, with the musket (although it was eventually a slightly shorter version with a rudimentary backsight). Only the specialist Rifle Regiments were equipped with the Baker rifle. Sharpe joined the 2nd Battalion of the 95th Rifles in July 1805. From then on, he regarded himself as a rifleman; he always carried a rifle and wore his patched, faded and often filthy green jacket no matter what his task, or what unit he was serving with. The depth of his commitment to this Regiment is all the more remarkable considering that, out of twenty-two years' service from 1793 to 1815, he served with the 2/95th for only three and a half years – all of them as Quartermaster. He was particularly loyal and protective to the riflemen who had been with him, cut off from the rest of the army, in Galicia during the winter of 1809. Typical of such men and the equipment they carried, was *Hagman* (*see* SKETCH 2, *p. 30*).

The 95th had three battalions in the Peninsula, for most of the time fighting in the Light Division. Riflemen were present at virtually every major engagement (and countless minor ones) of the war. They drank the toast 'First in the field and last out of it' for years after the war. Their dark green uniforms earned them the nickname 'The Sweeps', their agile skirmishing, 'The Grasshoppers'. Because they usually fought dispersed they carried no Colours and reacted to whistle blasts and bugle calls rather than the beating of drums. They concealed themselves, they fought in pairs, loaded their rifles kneeling or crouching behind rocks or trees, fired from the prone position and dodged from cover to cover in advance or retirement. They were the eyes and ears of the commander-in-chief. The standard of their marksmanship,

'FRIENDLY FIRE'

Casualties accidentally inflicted by troops on their comrades (currently called 'friendly fire' victims) have always been commonplace in battle. It is only recently with intense media coverage that they have been given such prominence. The 95th, skirmishing in front of Almeida in July 1810, were shelled by the Portuguese garrison's guns, and several deaths resulted. It was thought the dark green uniforms and the proximity of the riflemen to the enemy caused the error.

95th Riflemen

training, discipline, and internal unit administration was the envy of the army – not forgetting that riflemen did not have the vast amount of kit to polish like other soldiers. The standard of man-management and leadership expected of their officers was exceptional. They were undoubtedly an élite force. They were also very new, having been formed from 'An Experimental Corps of Riflemen' created from 443 volunteers of all ranks from fifteen Line Regiments, in March 1800.

Although Sharpe never considered himself anything but a rifleman it was with the *S. Essex* that he saw most of his fighting, and in this Regiment that he gained promotion to major. His experience of war, of command in battle and his leadership were gained primarily as a company officer in the Light Company of the *S. Essex*. He joined them in Spain in July 1809, as a lieutenant, just prior to the disaster at *Valdelacasa*. He left them early in 1814 to become a brigade major during the Battle of Toulouse. During that time his exploits had given the Regiment back its honour by taking the Eagle

at Talavera and thus changing its cap badge to that of an
Eagle in Chains. He secured for it the patronage of the Prince
Regent and its change of name to *The Prince of Wales' Own
Volunteers*. He had been responsible for the survival of the
Regiment not only on the battlefield but in the venal political
world of London. He had seen the *S. Essex* develop from an
ill-led, green battalion fresh from Fort Amherst in Chatham
(where they were stationed during their raising in 1808) to a
veteran unit with nine battle honours. It had, at times, been
a close-run thing.

The *S. Essex* provides an example of a single-battalion
regiment's struggle for life during the years 1809 to 1814.
Having arrived at Lisbon in May 1809 with about 950 all
ranks they were virtually at full strength. They looked a smart
unit in new uniforms, gleaming buttons, chins thrust forward
over stiff stocks, with well-burnished muskets. But, like all
fresh battalions, they were unfit. They needed time to accli-
matise to the searing heat of the summer; their stomachs
needed to get accustomed to strange local foods and dirty
water, and their feet and lungs needed to be hardened to
endless slogging over endless hills. They were not given time
for any of these things. The long march from Lisbon to
Plasencia (230 miles) under a blistering June sun was a grim
experience – men fell out, quenched their thirst with dubious
water, became sick and straggled, despite *Simmerson*'s re-
sorting to the lash for the laggards. When they paraded at
Plasencia to meet the Spanish battalion (DIAGRAM 1) they
had lost about 75 men. Sharpe and his 30 riflemen brought
the battalion back to over 800 – a strong unit.

The fiasco at *Valdelacasa* in which the *S. Essex* lost their
King's Colour was an appalling start to the Regiment's history. Wellington had given them an easy task, to destroy a
bridge well away from serious opposition. They were being
broken in gently, but within six months they suffered the
ultimate disgrace. They had also had 256 unnecessary casualties. Wellington punished them by making them a battalion
of detachments – the name *S. Essex* no longer appeared as a
Regiment in Wellington's army. This down-grading was not

SERGEANT'S PIKE

Except in Rifle
Regiments (where they
carried rifles) infantry
sergeants were not
issued with firearms,
carrying instead a
seven-foot pike, with a
cross-piece below the
point to prevent
over-penetration.
Sometimes known as
halberds they were
used to make a
triangle to which a
man was tied to be
flogged. Sergeants also
carried a sword but in
action seemed to prefer
the pike. The ex-
ception would be the
NCO in the 1/7th
(Royal Fusiliers) who
was running with his
pike, tripped, caught
the point in the
ground and fell
forward on the butt,
which went right
through his body.

In the Regiment's short life it had three sets of Colours. The King's Colour (lost at *Valdelacasa*) was the Union flag with the words 'South Essex' (no regimental number) surrounded by a wreath of roses, thistles and shamrocks embroidered in the centre. The Regimental Colour was yellow (facing's colour), with a small Union flag in the top corner adjacent to the pike, and the same device in the centre as the King's Colour. The second set, issued after Talavera, involved both Colours having the Eagle in Chains badge surmounted by the words 'South Essex', the whole surrounded by the wreath of roses, thistles and shamrocks in the centre. The third set was issued in August 1813 after the Prince Regent had granted them the title of *The Prince of Wales' Own Volunteers*. The device in the centre then incorporated the Prince of Wales's feathers and scroll. At this stage both Colours would have had the battle honours of Talavera, Badajoz, Salamanca (and possibly Vitória) embroidered on. The Colours were six feet six inches flying, and

S. Essex Regimental flag

deserved by their strength (at around 550 they were still a viable battalion) but was a way of punishing *Simmerson* for his incompetence when he could not be sacked because of his powerful political friends in London. Morale was abysmal; there was almost a mutiny at Oropesa.

No brigade commander wanted a battalion of detachments which had lost a Colour in a skirmish. At Talavera (MAPS 9 AND 10) they were in the 3rd Division, where General Hill moved them from Stewart's Brigade to Donkin's in an effort to keep them out of trouble. Their fortunes were redeemed when Sharpe captured the French Eagle, and were rewarded by regaining their name and seeing the departure of *Simmerson*. In the autumn of 1809 the army retired back to Portugal, and the *S. Essex* spent the winter patrolling the southern border before marching north in the summer of 1810 to Celorico. A year with little to do, a high wastage rate and no reinforcements took its toll on numbers. Then came a winter behind the Lines of Torres Vedras, still awaiting drafts which did not materialise. By March 1811, the battalion had been split into small company detachments on line of communication duties and was down to barely 400. They were not strong enough to participate in the Battle of Fuentes de Onoro (MAPS 14 AND 15) in May 1811, and although they were part of General Picton's 3rd Division, which was destined to carry out the assault on the main breach at Ciudad Rodrigo in January 1812, the *S. Essex* were desperately weak and were deliberately held back. Only the Light Company under Sharpe had a role to play. The battalion faced disbandment.

Switched to yet another division (Major-General Colville's 4th), they were saved by the arrival of several hundred reinforcements in February 1812, just in time for the blood-bath at Badajoz (MAP 16). They fought hard and suffered severely at Salamanca (MAP 22), bearing the brunt of the French counter-attack under Clausel. They were in the ghastly retreat from Burgos to Portugal in November 1812, during which discipline broke down in many units. As in so many battalions, their soldiers collapsed from fatigue, hunger and disease. Men looted wine cellars, became insensible and, in some instances, mutinous. The *S. Essex* survived, but only just. During that winter of discontent (1812–13), Wellington broke dozens of officers, hanged six and flogged sixty soldiers to restore discipline. The *S. Essex* were once again down to less than 400 men. By the spring, however, after several months at Lamego (MAP 26) on the Douro River, more drafts had brought them to a respectable strength of 600.

In 1813 the battalion was in the 5th Division under Major-General Oswald, and marched into Spain for the last time. At the Battle of Vitória (MAP 29) they were involved in the bitter fighting for the key bridge in the village of Gamorra Mayor (MAP 29), where heavy losses brought their numbers to an all-time low of 234 men on parade plus 96 in hospital. The problem all along had been the lack of a 2nd battalion at home to supply a regular infusion of recruits. What was not known during 1813 was that another battalion had been authorised, but that the corrupt activities of *Simmerson* and others had prevented the reinforcements from being sent to

six feet on the pike, which was nine feet ten inches long. The cords and tassels were crimson and gold mixed. A heavy burden for the ensign, especially in a strong wind.

S. ESSEX BATTLE HONOURS

The Regiment was entitled to nine battle honours for services during the period 1809–15. They were: Peninsula, Talavera, Badajoz, Salamanca, Vitória, Nivelle, Orthez, Toulouse and Waterloo. It is unlikely that all were emblazoned on their Colours before disbandment in 1817. The Regiment was not present at Fuentes de Onoro. It was not given Ciudad Rodrigo, as only the Light Company was engaged, or Pyrenees, as its numbers were small and it was employed mostly on guard duties awaiting reinforcements. Although Sharpe was not present, it participated in the Battle of Orthez in the 2nd Division, going into action east of the town. Quatre Bras was not awarded as a battle honour to any regiment, as they received Waterloo.

Regimental punishments in the 95th Rifles

PUBLIC PUNISHMENTS were for riflemen only; NCOs were reduced in rank, totally or partially. The least severe was Confinement to Barracks, with or without 'coat turning', which involved being taken to the tailor's shop and having the letter 'C' sewn on the offender's right sleeve, for which he was charged twopence. Next, was confinement in the 'black hole' (guardroom cells) for a maximum of eight days. This also involved coat turning and paying threepence.

The most severe was punishment at the triangles – flogging, and could be inflicted only by a court-martial. It was usually carried out after evening parade, the bugle-major obtaining the cat-o'-nine-tails from the quartermaster sergeant, the cost of which was charged to the soldier's account. The punishment was carried out and the sentence entered in the Court-Martial, or 'Black Book' of the Regiment. For some minor offences a company court-martial would be assembled. Sergeants could not be tried by them, but one for a corporal could be convened by a written order from the company commander to the sergeant-major instructing him to assemble a court composed of three sergeants and two corporals. A rifleman could be tried by a corporal, a 'chosen' man (later called a lance-corporal) and three riflemen. This court could pass sentences of extra duties, confinement to barracks, fines for the benefit of messes, and cobbing (spanking the backside with a tailor's sleeve board or similar object, done in private not in front of the troops, as with flogging).

REGIMENTAL AWARDS

The Peninsular War saw the introduction of good conduct, marksmanship and bravery awards by some regiments but not by the government. Some divided soldiers into two classes depending on behaviour, with the better class receiving privileges. Others instituted good conduct medals (5th, 7th, 22nd, 38th, 52nd, 71st, 74th, 88th, 95th,

Spain. Sharpe was able to sort matters out and bring over 400 men out in time for the crossing of the Nivelle (MAP 31) and the Battle of Toulouse (MAP 34) in April 1814. By that time the Regiment had royal patronage and had become *The Prince of Wales' Own Volunteers*.

As such they fought again at Quatre Bras and Waterloo. Two years later, on the principle of last formed, first disbanded, the *PWOV*, whose motto was *Caveat Actor* (Let the Doer Beware), was broken up as part of the general rundown of the army. Many soldiers returned to civil life, some transferred into the 9th Foot (Norfolks) or the 44th Foot (East Essex). The old depot at Chelmsford was burnt down in the Chartist Revolt of 1840, but their notorious training area on Foulness Island remains to this day Ministry of Defence property with restricted access. Some civilian veterans took up arms again; Sharpe and *Harper* fought in Chile in 1820. At about the same time a small group gave their services to Simón Bolívar, the revolutionary leader in South America who secured the independence from Spain of Venezuela, Colombia, Ecuador, Panama, Peru and Bolivia. Three ex-*S. Essex* soldiers settled in Nova Scotia. One elderly veteran, who was living in New Orleans, was persuaded to fight for Texan independence and died at the Alamo in 1836. In the year Sharpe died (1860) it was reported that an aged veteran was drilling militia volunteers in North Carolina. This was the last anyone heard of survivors of a long defunct Regiment. It is planned to create a *S. Essex* Regimental Museum, which will contain its Colours, silver, weapons, relics and records, in Fort Amherst, in Kent.

97th and some corps). The 52nd and 95th awarded a laurel wreath badge with the letters 'VS' (Valiant Stormer) beneath to survivors of the forlorn hopes at Ciudad Rodrigo and Badajoz. It was worn on the right sleeve.

3

Sharpe's Tiger

The story is set in India during the Fourth Mysore War against the Tippoo Sultan in 1799. Sharpe was a private in the 33rd Foot and Colonel Wellesley was an acting deputy commander of the British forces under Lieutenant-General Harris. The 33rd was under Major John Shee. The British forces advanced on Seringapatam (now Sriringapatna), the Tippoo's capital. As they approached the city Sharpe was flogged, but the punishment was stopped after 202 lashes to allow him to go on a special mission inside Seringapatam, with the promise of promotion if he succeeded. He 'deserted' and joined a French unit fighting for the Tippoo, but was betrayed (by *Sergeant Hakeswill*) and imprisoned. However, he escaped in time to prevent heavy British casualties in the storming of the breach by prematurely exploding a mine set to destroy them. He earned promotion to sergeant.

A WEEK BEFORE CHRISTMAS 1798, Colonel Arthur Wellesley obtained an important independent command – preparing the Army of Madras for an offensive against the Tippoo Sultan of Mysore. Two days before Christmas he was given the Arab horse, Diomed, which four years later was spiked under him at Assaye, an incident in which Sergeant Sharpe was intimately involved. These events were the direct result of the bizarre, indeed tragic, events of 16 December, when Colonel Henry Ashton, the officer tasked with assembling the troops, fought two duels.

Until recently, Ashton had been commanding the 12th Foot

(East Suffolk), but his headquarters' duties had compelled him to hand over to a Major John Picton. A misunderstanding arose between Picton (the elder brother of Sir Thomas Picton, who would be one of Sharpe's divisional commanders in the Peninsula) and Ashton. The dispute involved a minor problem concerning the other field officer with the 12th, a Major Allen. Touchy tempers and slighted honour led Major Picton to challenge the colonel to a duel, and early on the morning of 16 December they faced each other with pistols. Picton fired first and missed. Ashton, who was an excellent shot, deliberately and disdainfully fired in the air. Within hours, Allen challenged Ashton, who could have refused on both occasions but foolishly did not. So, twice in one day a colonel accepted to defend his honour against his subordinates – unique in the history of duelling. Again his opponent fired first, but this time with more effect. Ashton was hit in the side – a severe wound, probably through the liver. He remained standing, however, and once more fired into the air. On hearing the news of his friend's injury, Wellesley rode all night from Fort St George, Madras, to be with him. He arrived on the eighteenth and assumed command of the assembling troops while Ashton lay dying. Shortly before he died on the twenty-third, Ashton gave his charger – Diomed – to his friend.

WELLINGTON'S DUEL

Almost thirty years after Ashton's double duel, Wellesley (then the Duke of Wellington and prime minister) challenged Lord Winchilsea to a duel. The challenge was taken up and the two met in Battersea Fields early on the morning of 21 March 1829. Wellington's doctor produced a pair of duelling pistols as the Duke of Wellington did not own any. The doctor loaded both weapons. Wellington, anxious to proceed, said to his second, Lord Hardinge (who had lost an arm at the Battle of Ligny), 'Now then, Hardinge, look sharp and step out the ground. I have no time to waste, dammit!' An unsuccessful attempt was made to settle the affair, so the noble lords squared off. After a few seconds Hardinge said, 'Gentlemen, are you ready – Fire!' Wellington aimed his pistol but, seeing Winchilsea hesitate, deliberately fired wide of him. Winchilsea smiled, raised his arm and fired into the air.

English Duelling Pistols

Three months earlier, a seasick Private Sharpe, together with about 400 soldiers of the 33rd, had been hurled through the infamous surf onto the open beach below Fort St George. It was a frightening finish to an appalling voyage, which took twenty-five days instead of the normal five. The 33rd had been ordered south from Calcutta (Bengal) to stiffen the Army of Madras, and Wellesley and half the Regiment had the misfortune to sail in the Indiaman Fitz William. The ship went aground in the muddy mouth of the Hooghly River, and a thousand bags of saltpetre had to be thrown overboard while the troops heaved and sweated for hours to drag her off. Thereafter, the ship leaked dangerously, necessitating the manning of pumps day and night. The drinking water was contaminated, so Sharpe, with his commanding officer and virtually all on board, experienced the agonies of 'Bengal Belly' (dysentery). Fifteen died from it. The ship's barrels had probably been filled from the Lall Diggee, a large open pond which provided much of Calcutta's water supply. A correspondent to the Bengal Gazette wrote of this source, 'I saw a string of parria [sic] dogs without an ounce of hair on some of them, and in the last stage of mange, plunge in and refresh themselves very comfortably.'

Only experienced local boatmen, operating special raft-type vessels held together with rope, could get men or cargo ashore at Madras. Monstrous green waves, crested with foam, raced for the shore from the darker blue waters of the Bay of Bengal, with nothing to break their endless charge. Soaked, exhausted and terrified, the soldiers could do nothing but trust the boatmen to catch a crest at precisely the right moment. To be overturned was to drown.

By the end of the eighteenth century the British were the dominant European power on the Indian sub-continent. They had gone there for trade and that was the reason they remained, making immense fortunes. Their rivals had been the Dutch, the Portuguese and, particularly, the French. When Sharpe arrived after a ten-month sea voyage (broken briefly at the Cape of Good Hope) in February 1797, British control had long been exercised through the East India Company (EIC), which had grown into a government complete with trappings of authority, including an extensive civil service. All of which cost London nothing. To protect its assets, the EIC was allowed to raise its own military forces (native troops officered by Europeans), and its multitudinous activities, administration and personnel (civil and military) were self-financing. One of its most senior officials had the title of 'Collector' and indeed he collected revenue, principally land tax.

There were three British (EIC) Presidencies, or provinces, in India at that time. In the north-east was the Bengal Presidency based on Calcutta with the centre of power in Fort William. Eight hundred miles to the south was the Madras Presidency. Another 600 miles to the north-west was the third, the Bombay Presidency, facing the Arabian Sea and based on Bombay. At the head of the Madras and Bombay administrations was a governor who was subordinate to the governor-general in Fort William (Calcutta), although the huge distances made him more of a first among equals. Beyond and around these comparatively small enclaves were scores of native Indian rulers: the rajahs, the princes, and the sultans. These were absolute monarchs motivated by self-interest – the retention of land, wealth and authority – and controlled a patchwork quilt of states, some as large as Spain, others as small as Surrey.

One such ruler was the Tippoo Sultan of Mysore. In 1800 he was forty-six, a cruel, bigoted Muslim who claimed descent from the Prophet but ruled over an overwhelmingly Hindu state. His father, Hyder Ali, had been half-Afghan and comparatively light-skinned. His son was short, flabby and much darker, with a pencil moustache and thick neck. But he did not lack courage or ability as a soldier and administrator. He had been a soldier since he was a boy of fourteen, when he commanded a cavalry unit. He had fought for his father against the British in the First Mysore War, 1766–9, the Second Mysore War, 1780–3, and after his father's death he commanded the army in the Third Mysore War, 1789–92.

ship was in, checked cargoes. Not many survived the diseases and climate; it has been said that the odds of such a young man seeing home again were about the same as those of a subaltern leaving for the trenches in World War I.

THE BLACK HOLE OF CALCUTTA

Fort William was an immensely impressive fortification. It had been built to ensure that British Calcutta would never again be overrun, as it had been in 1756. Then the Nabob of Bengal had attacked the city, and there had been panic. Led by the governor, Roger Drake, most of the English fled in boats into the middle of the Hooghly River and steadfastly refused to return for the 146 men and their families left behind. The Nabob ordered these to be imprisoned in a small cell, said to be 18 feet long by 14 feet wide. Even if these measurements are understated, in the steamy, suffocating heat of an Indian summer night it is not surprising only twenty-three people were alive the next morning.

By 1799 the Tippoo was ready to recoup some of his lost land and authority – with the help of the French. Little Île de France (Mauritius) had declared its willingness, but could provide only about a hundred volunteers. Of greater significance was Bonaparte's victorious presence in Cairo. A French

Tippoo's Tiger

The Tippoo's tigers

THE WORD TIPU is Kanarese (a Dravidian language of western India) for tiger. The Tippoo Sultan was obsessed with them: in daily life the tiger served as a sort of armorial bearing. His royal throne (which he swore not to use until he had defeated the British) was in tiger form; the support was a large wooden tiger carrying the throne on its back, its head covered in gold and its eyes and teeth of rock crystal. The throne's frame was octagonal, surrounded by a low rail on which were ten small tiger heads made of gold, and beautifully inlaid with precious stones. The whole was covered in a thin sheet of gold and surmounted by a canopy fringed with thousands of pearls. Tiger stripes were incorporated in the uniforms of his troops; some mortars were in the form of crouching tigers, and the muzzles of cannons and hilts of swords were fashioned into tigers' heads. As we might keep watchdogs, the Tippoo kept tigers (one guarded Sharpe's dungeon at night). They were later shot by soldiers of the 33rd on Wellesley's orders. His two hunting cheetahs were not killed, but sent as a gift, with six Indian keepers, to King George III. Tippoo Sultan's tiger organ came to Britain and can be seen in London's Victoria and Albert Museum. It depicts a prostrate European soldier being savaged by a tiger, and when a handle is cranked it plays an organ inside the tiger, the sounds supposedly resembling the snarling of the beast and cries of the victim. Its voice, alas, is not what it was in Sharpe's day.

force landing at Mangalore (MAP 2) would receive the Tippoo's unstinting support – and the blessings of Allah. Unease was replaced by apprehension in Forts William and St George. This, at any rate, was the excuse the British needed to launch the Fourth Mysore War. If the Tippoo were deposed, British rule in southern India would be unchallenged.

Since May 1798, British India had been little short of a Wellesley family fiefdom. That was the month when Richard Wellesley, the Irish Lord Mornington, stepped ashore at Calcutta to a thunderous salute from the eighteen-pounder cannons on the walls of Fort William. The new governor-general had arrived. He brought with him as his private secretary his youngest brother, Henry. He had already met Arthur in Madras in April, during a brief stop on the voyage north. On the same ship was Major-General David Baird, an officer who was to play an aggressive and significant role in the coming hostilities. About fourteen years earlier he had been released after four years manacled in the Tippoo's cells at Seringapatam – the same cells which would house Sharpe, *McCandless, Lawford* and *Hakeswill*. Baird had little love for the natives: a characteristic which a year later cost him the military governorship of Seringapatam.

The campaign plan involved squeezing the Tippoo between two very unequal arms of a pincer, the hoped-for outcome being that he would be crushed in his capital, Seringapatam (MAP 2). In overall command of the Madras Army was Lieutenant-General George Harris, who had received a severe head wound when a bullet had furrowed his scalp at Bunker Hill during the American War of Independence (Sharpe later noticed that Harris was always lifting the edge of his wig to scratch the old scar). His deputies were Major-General Baird and Colonel Wellesley. In February 1799, the strength of the Madras Army was around 20,000, of which 4300 were Europeans. The plan envisaged Harris marching from his assembly area at Vellore to reach Seringapatam 250 miles to the west. Before he reached Mysore he would be joined from the north by the Nizam of Hyderabad (recently seduced from French sympathies) with 20,000 native troops. Harris would set off

MAJOR-GENERAL BAIRD

Born 1757; served as a captain in India in the 73rd Foot (2nd Royal Highlanders). Severely wounded in the battle against Hyder Ali at Conjeveram in 1780. Taken prisoner and chained for forty-four months in the same dungeons in Seringapatam that would house Sharpe, *Lawford, McCandless* and *Hakeswill*. When his mother heard that captives were chained in pairs, she was reputed to have said, 'I pity the man who is chained to ma Davie!' He served in India again in 1791, then in the Cape of Good Hope before returning to be Harris's senior deputy at the storming of Seringapatam in 1799. He was a large, powerful and courageous man, but had no liking for the Indians and was jealous of the authority given to young Colonel Wellesley. He returned to the Cape of Good Hope (1805–6) and Copenhagen (1807). Was second-in-command to Moore at Corunna, but was wounded shortly after Moore died. Promoted general 1814, but saw no more active service; died 1829.

The army on the march

TO MOVE AN ARMY in India required about five camp followers for every man with a musket. When Harris and the Nizam advanced into Mysore, they did so in a vast parallelogram about seven miles long by three wide, with infantry forming the flanks and cavalry the front and rear. Inside were the siege guns, the baggage, the carts, the *brinjarries* (grain merchants), servants, camp followers, their families, the grass-cutters (each cavalryman had one to procure fodder) – all jumbled in a immense sea of animals. These were the beasts of burden: elephants, camels and horses, but above all bullocks. The great majority were pack rather than draught animals, hired, together with their owners, to supply and carry the army. It is estimated that Harris's baggage and commissariat required 60,000 bullocks plus another 20,000 with his *brinjarries*. Add another 36,000 for the Nizam, and the staggering total is almost 120,000. In effect, the army fed from a gigantic, ponderously moving bazaar that crossed the dry countryside under a choking cloud of red dust. As they moved, they consumed. Such a mass of men and animals stripped the surrounding country of anything edible as thoroughly as a plague of locusts. When General Stuart's force joined Harris in mid-April there were about 50,000 soldiers, 120,000 followers and 120,000 bullocks encamped around Seringapatam.

on 13 February; moving at under 10 miles a day and resting every third day, he might expect to reach Seringapatam around mid-April – if the Tippoo did not intervene beforehand. The western arm of the pincer was flimsy, consisting of slightly over 6000 troops of the Bombay Army under local (an important distinction when seniority issues were so sensitive) Lieutenant-General James Stuart. From the west coast at Cannanore he had only half the distance to march so he would start eight days later than Harris, and take up a defensive position in a pass in the Western Ghats.

The glaring weakness in the strategy was obvious: the Tippoo was occupying what strategists call an 'interior lines' position. He was sitting between two opponents who were a long way away from each other and had virtually no means of communicating or co-ordinating their movements. He could strike one long before the other could intervene. And this is exactly what the Tippoo did. Selecting the weaker

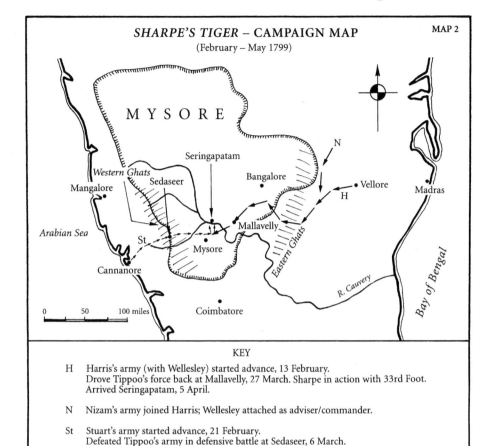

SHARPE'S TIGER – CAMPAIGN MAP
(February – May 1799)

MAP 2

MYSORE

Seringapatam

Western Ghats

Sedaseer

Bangalore

Mangalore

N

Vellore

H

Madras

Arabian Sea

St

Mallavelly

Mysore

Eastern Ghats

Cannanore

R. Cauvery

Bay of Bengal

0   50   100 miles

Coimbatore

KEY

H   Harris's army (with Wellesley) started advance, 13 February.
Drove Tippoo's force back at Mallavelly, 27 March. Sharpe in action with 33rd Foot.
Arrived Seringapatam, 5 April.

N   Nizam's army joined Harris; Wellesley attached as adviser/commander.

St   Stuart's army started advance, 21 February.
Defeated Tippoo's army in defensive battle at Sedaseer, 6 March.
Arrived Seringapatam 14 April and moved north of the Cauvery River.

enemy, Stuart, he attacked the British position in the high
pass near Sedaseer on 6 March. Because the pass was so long
and narrow, Stuart had been able to deploy only three
Bombay Infantry (EIC) battalions and six guns for its defence
under an extremely capable commander, Lieutenant-Colonel
John Montresor. In a four-hour battle, against odds of five
to one, Montresor's guns and native infantry smashed all
assaults. The Tippoo turned away to find Harris.

On 27 March, near an unknown town in Mysore named
Mallavelly, Sharpe the soldier killed his first enemy in close
combat. The Tippoo's army barred the British advance from

Pay-rate differences between Indian and British soldiers were enormous. Even so the sepoys, as the Indian troops were called, lived comparatively well compared with the average villager or urban worker. In Sharpe's time, an Indian rupee was worth about two shillings. Monthly pay rates:

Indian

Private	6 rupees
Corporal	8 rupees
Sergeant	10 rupees
Officers	16 – 60 rupees

British

Private	30 shillings (Rs15)
Corporal	40 shillings (Rs20)
Sergeant	55 shillings (Rs28)
Officers	120 shillings up (Rs60)

a low ridge. Wellesley and the 33rd had been attached to the Nizam's army, the colonel to 'advise' the Nizam (Meer Allum) and the battalion to add backbone to the native troops. Wellesley's column bumped the enemy first and came under artillery fire. Harris ordered him to push on, which he did with the 33rd leading a force of six EIC battalions. They formed line from column with each battalion echeloned back to the left rear of the one on its right. On the extreme right, out in front, was the 33rd under the temporary command of Major John Shee, an officer with a liking for the bottle. There were over 750 men advancing in a two-deep line, with the Light Company under *Captain Morris* on the left and Sharpe in the rear rank on the left of that. Wellesley had ridden forward on Diomed as a huge enemy column of between two and three thousand infantry poured over the crest of the rise and rolled down. Wellesley halted the 33rd and, with the enemy a mere sixty yards away, gave them a devastating volley followed by a bayonet charge. In the mêlée Sharpe confronted an Indian officer who, although he had a drawn sabre, fumbled to draw his pistol, then turned to run. Sharpe struck him in the side of the neck with his bayonet, parried a sabre slash, kicked him in the groin (which was to become a favourite tactic), and slammed his musket butt into the officer's face before driving his bayonet into his throat. He then looted the dying man of a few coins. It had been easy, it had been quick – and Sharpe had enjoyed it.

The British were then about a week's march from Seringapatam. On the day following the clash at Mallavelly, *Colonel Hector McCandless*, a senior EIC intelligence officer, was captured and taken to Seringapatam, and Sharpe was goaded into striking *Sergeant Hakeswill*, and was arrested pending a regimental court-martial. On 30 March Major Shee sent Sharpe 'to the halberds' to receive 2000 lashes, but apparently he exceeded his authority as a commanding officer in two ways. Firstly, hitting an NCO was so serious an offence that cases were heard by a general court-martial. A regimental court-martial at least should have been assembled, consisting of a minimum of three officers and excluding the

Flogging

MAJOR SHEE exceeded his powers in first trying Sharpe himself and then awarding 2000 lashes. He should have convened a drumhead regimental court-martial of three officers. There was certainly time for this on a rest day – General Crauford was known to hold them during a halt on the line of march. If it had found Sharpe guilty and handed down a punishment Shee, as his commanding officer, had the discretionary power to remit the whole, or part, of the punishment – something he was most unlikely to do. Sentences varied from 25 (a minimum) to 1200 lashes (maximum permitted), which was calculated to kill most men. It was normally reserved for desertion to the enemy, robbery with violence or striking an officer.

Only ten such awards were made during the Peninsular War, whereas over fifty received 1000 lashes. A surgeon was always present and could halt the punishment if he considered the man close to death. This was only a postponement (unless he had a humane commanding officer), the culprit had to receive the remainder (in one or more instalments) when pronounced fit. In theory, if a soldier died under the lash the sentence was to be completed on his lifeless corpse. Drummers flogged the prisoner and were supposed to carry a cat-o'-nine-tails in their pack. With heavy sentences several drummers would be involved, taking turns to give twenty-five lashes each.

Flogging – an example

THERE WERE a few men of iron who walked away from hundreds of lashes. One was Sergeant Thomas Mayberry of the 95th. He was sentenced to 700 for gambling with £200 of public funds, which had been entrusted to him to buy 'necessaries' for his men. A Corporal Morrisson and Rifleman Divine were also implicated. When Mayberry was tied up, he was offered (as was then customary) the option of banishment. He refused, despite Morrisson and Divine, who were to get 300 and 100 respectively, entreating him to accept. Incredibly, Mayberry took his punishment without a sound. Morrisson yelled and struggled so violently

that the halberds collapsed and he had to be held by two men. Divine looked so frail that the colonel took pity and he was let off with 25.

Mayberry, a man of immense strength and courage, almost won his stripes back in the breach at Badajoz. His company commander was so impressed by his actions (he had accounted for seven enemy) that he ordered him to the rear with the promise of his rank back. Mayberry, although covered in blood from several wounds, refused to retire, and was eventually killed by a sword-cut that split open his skull.

commanding officer – Shee should not have heard the case personally. Secondly, the maximum number of lashes that could be awarded by any court was 1200. Shee probably got away with these transgressions because the army was facing the enemy, and senior officers had more pressing matters. Also, he had the sentence carried out within two hours of passing it. Whatever the law, 1200 would have killed Sharpe as surely as 2000, but Wellesley's intervention on Harris's order after 202 lashes saved him. By the night of 31 March Sharpe and *Lieutenant Lawford* were in the cells in Seringapatam on their special mission to secure information from *McCandless*, having 'deserted' that morning.

Harris and the Nizam had encamped their armies west of the fortress of Seringapatam by the morning of 5 April (M A P 3). The Tippoo's fortress sat securely on Seringapatam Island protected on all sides by the north and south branches of the River Cauvery, although the river was fordable in most places. The Tippoo had to hold out until the monsoon would arrive – about the twentieth of May, which would bring immediate flooding and six months' security. If the British failed to take Seringapatam within eight weeks, they would have to withdraw. This was not long for a full-scale siege. The Tippoo had 30,000 men and hundreds of guns available. His troops were deployed, not just on the fortress walls, but within the fortified camp outside the eastern and southern walls, behind the Little Cauvery and as far west as the aqueduct. A particular strength of the fortress, of which the besiegers were unaware, was the hidden inner wall. Harris had to get his guns close enough, preferably within 400 yards, to the point in the walls selected for the breach. To avoid having to fight through the fortified camp, he chose the western side for the assault. This entailed considerable preliminary fighting to clear the enemy from behind the aqueduct and the Little Cauvery, virtually to the banks of the South Cauvery. Only then could he safely establish his main siege battery to begin the task of breaking in.

Harris ordered Wellesley to secure the area of Sultanpetah village, the wood to the north-west, and the line of the aqueduct in that area, by a night attack on 5 April. Wellesley put the Light and Grenadier Companies of the 33rd in the lead, followed by the rest of the battalion with the 1/11th and 2/11th Madras Native Infantry in reserve. Some 750 yards to the north Lieutenant-Colonel Shawe with the 12th Foot supported by the 1/1st and 2/3rd Madras Native Infantry were to carry out a similar operation. Wellesley personally led the 33rd.

Without meticulous planning and prior reconnaissance night attacks are often, if not always, chaotic, and this operation was Wellesley's only serious setback in his lengthy career. After failure at Sultanpetah, Wellesley contemplated a night attack only as a last resort.

There had been no proper reconnaissance; the night was pitch-black and the wood (tope) was found to be east of the aqueduct (itself fifteen yards wide and six feet deep on top of an embankment) instead of the west, as thought. The flank companies of the 33rd plunged through the water and blundered around in the thickets beyond, where they were fiercely attacked by the Tippoo's defenders. The first casualty on the British side was control. Captain West with the grenadiers ended up nearly a mile to the south; Major Shee with five battalion companies went a mile to the north, and eventually merged with Shawe's force. The Light Company was pushed back in confused close-quarter fighting in the tangled bamboo and brushwood of the tope. *Captain Morris's* leadership was ineffectual, and the only competent officer, Lieutenant Fitzgerald, had most of his arm torn away by a rocket and was then mortally wounded by a bayonet thrust – murdered by his own sergeant, *Hakeswill*. Sharpe, who had by then joined a French unit fighting for the Tippoo, added to the shambles by yelling conflicting orders in English. Although casualties were light – only about twenty-five, including eight prisoners, one of whom was *Hakeswill* – the attack petered out. An embarrassed but wiser Wellesley reported his failure to Harris personally. A similar assault in daylight the next day, again led by Wellesley with the King's

THUGS

Sleaman was made responsible for rooting out and destroying the Thugs – gangs of men who murdered and stole from travellers in the name of religion. A group would befriend a party of travellers then, on the signal of their leader (often a clap and a shout to 'Bring the tobacco!'), each thug pounced on his victim. They killed by strangulation, using a square hand-kerchief, in one corner of which was knotted a silver coin dedicated to the Hindu goddess Kali. Thugs believed they were carrying out a divine mission: one claimed to have murdered 719 people; his only regret was he did not reach 1000.

Scotch 'Brigade' (later the 94th Foot), easily drove off the enemy.

It was another month before Seringapatam was stormed. During those weeks Stuart's force arrived (14 April) and set up camp north of the river, and a series of British attacks drove the Tippoo's troops back towards the western walls of the fortress. By 2 May, after taking a number of key points such as the Mill Fort, two of the three main siege batteries were within 380 and 340 yards of their target. A total of 29 cannons and 3 howitzers commenced their pounding. Except for 2 24-pounders, these guns were throwing 18-pound iron balls. The sustained bombardment began to tear down 60 yards of curtain wall just south of the NW Bastion. Soon after the start, a huge explosion ripped the inside of the fortress as a magazine of rockets exploded.

Inside Seringapatam the Tippoo had presented Sharpe with a gold medallion for his efforts in the tope. However, on 25 April he and *Lawford* were betrayed. Thirteen British prisoners (eight captured on the fifth plus another five) from the 33rd had been paraded for execution by the Tippoo's musclemen bodyguards, the *jettis*. One by one they died, either by a terrible twisting of the head through 180 degrees, or having a nine-inch nail driven into their skulls. Each man had to wait his turn, watching his comrades die. *Hakeswill* was left to last, and was beside himself in a frenzy of fear and convulsions; he saved his neck (literally) by screaming his betrayal of Sharpe and *Lawford* just as the *jettis* began to turn his head.

The breach was pronounced practical on the evening of 3 May. The plan involved two assault columns attacking parallel to each other, both under the direct personal command of Major-General Baird (MAP 3). Wellesley commanded a reserve force in the rear. Each column was to clamber up the debris in the breach, and turn left and right to climb onto the walls before fighting their way round to encircle the fortress. Each column was headed by a 'forlorn hope' of volunteers. It consisted of a sergeant, carrying his Regiment's Colours, with twelve lightly equipped soldiers, followed by a

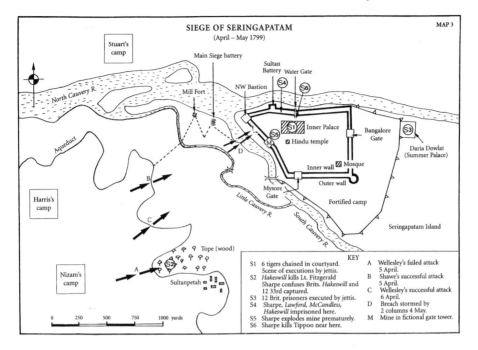

SIEGE OF SERINGAPATAM
(April – May 1799)   MAP 3

Stuart's camp

Main Siege battery

Sultan Battery   Water Gate

North Cauvery R.

Mill Fort

NW Bastion

S4   S6

Aqueduct

Inner Palace

S5   S1

Hindu temple

Bangalore Gate

S3

Daria Dowlat (Summer Palace)

D

Inner wall   Mosque

Outer wall

Harris's camp

B

Mysore Gate

Little Cauvery R.

Fortified camp

C

South Cauvery R.

Seringapatam Island

Nizam's camp

A

Tope (wood)

S2

Sultanpetah

KEY

S1   6 tigers chained in courtyard.
       Scene of executions by jettis.
S2   *Hakeswill* kills Lt. Fitzgerald
       Sharpe confuses Brits. *Hakeswill* and
       12 33rd captured.
S3   12 Brit. prisoners executed by jettis.
S4   Sharpe, *Lawford, McCandless,
       Hakeswill* imprisoned here.
S5   Sharpe explodes mine prematurely.
S6   Sharpe kills Tippoo near here.

A   Wellesley's failed attack
      5 April.
B   Shawe's successful attack
      5 April.
C   Wellesley's successful attack
      6 April.
D   Breach stormed by
      2 columns 4 May.
M   Mine in fictional gate tower.

0   250   500   750   1000 yards

subaltern (Lieutenant Lawrence on the left, Lieutenant Hill on the right) with another twenty-five men. The left column was commanded by Lieutenant-Colonel Dunlop from Stuart's force. Under him were six flank companies from Stuart's British regiments, the 12th and 33rd Foot plus ten companies of Bengal sepoy flankers. A matter of yards to the right the other column was under Lieutenant-Colonel Sherbrooke. His force was composed of the flank companies of the Scotch 'Brigade' and the Regiment de Meuron, the 73rd and 74th Foot and 14 flank companies of Bombay and Madras sepoys. About 5000 men, the majority of whom were Europeans, formed up in the trenches during the night of 3–4 May. They huddled, hidden but desperately hot and cramped, until 1 p.m. the next day.

At that precise time Baird drew his sword, stood and launched the assault. The attackers rushed forward under a galling fire and into the 300-yard-wide river, the passage of which had been marked out with white flags by Lieutenant Lalor of the 73rd. The water varied from ankle to waist deep.

SERINGAPATAM CASUALTIES

The British buried about 9000 of the Tippoo's soldiers after his defeat. The number of wounded is unknown. In the fort there were 287 cannons mounted on the walls plus 919 more in storage, together with 99,000 muskets, a large number of British manufacture. The price the British paid was comparatively small – just under 900 Europeans and 649 Indians killed, wounded and missing.

SUTTEE

Widow-burning
would possibly have
been the fate of *Mary
Bickerstaff* had she
married the Hindu
Kunwar Singh. It
arose from the Hindu
belief that a married
woman's husband is
her god on earth. To
be burnt on her
husband's funeral pyre
was the only certain
way to paradise for
both of them. It was
supposedly voluntary,
but enormous
pressure was put on
the widow to submit,
despite the terror and
agony in store. In
Bengal she was tied to
the often putrid
corpse, while men
stood by with poles to
push her back into the
flames should she
break free. In 1813 the
EIC tried to check the
practice by ordering
that an Indian police
officer be present to
certify the woman was
not drugged, pregnant
or a minor, and that
she went willingly. A
few did. William
Sleaman forbade *suttee*
in his district in the
1820s but one widow
insisted she was dead
already, that she
would feel no pain and
would neither eat nor
drink until Sleaman
gave permission. After
a week he did so. The
fire was lit, the
woman walked round
once, stepped in and
lay down without a

Within six minutes the forlorn hope had climbed the breach and Sergeant Graham planted his Colours in the rubble at the top and announced himself 'Lieutenant Graham!' (a promotion he would receive for being the first man into the breach). He was shot dead immediately. But there was no stopping the rush: men from both columns scrambled up onto the outer walls on either side of the breach. There was some dismay at the depth of the ditch behind the outer wall, and that the inner wall was undamaged and manned by the enemy in large numbers. It was at this stage, before the attackers had got down into the space between the walls, that Sharpe, who had escaped from the dungeons, prematurely exploded the mine intended to destroy the assaulting force in this gap. In reality there was no mine.

Captain Goodall, with the left column, found a narrow bridge across the gap and led his men across in single file, and once a lodgement had been secured on the inner wall the defenders were driven back. The Tippoo exposed himself to fire a succession of muskets from behind a traverse on the north wall, calmly firing shot after shot as the weapons were handed to him by his aides. With one, he killed Lieutenant Lalor, but despite his efforts resistance crumbled in the north and the Tippoo was wounded and forced to retire. Baird accompanied the right column which secured both the southern and eastern walls, including the Mysore and Bangalore Gates, within an hour.

It was thought that the Tippoo might be hiding inside the Inner Palace but a search proved fruitless. The exact circumstances of his death will never be known. The version given by the British army's historian, Fortescue, has the Tippoo, who had been twice wounded, borne back to the Water Gate in the north wall. His followers tried to lift him into his palanquin to get him away, but they were too late. He was hit again and attacked by British soldiers hand-to-hand, finally falling to a bullet through the temple, possibly fired by a soldier from the 12th Foot. He collapsed, and in the fury of the fighting by the inner wall Water Gate his body became covered with other corpses – possibly unrecognised. When the fighting was over, one of his aides, who had probably feigned death under the palanquin, crawled out and indicated where he had died. Corpse after corpse was lifted and examined by torchlight until the flabby and bloody body of the Tippoo was revealed. He was wearing no jewels. The man who killed him never claimed the credit. But neither did Sharpe.

sound. *Suttee* was officially prohibited in 1829 in all three presidencies, but it continued over a hundred years later.

The loot

WHEN WELLESLEY was made military governor of Seringapatam (over Baird's head) on the day following its fall, he flogged and hanged to restore order. It was too late, however, to prevent a night of pillage and rampage. Seringapatam was sacked. Sharpe secured the jewels the Tippoo wore at the time of his death – a minute fraction of the haul of treasure. The symbol of Mysorean power – the light green, silken standard with a red hand in its centre – was taken by Baird from the palace roof and sent to Fort William. The huge, gilded tiger's head from the Sultan's throne ended up in Windsor Castle, and the dreadful tiger organ is in the Victoria and Albert Museum.

The value of the treasure looted was estimated at £2 million, a fair proportion of which found its way into soldiers' hands as virtually every house in the city was raided. It was said that a single casket of jewels valued at £300,000 disappeared from the palace. The coins and jewels seized officially by the authorities were declared prize money for the army, which meant that most senior officers became rich. Baird was presented with the Tippoo's jewel-encrusted sword by a special prize committee. Harris, however, had a six-year legal battle with a penny-pinching EIC to keep his allocation. The Privy Council decided in his favour.

4

Sharpe's Rifles

In the bitter winter of 1809 the French were winning the war in Spain and the British army, under Sir John Moore, was retreating towards Corunna with Napoleon's forces in close pursuit. Lieutenant Sharpe and a detachment of about fifty riflemen from the 95th Rifles were cut off from the remainder of Moore's army and surrounded by enemy cavalry. In order to escape Sharpe joined forces with a Spanish cavalry officer, *Major Blas Vivar*, and his band of Cazadores. Sharpe was reluctantly persuaded to take part in a desperate attack on the French-occupied Galician city of Santiago de Compostela before making his way into northern Portugal and safety.

IN 1808 NAPOLEON, at the zenith of his power, resolved to add the kingdoms of Spain and Portugal to the territories under his rule. An expeditionary force under General Androche Junot marched across Spain to Lisbon, arriving to see the sails of the Portuguese fleet disappearing over the horizon on its way to Brazil with the royal court. Soon afterwards, the Spanish royal family was compelled to abdicate. Joseph Bonaparte, Napoleon's elder brother, was proclaimed king and French armies overran Spain. But the country at once flared into insurrection. The French suffered a series of defeats forcing them to retire behind the line of the Ebro river, abandoning Madrid and Junot with 25,000 men isolated in Portugal. Following the urgings of the Spanish and Portuguese authorities, the British government determined to send an expedition to expel Junot from Lisbon. At thirty-nine, the youngest lieutenant-general in the army, Sir Arthur Wellesley was delighted to get command of the tiny force earmarked for the task. Some 9000 men, virtually all infantry, would sail from Cork to be joined in Portugal by another 5000 sailing from Gibraltar under Major-General Brent Spencer.

At this time, Sharpe was still a 2nd lieutenant (Rifle Regiments did not have ensigns) acting as quartermaster-administrative officer to the four companies (or wing) of the 2/95th at Hythe. This wing of the battalion was under the command of Major Robert Travers. According to Rifleman Harris, Travers was 'a man much liked by the men of the Rifles, and, indeed, deservedly beloved by all who knew him. He was a tight hand; but a soldier likes that better than a slovenly officer . . . he was never a very good looking man, being hard-featured and thin.' As Quartermaster, Sharpe was pitched into the frantic scramble to get the companies kitted

Portuguese Cacadores
LEFT: *1st Battalion*
Rifleman
RIGHT: *Light Infantryman*

LIEUTENANT
BUNBURY

This officer came from
a distinguished
military family which
traditionally sent its
sons into the army.
Bunburys fought the
French, the Russians
(in the Crimea), the
Boers, the Germans
(twice) and the
Chinese. In more
recent times, the
author took over from
a Major Charles
Bunbury in Barbados
where he was serving
with the Barbados
Defence Force. His
father, Lieutenant-
Colonel Ramsey
Bunbury, had
commanded the Duke
of Wellington's
Regiment (Sharpe's
old 33rd) in the battles
for The Hook in
Korea.

SUBALTERNS' PAY

The basic daily pay of
junior infantry
officers was: ensign
5s 3d, lieutenant 6s 6d
and after seven years
7s 6d. Apart from the
quartermaster, who
got 6s 6d, officers with
special appointments
or skills were better
off, particularly
paymasters who held
the rank of captain.
The rates were: an
adjutant 8s 6d, an
assistant surgeon
7s 6d, a surgeon 11s 4d,
a paymaster (1st
battalion) 15s, 2nd
battalion 10s.

up for war. Bugles shrilled as the detachment marched briskly
to Dover where, on 8 June, the men were embarked for the
voyage to Cork. There the transports assembled, and the 9000
troops were jammed into the filthy, bilge-ridden holds of the
wallowing ships; there they waited.

The wait lasted nearly six weeks. Nobody was allowed
ashore except the Rifles, who were disembarked every day
for training. Harris again: 'Our merry bugles sounded over
the country, and we skirmished about in very lively fashion,
always being embarked again at night.' By the time the fleet
of transports with their escort of warships reached the coast
of Portugal at the end of July, all, except the 2/95th, had been
on board for eight weeks or more. Not that they had grounds
for complaint when their sojourn of seasickness and misery
was compared with their five sister companies of the 1/95th,
who had spent eleven months on transports in the recent
disastrous South American expedition.

On board the frigate HMS *Crocodile* on 1 August 1808, a
gaggle of officers stood by the rail peering and pointing at a
strip of Portuguese coastline. Wellesley, surrounded by his
staff, was watching the start of the army's ten-day disembar-
kation. The point selected was the mouth of the Mondego
River about 100 miles north of their objective, Lisbon (MAP
4). Modern technology has done little to change the problems
and techniques of amphibious landings. Portugal in 1808, the
Crimea in 1854 or the Falklands in 1982 would be equally
familiar in many ways to generals and soldiers of any century.
For the commanders, the choice of landing place, the arguments with the navy as to what is feasible, the overriding
need to avoid an opposed landing and the desire to disembark
as close to the objective as possible. For the troops the stuffing
of kit into haversacks, the endless cleaning of weapons, the
precarious clambering from big ships into little wallowing
boats, and the fruitless efforts to keep packs and feet dry.

Of all the officers with the 2/95th the busiest on board that
morning was the Quartermaster. The four companies of the
Rifles would be the first to disembark, and it was Sharpe's
job to ensure that each man carried precisely what the orders

Quartermasters

WHEN SHARPE EXCHANGED into the 2/95th as a 2nd lieutenant he was appointed Quartermaster (QM). This was one of the posts within an infantry battalion often given to an officer who had risen from the ranks. The others were adjutant and paymaster. In peacetime they could also expect postings as recruiting officer or barrack master. According to *The Regimental Companion*, published in 1811: 'The quarter-master is not to do any duty other than quarter-master while the regiment is on actual service. His duty is, to take care of the ammunition and stores of the regiment; to attend to all deliveries of coals, forage etc. and to prevent frauds from being committed against the public service.' A QM had responsibility for billeting, feeding, clothing, equipping and supplying ammunition within his battalion. He kept stocks and, in peacetime, maintained a central store from which issues were made. In effect he was the supply staff officer to the colonel. It was an administrative job of crucial importance but a non-combatant post. As such, it was looked down on by others and this irked Sharpe considerably.

Sharpe had won his commission on the battlefield as a sergeant and it seemed logical that his fighting ability would have secured him a combat role, but the army saw things differently. As an ex-ranker and senior NCO, Sharpe knew soldiers intimately, he understood company and battalion administration, knew every piece of equipment and weapon, and understood the cheating and trickery in the ranks. The system of having ex-rankers as quartermasters has persisted to the present day, and become entrenched in that special quartermaster commissions are given to senior warrant officers who have worked their way up the NCO promotion ladder. No officer with a combatant commission can be a quartermaster. Likewise a quartermaster would never command troops in a combat role, except in dire emergency when no other officer was available. Although they hold identical ranks to other officers and can rise to lieutenant-colonel, they are listed separately in the Army List. They always have the letters (QM) written after their rank, thus: Captain (QM).

Major Dunnett was far from exceptional in his dislike of ranker officers. This was based on the prejudice that only a gentleman could be an officer. But Sharpe, as Quartermaster, was accepted by most for what he was – a courageous NCO who had been rewarded with a commission, and given a job that fitted his background and experience. The position of promoted sergeants was invariably difficult and required a man of exceptional character to make good. Even the soldiers preferred a 'proper' officer. Rifleman Harris had this to say: 'I know from experience, that in our army the men like best to be officered by gentlemen, men whose education has rendered them more kind in manners than your coarse officer, sprung from obscure origin, and whose style is brutal and overbearing.'

decreed. Full haversacks and canteens, tin camp kettles to be issued, each man to land with one spare shirt, one spare pair of shoes, comb, razor and a brush, three days' bread plus two days' cooked meat, eighty rounds of ammunition instead of the usual sixty, and three good flints. Three days' oats were required for each horse. An army reserve of half a million musket cartridges was to go ashore. Each company in the half battalion was up to establishment with a captain commanding, three subalterns, five sergeants, two buglers and 100 riflemen. That left Major Travers, Sharpe and a quartermaster-sergeant as the headquarters. A total of 447 all ranks.

The landings were lengthy and laborious as well as dangerous. The treacherous surf claimed boats, equipment and several lives, including those of two MPs. Fortunately, there was not a Frenchman in sight. After five days, more ships arrived with Spencer's troops. By the tenth of August the 14,000 troops in six brigades, with the 2/95th in Major-General Fane's brigade leading the advance, began to uncoil themselves and march south: an endless infantry column trudging through the ankle-deep sand under a blistering sun. A handful of horses pulled the three artillery batteries and carried the only cavalry available: 240 men of the 20th Light Dragoons who provided the thin screen for the force. Weeks of inactivity in the cramped conditions on the transports had a debilitating effect; the heat, the hot sand and the heavy loads took their toll. The pace slowed, units began to straggle and the red tunics and new grey trousers darkened with sweat. Even the Riflemen, much fitter than most, suffered. Harris, up front with the Rifles, commented:

> The weight I myself toiled under was tremendous ... I am convinced that many of our infantry sank and died under the weight of our knapsacks alone. For my own part, being a handicraft [shoemaker], I marched under a weight sufficient to impede ... a donkey, so awkwardly was the load our men bore in those days placed upon their backs, that the free motion of the body was impeded, the head held down from the pile at the back of the neck ...

A modern infantryman would sympathise.

Wellesley was making for the small town of Leiria. There his troops would get off the sand onto a reasonable road, and he had arranged to link up with his Portuguese allies under General Bernardin Friere. The Portuguese had promised to co-operate and to hand over a magazine of supplies. Having recently given them 5000 muskets and sets of personal equipment, Wellesley was hopeful, but his optimism was misplaced. Friere was difficult, his force of 6000 had consumed the supplies, and he proposed to disappear into the hills and approach Lisbon from the north-east rather than take the direct route down the coastal plain. This was an impossibility for the British as they were dependent on their ships for food and had to hug the coast until a viable supply system had been established on land. As the price for marching with Wellesley, Friere demanded that his force draw rations and equipment from the British fleet. The impasse was resolved by compromise. The bulk of the Portuguese would sit on their hands at Leiria until the outcome of the first clash with the French was known, but a force of 1500 light troops and a few cavalry under an Irish mercenary, Colonel Nicholas Trant, would be 'loaned' to Wellesley. (The British commander was to get to know Trant well in the coming years. In 1839, on hearing the news of his death in comparative poverty, he exclaimed, 'Trant, poor fellow! A very good officer, but as drunken a dog as ever lived!')

Sharpe's duties during this time revolved around rationing the companies. No ammunition had been expended, but the men needed to eat – and drink. Every soldier was entitled to a daily ration of a pound of bread or biscuit (bread baked twice, making it lighter, drier and longer lasting) plus a pound of fresh or salt meat. Of greater consequence was the pint of wine. The wives accompanying the troops (limited to six per company at this stage) got half rations, children a quarter. During the day supplies were landed from the transports and carried forward in carts under the control of the chief commissary. Sharpe had to organise working parties under

PREMONITIONS OF DEATH

Harris records how a Corporal Murphy who, when the order to fall in was given before the Battle of Vimiero, '. . . appeared quite dejected and out of spirits. He had a presentiment of death, which is by no means an uncommon circumstance . . . Others besides myself noticed Murphy on this morning and, as we had reason to know that he was not ordinarily deficient in courage, the circumstance was talked of after the battle was over. He was the first man shot that day.' When this foreboding is felt, it is usually impossible to shake off and frequently, though not always, turns out to be true.

senior NCOs from each company to collect the rations from the brigade commissary, Assistant-Commissary Lamont. Sharpe's task, and that of the other quartermasters, was made easier during the first few days by the generosity of the villagers who brought in oranges, grapes, melons, figs and strange delicacies never before tasted by British soldiers. At the end of the first day's march Sharpe was given a live calf for the 2/95th. According to Harris, the Rifles 'feasted in our first entrance to Portugal like a company of aldermen'. It was a situation that did not last.

The need for the British to land so far from Lisbon, and the agonisingly slow process of disembarking, gave Junot a considerable amount of that most precious of commodities in war – time. He needed to assemble an army to confront the invaders. Strongly escorted gallopers spurred from Lisbon to summon General Loison from Badajoz with his 7000 men. An energetic, if brutal and rapacious officer, Loison had, at the end of July, done much to inflame the hatred of the populace against the French by massacring hundreds of men,

*French
Dragoons*

women and children at Evora. The city was sacked with every kind of sacrilege and brutality; its fate was the forerunner of many similar scenes in the coming years. While awaiting the arrival of his subordinate on 6 August, Junot sent General Henri Comte Delaborde with about 5000 men north from Lisbon on a delaying mission. With so few men in comparison with his enemy, Delaborde looked for a suitable defensive or blocking position. By the tenth, when Wellesley started his march south, Delaborde was fifteen miles south of Leiria. But there was no suitable position there so, as the British trudged towards him, he pulled back to the hills at Rolica, leaving a small rearguard near the village of Obidos four miles to the north. The first clash between British and French troops of the Peninsular War was approaching – an engagement Wellesley called 'a little affair of advance posts'.

Although not in a strictly combat role, Sharpe was with the Rifles when the first shots were fired. As we have noted, despite being the Quartermaster and an officer, he always carried a rifle, a habit that he was to maintain throughout his years in the Peninsula. On the evening of 15 August, the leading companies under Travers, with others from the 5th/60th, were shot at from the tiny hamlet of Obidos, perched atop a hill and surrounded by apple orchards and melon vines. There was a brisk exchange of fire and Lieutenant Bunbury of the 2/95th was hit in the head, dying almost immediately. He had the unfortunate distinction of being the first British soldier to be killed in the war. Travers (probably assisted by Sharpe) urged on his men who skirmished forward in grand style, working in pairs and darting from cover to cover, firing as they went. The French withdrew and, in the eagerness of this first encounter, the Rifles chased the enemy well south of the village. Racing ahead a mile or more, they were in trouble when enemy appeared on both flanks. General Spencer had to lead his brigade forward to extricate them; the Rifles had three killed and seven wounded in this skirmish.

Four miles to the south, Delaborde made his stand at Rolica. This, the first of Wellesley's battles, took place on 17

LIEUTENANT WILLIAM HUMBLEY

Lieutenant Humbley of the 2/95th was a contemporary of Sharpe. Like Sharpe, he served under Major Travers at Rolica and Vimiero and continued to serve throughout the Peninsular and Waterloo campaigns. He was present at virtually every battle, and when at last, in 1848, a silver medal was awarded to Peninsular veterans his had thirteen clasps (Sharpe got twelve). He was severely wounded at Waterloo – still only a lieutenant. When he died in 1857 however, he was a lieutenant-colonel on half-pay.

LIEUTENANT FITZROY SOMERSET

Present with Wellesley as an ADC was a young Guards officer, Lieutenant the Honourable Fitzroy Somerset, who in 1854 (as Lord Raglan) commanded an almost identical operation – the landings in the Crimea.

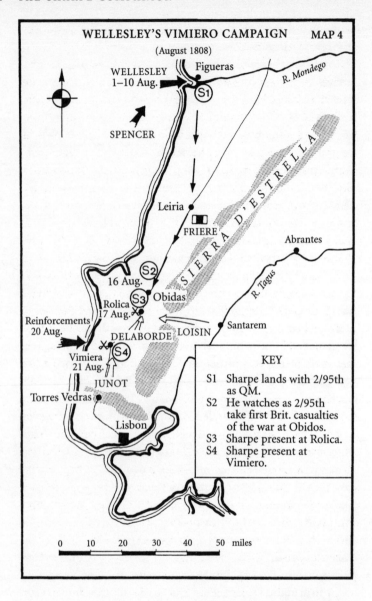

WELLESLEY'S VIMIERO CAMPAIGN   MAP 4
(August 1808)

WELLESLEY
1–10 Aug.

Figueras
S1
R. Mondego

SPENCER

Leiria

FRIERE

SIERRA D'ESTRELLA

Abrantes

S2
16 Aug.

S3 Obidas

Rolica
17 Aug.

R. Tagus

Reinforcements
20 Aug.

DELABORDE LOISIN

Santarem

Vimiera
21 Aug.

S4

JUNOT

Torres Vedras

Lisbon

KEY

S1 Sharpe lands with 2/95th
    as QM.
S2 He watches as 2/95th
    take first Brit. casualties
    of the war at Obidos.
S3 Sharpe present at Rolica.
S4 Sharpe present at
    Vimiero.

0   10   20   30   40   50 miles

August with the 2/95th hotly engaged. Sharpe accompanied
his battalion as it fought in the broiling sun among the gullies
and terraces of steep hills. The green-jacketed Riflemen were
young and inexperienced but thoroughly trained. They
fought hard, dashing forward, fixing their sword-bayonets as

they ran, to the cry of 'Over, boys! Over, over!' One officer and seventeen men died; another thirty were wounded.

Rolica was a British victory, perhaps inevitably, as the French were outnumbered by more than two to one. The next day Wellesley moved south to Vimiero to cover the landing of two brigades of reinforcements which would bring his strength up to 17,000 men and 18 guns. Lisbon was within his grasp. Unfortunately, at this time, Lieutenant-General Sir Harry Burrard appeared, to assume command, and there was to be no further advance until yet more reinforcements under Sir John Moore arrived. Wellesley, however, had a temporary reprieve; the French attacked him, and Sir Harry stayed on board his ship, allowing Wellesley to fight his second battle.

The Battle of Vimiero, on 21 August, was significant. Veteran French troops advanced using the Napoleonic tactics of the attacking column, preceded by clouds of skirmishers, which had been successful throughout Europe, but they were destroyed by the controlled, rolling musketry of steady infantry deployed in line. In his despatch and General Orders after the battle, Wellesley praised the valour and discipline of the 2/95th. They had suffered severely, having thirty-seven men killed and four officers and forty-three riflemen wounded. Within a week, almost a third of the original four companies had become casualties. (Sharpe now had over five years' service as an officer, and Major Travers was instrumental in securing his promotion to acting Lieutenant shortly after the Battle of Vimiero. But he kept him as Quartermaster. His promotion brought him no financial reward – lieutenants and quartermasters both received 6s 6d per day.)

By the end of August, Junot had capitulated with honour on terms which caused a scandalised outcry in England. Not only were the enemy allowed to keep the loot they had plundered from the Portuguese under the guise of 'personal effects', but the entire army was repatriated to France in British ships. All this was part of the Convention of Cintra signed on 31 August. Wellesley had now been outranked by several more senior lieutenant-generals, including Sir Hew Dalrymple who took over as commander-in-chief on 23

MAJOR TRAVERS

An amusing incident concerning Major Travers at the Battle of Vimiero is told by Rifleman Harris: 'The major had just now disclosed what none of us, I believe, knew before, namely, that his head was as bald as a coot's, and that he had covered the nakedness of his nob, up to the present time, by a flowing Caxon [wig] which, during the heat of the action, had somehow been dislodged ... The Major [was] riding hither and thither, digging the spurs into his horse's flanks, and just as busy as before the firing had ceased. "A guinea", he kept crying, "to any man who will find my wig!" The men ... burst into shouts of laughter ... and "A guinea to any man who will find my wig", was the saying amongst us long after that affair.'

The duel

FIGHTING as a light infantryman was frequently an individual affair. Skirmishing ahead of the battalion or 'firing and retiring' in retreat, riflemen often fought against one or two enemy who were clearly visible as if they were a personal opponent. What amounted to a duel was fought. After the battle of Vimiero Harris was involved in such an affair when engaged in looting the dead.

'. . . [I] pulled one of his shoes off . . . It was not much better than my own; however, I determined on the exchange, and proceeded to take off its fellow. As I did so, I was startled by the sharp report of a firelock, and, at the same moment, a bullet whistled close by my head . . . There was no person near me in this part of the field . . . I looked to the priming of my rifle and turned to the dead officer of the 50th. It was evident that some plundering scoundrel had taken a shot at me . . . Hardly had I affected the exchange, put on the dead officer's shoes, and resumed my rifle, when another shot took place, and a second ball whistled past me. This time I was ready, and turning quickly, I saw my man as he was just about to squat down behind a small mound, about twenty paces from me. I took a haphazard shot at him, and instantly knocked him over. I immediately ran up to him; he had fallen on his face, and I heaved him over onto his back, bestrode his body, and drew my sword bayonet. There was, however, no occasion for the precaution as he was even then in the agonies of death . . .'

August. Sir Hew and Sir Harry, together with Wellesley, were summoned home in September to face an enquiry into their unseemly generosity to the French, and the dithering and delay that characterised the high command after Vimiero. Sir Hew was sacked, Sir Harry retired and Wellesley absolved. Meanwhile most of the army, including Sharpe and the 2/95th, descended on the fleshpots of Lisbon where they fraternised with the French in the relentless pursuit of whores and drink. On 6 October, Sir John Moore took command in Portugal.

Portugal was free of the French. Moore's task was to drive them from Spain (MAP 5). They had vacated Madrid and were concentrated behind the line of the Ebro where some 90,000 soldiers under the overall command of Joseph were deployed in eight separate corps. Opposed to them were three

Spanish armies totalling about 76,000 men. Moore's 20,000 were to be reinforced by 8000 under Sir David Baird (of Seringapatam fame), who would disembark at Corunna. These forces would unite and co-operate with the Spanish armies to push the French back. Moore's plan involved no less than five separate columns (including Baird's) converging on Burgos; his march began in late October, with Sharpe (still Quartermaster) and the 2/95th, a part of Major-General Fraser's command, taking the Abrantes–Guarda route. Within a week, the situation changed dramatically and 200,000 veterans, including the Imperial Guard, poured over the French border at Bayonne under Napoleon's personal command. The Spanish armies were scattered and the Emperor, brushing aside all opposition, marched into Madrid on 4 December. Almost immediately he turned north-east, to cut off the British from Portugal and drive them into the sea.

The 2/95th reached Salamanca on 13 November, after

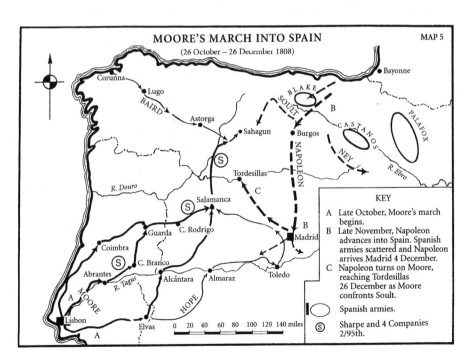

MOORE'S MARCH INTO SPAIN
(26 October – 26 December 1808)
MAP 5

KEY

A Late October, Moore's march begins.
B Late November, Napoleon advances into Spain. Spanish armies scattered and Napoleon arrives Madrid 4 December.
C Napoleon turns on Moore, reaching Tordesillas 26 December as Moore confronts Soult.

Spanish armies.

(S) Sharpe and 4 Companies 2/95th.

marching 320 miles at about eighteen miles a day. There was another hundred miles to go before they faced the French under Soult near Sahagun. On 20 December Sharpe's four companies were reunited with the four companies under Lieutenant-Colonel Hamlet Wade which had marched from Corunna with Baird. Similarly, the two wings of the 1/95th had been united under Lieutenant-Colonel Andrew Barnard. This battalion was placed in the reserve under Sir Edward Paget while the 2/95th formed part of the Light Brigade commanded by Major-General Robert Crauford with the 1/43rd and 2/52nd. By Christmas Eve, Moore decided that he had no option but to retire, to escape being cut off by Napoleon's rapid advance. With the countryside white with frost and snow, the infamous retreat to Corunna began. The Light Brigade was committed to rearguard duties fighting off French cavalry patrols, destroying bridges, sweeping up stragglers and drunkards from other units – always the last to leave a position. Sharpe witnessed a small example of Crauford's ferocity when he spotted an officer of the Rifles avoiding walking through a freezing stream; he was made to walk backwards and forwards through the water several times in front of his men.

The orders to retreat brought disgraceful lapses of discipline. With the notable exception of the light troops, pillage and wanton destruction were common, and officers made little or no attempt to control their men. Troops refused to

March discipline

GENERAL CRAUFORD was notorious for his ruthlessness in enforcing march discipline. Stragglers who trailed into camp after their battalions were, on the general's insistence, paraded by the orderly sergeants in front of the surgeon. If pronounced skulkers, they were court-martialled. Another Crauford speciality was confiscating stragglers' ramrods on the march, and riding off with them. At times he collected as many as a dozen. In bivouac, battalion adjutants were ordered to find all men without ramrods; the culprits received twenty-four lashes.

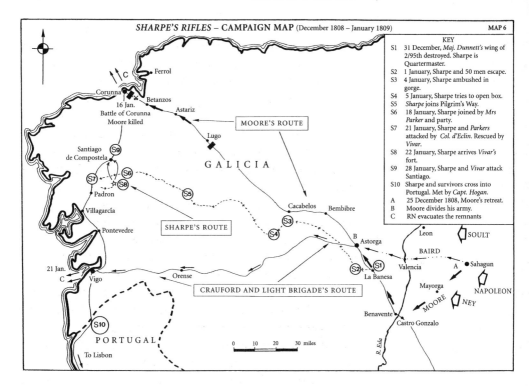

SHARPE'S RIFLES – CAMPAIGN MAP (December 1808 – January 1809)   MAP 6

KEY
S1 31 December, *Maj. Dunnett's* wing of 2/95th destroyed. Sharpe is Quartermaster.
S2 1 January, Sharpe and 50 men escape.
S3 4 January, Sharpe ambushed in gorge.
S4 5 January, Sharpe tries to open box.
S5 *Sharpe joins Pilgrim's Way.*
S6 18 January, Sharpe joined by *Mrs Parker* and party.
S7 21 January, Sharpe and *Parkers* attacked by *Col. d'Eclin*. Rescued by *Vivar*.
S8 22 January, Sharpe arrives *Vivar's* fort.
S9 28 January, Sharpe and *Vivar* attack Santiago.
S10 Sharpe and survivors cross into Portugal. Met by *Capt. Hogan*.
A   25 December 1808, Moore's retreat.
B   Moore divides his army.
C   RN evacuates the remnants

wait for the regular distribution of food or fuel, seizing what they could find and stripping houses of furniture for fires. Deplorable scenes occurred in villages such as Mayorga, Benavente, La Baneza and Bembibre.

At the start of the withdrawal, Wade had divided his battalion into two separate wings of four companies each. They alternated as the rearguard. When the battalion had been reunited there were two quartermasters and Sharpe hoped that he might be sent to a company. The splitting into two wings put paid to that idea as each sub-unit needed an administrative officer. Sharpe was particularly embittered when he was switched from Major Travers' wing to *Major Warren Dunnett*'s. *Dunnett* detested 'other rank' officers and let Sharpe know it.

On 31 December, *Dunnett*'s companies were deployed west of the stone bridge over the river just north of La Baneza (MAP 6). About a hundred stupefied redcoats and some

SHRAPNEL

At Vimiero spherical
case-shot, hollow
cannon balls filled
with musket balls,
were used for the first
time. They were fired
at a high angle from
howitzers and fused to
explode in the air over
the target. Wellesley
wrote to the inventor
(Lieutenant-Colonel
Shrapnell after whom
the shell was named)
saying he had,
'... every reason to
believe that they
[spherical case] had
the best effect in
producing the defeat of
the enemy at Vimiero'.
Shrapnel has
continued to be one of
the most effective types
of shell for use against
soft (human) targets.

besotted women could not be roused and were abandoned where they lay. Sharpe went about his duties, distributed spare ammunition, and tried to avoid the irritable *Dunnett*. That was the day the advance guard of General Colbert's light cavalry brigade caught up with the 2/95th. It was a typical rearguard action, mishandled by *Dunnett*: the wing was destroyed, and Sharpe and fifty survivors were separated from Moore's army. Three days later, at Cacabelos, the 1/95th handled an identical situation more successfully – they even killed General Colbert.

Sharpe was cut off from the army throughout the month of January 1809. He was unaware that the day following the débâcle at La Baneza Moore had ordered Crauford's Light Brigade and his other German light troops to head for the coast at Vigo, while the bulk of the army continued to march to Corunna, where it arrived on 11 January. Part of the army's immediate duties was the destruction of stores, clothing and equipment which could not be loaded on the transports. This included blowing up 4000 barrels of gunpowder. The explosion was awesome: the largest and loudest in the world until that time, it smashed virtually every window in the city. The 1/95th stayed with Moore, and took part in the Battle of Corunna on 16 January.

The remnants of Sharpe's old battalion took the southerly route through Orense. Although it was a terrible march, with Crauford having men flogged in the snow by the roadside and many dying of exhaustion in blizzards, the enemy did not pursue them. On 21 January Sharpe's compatriots sailed for Portsmouth. By early February they were back in their billets in Hythe. Moore was killed at Corunna, but he had won a victory and bought sufficient time for the fleet to evacuate what was left of his army on 17 January. The operation was like a miniature Dunkirk: in 1940 small groups of British troops were left behind in France, as Sharpe and his men were left in Spain in 1809.

Sharpe's wanderings and experiences with the guerrillas in Galicia, culminating in his participating in the attack on Santiago de Compostela, although fictional, were typical of

General Colbert's death

ALL REGIMENTS have their characters, their rogues, men whose deeds (or misdeeds) shout from the pages of regimental histories. The 95th Rifles had such a man in the Peninsular War by the name of Tom Plunket, an Irishman. He served with the 1/95th during the retreat to Corunna, and was present at the rearguard action at Cacabelos.

In fading light General Colbert was seen encouraging his dragoons to press home a final assault. Plunket, an excellent marksman, went forward, announcing that he 'would bring that fellow down'. He lay on his back in the snow and, placing his foot in his rifle sling, took deliberate aim. His shot killed the general. He next brought down a trumpeter. It is alleged that Sir Edward Paget, the commander of the reserve division, witnessed the shooting and tossed his purse to Plunket. Drink was his downfall; as a sergeant, he was drunk on duty and threatened to shoot his company commander. He was broken to rifleman and sentenced to 300 lashes but only received thirty-five. He subsequently regained the rank of corporal and was badly wounded in the head at Waterloo.

Some months after Waterloo he married a woman without a face. This unfortunate had been standing too close to an ammunition wagon at Quatre Bras when it exploded. Her features, according to Edward Costello, were 'rendered a blue, shapeless, noseless mass'. She received a shilling a day disability pension – double Plunket's. He re-enlisted, was promoted corporal after being recognised by his former commanding officer on an inspection parade, then left on a better pension which he exchanged for land in Canada. Plunket was no farmer and soon returned, penniless, to roam the streets of Colchester selling matches. He died in the street a few years later.

---

the small-scale operations which bled the French armies of occupation in the following years. *Mrs Parker,* her husband and her lovely daughter *Louisa* were, in reality, Lord and Lady Holland, who had arrived at Corunna on HMS *Amazon* on 5 October. After many weeks with Baird's force, they were making their precarious way south to Lisbon when they met Sharpe.

Troops from Marshal Ney's VI Corps sacked and garrisoned Santiago de Compostela. The mission of his superior, Soult, was to turn on Portugal, but before moving south he received the surrender (after a token twenty-four hours of feeble resistance) of the vital port of Ferrol. Enormous

The Santiago Pilgrimage

ACCORDING TO LEGEND St James (Santiago) came to Spain to spread the gospel between the Crucifixion and his martyrdom in Jerusalem in A.D. 44. Two of his disciples removed his corpse to Jaffa and took it by boat to Padron, south of Santiago. The body was buried and forgotten until the year 813, when the grave was revealed to the Bishop of Padron by a star. The rediscovery was timely. During the previous century the whole of Spain, apart from the northern kingdom of Asturias, had been overrun by the Moors who, fighting in the name of Mohammed, introduced the idea of a Holy War to the West. The Christians had their own champion – St James. An apparition of St James on a snow-white horse slaughtered thousands of Moors at the decisive Battle of Clavijo (now in La Rioja). The peaceful fisherman from Galilee was, from then on, Matamoros (the Moor-slayer), the knightly scourge of the Arabs.

A church was built on the site of the grave and pilgrims began to arrive. It was a lucrative business for the church, but pilgrimages came to an abrupt halt in 1589 when Francis Drake attacked Corunna and the bishop of Compostela hid the remains of Matamoros in Santiago's cathedral, where a workman found them in 1879. The question of authenticity was quickly settled: there was a nick in the skull, and a sliver of bone in Rome turned out to be a perfect match! The relics were blessed by the pope. Pilgrimages flourished; even today pilgrims come from all over the world, especially in holy years when 25 July falls on a Sunday, when Santiago can have up to two million visitors.

quantities of stores, equipment, 20,000 muskets, 4000 sailors and the ships in harbour were meekly handed over on 26 January. Two days later Sharpe and *Blas Vivar* attacked Santiago (MAP 7), and two days after that Soult marched south. He and Sharpe had the same objective – Lisbon.

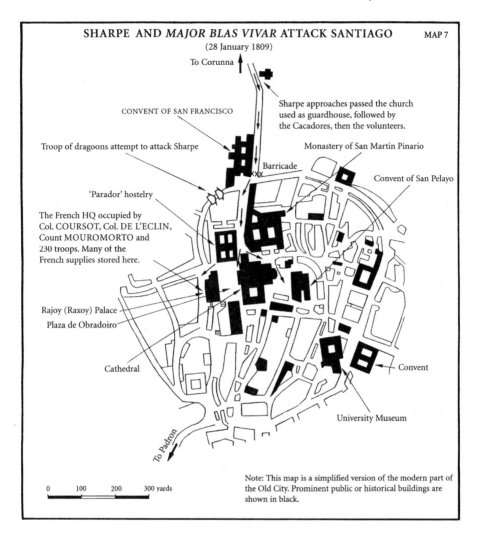

SHARPE AND *MAJOR BLAS VIVAR* ATTACK SANTIAGO MAP 7
(28 January 1809)

To Corunna

CONVENT OF SAN FRANCISCO

Sharpe approaches passed the church
used as guardhouse, followed by
the Cacadores, then the volunteers.

Troop of dragoons attempt to attack Sharpe

Monastery of San Martin Pinario

Barricade

Convent of San Pelayo

'Parador' hostelry

The French HQ occupied by
Col. COURSOT, Col. DE L'ECLIN,
Count MOUROMORTO and
230 troops. Many of the
French supplies stored here.

Rajoy (Raxoy) Palace
Plaza de Obradoiro

Cathedral

Convent

University Museum

To Padron

0   100   200   300 yards

Note: This map is a simplified version of the modern part of
the Old City. Prominent public or historical buildings are
shown in black.

5

Sharpe's Eagle

**The S. *Essex* arrive in the Peninsula under the aristocratic
and incompetent *Lieutenant-Colonel Sir Henry Simmerson.*
The battalion is immaculately dressed, perfectly drilled,
but can barely fire its muskets until Sharpe gives the men
instruction. In their first operation – the blowing of the
bridge at *Valdelacasa* – the S. *Essex* lose their King's
Colour. Sharpe is promoted to temporary captain for his
actions at the bridge and given command of the Light
Company. At the Battle of Talavera, *Simmerson* is relieved
of command for retiring from the line and Sharpe captures
a French Eagle.**

10 JULY 1809 was the day that the S. *Essex*, bivouacked in
the hot, dusty wheatfields outside Plasencia, formally met the
Spanish battalion with which it was to co-operate in the
destruction of the bridge at *Valdelacasa*. It was also the day
that Wellesley rode forty miles south to meet the Spanish
captain-general at his headquarters at Casa del Puerto, just
south of the Tagus. He urgently needed to agree plans for
the advance on the French.

It had been an exhausting, indeed frustrating, ride. As he
and his small escort clattered over the Roman bridge at Almaraz, it was getting dark and he was nearly five hours late. His
guide had got lost and the map was inaccurate. On arrival
he found that General Don Gregario García de la Cuesta had
paraded an overlarge contingent of his army for review, and
the troops had been waiting a long time. Nevertheless,
Wellesley was not impressed with what he saw as he peered

at the men by the light of spluttering torches. Four days earlier he had read a report on the Spanish army from Colonel Roche, a liaison officer with Cuesta. Roche said that, in his opinion, 'Anything like order, system, or discipline is out of the question; and when one adds that, with few exceptions, the officers are more ignorant than the men, it is impossible not to feel apprehensions for the issue.' After his inspection, and watching some clumsy attempts at drill, Wellesley realised Roche had not exaggerated.

In the early hours of the eleventh, as the *S. Essex* paraded in readiness to follow the *Regimiento de la Santa Maria* south towards *Valdelacasa* and their deplorable encounter with the French, Wellesley and Cuesta held a four-hour conference. This was not easy since neither could speak the other's language. The prolonged, and at times heated, exchanges were conducted partly in the language of the enemy and partly through Cuesta's chief-of-staff, yet another of Irish origins – General O'Donoju. Wellesley, a successful general of forty, faced an old man of almost seventy, described by one observer as 'the most murderous looking old man I ever saw'. He had been defeated in three major battles, and in the last (Medellin) had been ridden over by his own routed cavalry. Since then he had travelled around in a huge wagon drawn by nine mules.

Sergeant's Halberd

In June, when *Hogan* had briefed Sharpe for the bridge-blowing operation at Ponte Cardenal (*Valdelacasa*), Wellesley had hoped to trap Marshal Victor south of the Tagus, where he then was. If Wellesley advanced eastwards, north of the river, and seized or destroyed the bridges while Cuesta pressed him frontally, Victor's communications could be severed and he would be cut off from Madrid. There had been delays; there had been arguments and finally Victor had withdrawn north of the Tagus and taken position behind the Alberche. Wellesley had not cancelled *Hogan*'s and Sharpe's mission. There was still value in destroying this bridge. He could not afford to guard it, his priority was the more dangerous left (northern) flank. It would be a simple task and would break in one of his greenest battalions (the *S. Essex*); it was

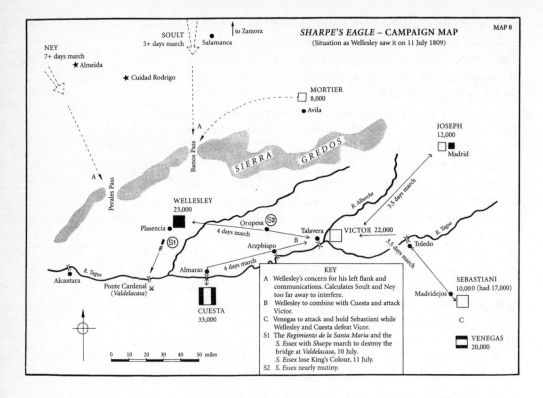

SHARPE'S EAGLE – CAMPAIGN MAP
(Situation as Wellesley saw it on 11 July 1809)

MAP 8

KEY
A   Wellesley's concern for his left flank and communications. Calculates Soult and Ney too far away to interfere.
B   Wellesley to combine with Cuesta and attack Victor.
C   Venegas to attack and hold Sebastiani while Wellesley and Cuesta defeat Victor.
S1 The *Regimiento de la Santa Maria* and the *S. Essex* with *Sharpe* march to destroy the bridge at *Valdelacasa*, 10 July. *S. Essex* lose King's Colour, 11 July.
S2 *S. Essex* nearly mutiny.

also politically expedient to involve a Spanish battalion in an 'important' operation. The chances of meeting the enemy were small, success was almost inevitable and would boost British–Spanish relations, which were far from happy.

According to Wellesley's intelligence the situation resembled that shown on MAP 8. Having been delayed for three weeks at Abrantes, for lack of cash to buy supplies or carts and hire mules, Wellesley reached Plasencia with 23,000 men and 30 guns. Cuesta, with 33,000 troops, was just south of the Tagus near Almaraz. Both were about four days' march from Victor, with 22,000 men, encamped east of Talavera. If Wellesley could combine with Cuesta at Talavera before reinforcements reached Victor, the massive superiority in numbers should ensure a crushing defeat for the French. There were two major events that might frustrate this plan. First, Victor could be reinforced by Joseph Bonaparte from

Madrid or General Sebastiani from Madridejos – or both. These two small armies were only three and a half days' march from Victor, so this would be the most likely, almost knee-jerk reaction, of the French to an Allied advance. The second problem was Wellesley's open left flank. If, while he was engaged with Victor, Marshals Soult, Ney and Mortier should burst through the Banos or Perales Passes he would be in dire trouble – cut off from Portugal, his supply line severed, and surrounded by enemy armies.

The answer to the first difficulty was for the Spanish General Venegas to engage Sebastiani vigorously, to ensure that he had no troops to spare to help Victor. If Sebastiani were pushed, and fell back, Joseph might think it imprudent to despatch reinforcements away from Madrid. With the second threat Cuesta refused to detach any sizeable force to guard the key passes on the left flank. Wellesley therefore relied on time and space calculations: not only did he consider Ney involved in Galicia and Soult not fully recovered from his recent defeats in Portugal, but he calculated that neither could intervene on the Tagus before Victor was defeated. If the British and Spanish marched south immediately, Soult was over five days away around Zamora while Ney was over seven. The strategic plan was agreed in outline, but Wellesley was unable to move from Plasencia until 17 July. His Portuguese and Spanish allies failed to provide minimum transport or animals, and his military chest and reserve ammunition were stuck at Abrantes for want of carts.

Meanwhile *Captain Hogan*, accompanied by Sharpe and escorted by the *S. Essex* and the *Santa Maria Regiment*, descended, with Colours flying and drums beating, on the bridge at *Valdelacasa*. The tactical blunders perpetrated around that bridge by both the Spanish and the British illustrate how deadly was the game of chess between infantry and cavalry on the Napoleonic battlefield. There were rules for both sides. If both knew and played by the rules, the game would be drawn. If either flouted them, an opportunity was presented to the opposition to take or ignore according to the ability of the officer giving the orders.

A RIFLEMAN'S LOAD

Costello listed the kit carried by each rifleman on the march to Talavera as: knapsack, straps, 2 shirts, 2 pairs stockings, 1 pair of shoes, ditto soles and heels, 3 brushes, box of blacking, razor, soap-box, extra pair of trousers, mess tin, centre tin, haversack, canteen (full), greatcoat, blanket, powder-flask, ball-bag (30 loose balls), wooden mallet, belt, pouch (50 rounds), sword-belt and rifle plus personal items. The men in each squad (8) took turns to carry 4 6-pound bill-hooks. Costello gave a total weight of 70–80 pounds per man.

French Eagle

Cavalry relied on mobility and shock action, and could avoid infantry with ease. They awaited the chance to close quickly so that the weight of the horses, the hooves and heavy sabres wielded by a rider striking down could trample and smash the foot soldier. In a mêlée the mounted man was king. Their problem was to break into the infantry formation. The infantry's advantage lay with their muskets and their numbers. With very few exceptions, a battalion in a square, firing controlled volleys, had little to fear from even determined enemy horsemen, but the problem with a square was two-fold. First, it moved only at a crawl and – of far greater importance – its densely packed ranks provided artillery with

---

French Eagles

THE EAGLE was to a French regiment what the Colours were to a British: the sacred standard which gave the Regiment its life. To carry it, to defend it, to sacrifice one's life for it was the ultimate honour; To lose it to the enemy, the ultimate disgrace. The Eagle symbolised the Emperor's presence and the rallying point in battle; as long as it was there, the Regiment existed, no matter how high the casualties. From 1804 Eagles were ceremoniously presented to all Guard and Line Regiments by the Emperor personally – they became objects of worship.

The Eagle was made of bronze and usually topped the pole that carried the regimental standard. Sergeant Thirion of the 2nd Cuirassiers, who carried one in Russia, described it simply as, 'At the end of a fairly long staff was a bronze eagle with open wings . . .' Great precautions were taken to prevent their loss. In 1806, and again in 1807, Napoleon issued instructions to light cavalry and light infantry units, whose tactical duties and formations rendered protection problematic, to leave them at depôts when going on campaign. This order was widely ignored. In 1808 the Emperor decreed the establishment of special 'Eagle-bearing parties': men whose sole duty was to carry and protect it. They were the French equivalent of British Colour parties. A new appointment, that of a '*porte aigle*', ranking as an ensign, was created for all infantry regiments. Napoleon decreed that he had to be a veteran of ten years' standing who had fought at Ulm, Austerlitz, Jena and Friedland. This first 'Eagle bearer' was to be supported by two veteran senior sergeants who became the second and third Eagle bearers. The Emperor approved individual appointments and designed their special weapons: a spontoon, a short sword and two pistols carried in an open breast holster.

the perfect target. If the infantry formed line or column to move, cavalry had a chance to charge home.

Solid shot

Lieutenant-Colonel Sir Henry Simmerson and the Spanish commander had little tactical knowledge and no experience. When *Simmerson* ordered Sharpe's riflemen to advance against the chasseurs in a dispersed skirmish line, he was inviting their destruction. Sharpe, rightly, refused to oblige, and was later backed by Wellesley. The adoption of squares was the correct decision when the French horsemen threatened, but the Spanish were panicked into breaking another rule: they fired too early, and one whole side of the square fired simultaneously. At two hundred yards the musket did virtually no damage, and all the weapons were unloaded. A better trained battalion might have got off another volley before the horsemen hit them, and only one rank would have fired at a time – but not the *Santa Maria*. The Spanish threw away their firepower and exposed themselves to the mobility and shock action of the enemy. Even then, they might have survived had the square bristled with an unflinching hedge of bayonets; it did not.

Mortar shell

Once the French deployed a gun, the odds swung dramatically in their favour. Canister and roundshot could tear terrible gaps in tightly packed infantry, while dispersion invited the cavalry to charge. Sharpe's use of his men as snipers, with their more accurate and longer range rifles to pick off individual gun crews, was the only effective answer. *Simmerson*'s blowing of the bridge too soon, with a large number of his men on the wrong side, was an almost appropriate ending to a disastrous day, although on occasion such a decision is taken to prevent a bridge falling intact to the enemy. *Simmerson*'s dilemma is not uncommon in military history. (The British blew the bridge over the Sittang river in Burma in 1942 with the bulk of one division trapped on the wrong side, and the Germans failed to destroy the Remagen bridge over the Rhine in 1944 before the Americans charged across.)

Canister

Simmerson was very lucky to keep his command after

Valdelacasa. His battalion had lost almost a quarter of its
strength, plus its King's Colour, in a minor skirmish. This
was an unheard-of disgrace. The *S. Essex* was newly arrived
in the Peninsula and there was no second battalion to supply
reinforcements. Like all battalions fresh from barracks in
England, too many men reported sick, too many fell out on
the march from the heat and the distances that had to be
covered. It took several months to make a hard-marching
battalion. However, Wellesley needed the manpower, so,
instead of sending it home to recruit or disbanding it, he
downgraded the *S. Essex* to a battalion of detachments. It
lost its title and its identity, and became the receptacle for
any group of soldiers that needed a unit. It would have its
numbers made up by the 'odds and sods', the flotsam of
war, the stragglers of other regiments, small drafts awaiting
postings and anyone else who could be pressed in. Officers
would come and go and any sense of unit pride would be
hard, if not impossible, to foster. The *S. Essex* (still called
this as 'battalion of detachments' is cumbersome) was posted
to Major-General Hill's 2nd Division. Initially it was grouped
with the 29th (Worcestershires) and 1/48th (Northamptons)
in Brigadier-General Stewart's brigade.

Wellesley's march into Spain in the summer of 1809 was
a logistical nightmare. The commissariat could not cope. For
the army to move and fight there were two basic requirements
– food, and transport for supplies. If these existed, they had
to be paid for in coinage acceptable to the local people. The
French took what they wanted by force, the British could
not do this – well, not at the start of the war. Theft of
even a chicken was punishable by death by hanging. The
Portuguese and Spanish were allies and undertook to provide
(for payments) supplies and wagons, carts and mules to move
them. The long march to Talavera (and back again) saw some
of the worst hardships of the entire war due to hunger.
The commissariat officer giving Sharpe's men half rations at
Oropesa seemed lavish when compared with what they got
a few weeks later. Cuesta was unable to keep his promises
with regard to food and transport, Wellesley lacked coinage

(proper silver dollars) and, although it was the harvest season, the countryside east of Talavera was expected to sustain three armies and the civilian population. Not surprisingly, the *S. Essex* were not the only troops with empty stomachs.

Incidents of indiscipline were frequent. Some men stole, a few deserted and a handful, like *Corporal Moss* and *Private Ibbotson*, were caught and shot. Shooting was almost exclusively reserved for desertion. Soldiers who murdered, mutinied, looted or struck their superiors were invariably hanged from the nearest tree. George Bell, an officer in the 34th, recalled, '. . . seeing three soldiers hanged one morning, on the long projecting arm of a cork tree, for robbing some muleteers; men who had fought to the death in the battlefield. It was a melancholy sight, as we marched away, to see three red-coats dangling in the air, awaiting the vultures . . .'

Although Wellesley vehemently insisted that he would stamp out looting with draconian punishments, he was striving for the impossible. The men were months in arrears with their meagre pay, and for much of the time in a state of semi-starvation. Theft became rampant; those caught picking up a stray pig or duck were flogged, those who robbed a person were hanged. Wellesley's 'bloody provost' arrested a man staggering out of a house with a huge gilt mirror. The mirror and the man were both hung up, the soldier being forced to watch his own strangulation.

On 22 July, two seemingly endless parallel columns of troops wound their way through the cornfields and cork and olive orchards of the last few miles to Talavera. The British, led by Hill's division, were on the right, the Spanish on the left. French dragoons retired before them. Wellesley's plan of uniting with the Spanish army and crushing an isolated Victor before he could be reinforced was unfolding perfectly, despite administrative chaos and Cuesta's begrudging co-operation. By the evening of the twenty-second, both armies were facing the French along the line of the Alberche River. Sharpe and his Light Company joined the other skirmishers on the banks of the stream. Behind, bivouacking under the trees, was the rest of the battalion and the 29th and 1/48th.

EXECUTIONS BY HANGING

Hanging was the penalty for all capital offences except desertion. Only about forty cases are reported, plus a few carried out on the spot when the provost caught a soldier attacking a peasant for loot. Stealing without violence was punished with the lash, armed robbery with death. The same was true if the items stolen were valued at more than forty shillings. Men were hanged for robbing the commissary-general's chest, absconding with a senior officer's baggage and purse, and one for sodomy – a capital offence until the 1840s.

The following day, a Sunday, would see serious fighting – that much was obvious to the greenest of recruits.

This was also the day that Napoleon's brother Joseph in Madrid received the first definite intelligence that the allies had closed up to Victor. His knee-jerk reaction had been predicted. Marshal Jourdan, his chief-of-staff, sent despatches summoning Sebastiani and, more critically, Soult. The latter was to collect his corps and march at once to Plasencia. Joseph would march that evening for the Alberche.

Wellesley and Cuesta had to attack at once, and Wellesley was up until midnight urging his aged ally to do just that. Only at that late hour did Cuesta grudgingly assent. By three o'clock the next afternoon the Spanish had not moved. Wellesley found Cuesta seated on a pile of cushions near the bridge across the Alberche. He poured forth a string of feeble excuses for his lack of action – and anyway tomorrow would be soon enough. When tomorrow came, the enemy had vanished. It was now Wellesley's turn to refuse to move while Cuesta, perhaps conscience-stricken, set off on 24 July in pursuit of Victor, under the deluded conviction that the French were fleeing from him. By the 26th he scrambled back, with a reinforced enemy snapping at his heels. Cuesta proposed to stand on the Alberche, and he insisted on doing so with his back to the river. Only when Wellesley went down on his knees, literally, and pleaded for some minutes did the Spanish captain-general give the necessary orders to retire to the Talavera position.

Wellesley considered that the Battle of Talavera was one of the hardest fought of modern times. George Napier has written, 'I never saw a field of battle which struck me with such horror as Talavera.' Wellesley's army, out-numbered two to one, suffered 5000 casualties – a quarter of his force. Only Waterloo, six years later, dwarfed Talavera in terms of massed French artillery bombardments and repeated frontal assaults by huge columns of infantry. If ever a battle illustrated the Napoleonic tactics of column (French) v line (British), this was it. There was a period of perhaps thirty minutes on the afternoon of the second day when the French

Crauford's March to Talavera

THE LIGHT BRIGADE under Crauford, consisting of the 1/43rd, 1/52nd and 1/95th, missed the battle by a few hours, having been marching to the sound of the guns throughout 28 July. During the final twenty-four hours, they covered about forty-two miles, much of it in the broiling sun, with each man carrying 50–60 pounds. It was an epic achievement done, for the most part, at the special light infantry pace of three steps running and three walking, and the more remarkable because it was the end of a gruelling march of some 250 miles in the hottest month of summer.

Starting at Lisbon, Crauford packed the brigade into flat-bottomed boats for the first forty miles up the Tagus. Many hours jammed together, unable to stretch, caused crippling leg cramps which, coupled with a plague of frogs, made their first bivouac memorable. Then on foot through Santarém and Castello Branco – a squalid town where millions of flies descended on the sweating soldiery. From here, on 17 July, the serious marching began: ten days of continuous, grinding effort, each day covering 20 miles, sometimes 25, instead of the regulation 15. Captains marched at the rear of their companies, majors at the rear of their wings, while the colonels rode up and down the line. March discipline was harsh: to fall out without a pass was a court-martial offence. As a straggler came in he was tried and flogged immediately; if he was ill, he was flogged when he had recovered. The next day it was easy to know the number who had been flogged by counting those with knapsacks on their heads.

The longest marches were done at night. On the evening of 27 July at Navalmoral, news was received of fighting near Talavera. Crauford resolved on a forced march to cover the forty-two miles in twenty-four hours. They started before dawn, and at midday, at Oropesa, the baggage was left behind with those men commanding officers felt could not make it. The majority, about 3000, pressed on, meeting en route innumerable Spanish fugitives plus a few British commissary clerks. On and on through the afternoon, evening and into the night, without food, without rest, the brigade stepped out, and early on the morning of 29 July Talavera was reached. Only seventeen men had fallen out. The Light Brigade arrived too late for the fighting, but it is a march that history remembers.

had victory in sight: a huge hole appeared in the allied centre, made worse by the deliberate withdrawal of the *S. Essex*, which Wellesley was able to plug only at the last moment.

The fighting began on 27 July (MAP 9). The morning was notable because Wellesley only just avoided capture; the afternoon for Spanish panic and flight; the night for a French surprise attack which almost succeeded. Wellesley was watching the retirement of his rearguard east of Talavera. Unknown to him, Donkin's brigade had been caught dozing in the shade of the cork trees by an energetic enemy; the 2/87th and 1/88th panicked and retreated in some confusion. An ADC informed Wellesley what had happened, and he spurred forward to the ruined buildings of the Casa de Salinas to see for himself. Clambering to the top of the walls, he had barely time to steady his telescope when French skirmishers swarmed around the building. He was forced to dash down

Bivouac life

SOLDIERS OF ALL RANKS and all armies in the Peninsula slept either in billets (buildings), tents (which were not general issue until 1813) or bivouacs. On active campaigning, the bivouac was the most common. This meant sleeping in the open, providing oneself with what shelter nature could supply. Trees, bushes, grass, stones were all used to protect the individual from the elements, particularly wind and rain. Large trees with thick foliage (protection from rain and sun) were so coveted that, on halting for the night, officers were known to choose their trees by seniority. Some went to extraordinary lengths to keep dry, believing the old army adage, 'any fool can be uncomfortable'. One subaltern stretched out on the grass and got his servant to thatch him by bending twigs and covering the arch with straw or sedge.

Next to his musket, the blanket was probably the soldier's best friend. Portuguese troops were lucky to be issued with extra large blankets, with loops already provided at the corners to make it easy to build a makeshift roof. Three men sharing could find some shelter under one blanket and warmth wrapped in the other two. Eventually Wellington instructed commanding officers to have the corners and edges of blankets strengthened so they could be pitched without tearing. Winter was the worst, when wood represented warmth and claimed equal priority with food. Sleeping, or trying to sleep, under the stars on a clear frosty night was a dreadful experience. Many made no attempt to sleep, but huddled around a fire. Those who tried found their cloak or blanket frozen to the ground by dawn. Dead bodies were rock hard, with hair and clothing cemented to the ground. Living rough in the open, endless marching and physical effort on meagre rations kept the Peninsular Army exceptionally lean and hard. There were no fat soldiers on campaign.

the steep steps, scramble into the saddle and gallop out of the courtyard pursued by shouts and several shots. It was his narrowest escape of the war, and one of the few occasions when he drew his sword.

Sharpe and *Harper* witnessed the Spanish débâcle from the top of the city's east gate (not west as in the book). The Spanish army had been drawn up with its first line just east of the city and extending north for over a mile to the fortified farm of Pajar (MAP 9). Most were comfortably behind the obstacle belt constructed under the supervision of British engineers like *Hogan*. Around seven o'clock in the evening several squadrons of French dragoons were seen approaching east of the city at a range of half a mile. What seemed like the entire front line of Spaniards fired one enormous, but useless, volley. The noise was shattering, the smoke clouds dense and the effect on the enemy zero. But for four Spanish battalions it was enough. With cries of 'Traitor! Traitor!' they fled through the city, abandoning their weapons but pausing to plunder the British baggage as they passed. Sharpe's Light Company, on duty at the gate, were ordered not to try to stop them, but retribution was swift and severe. Spanish cavalry were sent to round them up to be decimated (1 in 10 to be shot). Cuesta commuted it to 1 in 20 after Wellesley intervened.

The third event of 27 July, in which Sharpe and the *S. Essex* were heavily involved, was the night attack by Ruffin's Division through the King's German Legion (KGL) up onto the key feature of the British line, the Cerro de Medellin. Like so many night attacks, it went wrong. This was fortunate for Wellesley as in the confusion of taking up position much of the high ground was unoccupied. Battalions that thought they were in the second line were in the first, generals and staff did not know unit locations and Donkin's demoralised brigade from the 3rd Division became mixed up with the 2nd Division. Night attacks are notoriously difficult to mount: many flounder on navigation errors or noise – or both. Ruffin's attack was ruined by navigation difficulties. Nine battalions, in three regiments, participated (MAP 9).

WOUNDED BURNT

The intense heat in summer, coupled with gunpowder and the flames and sparks of heavy firing made grass fires an unpleasant hazard for wounded on Peninsula battlefields. Rifleman Harris described a French victim at Rolica: '... this man was as completely roasted as if he had been spitted before a good kitchen fire. He was burnt quite brown, every stitch of clothes was singed off, and he was drawn all up like a dried frog ... we examined him, turning him about with our rifles ... the poor fellow called forth from us very little sympathy, but seemed only to be a subject of mirth.'

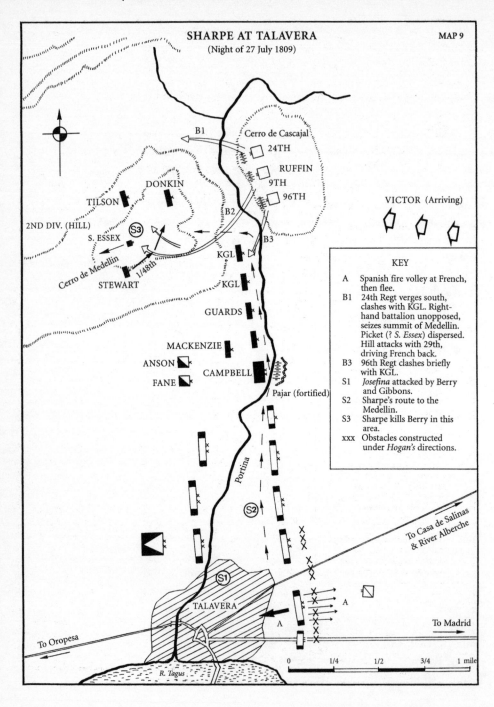

SHARPE AT TALAVERA
(Night of 27 July 1809)

MAP 9

Cerro de Cascajal

24TH

RUFFIN
9TH

96TH

VICTOR (Arriving)

B1

B2

B3

DONKIN

TILSON

2ND DIV. (HILL)

S3

S. ESSEX

Cerro de Medellin

1/48TH

STEWART

KGL

KGL

GUARDS

MACKENZIE

ANSON

FANE

CAMPBELL

Pajar (fortified)

Portina

S2

S1

TALAVERA

A

To Casa de Salinas
& River Alberche

To Madrid

To Oropesa

R. Tagus

0   1/4   1/2   3/4   1 mile

KEY

A   Spanish fire volley at French, then flee.
B1 24th Regt verges south, clashes with KGL. Right-hand battalion unopposed, seizes summit of Medellin. Picket (? *S. Essex*) dispersed. Hill attacks with 29th, driving French back.
B3 96th Regt clashes briefly with KGL.
S1 *Josefina* attacked by Berry and Gibbons.
S2 Sharpe's route to the Medellin.
S3 Sharpe kills Berry in this area.
xxx Obstacles constructed under *Hogan's* directions.

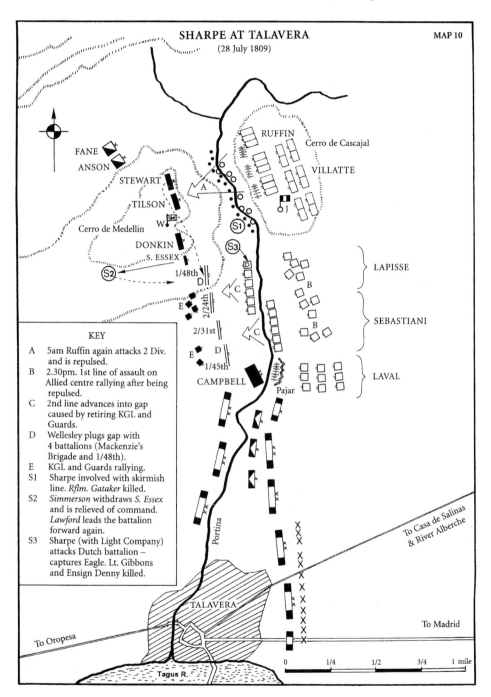

SHARPE AT TALAVERA
(28 July 1809)

MAP 10

RUFFIN
Cerro de Cascajal
VILLATTE
FANE
ANSON
STEWART
A
TILSON
W
Cerro de Medellin
DONKIN
S. ESSEX
J
S1
S3
S2
1/48th
D
E
2/24th
B
LAPISSE
C
2/31st
C
B
SEBASTIANI
E
D
1/45th
CAMPBELL
Pajar
LAVAL
Portina
To Casa de Salinas
& River Alberche

TALAVERA

To Madrid

To Oropesa

0   1/4   1/2   3/4   1 mile

Tagus R.

KEY
A   5am Ruffin again attacks 2 Div.
     and is repulsed.
B   2.30pm. 1st line of assault on
     Allied centre rallying after being
     repulsed.
C   2nd line advances into gap
     caused by retiring KGL and
     Guards.
D   Wellesley plugs gap with
     4 battalions (Mackenzie's
     Brigade and 1/48th).
E   KGL and Guards rallying.
S1   Sharpe involved with skirmish
     line. *Rflm. Gataker* killed.
S2   *Simmerson* withdraws *S. Essex*
     and is relieved of command.
     Lawford leads the battalion
     forward again.
S3   Sharpe (with Light Company)
     attacks Dutch battalion –
     captures Eagle. Lt. Gibbons
     and Ensign Denny killed.

FRENCH
CASUALTIES

Although their 7000
casualties at Talavera
exceeded the British
by 2000, it represented
only one sixth of the
total engaged rather
than one quarter. The
96th Regiment lost
600 (50 per cent), the
24th and 54th lost 500.
Generals Lapisse and
van Porbeck died. All
the colonels and seven
out of twelve battalion
commanders (majors)
in Sebastiani's
division were
wounded. Most of the
French casualties were
from musketry,
whereas a high
proportion of British
were from cannonshot
and shell.

The darkness, the wooded hillsides and the steepness of the Portina ravine were confusing. The 24th Regiment went too far north, missed its objective entirely and made no contact. The 96th sent too far south, and slowly, thus only making light contact later with the KGL. The 9th Regiment, in the centre, was more successful. Although losing direction and clashing with the slumbering Germans, at least one battalion secured the summit of the Medellin feature, brushing aside the picket (which may have been found by the *S. Essex*).

In the darkness and confusion, with the *S. Essex* surprised and pulling back, Sharpe settled a personal vendetta by killing *Lieutenant Berry* for raping *Josefina* in Talavera. In reality, the divisional commander, General Hill, after nearly being killed due to mistaken identity of units, brought forward the 1/48th, who drove the French back and retook the summit. By 5 a.m. on the twenty-eighth, Sharpe and his men had joined the Light Companies of the other battalions in their skirmishing role along the line of the Portina. At some stage during the night, the *S. Essex* were switched from Stewart's brigade to Donkin's 3rd Division. The reasons are unclear: perhaps it was felt necessary to bolster Donkin, or to get the *S. Essex*, who had not done well during the night, to a less exposed part of the line. At dawn on 28 July, *Simmerson* had the battalion on the right flank of the brigade, on the southern slope of the Medellin, looking down on the backs of the Germans and Guards in the centre of the British line (MAP 10).

The slowly rising sun illuminated a sight of unusual military splendour. The mile between the Cerro de Cascajal and the Pajal farm was packed with 40,000 Frenchmen on the east bank of the Portina. Bands played, trumpets shrilled and drums rumbled as the dark blue masses formed up under the Eagles for the first of several assaults on the allied position. But first the guns: in typical Napoleonic fashion, a single cannon shot signalled a massive preparatory bombardment by fifty-four French guns. The infantry then came on in heavy columns behind clouds of skirmishers, with drummers frantically beating the *pas de charge*, first on the Medellin through to seven o'clock, then south as far as Pajar.

Sharpe and his light troops, together with the other British skirmishers, fought with great skill and tenacity, often with the head of enemy columns only a hundred yards behind as they withdrew through the main position. It was during this fighting that *Rifleman Gataker*, one of Sharpe's original band of escapees from the Corunna retreat, was killed. The long scarlet lines held their fire until the French were a mere sixty yards away – then the devastating volley, then the rolling volley by half companies rippling along the lines. As the French reeled and shuddered to a halt, British battalions went in with the bayonet. Nowhere did the French penetrate the position.

By 10 a.m. there was a de facto truce along the Portina. Soldiers of both sides paused in the intense heat to slake their thirst side by side from the dirty, stagnant pools. Wounded were carried away, some dead were buried, enemy shook hands with enemy. For perhaps an hour British, French and Germans mingled amicably, united in their exhaustion and burning thirst. Then the drums and trumpets sounded the recall. With a final shouted remark, a final backward wave, the blue and the scarlet separated to settle the outcome.

Against the advice of Jourdan and on the insistence of Victor, Joseph agreed to one more massive attack. They would hit the centre of the British line between the Pajar and the Medellin with 15,000 bayonets. The divisions of Generals Lapisse and Sebastiani had twelve battalions each (MAP 10). They were deployed side by side, each with six battalions in the first and six in the second line. These were formed in double company columns – rectangular blocks of men ('column' is the term, but is something of a misnomer) with a frontage of about sixty men and a depth of nine. As the first line of some 8000 troops, supported by light, four-pounder artillery pieces, began their ponderous but awesome advance, *Simmerson* gave his order to withdraw the *S. Essex*. This assault met the same fate as those before it. The blocks of blue dissolved in the maelstrom of close range musket fire, followed by a furious bayonet charge. On this occasion,

FRATERNISATION

Thousands of instances of fraternisation, such as those witnessed by Sharpe along the Portina, occurred during the war. Lieutenant Wood of the 82nd described an unusual one: 'Just before dusk . . . many of our soldiers run into a field between the hostile pickets, and dig with their bayonets. Soon after I saw many of the enemy do the same thing: [they] appeared even familiar, laughing and joking . . . men, who tomorrow would be slaying each other, should now be so good-humouredly employed together. They were digging potatoes.'

however, the battalions of Guards and KGL, wild with enthusiasm, gave chase over the Portina. Officers lost control, units became split up, disorganised and fragmented. And at this moment they came up against the unbroken second French line. It was the Guards and Germans who were now pushed back; about 600 guardsmen out of 2000 fell. They were tumbled back over the stream: the British centre was crumbling and a huge hole opening.

While this drama was unfolding, *Simmerson* had been relieved of his command and replaced by *Lieutenant-Colonel Lawford*, who turned the *S. Essex* around and marched them back towards the action. For Wellesley the real crisis of the battle had arrived. The 1/48th were doubled down from the

The Barossa Eagle

THE HONOUR of capturing the first Eagle in the Peninsular War went, not to Captain Sharpe and *Sergeant Harper* of the *S. Essex* at Talavera, but to Ensign Keogh and Sergeant Masterman of the 1/87th (now the Royal Irish Rangers) at the Battle of Barossa on 5 March 1811. The 1/87th became involved in close combat with the French 8th Regiment when Keogh spotted their Eagle surrounded by Frenchmen. Shouting to Masterman to follow him, he immediately attacked the *porte aigle* with his sword and grabbed for the staff with his left hand. While trying to wrench it free, the young ensign went down, shot and bayoneted in the side. The struggle became desperate; according to French accounts no less than seven officers or senior NCOs fell defending the Eagle, the last (a Lieutenant Gazan) clinging to it with both hands until, terribly wounded, Masterman tore it from him. Major Hugh

Gough, the commanding officer of the 1/87th, later described it thus: 'It is brass, well gilt; the wreath [awarded by the city of Paris for service at the Battle of Friedland] is pure gold ... It is much heavier than the colours of a regiment, and from the weight being all at the top is very unwieldy.' The Gough family kept a piece of the gold wreath which had been broken off during the fight.

This Eagle was paraded in London and eventually deposited, with other trophies of the war, in the chapel at the Royal Hospital, Chelsea. It was stolen in 1852 by a thief who used a workman's ladder to get into the organ loft and break the Eagle from its pole. It was never recovered. The 1/87th became known in the Peninsula as the 'Aigle-Takers', and later adopted an eagle with a wreath as a badge. Masterman was promoted sergeant-major and commissioned shortly afterwards.

Medellin to join the three battalions of McKenzie's brigade: four battalions – perhaps 3000 men – strung out in two ranks deployed to plug the half-mile gap. It was enough – just. In the turmoil and vicious hand-to-hand fighting, Sharpe led the volunteers from his Light Company into the Dutch battalion and took its Eagle. It was then that sixteen-year-old *Ensign Denny* died. The *S. Essex* arrived in time to join the final rout of the French. During this fighting *Lieutenant Gibbons* (*Josefina*'s other rapist) attacked Sharpe, but was bayoneted by *Sergeant Harper* from behind.

The butcher's bill for Talavera was high: 5000 British and 7000 French casualties. Sharpe's company was down from 89 to 51, most of whom were injured. Many wounded on both sides were burnt in the grass fires that raged across the Portina valley after the battle, and fully two-thirds of the British survivors were employed bringing in the wounded. It was the age of amputation; any serious wound to a limb and the surgeon invariably reached for his saw. The growing pile of arms and legs that Sharpe saw outside the hospital building was not exaggerated.

The *S. Essex* had got off lightly in terms of casualties. *Simmerson* was sent home, supposedly in disgrace. Wellesley, still without food for his army, found that Soult, Ney and Mortier had descended on his communications at Plasencia and that the Spanish army was more of a hindrance than a help. Thus, despite a victory which gave him the title of Viscount Wellington of Talavera, he was obliged to begin a long and bitter retreat to Lisbon. There would be no further set-piece battle for fourteen months.

THE SALAMANCA EAGLE

The namesake of the *S. Essex* was the East Essex, or 44th Foot. They captured the Eagle belonging to the French 62nd Regiment at the Battle of Salamanca on 22 July 1812. The officer who took it, Lieutenant Peirse, claimed to have scratched his name on the base. Many years later this Eagle disappeared, then was found and restored to the Essex Regiment. The puzzle today is why the Eagle kept at Chelmsford museum has neither the number '62' nor any name scratched on its base.

6

Sharpe's Gold

'CROAKING'

It was not only the Spanish who became defeatist and proclaimed bitterly that they were being abandoned after Masséna's invasion of Portugal in the autumn of 1810. Rumours and grumbling were rife within the British army, and Wellington's strategy was openly criticised. Much information valuable to the enemy got into the press via letters home. This complaining (130 years later Montgomery called it 'bellyaching') was called 'croaking'. Some senior officers such as Charles Stewart, the Adjutant-General, and Major-General Crauford were guilty. Wellington eventually got rid of the former after reducing him to tears; Crauford on his death-bed (he died of wounds received at the Siege of Ciudad Rodrigo in 1812) apologised profusely for his mischief-making.

Captain Sharpe and the *S. Essex* march up from the southern borders of Portugal to join Wellington's main army grouped around Celorico. Arriving in mid-August 1810, Sharpe, with the Light Company, is given a secret mission: the securing of a considerable quantity of gold. The gold was in the hands of a Spanish guerrilla leader (*Cesár Moreno*), over the border in French-held Spain, east of the Portuguese fortress of Almeida. Sharpe knew only that the ability of the British to continue the war depended on securing the gold. He was not told that it was required to finance the completion of the Lines of Torres Vedras – fortifications stretching across the Lisbon peninsula about fifteen miles north of the city. If necessary, Wellington intended to retire behind these lines and defy the French to throw the British out of Portugal.

EARLY IN 1810 Napoleon was preoccupied with two problems: first, the war in Spain had become a running sore, a constant bleeding of men and resources he could ill afford; second, Josephine had failed to produce an heir.

On the former, he reasoned that as long as the British remained in Portugal the Spanish would continue to resist. French armies had overrun Spain; France was an occupying power; Napoleon's brother (Joseph) sat on the Spanish throne; French soldiers roamed the city streets; and Wellington had retired over the border. But Spain was not conquered. In January of 1810, 325,000 French troops had been necessary to hold down the populace, seek out the countless guerrilla bands, forage and protect the endless supply convoys and couriers. France ruled the towns, Spain the countryside. To ensure a mounted messenger had a better than even chance of reaching his destination two squadrons of cavalry had to accompany him. The solution – Invade Portugal. Drive Wellington into the sea.

Such a decisive offensive merited the Emperor's personal supervision, but plans to take the field were disrupted by his second difficulty. Arrangements to divorce Josephine and marry Marie-Louise of Austria took time and much delicate diplomacy. By mid-April he resolved to give the optimistically named 'Army of Portugal' to Marshal Masséna, fifty-two-year-old Duke of Rivoli and Prince of Essling (also known as the 'Spoilt Child of Victory' or 'The Old Fox'). He took command in Spain on 10 May.

Marshal Masséna

BORN 1758 NEAR NICE. His father was dead, and he was abandoned by his mother. Worked in a soap factory before running away to sea at thirteen. In 1775 he enlisted in the French army's Royal Italian Regiment and rose to regimental sergeant-major in nine years. Denied further promotion, he left the army to become a grocer, which was rumoured to be a front for smuggling. Made a lieutenant-colonel of Volunteers in 1791, he was a divisional general within two years. Fought in Bonaparte's Italian campaign and was noted as a tough, courageous, 'hands-on' leader, always at the front. Made a marshal in 1804. Commanded the IV Corps at the battles of Landshut, Eckmuhl, Ebersberg, Aspern-Essling and Wagram. By the time Napoleon sent him to Spain, he had lost his fire.

He was a notorious lecher and looter. His mistress, Madame Leberton, travelled with him to Spain, dressed as a dragoon. Although the Emperor rewarded him handsomely, he was always after a quick franc. Napoleon was aware of Masséna's 'little savings' and frequently had them transferred to the army paymaster. Uneducated, a poor reader, Masséna was an instinctive general who needed the stimulation of combat to show his energy and ability. Despite the devastated countryside, he kept his army close up to the impregnable Lines for five weary months. Recalled in disgrace after defeat at Fuentes de Onoro in 1811, Masséna never received another field command. During the 100 days culminating in Waterloo, he remained as commandant of the Marseilles district. He refused to sit on Ney's court-martial and died two years later, in 1817. His tombstone bears the single word 'Masséna'.

MULETEERS

Mules were used for virtually all forward transport for the army (except artillery). Wellington's army of 47,000 required almost 7000 in 1812. A muleteer was entitled to a dollar a day plus a dollar for each animal he provided. In 1813, their pay was, in some cases, up to twenty-six months in arrears. Hardy, cheerful men on the road, always singing, dressed in large black felt hats, short jackets, a blanket with a hole in the middle for their heads, blue breeches and sandals, they served the British well but often refused to carry supplies for the Portuguese.

When Wellington summoned the *S. Essex* north in August and selected Sharpe for a special mission, he was putting the finishing touches to a strategic plan that was, ultimately, to lead to the liberation of Spain and see British troops storming the passes of the Pyrenees just over three years later. It was a defensive plan. If Masséna massed his forces and advanced into Portugal, his very strength would be his undoing. Spain and Portugal were countries where large armies starved and small ones were defeated. To beat the British on the battle-field, the French had to concentrate large numbers of troops. Putting 65,000 men, 20,000 horses and vast hordes of mules and oxen within a few miles of one another is like having plagues of locusts descend on the area. Far more so than the British, the French 'lived off the land'. The nearby towns, villages and countryside were their primary source of food and forage. Masséna had to unite to fight, but disperse to eat.

Wellington's strategy had been devised many months before. It had three strands. Any French advance would be across a scorched countryside, devoid of provisions. They would find bridges broken, mills destroyed, boats burnt, fields laid waste and the population gone with their livestock – to the hills, or behind Wellington's second strand, the Lines of Torres Vedras (MAP 11). This double line of fortifications (with a third close to Lisbon to cover an evacuation by the Royal Navy) stretched from the Atlantic coast to the Tagus estuary and would present Masséna's ravenous army, after marching across 'miles and miles of threadbare carpet', with an impregnable, unassailable barrier. Portuguese militia would man the fixed defences, while the British army was held back to strike as necessary and to follow up the retreating French. Retreat they surely would; blocked by so formidable an obstacle and unable to feed themselves, the Eagles must turn and take flight.

The final strand which, entwined with the other two, was to produce a war-winning strategy was harnessing the hatred of the Portuguese and Spanish peasants for the French. A Portu-guese regular army of 45,000 was retrained and reorganised by

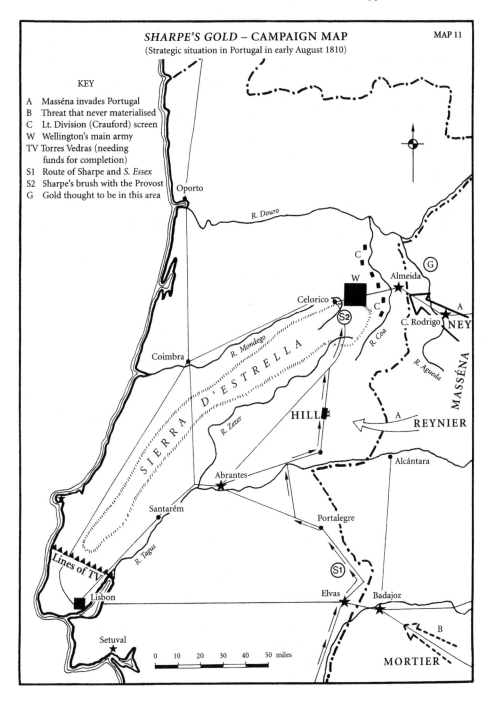

SHARPE'S GOLD – CAMPAIGN MAP
(Strategic situation in Portugal in early August 1810)

MAP 11

KEY

A   Masséna invades Portugal
B   Threat that never materialised
C   Lt. Division (Crauford) screen
W   Wellington's main army
TV Torres Vedras (needing
    funds for completion)
S1 Route of Sharpe and *S. Essex*
S2 Sharpe's brush with the Provost
G   Gold thought to be in this area

R. Douro

Oporto

C

W   Almeida   G

Celorico   C   A   NEY

S2   C. Rodrigo

R. Coa

R. Mondego   R. Agueda   MASSÉNA

Coimbra   S I E R R A   D' E S T R E L L A

R. Zezer   A   REYNIER

HILL

Alcántara

Abrantes

Santarém   Portalegre

R. Tagus

Lines of TV   S1

Lisbon   Elvas   Badajoz

B

Setuval   0   10   20   30   40   50 miles

MORTIER

DESERTION

Two types: desertion to the enemy, and desertion which only involved absconding from a unit. In the first instance, the culprit was invariably shot. With the second, executions sometimes took place but for many the sentence was flogging or transportation. In 1811, of the ten deserters who absconded together four were shot and six flogged. A high proportion were Irish; it was not hard to persuade Irish prisoners to change sides, although many reverted at the first opportunity. Desertion was prevalent from the foreign corps – the Brunswick Oels Jägers, whose recruits were originally German but soon included Poles, Swiss, Danes, Dutch and Croats, and the Chasseurs Britannique. This regiment was originally composed of French royalists but soon recruited deserters from any country. Not surprisingly, it had the highest incidence of desertion of any regiment in the British army, and tended to melt away whenever it came near French lines. A standing order forbade it to do out-post duty. Of the eighteen chasseurs who deserted as a body in 1812, all but two were Italians.

Major-General Beresford under British officers (many, like Sharpe's old friend from India, *Lieutenant Tom Garrard*, former sergeants commissioned on transfer). Another 45,000 militia were deployed. Portuguese battalions were brigaded with British battalions and thousands of Portuguese peasants were persuaded to roll out the 'threadbare carpet' in central Portugal. Wellington had used his powers as the Portuguese Marshal-General to call to arms the entire male population of the kingdom. Thousands became guerrillas in the hills – the Ordenanza. These, and their Spanish equivalents such as *Cesár Moreno* and *El Catolico*, harried foraging parties, cut down couriers, attacked pickets, plundered wagons and – of critical importance – provided Wellington with accurate and timely intelligence.

Sharpe was never told the true destination of the gold he was to secure. In August 1810, he would never have heard of Torres Vedras, an obscure castle in the centre of the Lisbon peninsula. By that date the Lines were nearing completion but their existence was known to few outside the Portuguese labourers and their supervising engineers who were constructing them. When Wellington finally withdrew behind them in October, their existence was as much a surprise to his soldiers as they were a shock to the French.

Exactly a year before, in October 1809, Wellington had issued orders for their construction. Talavera had been won, Sharpe had taken the Eagle, the *S. Essex* were under the command of *Lieutenant-Colonel Lawford*, and *Simmerson* had gone home in disgrace. The allied army had nevertheless been ordered to retire behind the Tagus. They had gone in a truculent mood, hungry and not understanding why triumph at Talavera was followed by demoralising retreat. There were ugly scenes on the march, looting was common and the lash was applied with ferocity. With his army sullen and dispirited, Wellington took two weeks off to ride around the hills and valleys north of Lisbon with his chief engineer, Lieutenant-Colonel Richard Fletcher.

Continually in the saddle from dawn to dusk, Wellington

and Fletcher ranged across the rugged hills that choke the Lisbon peninsula north of the city. Nature had been kind in providing obstacles to invaders approaching from that direction. Wellington instructed Fletcher to use military engineering to augment the natural barriers: artificial inundations, palisades, scarped slopes, trenches, abatis, redoubts and hilltop forts, Wellington required them all. The detached redoubts were the cornerstones of the system. They were closed earthworks designed to hold from three to six guns and up to 300 men. All possible cover in front of the Lines was removed and the countryside turned into a huge glacis. To achieve this mounds were levelled, sunken roads filled, vineyards cut down and buildings demolished. The landowners were paid compensation for this destruction. Lateral roads were built to facilitate the speedy movement of troops to threatened points, and the defensive system was linked by semaphore stations. When complete, a signal from the Atlantic would reach the Tagus in seven minutes, while a galloper from headquarters could deliver a written message anywhere within an hour. It was a splendid achievement, the linchpin of Wellington's plan.

War is costly in terms of cash as well as lives. The British Treasury had to fund every allied endeavour. Spain and Portugal were allies, but poor ones; neither could pay for a war on the scale of that which raged for six years in the Peninsula, so the burden shifted to the British. Not only did British troops have to be paid and maintained; so did the Portuguese – every soldier, every labourer, every contractor, every muleteer and every peasant who provided food or forage. The British government was shaken by the cost of the war. By April 1810, the subsidy to Portugal alone was running at £1.5 million annually, and the problem was exacerbated because paper money was seldom acceptable, and treasury bills (IOUs/receipts) even less so. What everybody wanted was coinage (specie): shiny silver dollars or gleaming gold coins. Wellington complained bitterly and often that his troops' pay was in arrears, that huge debts were mounting, and that without sufficient coinage the war was lost. Hence

GERMANS EAT DOGS

Costello tells how the Brunswick Oels Jägers were 'gifted with a canine appetite that induced them to kill and eat all the dogs they could get hold of...' The 95th had a pet dog named 'Rifle' which accompanied them into action and dashed about barking as though it was all a grand game. He survived the bullets, only to 'be devoured by the insatiable jaws of the Brunswickers'.

the importance he attached to Sharpe's mission. Sixteen thousand gold doubloons (each valued at £3.5) was the equivalent of perhaps £100 million in today's money. Certainly enough to complete the Lines of Torres Vedras with plenty to spare. For such a sum kingdoms are bought and sold, as the power-hungry guerrilla leader *El Catolico* appreciated.

Important though Sharpe's mission was, it was but a tiny facet of a growing nightmare for Wellington and, more particularly, for his chief Treasury official Mr (later Sir Richard) Kennedy, the Commissary-General. During Kennedy's tenure some £6 million worth of coins were shipped to Lisbon towards the £54 million he was later found to have disbursed. Although Britain was the richest country in the world, her

The Commissaries

THESE MUCH-MALIGNED Treasury officers (whose grades were equated to military ranks in 1815) were responsible for buying, storing, forwarding and issuing the supplies needed to keep the army functioning. The commissary-general (brigadier) with his deputy (lieutenant-colonel or major) were attached to army headquarters, and with each division was an assistant (captain) and each brigade a deputy-assistant (lieutenant). Under them came commissary clerks (sergeant-majors). They had a thankless and stressful life. The commissary with a division was expected to provide daily 10,500 lbs of bread (or 7000 lbs of biscuit), 7000 lbs of meat and 7000 pints of wine. They also had responsibility for the 500 slaughter beef on the hoof and the 600 divisional mules.

Picton (3rd Division) had his assistant-commissary report at 3 a.m. every morning while on the march. These red-jacketed young men were sometimes only sixteen years old. In 1810 their conditions of service were regulated, with new entrants having to do a year as probationary clerks before commissioning. They dispersed huge sums, usually in the form of receipts, for every purchase of goods or services, and had to keep meticulous accounts of public money. Auditors would probe and question for years after transactions had been completed, and death was no escape: debts were passed down to dependants. Perhaps not surprisingly, many commissariat officers were not overscrupulous and did not come from the best elements of the commercial world. As one remarked, 'Gentlemen, if a commissary is expected to starve in the midst of all his stores, then the devil take the whole business.'

'The Honeysuckers'

WELLINGTON MADE FULL USE of the 'Bloody Provost' to keep looting in check. There was a provost marshal at his headquarters and an assistant on the staff of every division, who had charge of prisoners to be tried by general court-martial, and of deserters and prisoners of war. The provost's mounted patrols were wide ranging and ruthless in dealing with offenders, as Sharpe and *Batten* discovered. During the retreat to the Lines of Torres Vedras, the provost twice exercised their right to carry out summary executions of men caught in the act of committing a capital crime – a dragoon and a Portuguese soldier were hanged.

Normally Wellington was unbending when his orders against looting were flagrantly disregarded, but on one occasion his sense of humour overruled his sense of discipline. He was out riding when he came upon a soldier of the Connaught Rangers rushing along with his greatcoat wrapped around his head and a beehive balanced on top, around which swarmed an angry host of bees. The commander-in-chief challenged him furiously, 'Hey, you sir, where did you get that beehive?' Muffled by his coat and unable to see his questioner, and failing to detect the tone of authority due to the buzzing around his head, the soldier yelled back, 'Just over the hill there, and, by Jasus, if ye don't make haste they'll be all gone.' Wellington let him hurry on. Several men of the 53rd were caught a few days later at the same game, but this time the humourless provost spotted them. A general court-martial sentenced each to 700 lashes, and the Regiment acquired a nickname: 'The Honeysuckers'.

---

stocks of gold and silver were limited. Paper money, which Britain had introduced in 1797, was fraught with inflationary risks (the temptation being to keep printing more), and in 1810 a parliamentary committee recommended (unsuccessfully) that banknotes be withdrawn within two years. Government agents travelled the world in search of Spanish and Portuguese dollars. In the year before Sharpe secured his hoard, Spanish dollars had been bought in China but had to be reminted as they were defaced by Chinese hieroglyphics. (In 1813 the problem was partially solved by obtaining a steady supply of gold pagodas from India which were turned into guineas.)

If the *S. Essex* wanted a wagon, a horse, bread or anything from a Portuguese smallholder, it had to be paid for. The farmer wanted cash but was invariably given a receipt, which he had to go to Lisbon to exchange for real dollars. A wait of weeks there might be required before coins were available, so the Portuguese peasant usually sold his receipt to a dealer – at a considerable loss – and when the dealer had enough to make his journey worthwhile he went to Lisbon, where he bought more receipts from people fed up with waiting. It was a lucrative business.

Theft could be punishable by death, as *Private Batten* discovered when he was caught in the act of 'winning' a scraggy chicken in the deserted village outside Celorico. The inhabitants had gone south in response to Wellington's 'threadbare carpet' appeal, but their property was still protected. The provost was entitled to hang a looter on the spot if he was caught red-handed in the act of stealing from a person, and using violence to do so. In this instance *Lieutenant Ayres* would have exceeded his powers had he hanged *Batten* because the owner of the chicken was not threatened, indeed was not even present. Sharpe knew his military law, and threatening to shoot the officer was a long way outside it. Had *Batten* really been caught committing a capital crime and Sharpe had prevented *Ayres* from hanging him, he would not have got away with a mere apology.

When Sharpe set out to find the gold in mid-August 1810, Masséna's army had been on the move for more than a month. The great Spanish fortress of Ciudad Rodrigo had fallen to Marshal Ney's troops on 9 July, and Almeida was his next objective. Wellington had done nothing to relieve Ciudad Rodrigo. More than any other act or omission, this 'failure' led to the widespread belief by Spaniards that he was abandoning them to the French. The only way *Moreno*, *El Catolico* or any other guerrilla leader would be persuaded to hand over gold to the British was if he was absolutely certain that it would go into Spanish coffers – hence Sharpe's impression that it was destined for Cadiz. Had the guerrillas known it was needed to compensate Portuguese landowners and pay Portuguese workers near Lisbon, Sharpe would have met with total hostility.

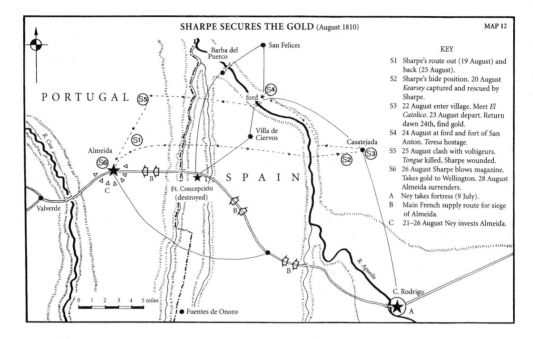

SHARPE SECURES THE GOLD (August 1810)   MAP 12

KEY

S1 Sharpe's route out (19 August) and back (25 August).
S2 Sharpe's hide position. 20 August *Kearsey* captured and rescued by Sharpe.
S3 22 August enter village. Meet *El Catolico*. 23 August depart. Return dawn 24th, find gold.
S4 24 August at ford and fort of San Anton. *Teresa* hostage.
S5 25 August clash with voltigeurs. *Tongue* killed, Sharpe wounded.
S6 26 August Sharpe blows magazine. Takes gold to Wellington. 28 August Almeida surrenders.
A   Ney takes fortress (9 July).
B   Main French supply route for siege of Almeida.
C   21–26 August Ney invests Almeida.

The garrison of 5500 Spanish regular and militia troops in Ciudad Rodrigo was commanded by a vigorous, if ancient seventy-year-old veteran, General Andrès Herresi. He had held out for six weeks, sustained by the belief that the British would arrive to raise the siege. As time passed, as Ney's guns crept closer, as casualties mounted and as help failed to appear, the distraught Herresi smuggled out a distraught note for Wellington: '*O venir luego! luego! luego! a secorrer esta plaza.*' (O come now! now! now! to succour this place.) Wellington was not drawn; his overriding aim was the defence of Portugal. To chance his army in Spain against at least double his numbers was to risk the very continuation of the war. He would fight when he chose, where he chose. In a despatch he wrote, 'It was impractical to attempt it [relieving Ciudad Rodrigo] unless it could be supposed we should beat an army nearly double the strength of the allied army, having nearly four times the number of cavalry, in a country admirably adapted to the use of that arm.'

Militarily, there was nothing spectacular in Sharpe's

SEMAPHORE
SIGNALLING

The army adopted
semaphore signalling
from the RN and, as
noted by Sharpe, the
stations were
sometimes manned by
a midshipman or a
senior naval rating
who was familiar with
the codes. (Almeida
had such a station.)
Large code books
(Home Popham's
*Telegraph
Vocabularies*) were
needed, where
common (and not so
common) messages
and military
phraseology were
reduced to a few
numbers. Most hoisted
balls rather than
inflated sheep's
bladders, but the
system was of no use
in bad weather or at
night. Semaphore was
used extensively while
awaiting Masséna's
offensive during the
summer of 1810, and
again within the Lines
of Torres Vedras. By
1813 the system had
been established on a
divisional basis with a
telegraph officer,
NCO and three
soldiers complete with
equipment. It was the
start of the modern
Royal Corps of
Signals.

mission (MAP 12). Although the securing of gold was unusual, the operation and tactics used were typical of hundreds of small-scale ventures behind enemy lines. It was, in effect, a fighting patrol with a specific task. Sharpe was told only what he needed to know, given a guide (*Major Kearsey*), and allowed to use his initiative to complete the task. It was one small example of how Wellington used his extensive intelligence network to pinpoint a task (in this case securing gold coins). *Kearsey*, the 'exploring' or 'observing' officer, provided the information, had the contacts with the guerrillas and knew the local terrain; Sharpe provided the firepower.

Wellington employed many men like *Kearsey*, the most famous being Captain (as he was in 1810) Colquhoun Grant. Sometimes in uniform, sometimes not, these men rode deep into enemy territory alone or with a handful of Spanish companions. Their job was to discover everything about the French: how many infantry, cavalry, guns, where they were, where they were going and by what route; what were their intentions? Often they would be away for weeks, even months at a time.

Occasionally they had a specific task of critical strategic significance. After Sharpe had delivered the gold, after Almeida was blown up, and while Sharpe was on leave in Lisbon, Wellington needed to know what route Masséna would take when he moved south-west towards Coimbra. Would he march on the northern or southern bank of the Mondego River? Two officers were left behind to provide the answer as the allied army pulled back. Captain Somers Cocks and Lieutenant Lovell Badcock watched the French columns from high in the northern hills of the Sierra da Estrela (MAP 4), not far from the village where *Batten* was so nearly hanged. In early September, Ney's men were south of the river and marching east, then suddenly they swung north and crossed the river near the village of Fornos. A column which continued along the south bank was watched carefully and discovered to be a feint: the enemy had gone north. The 'observing' officers spurred away. Wellington moved his army north of the river and awaited the confrontation at what became known as the 'bloodstained hill of Bussaco' – one of the few battles at which Sharpe was not present.

Lieutenant-Colonel William Cox was the British commander of a Portuguese garrison of around 5000 soldiers and over 100 guns in Almeida. He had the rank of brigadier in the Portuguese army. He intended, and Wellington expected, to hold the fortress blocking access to Portugal for several weeks, at least until the September rains arrived to make the bad roads worse. It was a neat little fortress with six bastions, almost circular and with a diameter of 700 yards. Inside was a small township, a castle (on top of which was the semaphore station) and a cathedral, which Cox was using as the main magazine. Stored in the vault were hundreds of barrels of gunpowder, which had to be manhandled to the guns on the walls. This was not as dangerous as might be supposed

THE KING'S GERMAN LEGION (KGL)

When Hanover was overrun in 1803, King George III (as Elector of Hanover) authorised the formation of a King's German Regiment from the citizens of Hanover. It quickly expanded into the KGL, eventually comprising 8 line and 2 light battalions, 5 regiments of cavalry (3 hussars, 2 dragoons) plus 6 artillery batteries and a handful of engineer officers. They fought with great distinction in the Peninsula and at Waterloo. Their dragoons gained lasting fame for breaking two French infantry squares at García Hernandez in 1812.

Polish Lancers

FRENCH
VOLTIGEURS
The equivalent of
British light infantry,
with one company per
battalion, their tasks
were scouting and
skirmishing. They
were usually the first
troops to clash with
Sharpe's riflemen in a
set-piece battle such as
Talavera. Short, tough
soldiers, they ranked
second only to
grenadiers, officially
assigned the second
position of honour on
parade: the left of the
line. They got their
name from the word
'to vault', being
recruited for smallness
and agility which
facilitated vaulting up
behind a cavalryman
if necessary.

because the cathedral was immensely strong and could withstand a direct hit by the most powerful artillery of the besiegers.

When Sharpe arrived with the gold on 25 August he had to use utmost caution: the French had been digging their parallels since the fifteenth and their fifty-four heavy cannons and mortars were almost ready to fire. On the morning of the twenty-sixth they did so, pounding the walls and lobbing shells over them continuously for twelve hours. The siege of Almeida started and ended in one day, terminated at about 7 p.m. by a monumental, volcanic eruption as the tons of gunpowder in the cathedral vaults exploded. It was an accident, not deliberate as in Sharpe's story. Throughout the day men had been hauling barrels of powder from the vault to be delivered to the magazines near the cannons on the walls. Most of them were carried through the streets on mules. At some stage a barrel had leaked a trail of powder from the cathedral doors, which had been opened to facilitate loading. By the entrance were stacks of filled cartridges awaiting the next mule. A French mortar shell exploded in the street, ignited the powder trail which flared back to the cartridges, which exploded. A few seconds later, the entire building disappeared in one of the biggest explosions the world had thus far witnessed.

The cathedral ceased to exist; every house had its roof sheared off, and about 500 defenders on the walls were killed. One man near the cathedral survived; he had the presence of mind to dive into a large oven after the first explosion. The fountain of debris that soared into the sky produced a deadly rain of granite blocks and stones which caused about forty casualties in the French lines. To this day, many of the blocks lie where they fell. Cox tried to persuade his officers to carry on the fight, but it was useless without guns, ammunition, or artillerymen. On 28 August he surrendered, by which time Sharpe (with the gold) had used the chaos and darkness to slip away to Wellington. The commander-in-chief's despatch dated 31 August sums up neatly what happened at Almeida:

The explosion of the magazine destroyed the whole town, made a breach in the place, blew all the guns excepting three into the ditch, destroyed all the ammunition ... killed or wounded the greater part of the artillerymen. The major commanding the artillery was the person employed by Cox to settle the capitulation for him. He went out and informed the French of the exact state of the place after the explosion, and never returned! Masséna has made him a colonel!!

French Voltigueurs

Sharpe's Battle

The *Real Compañía Irlandesa (Royal Irish Company)* did not exist. However, the Spanish maintained four Royal Guard companies, each of a different nationality, distinguished by the colour of its carbine bandolier – Spanish red; American purple; Italian dark green; Flemish yellow. There were three Irish regiments serving in Spain: the Hibernia, Irlanda and Ultonia. Thousands of Irishmen left home every year for foreign service to escape the 'Penal Laws' and for the chance to take a shot at the hated redcoats. *Sergeant Harper* enjoyed fighting, but did so for the English with great reluctance. It was not unusual for a third of a British battalion to be Irish, so attempts to subvert them, such as Sharpe detected, were taken very seriously.

In the spring of 1811 the French, under Marshal Masséna, had retreated from the Lines of Torres Vedras, and their only remaining Portuguese possession was the fortress of Almeida. Captain Sharpe and the forty men of his Light Company were tasked with training the Spanish *Real Compañía Irelandesa (Royal Irish Company)*, which had been attached to Wellington's headquarters. They were sent to garrison a disused and partially derelict fort (*San Isidro*) on the border. They defended the fort against *Brigadier Loup's brigade of 'Grey Wolves'*, by blowing up the ammunition wagons and sustaining heavy losses. A court of inquiry was to be set up to investigate the disaster and Sharpe feared being blamed. He was sent to guard the army's ammunition reserve before the Battle of Fuentes de Onoro, but became involved in the ferocious fighting for the village and in the Light Division's famous three-mile withdrawal in close column of companies covering the threatened British right flank. The action ended with Sharpe once again in Fuentes de Onoro where he succeeded in drowning *Loup* in a hand-to-hand struggle.

THE *S. ESSEX*, much depleted in numbers, had been split into small company packets on line of communication duties as Wellington followed up Masséna's retreat from Portugal. When the green, and grey-faced, reinforcements gratefully disembarked from England on 2 March 1811, none was drafted to the *S. Essex*. From October 1810 to the end of February 1811, the battalion spent a dull, if reasonably comfortable,

ABOVE The Duke of Wellington.

RIGHT Napoleon Bonaparte, from a painting by Robert Lefèvre.

A somewhat apocryphal but interesting impression of the assault on the breach at Seringapatam in May 1799. In the centre is General Baird directing the attack. Note how the attackers are clambering up the broken wall on the left. The man on the top left with the Colours represents Sergeant Graham moments before he was killed. Bottom left and in the centre are excellent examples of the Tippoo's tiger-mouthed cannons and, bottom right, a soldier in a tiger-striped uniform.

A modern view of the 'dungeons' of the Sultan Battery under the north wall of Seringapatam. It was here that Sharpe, *Lawford*, *McCandless* and *Hakeswill* were imprisoned and guarded at night by a prowling tiger. These 'dungeons' were a magazine for the gun battery.

RIGHT A picture of the Tippoo's famous working model of a tiger mauling a prostrate European, with a clear view of the organ built inside to provide suitable noises when the handle was cranked.

The principal Peninsular War generals. *Top row, left to right*: Sir Thomas Picton, General Crauford, Sir Thomas Graham, Sir Henry Clinton. *Second row*: Sir Rowland Hill, Sir John Moore, Marshal Lord Beresford. *Third row*: Napoleon, Wellington. *Fourth row*: Marshal Soult, Marshal Massena, Marshal Ney. *Fifth row*: Marshal Marmont, General Junot, Marshal Victor, Marshal Suchet. (From *A War in the Peninsula* by H. R. Clinton, London).

Some of the British, French and Prussian infantry and cavalry weapons used at Waterloo. Many of the arms were of old patterns, made in the previous century, renovated and modified for the war. *From left to right*: British pattern 1796 heavy cavalry sword; British India pattern musket with shortened barrel and long bayonet; Prussian model 1809 infantry musket; French heavy cavalry sword; British light dragoon pistol; French cavalry pistol; British pattern 1796 light cavalry officer's sword; British Baker rifle; French infantry musket, model 1777 with later modifications; French light cavalry sword.

French dragoons ambushed in the streets of Madrid during the uprising of May 1808. Note the priest in the right foreground with dagger and blunderbuss. Priests played a prominent part in guerilla activities throughout the war.

The Battle of Vimiero, 21 August 1808, where Wellesley defeated the French General Junot. Sharpe was present at this battle as the quartermaster of the 2/95th. He was a 2nd Lieutenant but was promoted the next day to fill a casualty vacancy.

Tom Plunkett of the 95th Foot picks off French General Colbert with his Baker rifle during the retreat to Corunna in 1809. Illustration by Harry Payne.

The seminary and cathedral at Santiago de Compostela. Sharpe and *Major Blas Vivar* were involved in heavy fighting with the French around these buildings when they briefly took the city on 28 January 1809.

The Battle of Talavera, 27–28 July 1809. It was here that *Sharpe* captured an enemy Eagle and the *S. Essex* to some extent redeemed themselves (after *Lt-Col. Simmerson* had been relieved of command).

The small but typical Portuguese town of Torres Vedras with part of the famous 'Lines' (fortifications) crowning the hill behind. Wellington successfully defied Massena's army from behind the Lines of Torres Vedras throughout the winter of 1810–11.

The Battle of Fuentes de Onoro, 3–4 May 1811. The picture shows a Light Division square repulsing a French cavalry attack during that division's famous battlefield withdrawal of three miles. Sharpe participated in this withdrawal and finished his battle by drowning *Brigadier Loup* in the stream at Fuentes de Onoro.

The bridge in Fuentes de Onoro village looking west. Some 14,000 Frenchmen were eventurally absorbed in the bloody and prolonged struggle for this handful of houses. Near this bridge Sharpe was wounded in the shoulder by *Juanita*. She was then shot by *Harper* and Sharpe drowned *Brigadier Loup* in the stream.

Wellington's Divisions

WITH THE CREATION of the 7th Division in March 1811, the divisional structure of the army was complete, with eight infantry (including the Light Division) and two cavalry divisions (from early 1812). The infantry were usually under a lieutenant-general and had two British and one Portuguese brigade in each. Over the years they acquired nicknames:

1st Division   The largest at 7000 normally commanded by the senior lieutenant-general (Spencer in 1811). Known as 'The Gentlemen's Sons' because it contained Guards Regiments.

2nd Division   GOC W. Stuart. Usually formed the bulk of Hill's semi-independent command operating on the right flank of the Army, nicknamed 'The Observing Division'.

3rd Division   GOC Picton, whom Wellington described 'as rough, foul-mouthed a devil as ever lived, but he always behaved extremely well on service'. Known as 'The Fighting Division'; ranks drawn mainly from Irish peasantry; hard fighting record on and off the battlefield.

4th Division   GOC Cole. Nicknamed 'The Supporting Division' as it so often supported the 2nd Division with Hill. After Battle of Albuera earned new name of 'The Enthusiastics'.

5th Division   GOC Leith. 'The Pioneers'; origin uncertain but possibly due to the amount of road-making it did in 1810.

6th Division   GOC A. Campbell. 'The Marching Division', due to its extensive marching and counter-marching without engaging the enemy prior to the Battle of Salamanca in 1812.

7th Division   Last division formed. GOC, initially Houston, but changed often. Sometimes called 'The Mongrels' because it had only two British and four foreign battalions. The Brunswick Oel Jägers and Chasseurs Britanniques earned it a bad reputation for desertion. After a poor showing at Fuentes de Onoro it was not used much for two years, but redeemed itself in the Pyrenees battle of 1813.

Light Division   GOC Robert Crauford (until killed in 1812). Called themselves '*The* Division'. Screened the army in advance and withdrawal. Often mustered only 4000 compared with the others at 6000. Regarded as the élite formation in the allied army.

time behind the Lines of Torres Vedras waiting for winter and starvation to defeat the French.

It had been a long five months. As early as December 1810 Wellington, in a despatch to Lord Liverpool, wrote:

It is certainly astonishing that the enemy have been able to remain in this country so long; and it is an extraordinary

CATTLE CULL AT
ALMEIDA

The French garrison had a herd of cattle which was put out to graze on the glacis. From 10–15 April, two companies of the 1/95th had the daily duty of parading before dawn to shoot the cattle. From behind rocks they sniped the defenceless beasts, provoking an enraged artillery reaction which killed a sergeant. The cull was successful, however, as the surviving cattle were withdrawn behind the walls.

instance of what a French army can do. It is positively a fact that they brought no provisions with them and they have not received even a letter since they entered Portugal . . . I could not maintain one division in the district in which they have maintained not less than 60,000 men and 20,000 animals for more than two months.

Masséna's men were master scavengers; ruthless, and with seventeen years' experience of rooting out hidden stocks. The truth was that the 'threadbare carpet' policy had not been thoroughly implemented; destruction of everything useful to the enemy had been diluted to concealment, by the frugal peasants. Grain was stored in caves or walled up in cottages, mill machinery was buried, and livestock hidden in the hills. During the winter British commissaries sallied forth with cavalry escorts to try to enforce the 'scorched earth' edict. Assistant-commissary Schaumann took part in these raids and described what was involved:

> My duty was to clear the ground between us and the enemy of all possible victuals . . . I was given a detachment of hussars . . . my people followed us with mules and empty sacks . . . when we reached a village we sent patrols to the left and right . . . and proceeded to plunder the houses and barns which had long lain deserted by the inhabitants. As a rule the owners had concealed their property badly; everywhere one could see from large damp patches on the walls that something had been recently walled up . . . We often found large supplies of corn, wheat, oil, ham, pork, sausages and vegetables.

Cunning and resourceful the French undoubtedly were, but this was not enough. There developed a cruel and barbaric struggle for survival between the guerrillas (such as *El Castrador*) allied with the peasants who had ignored instructions and stayed north of the Lines, and the French. It was a war in which torture, followed by execution, was commonplace. Reprisal followed reprisal as the French sought food, and the Portuguese sought vengeance.

Some Frenchmen were called 'diviners': men who claimed

Brunswick Oel Jägers

FORMED 1809 from Duke of Brunswick's men evacuated from North Germany after the Wagram campaign. Originally had excellent Prussian officers and German rank and file volunteers. However, when this source dried up, replacements came from British prisoner-of-war camps. A motley assortment of German, Polish, Swiss, Danish, Dutch and Croatian turn-coats was recruited, and desertion became a problem. Jägers wore green, rather than the usual Brunswick black, with a skull and crossbones badge; at the start, they were good fighters, providing several of the detached companies of riflemen with which Wellington strengthened the light companies of his divisions.

they could sniff out food caches. Woe betide the wretched individual who failed to produce any. The treatment meted out involved mutilation (including castration), and the fiendish murder of mothers and their children hung up together and a fire lit under them. *Loup*'s horrific activities were not untypical. But, even Masséna's hardened campaigners could not withstand indefinitely exposure to torrential rain, hunger, the partisan's knife and sickness. To haemorrhage 500 dead a week was more than any army could sustain and remain a fighting force. On 14 November 1810, under cover of a thick fog, the French decamped, pulling back thirty miles beyond Santarém, leaving behind sentries of straw and shakos stuck on sticks to deceive the Light Division pickets. Neither Sharpe, the *S. Essex* nor any soldier had heard a shot fired.

Both sides were isolated. The French more so than the British, who had their tiny toehold on the Lisbon peninsula securely connected to England by their fleet. Masséna, however, was cut off in Portugal by hundreds of miles of hostile countryside over which one important messenger (General Foy travelling to Paris, for example) required 2000 men as escort. Both sides needed reinforcements. Twice during the winter more Frenchmen marched into Portugal. The first attempt in November was aborted, the second saw D'Erlon's 9th Corps of 11,000 troops arrive in December with plenty

FRATERNISING WITH THE FRENCH

This was condoned throughout the war. Examples were chatting, exchanging souvenirs, bathing together, sharing rations, playing games and exchanging British tobacco for French brandy. Costello describes how, after the Battle of Fuentes de Onoro, Crauford recognised a French soldier puffing on his pipe in a British blacksmith's forge on the west bank of the Dos Casas. Costello told his general the Frenchman had come over for a light. 'Indeed', replied Crauford, 'let him go about his business, he has no right here, nor we either' – and walked away.

INFANTRY
MOUNTED BEHIND
CAVALRY

The 95th being given a
ride behind cavalry
when chasing Masséna
out of Portugal was
not uncommon, but it
was unpopular with
the riflemen.
According to Costello
it was 'particularly
galling to the infantry
... the friction alone
produced on the legs
and seat by the
dragoon's saddle-bags,
it was sometime
before the footsoldier,
when placed upon his
legs, could move with
anything like despatch
... this method of
riding was generally
attended by the loss of
the men's mess tins,
which became shaken
off by the jolting.'

of ammunition – but no food. The additional mouths added
to the misery. Despite these extra men Masséna had a weaker
army in the new year than when he had arrived three months
earlier.

The weeks of winter inactivity were frustrating for Wellington: the home government failed to reinforce his army;
relations with the Portuguese Regency Council soured; a host
of his general officers took ship for home leave, and his junior
ones (including Sharpe) found every reason to sample the
fleshpots of Lisbon. Not until the beginning of March did
Wellington receive his new battalions. Perhaps these reinforcements, perhaps the impossibility of smuggling more
coffee and sugar through the English lines for his mistress,
finally broke Masséna's resolve. More likely his troops' endur-
ance had cracked. On 4 March the depleted and demoralised
French regiments were ordered to turn their backs on the
Lines. The long race north had begun.

Although Sharpe did not play any part in chasing the
French from Portugal, his old Regiment (the 95th) did. As
always, the Light Division led the advance behind the cavalry
screen, although it (and the cavalry) were temporarily commanded by one of the most incompetent fools in the army
(Sir William Erskine) because Crauford and Major-General
Cotton had yet to return from leave. Despite this, the division,
with the 95th in the van, kept in close contact with the French
rearguard for the next month. At times the riflemen jolted
along on horseback, clinging uncomfortably and reluctantly
to a cavalryman. In twenty-eight days they fought and
marched about 200 miles from the Lines to the Coa River.
Skirmishes were daily occurrences as the French were pressed
hard and turned at bay.

On 11 March Captain O'Hare's company captured the personal baggage of Colonel Soult, nephew of the marshal. The
contents, except for his medals which were presented to
O'Hare, were auctioned off in bivouac that night. In the fight
for the village of Casal-Nova a popular officer, Lieutenant
Strode, died of his wounds. Like Sharpe, he had made his
name by always carrying a rifle and being a formidable shot.

Portuguese Cacadores

CACADORES were riflemen trained to skirmish. Eventually 12 battalions (including the three light infantry battalions of The Lusitanian Legion). Apart from these latter, whose uniforms were ivy-green, they wore brown, which contrasted starkly with the bright blue and white of the line battalions. Initially armed with muskets and short swords, later with rifles and sword-bayonets. Eight battalions raised and commanded by British officers. Full strength battalion 770 in six companies, but 500 more normal. Generally fought well.

During this action, which took place on the fourteenth, the 95th found that they had been opposed by the French 95th Regiment. That night souvenir hunters snipped dozens of buttons from dead men's jackets. Three days later General Loison's ADC, a Portuguese officer, was taken with his Spanish wife, who had, like Masséna's mistress, disguised herself as a hussar. Lieutenant Kincaid put the situation neatly, 'He was a Portuguese, and a traitor, and looked very like a man who would be hanged. She was a Spaniard, and very handsome, and looked very like a woman who would get married again.'

Masséna had wanted to cross the Mondego River and go north into countryside still capable of feeding his army. He was prevented by Portuguese under Colonel Trant on the north bank and compelled to swing north-east towards Celorico. To speed up the retreat, Masséna ordered all wheeled transport except gun carriages and caissons to be destroyed and all useless animals hamstrung. The latter was a cruel and unnecessary order as the wretched beasts were of no use to Wellington: bundles of skin and bone that could barely walk, let alone carry a load. Grattan, a subaltern in the 88th recorded, 'The most disgusting sight was the asses [mules] floundering in the mud, some with throats half cut, the rest most barbarously houghed [hamstrung] ... Their meagre appearance, with backbones and hips protruding through their skin, and their mangled limbs, produced a feeling of disgust and commiseration.'

OFFICERS' DONKEYS

As Masséna retreated from Portugal in March 1811, the British commissariat and baggage were invariably far to the rear of the Light Division, so many company officers recruited Portuguese boys with donkeys. The animals carried the officer's small comforts. Each boy was given a pigskin for wine, canteen for spirits, tea and sugar, a goat tied to the donkey plus a dollar or two to purchase bread or other luxury items which might come his way on the march. Kincaid commented, 'They were singularly faithful and intelligent in making their way to us every evening...'

Marshal Ney commanded the French rearguard with considerable defensive skill, but he could not work miracles, neither could he get on with a superior whom he despised and distrusted. On one occasion a rumour that Masséna had been captured was passed to Ney, who instantly exclaimed, *'Pardieu! Tant mieux!'* ('So much the better, that's fine!'). On 22 March the French staggered into Celorico and opened up communications with Almeida. Both armies were disintegrating with the combined effects of exhaustion, hunger and indiscipline, and a halt was called. Masséna summoned his generals, and announced to an incredulous audience an immediate march towards Plasencia and thence into Portugal again. Ney, who knew the barrenness of that part of Spain, refused point-blank to budge. It was a ludicrous order. Masséna persisted, giving Ney an hour to reconsider his insubordination. Again Ney refused. He was relieved of command of the 6th Corps, which he had held for seven years, and began the long journey to Paris in disgrace, but his career was far from over. Ney, 'the bravest of the brave', reappeared the following year in a familiar role – commanding the rearguard for his Emperor in the retreat from Moscow.

Within a few days Ney was proved right. The sheer impossibility of the march was recognised by Masséna and after a defeat at Sabugal (despite Erskine's bungling) on 3 April, he swung east. On the eleventh, he reached Salamanca, where the governor gave a dinner in honour of his ADC (mistress). On the tenth, Wellington issued a proclamation that the invader had gone.

To the People of Portugal

10th April, 1811

The Portuguese nation are informed that the cruel enemy who had invaded Portugal, and had devastated their country, have been obliged to evacuate it ... The inhabitants are therefore at liberty to return to their occupations.

Wellington

With the small exception of 1500 Frenchmen in Almeida, it was true.

About a week after the proclamation, as Sharpe and his forty men confronted *Loup's brigade* and executed two Frenchmen in the hills near Villar Formoso, Masséna had decided to advance to the relief of Almeida (MAP 13). Unbeknown to him, Napoleon had already replaced him with Marshal Marmont. This news would be some time arriving, so Masséna proceeded to try to get supplies into Almeida. By 26 April, his army was rested, fed and reinforced to a strength of 48,000. His main weakness was in artillery, with only thirty-eight guns compared with Wellington's forty-eight, and to a lesser extent in cavalry. He had deployed horsemen forward along the Agueda River, where they had exchanged shots with the Light Division. On the twenty-third there had been

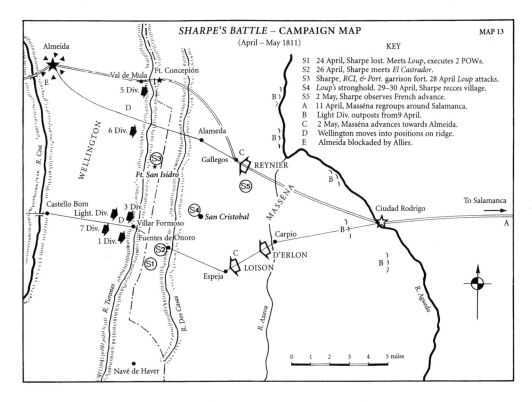

SHARPE'S BATTLE – CAMPAIGN MAP
(April – May 1811)

KEY   MAP 13

S1 24 April, Sharpe lost. Meets *Loup*, executes 2 POWs.
S2 26 April, Sharpe meets *El Castrador*.
S3 Sharpe, *RCI, & Port.* garrison fort. 28 April *Loup* attacks.
S4 *Loup's* stronghold. 29–30 April, Sharpe recces village.
S5 2 May, Sharpe observes French advance.
A   11 April, Masséna regroups around Salamanca.
B   Light Div. outposts from 9 April.
C   2 May, Masséna advances towards Almeida.
D   Wellington moves into positions on ridge.
E   Almeida blockaded by Allies.

ROYAL WAGON
TRAIN

Colonel Runciman's
former post of Wagon
Master-General had
been a thankless and
stressful if critical
appointment. The
Royal Wagon Train,
formed in 1800, was
that part of the army
which, in theory,
provided transport to
stock supply depots
on the lines of
communication. It
grew from eight to
fourteen troops each
consisting of a captain,
paymaster, adjutant,
surgeon, veterinary
surgeon, eleven
NCOs and 60 drivers.
The British wagons
sent to the Peninsula
were useless for
load-carrying, but as
they had elementary
springs they were used
for carrying wounded
whenever possible. By
1813 the Train was
treated as an
Ambulance Corps.

a clash near the bridge over the Azava, close to Carpio, when
two infantry battalions and some cavalry had been repulsed
by the British 52nd Regiment. Then Masséna moved forward
to Ciudad Rodrigo.

It was probably Wellington's shortage of cavalry (he had
1850) and their poor handling by Erskine, coupled with
the large area involved, that permitted *Loup* to raid up to
the Turones during the second half of April. By the ninth
the Light Division was well forward on the Agueda, so *Loup*
was operating behind enemy lines. There is no trace of such
a brigade in Masséna's army, but the marshal certainly made
use of dragoons, sometimes supported by infantry, to hunt
guerrillas and terrorise villagers. Because of a shortage of
horses after the recent retreat, *Loup*'s two battalions of infantry were in all probability dismounted dragoons. Until 1806,
Napoleon had two divisions of dismounted dragoons nicknamed 'the walkers' or 'the wooden swords'. In Austria they
had marched as the baggage guard for the Grande Armée,
armed with light muskets. *Loup*'s mixed brigade was tasked
with escorting the supplies in the final push for Almeida,
possibly because Masséna remembered 'the walkers' had done
the same for the Emperor. Dragoons, in green rather than
grey uniforms, provided the backbone of French anti-
guerrilla activity; mobile and well armed they tended to serve
in small detachments protecting supplies and couriers. They
wore brass helmets, hence the Spanish nickname 'golden
heads', although often the helmets were covered in linen
cloth or a horsehair mane.

The villages of Val de Mula, Castello Bom, Gallegos, Carpio, Villar Formoso (where Wellington had his HQ for the
battle) and Fuentes de Onoro were as familiar to the Light
Division (particularly the 95th) as their villages and hamlets
in rural England or Ireland. The riflemen had been billeted
there in the past for weeks on end, got drunk in the local
wine shops, flirted with local girls, patrolled the nearby hills
and streams, and knew many inhabitants by name. *Fort San
Isidro* and *San Cristóbal* did not exist, but had they done so
their locations would have been approximately as shown on

MAP 13. Fort Concepción was (and is) very real. In April 1811 it was half demolished and normally deserted except when used as a temporary defensive post by either side operating in the area. *Loup* occasionally found it a useful overnight shelter, while for Wellington it dominated the main road from Ciudad Rodrigo to Almeida. Ten months earlier, just before Almeida fell to Ney, Captain O'Hare, with two companies of the 95th, was occupying Fort Concepción, and had watched engineers preparing the Almeida defences for demolition. On 21 July, he was ordered to withdraw; after marching a mile a huge explosion shook the ground as a fountain of earth, stones and rubble soared upwards. To this day it is worth a visit; some stone blocks still lie where they landed nearly 200 years ago.

When Sharpe and *Hogan* went forward to observe the French advance on 2 May, they were looking down on Reynier's 2nd Corps. Merle's division of nine battalions, followed by Heudelet's of twelve – 10,000 men, stretched for nearly three miles. An endless cloud of choking, grey dust hung over it all, so the watchers could not be sure of individual units. Soult's nephew's three regiments of cavalry trotted ahead and to the flanks (their colonel minus his medals). Peering hard through his telescope, Sharpe picked out the ponderous, plodding column of ox-wagons dragging the supplies to keep Almeida going through the summer. With the distance, dust and haze he failed to distinguish the grey-uniformed escort – *Loup's brigade*. At that time, about 5 p.m., the head of the column was entering the village of Gallegos, marching on the main route from Ciudad Rodrigo to Almeida. Within five miles it would have to pass under the broken walls of Fort Concepción, cross the Turones at Val de Mula, climb the next rise and the fortress would be in sight. The Corps had taken the most direct route to their objective. What neither Sharpe or *Hogan* could know was whether this thrust would be hammered home.

It was not. Masséna, out of sight of the watchers due to distance, had chosen the minor, more southerly route through Carpio and Espeja towards Fuentes de Onoro for the bulk of his army. Some 28,000 infantry (Ney's old Corps, the 6th, now under Loison, plus D'Erlon's 9th) and his cavalry division were marching by the indirect route to approach Almeida via Wellington's southern flank.

If Sharpe was unable to convey this crucial information to his commander-in-chief, others could. Wellington was aware of the relative strengths of both advancing columns from gallopers hurrying back from cavalry and Light Division outposts. He had resolved to fight a defensive action with six infantry and one small cavalry division – a total strength of 37,000 – while Pack's Portuguese blockaded Almeida. His chosen position was the high ground between the two parallel streams of the Turones and the Dos Casas (MAP 13). The length of this rectangular plateau, from Fort Concepción in the north to Fuentes de Onoro in the south, was eight miles, the width two. It straddled the border between Spain and Portugal. Although the two streams were fordable, they flowed through narrow valleys, almost gorges. Attackers advancing across the Dos Casas from the east would be confronted with a stiff, lung-bursting climb of almost 200 feet before they reached the top. There were three places in this 'wall' where passage was comparatively easy. In the north the road passed Fort Concepción, in the centre the rough track from Gallegos via Alameda and in the south the route through Fuentes de Onoro.

Wellington's position may have looked formidable, but there were serious drawbacks. The first was that he would fight with his back to an obstacle: the Coa River, which flowed through a steep gorge, bridged only at Castello Bom and near Almeida. His army also had its back to the Turones, but this was not so serious as it was easily fordable at most places. Having a difficult obstacle behind does not matter if the force wins, but defeat can lead to annihilation. If Wellington were defeated and had to retire across the Coa he might well be crushed in the scramble to cross the bridges. The next problem was his southern flank (see MAP 14). It 'hung in the air', and invited a turning movement from the French. The ground between Fuentes de Onoro and Navé de Haver

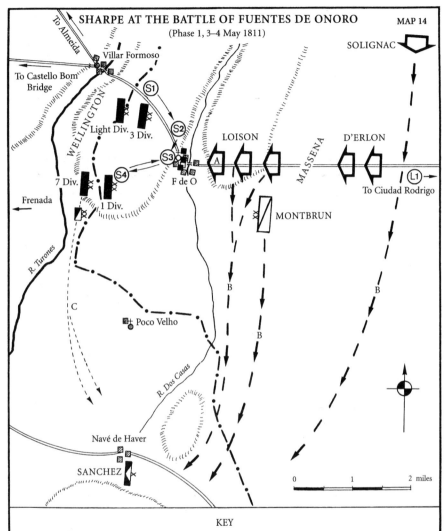

SHARPE AT THE BATTLE OF FUENTES DE ONORO   MAP 14

(Phase 1, 3–4 May 1811)

To Almeida

Villar Formoso

To Castello Bom
Bridge

SOLIGNAC

WELLINGTON

Light Div.   3 Div.

LOISON   MASSENA   D'ERLON

7 Div.

Frenada

1 Div.

F de O

To Ciudad Rodrigo

MONTBRUN

R. Turones

C

Poco Velho

B

B

B

B

R. Dos Casas

Navé de Haver

SANCHEZ

0   1   2 miles

KEY

A   3 May. Férey's Div. assaults Fuente de Onoro,
    defended by Col. Williams with Light
    Companies of 1 & 3 Divs. Attack repulsed.
B   Night 4–5 May. Marchand, Mermet and
    Solignac's Divs. march to turn Wellington's
    vulnerable flank.
C   4 May. Wellington sends 7 Div. and cavalry to
    guard flank.

S1 Sharpe and *Real Campanía Irlandesa* guard
    ammo reserve.
S2 Sharpe recces route forward. Observes French
    attack forming. Sharpe and *Sgt. Harper* move
    to Fuentes de Onoro and join fight.
S4 Sharpe sent for reinforcements and returns to
    fight in village.
L1 *Loup's* brigade and supplies for Almeida
    off map.

QUALITY OF
FRENCH OFFICERS

The high proportion
of officer losses at
Fuentes de Onoro
spoke well of their
courage and
leadership; they were
generally men of
exemplary honour and
spirit. One cuirassier
regiment devised a
unique test for new
officers: they were
given three horses,
three bottles of
champagne and three
willing wenches, and
had three hours to ride
a rough twenty-mile
course, drink the
champagne and bed
the women, choosing
their own order of
events.

BRITISH
GENEROSITY

The village of Fuentes
de Onoro was
virtually destroyed in
the battle. On 22 May
Wellington wrote to
the Prime Minister,
'My soldiers have
continued to show the
Portuguese nation
every kindness . . .
The village of Fuentes
de Onoro having been
the field of battle . . .
and not having been
much improved by the
circumstance, they
immediately and
voluntarily subscribed
to raise a sum of
money to be given to
the inhabitants as a
compensation for the
damage.'

is comparatively open, level and almost five miles wide. From the right flank of the 1st Division to the Spanish cavalry under Sanchez at Navé de Haver there were no troops, no defences, no real natural obstacles. This presented Wellington with tactical problems and Masséna with tactical opportunities – in military terms, it was the tactical flank of the allied position. It was also the strategic flank. Wellington's lines of communication lay to the south and south-east, so a successful French turning movement around Poco Velho would push the allied force off its supply route, up against the Coa. The tactical and strategic flanks coincided. The situation cried out to be exploited; it was.

As Sharpe watched the French preparations for an attack, he was apprehensive of the dangers posed in the south (MAP 14). Unbeknown to him, the south was safe for a while. Masséna had ordered Loison to seize Fuentes de Onoro while Reynier, far to the north, made a feint along the main road. The corps commander committed the leading division, Férey's, to the daunting task of fighting uphill through a heavily defended village where formations were impossible. Every advantage, bar numbers, was with the defenders crouched behind walls, in cottages, gardens and alleyways. Typically, Sharpe and *Harper* ventured into the village, noting the mixture of British, German and Portuguese light troops – the cream of two divisions – awaiting the onslaught. Férey had ten battalions; he threw five into the first assault, the weight of which carried the attackers up to what was to become the high watermark of the struggle for the village – the church.

Colonel Williams had held back a reserve of several companies which he used to drive the French back in vicious, bloody, close-quarter street fighting where the bayonet and sword were as deadly as the bullet. *Harper's* Nock gun was used with great effect, but took too long to reload to be of much use after the first discharge. When Férey launched his second brigade, its battalion of the Hanoverian Legion caused confusion to both sides with their scarlet jackets. French artillery and their 66th Regiment opened fire on them assuming

*74th Highland Light
Infantry advancing*

them to be British. An allied unit refrained from firing on
them for the same reason until it received an unexpected
volley. Despite these errors, numbers again favoured the
French and the fighting slowly climbed back towards the
church. Williams was wounded about this time, although
whether just before or just after sending Sharpe for reinforcements from the 1st Division, is not clear. The 1/71st (Highland
Light Infantry), 1/79th (Cameron Highlanders) and the
2/24th (Warwickshires) arrived in time to push the enemy
back over the stream. At the end of the day the French were
still on the east bank of the Dos Casas.

There was a lull on 4 May, although Sharpe, *Hogan* and
Harper had an eventful afternoon. They had attended the
funeral of *Lord Kiely* who had shot himself in the church at
Villar Formoso two days before. The service ended with the

CASUALTIES AT
FUENTES DE
ONORO

Casualties on both
sides were
surprisingly light
considering that nearly
80,000 troops were
involved. The inability
of cavalry, on its own,
to inflict serious losses
on well-ordered
infantry, even in
retreat, was well
illustrated. The seven
battalions of the Light
Division suffered only
67 casualties on 5 May.
Total losses for the
battle were: British
1522 (including 259
Portuguese); French
2192. A feature was
that the French losses
of officers was triple
that of the British – 28
killed and 151
wounded, as against 9
and 57. Most losses
occurred in the village.

priest (*Father Sarsfield*) being shot dead by Sharpe as he was
about to kill *Hogan*. It was a happier day for the Light Division. They welcomed Crauford back from leave. When the
3rd Cacadores saw him they yelled, 'Long live General Crauford, who takes care of our bellies.' Unfortunately, the gods
were not listening: he had under a year to live.

All this was far removed from Masséna's deliberations two
miles to the east. Montbrun's cavalry reconnaissance that
morning had revealed the huge gap on the allied right, and
Masséna resolved to exploit it. His plan was well conceived,
and had it succeeded could have given the French the war
(MAP 13). Wellington was to be deceived into thinking
Fuentes de Onoro would again be the focus of attack. Férey
would make as if to cross the stream while the two divisions
of D'Erlon closed up behind to replace those of Marchand
and Mermet. These two were to slip south during the night
to be ready to attack between Poco Velho and Navé de Haver.
Wellington had been advised of the French cavalry's presence
in the south, and had agreed with Spencer that he needed to
protect that flank. Surprisingly, for such a crucial task, he
sent the inexperienced, newly formed and largely foreign 7th
Division under Houston, which took position overlooking
Poco Velho. It was isolated and insufficient.

When the heavy French presence was revealed in the south
on the morning of the fifth, Wellington immediately had to
send the Light Division to extricate the 7th. First Montbrun,
and then Loison's infantry pressed into the gap (MAP 15).
Heavy fighting was anticipated, so Sharpe was ordered to take
ammunition to Crauford. Having spoken with the general, he
enthusiastically joined with the skirmishers of his old Regiment in covering one of the most famous and well-conducted
battlefield withdrawals in the Napoleonic Wars. Fortunately,
there had been an inexcusable pause by the French after
taking Poco Velho, which allowed the 7th to pull back almost
unscathed, and the Light Division time to arrive and deploy.
It was this delay – this failure to grasp the opportunity and
reinforce success – that prompted Wellington's remark about
how things would have been different if 'Boney' had been

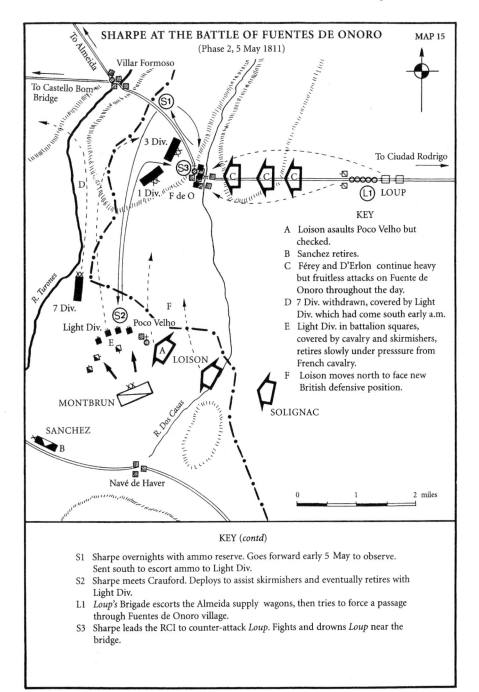

SHARPE AT THE BATTLE OF FUENTES DE ONORO   MAP 15
(Phase 2, 5 May 1811)

To Almeida

Villar Formoso

To Castello Bom
Bridge

To Ciudad Rodrigo

S1

3 Div.

S3

D

1 Div.   F de O

LOUP   L1

KEY

A   Loison asaults Poco Velho but
    checked.
B   Sanchez retires.
C   Férey and D'Erlon continue heavy
    but fruitless attacks on Fuente de
    Onoro throughout the day.
D   7 Div. withdrawn, covered by Light
    Div. which had come south early a.m.
E   Light Div. in battalion squares,
    covered by cavalry and skirmishers,
    retires slowly under presssure from
    French cavalry.
F   Loison moves north to face new
    British defensive position.

R. Turones

7 Div.

S2   F

Light Div.   Poco Velho

E   A   LOISON

MONTBRUN

SANCHEZ

B

R. Dos Casas

SOLIGNAC

Navé de Haver

0   1   2 miles

KEY (contd)

S1   Sharpe overnights with ammo reserve. Goes forward early 5 May to observe.
     Sent south to escort ammo to Light Div.
S2   Sharpe meets Crauford. Deploys to assist skirmishers and eventually retires with
     Light Div.
L1   *Loup's* Brigade escorts the Almeida supply wagons, then tries to force a passage
     through Fuentes de Onoro village.
S3   Sharpe leads the RCI to counter-attack *Loup*. Fights and drowns *Loup* near the
     bridge.

MASSÉNA'S
DISMISSAL

The man of whom
Wellington later said,
'When Masséna was
opposed to me, I never
slept comfortably'
retired to Ciudad
Rodrigo and
announced a victory!
But he fooled no one,
least of all his master.
'His Majesty [was]
distressed to see his
Army retire before a
British force so inferior
in numbers.' On the
same day that
Brennier, by good
fortune and British
incompetence, crossed
the Agueda (see
'Escape from the
Almeida garrison'),
General Foy arrived
from Paris carrying
Masséna's letter of
dismissal. The new
commander of the by
now misnamed 'Army
of Portugal' was
Marshal Marmont,
Duke of Ragusa.

there. Eventually, as the Light Division withdrew in four battalion columns (of companies) with parade-ground steadiness and ready to form square instantly, the French cavalry surged forward to overwhelm them. It was a classic example of infantry thwarting the efforts of horsemen to get to grips. Slowly, deliberately, the division marched the three miles to its new position. Lack of artillery and infantry support robbed the French of victory. The dragoons and chasseurs could harry and threaten but could not close.

Wellington had formed a new line on the high ground west of Fuentes de Onoro but in so doing had abandoned his line of communication to the south. The assault on Fuentes de Onoro renewed, and once again the fighting flowed up to the church, once again reserves on both sides joined the senseless struggle. Sharpe, who had returned with the Light Division, was soon sucked into the street fighting. His anxiety over a possible inquiry into the *Fort Isidro* reverse, and Crauford's words of encouragement when he delivered the reserve ammunition, had combined to make him determined to redeem himself in the thick of battle. The French were fought to a standstill. There was never any chance of *Loup*, or anybody else, forcing a passage for supply wagons through the village. Three French divisions, 14,000 men, had been absorbed, as a sponge soaks up water, in the bloody and prolonged battle for the handful of houses that was Fuentes de Onoro.

Escape of the Almeida garrison

IT WAS CUSTOMARY for Parliament to move a vote of thanks for a victory in the Peninsular War. For Fuentes de Onoro it did not do so: the reason was the escape of the French garrison from Almeida six days later. Wellington described it as 'the most disgraceful military event that had yet occurred to the British Army in the Peninsula'.

Masséna, having abandoned hope of supplying the garrison, offered 6000 francs to each of three volunteers who would take a message to the commander, Governor Brennier, to break out. Two were caught and shot as spies, the third got through. On 10 May a pre-arranged salvo of guns fired from Almeida told Masséna his message had arrived. He retired behind the Agueda. In the early hours of the eleventh the entire garrison of 1400 slipped out and headed for the bridge over the Agueda at Barba de Puerco ten miles north-east, having mined the defences to detonate after their departure.

Wellington had taken steps to prevent such a sortie, including an order that the bridge be secured. The order was sent to Erskine, who was dining with Spencer. At first he made the ludicrous suggestion of sending a corporal and four men before agreeing to send the 1/4th (King's Own) under Lieutenant-Colonel Bevan. Typically, he stuffed the order in his pocket and forgot it, so it was midnight before Bevan received it. He was persuaded there was no need to move until dawn, by which time Brennier was at, and over, the bridge. Wellington was livid. Erskine lied about the time he sent the message and blamed Bevan for getting lost (though had Bevan reacted immediately he could have beaten the French to the bridge). Accusations and recriminations flew for weeks until the unfortunate Bevan shot himself to avoid a pending court-martial.

Sharpe's Company

The backdrop to this book is the sieges of Ciudad Rodrigo and Badajoz – two Spanish border fortresses that blocked the main routes to Madrid from Portugal. At the first, Captain Sharpe had temporary command of the *S. Essex* Light Company, but before Badajoz he lost this to an officer who had paid for the vacancy. Nevertheless, Sharpe was heavily involved in the bloodbaths of the breaches at both places. The *S. Essex* also changed commanders, with *Lieutenant-Colonel Windham* replacing *Lawford* who was badly wounded at Ciudad Rodrigo. Wellington's assault in winter, when active warfare was not normally a military option, surprised the French. The campaign revolved around whether the allies could take the fortresses before the French could assemble their scattered forces and go to their assistance.

ON THE MORNING OF 19 JANUARY 1812, Sharpe had gone forward to a position just to the left of the twenty-four-pounder iron siege guns of No. 5 Battery on a small, low ridge called the Little Teson, a mere 300 yards from the breaches in the wall at Ciudad Rodrigo. Even without his telescope, the view was startlingly clear – and what he saw is shown in SKETCH 3. The view today is not dissimilar: the same skyline, the same medieval walls, even the outline of the breaches can be picked out where Wellington later had the masonry repaired. Sharpe, *Hogan, Harper,* indeed any of their men, would have no difficulty in pointing out the key landmarks of this battle of long ago, or in negotiating the

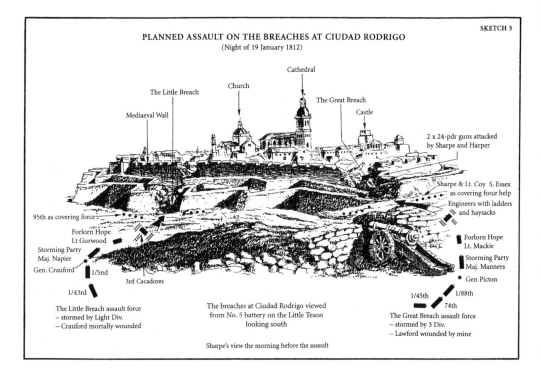

PLANNED ASSAULT ON THE BREACHES AT CIUDAD RODRIGO
(Night of 19 January 1812)

SKETCH 3

Cathedral

Church

The Little Breach

The Great Breach

Mediaeval Wall

Castle

2 x 24-pdr guns attacked
by Sharpe and Harper

Sharpe & Lt. Coy S. Essex
as covering force help
Engineers with ladders
and haysacks

95th as covering force

Forlorn Hope
Lt Gurwood

Storming Party
Maj. Napier

Gen. Crauford

1/5nd

3rd Cacadores

1/43rd

Forlorn Hope
Lt. Mackie

Storming Party
Maj. Manners

Gen Picton

1/45th   1/88th

74th

The Little Breach assault force
– stormed by Light Div.
– Crauford mortally wounded

The breaches at Ciudad Rodrigo viewed
from No. 5 battery on the Little Teson
looking south

The Great Breach assault force
– stormed by 3 Div.
– Lawford wounded by mine

Sharpe's view the morning before the assault

narrow streets of the old town using a nineteenth-century map.

Ciudad Rodrigo is one of the most attractive of the small towns in Spain. It sits on a hill overlooking the Agueda River as it meanders lazily northwards before crashing through the gorges to join the Douro and the sea. The Moors knew the place; indeed they built the original battlements that surround it, on which the modern visitor can circle the city. Today, the castle is an up-market hotel for tourists. From a bedroom window it is possible to throw a coin onto the precise position of the two French guns which Colonel O'Toole took after dashing across the old Roman bridge (see MAP 17).

The city was significant for strategic reasons (MAP 16). It was only a few miles from the Spanish border with Portugal, astride the main northern route between the two countries. An army, or more accurately its heavy guns and supply

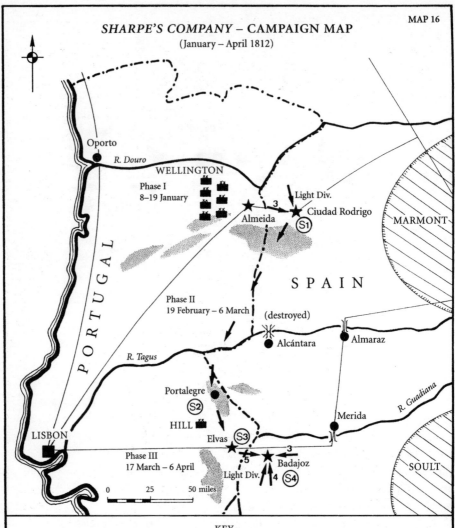

SHARPE'S COMPANY – CAMPAIGN MAP
(January – April 1812)

MAP 16

Oporto

R. Douro

WELLINGTON

Phase I
8–19 January

Almeida

Light Div.

3

Ciudad Rodrigo

S1

MARMONT

S P A I N

Phase II
19 February – 6 March

(destroyed)

Alcántara

Almaraz

R. Tagus

Portalegre

S2

HILL

Merida

R. Guadiana

LISBON

Elvas

S3

Phase III
17 March – 6 April

5

Badajoz

3

Light Div.

4

S4

SOULT

P O R T U G A L

0   25   50 miles

KEY

4

Assault division.

Phase I   Wellington concentrates
7 divisions to take Ciudad
Rodrigo. Hill watches the
south.

Phase II   Wellington moves south to
the Elvas area.

Phase III Wellington takes Badajoz.
Both main routes into Spain
now open.

S1   Sharpe and *Harper* attack 2 guns in the Great Breach.
     Lt. Col. Lawford, CO of *S. Essex* badly wounded.

S2   Sharpe and S. *Essex* billetted for 3 days in Portalegre.

S3   *Ensign Matthews, Sgt. Hakeswill* and new recruits
     join the *S. Essex.*
     Sharpe loses his company to *Capt. Rymer.*
     Sgt. Hakeswill tries to rape Sharpe's wife, *Teresa.*

S4   Sharpe and *S. Essex* assault the central breach at
     Badajoz.

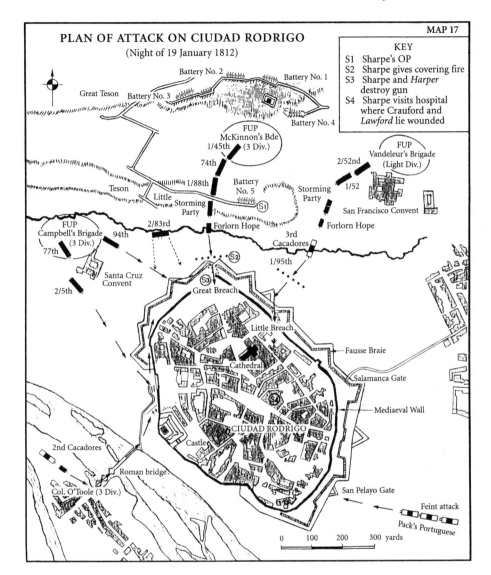

PLAN OF ATTACK ON CIUDAD RODRIGO
(Night of 19 January 1812)

MAP 17

KEY
S1 Sharpe's OP
S2 Sharpe gives covering fire
S3 Sharpe and *Harper* destroy gun
S4 Sharpe visits hospital where Crauford and *Lawford* lie wounded

Battery No. 2
Battery No. 1
Great Teson
Battery No. 3
Battery No. 4

FUP
McKinnon's Bde
1/45th (3 Div.)
74th

FUP
Vandeleur's Brigade
(Light Div.)
2/52nd
1/52

Teson
Little Storming Party
1/88th
Battery No. 5
Storming Party
San Francisco Convent

FUP
Campbell's Brigade
(3 Div.)
77th
94th
2/83rd
Forlorn Hope
3rd Cacadores
Forlorn Hope
1/95th

Santa Cruz Convent
2/5th
(S2)
(S3)
Great Breach
Little Breach
Fausse Braie
Cathedral
Salamanca Gate
Mediaeval Wall

CIUDAD RODRIGO

Castle
2nd Cacadores
Roman bridge
Col. O'Toole (3 Div.)
San Pelayo Gate

Feint attack
Pack's Portuguese

0 100 200 300 yards

wagons, wanting to invade either country and strike for Madrid or Lisbon would have to follow either the northern or the southern route. Ciudad Rodrigo, with a garrison of 2000, and its Portuguese equivalent, Almeida, just across the frontier, blocked the northern road. Badajoz, defended by 5000, and Elvas fulfilled the same role 140 miles to the south.

Two pairs of fortresses opposite each other, watching and waiting, like castles on a chess board, for the other to make a move.

Towards the end of 1811, Napoleon, who had already decided on war with Russia, began to drawn off men from Spain for the impending campaign in the east. The élite infantry of the Guard and all the Polish cavalry were ordered out; some 27,000 veterans marched away. Marshal Marmont, commanding the French army nearest to Wellington in the Tagus valley, received the Emperor's orders to send 10,000 men east to help Suchet take Valencia. When Wellington

Siegecraft – the defence of a fortress

FORTRESSES WERE SITED to serve strategic purposes, such as covering important routes, defiles or river crossings. This meant that they had to be built on or within gunshot range of the point they were guarding. This limited the selection of the site, with the builders often being forced to choose a position dominated by higher ground within cannon range. Guns positioned as high as, or higher than, the walls rendered the defence decidedly parlous. A partial solution was to construct outlying redoubts on the higher ground to keep the besiegers at bay for as long as possible. Interestingly, these outlying forts had no serious defences in the rear so that, if lost, the guns on the fortress walls could blast their new occupants with ease.

Vauban, the Frenchman who had made fortress construction an exact, asymmetric science, devised an intricate pattern of defensive works based on star shapes (DIAGRAM 3). Nearest the attackers an open slope or glacis was developed

(DIAGRAM 4) so that an attacking gun positioned on it would be forced to fire uselessly over the walls. Next came the ditch, twelve feet deep and often dry. Then there might be a counterguard, an earth bank to protect the curtain walls or, as at Badajoz, a ravelin, which was a triangular earthwork in the ditch. (Sharpe scrambled over, while *Hakeswill* cowered behind it, at Badajoz.) Sometimes there would be a cunette, a ditch within a ditch, too wide to jump, and deep, often filled with water. Such an unforeseen obstacle protected the central breach at Badajoz and a number of attackers drowned in it. Then there was the scarp, or defenders' wall, of the ditch, which added considerably to the height of the curtain walls on top of it. Sometimes there was a berm, or ledge, where the two walls joined, linking together massive bastions that jutted out, enabling the garrison to bring flanking fire to bear. The focal point inside was the castle, housing magazines, stores and the garrison commander's residence.

heard this news, he determined to strike. At noon on 8 January 1812, the Light Division sucked breath through clenched teeth as its infantry waded through the freezing waters of the Agueda and invested Ciudad Rodrigo, to the astonishment of its defenders.

Sharpe and the *S. Essex* were in the 3rd Division, although the battalion was not destined to take part in the assault. Their divisional commander was Lieutenant-General Sir Thomas Picton – a coarse, moody, but competent officer who was to be wounded at Badajoz and killed at Waterloo. Their brigade commander was Major-General 'Dan' McKinnon. Their fellow battalions were the 1/88th (Connaught Rangers), packed with the wild compatriots of *Sergeant Harper*, whose regimental nickname became 'The Devil's Own'; the 1/45th (Nottinghamshire), known in later years as The Sherwood Foresters. The third battalion was the 74th, full of unruly ruffians from the back streets of Glasgow, which eventually became the hard drinking, hard brawling, hard fighting Highland Light Infantry.

Wellington was in a hurry. He wanted to take the city before Marmont could march to its relief so, after a mere ten days' bombardment, he went forward for a final reconnaissance with his siege gunner, Major Alexander Dickson, and chief engineer, Lieutenant-Colonel Richard Fletcher. Sharpe's friend and mentor, *Major Hogan*, would certainly have accompanied them (MAP 17). The forward French outpost called the Renaud Redoubt on the Great Teson, and those at the Convents of Santa Cruz and San Francisco had already been taken. It was now a matter of deciding if the iron guns of the new siege train had done their job. On that morning, the eighteenth, with No. 5 Battery only 300 yards from the wall, twenty-three 24-pounders and two 18-pounders battered the Great Breach, while seven 24-pounders opened on the Little Breach. Although dense smoke clouds obscured the view as the gunnery duel continued throughout the day, Wellington had seen enough. The artillery would continue the pounding on the nineteenth and the infantry would attack after dark. H-hour (the time the troops

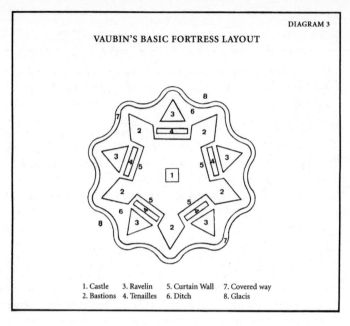

DIAGRAM 3

VAUBIN'S BASIC FORTRESS LAYOUT

1. Castle   3. Ravelin   5. Curtain Wall   7. Covered way
2. Bastions   4. Tenailles   6. Ditch   8. Glacis

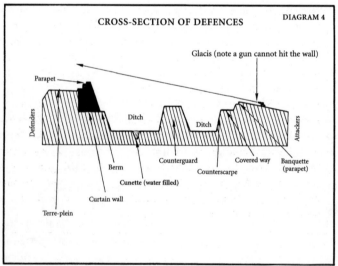

CROSS-SECTION OF DEFENCES   DIAGRAM 4

launched their attack) was set for 7 p.m. but nobody was told. The time was chosen with care, to give enough darkness for the attackers to form up, but not enough for the French to repair much of the damage to the walls.

Siegecraft – the attack on a fortress

THE FIRST TASK of besiegers was to surround the fortress and cut off its communications: to invest it. Complete isolation was not always achievable, particularly if the defenders had control of the sea. Next, a proportion of the besieging army would be deployed as a covering force to delay the approach of an enemy field army. Before a siege could get underway, outworks had to be taken. At Ciudad Rodrigo, these were Forts Renaud, Santa Cruz and San Francisco; at Badajoz, Picurina, Pardaleras and San Cristobal. Next came the digging. Digging trenches was a prerequisite for getting the guns forward. The siege train had to be positioned opposite the right spot in the walls with a direct line of sight and as close as possible.

This trench was the first 'parallel'. It was literally parallel to the wall to be attacked. At night, engineer officers pegged out the trench line with white tape. A covering force, perhaps with riflemen, would deploy, and the battalions came forward in the dark to do the spadework. The first parallel had to be finished by daylight. Communication trenches were then cut back to dead ground, so that movement in daylight was possible with a degree of safety. Simultaneously, trenches were dug forward on a line which, if extended, would miss the fortress, thus preventing the garrison from firing down the whole length of them. These trenches were called 'saps' – hence the term 'sappers'. When the saps had reached the required spot, a second 'parallel' would be started. Sometimes a third or more were needed, extending right up the glacis, to get the guns really close to the intended breach. As part of the 3rd Division at Ciudad Rodrigo, the *S. Essex* formed up in, or behind, the second parallel.

Digging was continuous, divisions working on a twenty-four-hour shift system. At Badajoz on 28–29 March, the duty division had to provide working parties of 1200 men by night and 1000 by day. The fire of the heavy guns would eventually weaken the base of the wall, bringing it down, the resultant rubble providing a slope to scramble up. When the breaches were big enough, they were stormed. Invariably the assault was a combination of storming, escalades and feint attacks, and the major problem with a breach was that the enemy knew precisely where the attack would come. The majority of his guns were sited there, and there he erected chevaux-de-frise, retrenchments and other obstacles.

Sharpe had toyed with the idea of volunteering for the Forlorn Hope ('The Hope') for the assault by the 3rd Division on the largest breach. If he survived he would almost certainly receive an immediate promotion, or at least be confirmed in his position as company commander of the *S. Essex* Light

'FORLORN HOPES'

In the 95th, at San Sebastian in July 1813, only two volunteers were needed for 'The Hope' from each company, but many more stepped forward. Lots were drawn to find the 'lucky' men – Privates Royston and Ryan. They were offered £20 to exchange places but refused. At about this time survivors of 'The Hope' from Ciudad Rodrigo and Badajoz were recognised in the 52nd Regiment by a badge of laurel with the letters VS (Valiant Stormer) underneath. This was worn on the right arm, but it was a commanding officer's award not given outside this regiment. The French were more generous. Such volunteers, 'Enfants perdu' ('Lost children'), were usually commissioned and received the Legion of Honour, which obliged their comrades to salute them. A Private Burke (95th) survived 'The Hope' at Ciudad Rodrigo, Badajoz and San Sebastian only to be mortally wounded at Quatre Bras in the Waterloo campaign.

Company. He did nothing about it, however, and that almost suicidal post went to Lieutenant Mackie of the 88th. 'The Hope' always led the assault: a party of about 25–30 soldiers led by a subaltern and a couple of sergeants, to draw the enemy fire. They were to be the first into the breach and, usually, the first to die. It was a post of the utmost honour and there was seldom a lack of volunteers. If the officer survived, he was virtually assured of promotion. The sergeants could normally expect battlefield commissions as ensigns. The soldiers got nothing. One of those who volunteered at Ciudad Rodrigo and again at Badajoz was Edward Costello of Sharpe's original Regiment, the 95th. He described the selection procedure: 'On the eve of the storming of a fortress, the breaches, etc., being all ready, captains of companies, on their private parade, give the men to understand that such and such a place is to be taken by storm. Every man then who wishes to volunteer to head the stormers [the Forlorn Hope was in front of the stormers] steps forward to the front, and his name is immediately taken down by the officer . . .'

The attacking columns on the two breaches at Ciudad Rodrigo were composed according to the tactical teaching of the time. First, engineers and a covering party; next 'The Hope', followed by the 'stormers' and then the bulk of the attacking battalions one after the other, with one at least held back as a reserve.

In the 3rd Division a handful of engineers would be among the first men up the glacis, carrying sacks stuffed with hay and a few ladders. There were never enough engineers, so infantry were drafted in to assist. In this instance Sharpe's Light Company got the task. It was not such a hazardous undertaking as being in the assault proper, as the men had only to go forward to the lip of the glacis and throw their sacks down into the ditch to soften the landing of those who had to jump in (DIAGRAM 5). The ladders were also placed down the counterscarp (side of the ditch). Having done that, the infantry could expect the comparatively easy job of spreading out on the edge of the glacis and supporting their

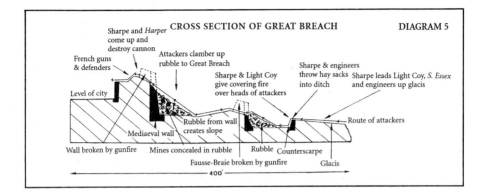

CROSS SECTION OF GREAT BREACH   DIAGRAM 5

Sharpe and *Harper*
come up and
destroy cannon

French guns   Attackers clamber up
& defenders   rubble to Great Breach   Sharpe & engineers
                                                    throw hay sacks   Sharpe leads Light Coy, *S. Essex*
                          Sharpe & Light Coy   into ditch   and engineers up glacis
                          give covering fire
Level of city   over heads of attackers

                              Rubble from wall   Route of attackers
                              creates slope
         Mediaeval wall

Wall broken by gunfire   Mines concealed in rubble   Rubble Counterscarpe
                          Fausse-Braie broken by gunfire   Glacis
                    — 400' —

The Escalade

THIS MEANT climbing walls with ladders. It was employed with great skill at Ciudad Rodrigo and Badajoz: at the first, Colonel Colborne's surprise seizure of the Renaud Redoubt, and Lieutenant-Colonel O'Toole's charge across the Roman bridge; at Badajoz, it meant the taking of the castle by *Captain Knowles* (Colonel Ridge). The principal advantage of the escalade was that it gave the attackers the possibility of surprise, because they could choose the section of wall at the last moment. There was no need for a lengthy bombardment, which alerted the garrison where the assault would come.

But there were problems. Ladders are extremely heavy and unwieldy, and an accurate estimate had to be made of the height of the wall: the late discovery that a ladder was too short could be disastrous. At Badajoz, the order was given that 30-foot ladders were required (for the castle, 12 were taken) but some were found to be 32 feet, others only 28. Six men were needed to carry each, and as they were at the front of the attack, they were likely to be among the first casualties. A dropped ladder had to be picked up again; delays resulted.

Climbing a ladder with someone dropping rocks on you, or trying to push the ladder over, was a thoroughly unpleasant experience. A soldier had to sling his musket because both hands were needed to hang on (*Knowles* resorted to holding his sword in his teeth). The knack lay in placing the ladder with the bottom as far from the base of the wall as possible and the top just below the battlements. This made pushing the ladder away from the wall much harder. With a hand-to-hand fight at the top, the man on the wall had a distinct advantage over a man on the ladder. The climber's comrades on the ground endeavoured to pick off the defenders as they struggled to tip over the ladder. Once a man secured a foothold on the wall, he had simply to hold his ground until more men clambered up. If the escalade got this far, it was invariably successful.

THE SURRENDER OF
CIUDAD RODRIGO

There was controversy
over who received the
surrender of the city
from General Barrie.
The two officers,
Lieutenants Gurwood
(52nd) and Mackie
(88th) who had led
'The Hopes' of the
Light and 3rd Divisions
respectively, both
claimed the honour.
Gurwood chased
French fugitives into
the castle and received
Barrie's sword as the
token of formal
surrender. Mackie,
who escaladed the
castle, took the sword
of Barrie's ADC, who
gave it on behalf of his
general. As Gurwood
had custody of Barrie,
he got the credit and
was given the sword
in the breach by Lord
Fitzroy Somerset on
behalf of Wellington.
Gurwood, who was
thirty-third on the
seniority list of
lieutenants in the
52nd, was also
rewarded with a
captaincy in the Royal
African Corps – a
promotion Sharpe
would surely have
spurned.

comrades with musket or rifle fire. In the Light Division, attacking the smaller breach, some of the 1/95th were out in front to give supporting fire while the division's Portuguese regiment, the 3rd Cacadores, were carrying the sacks and ladders.

Behind the 'sack and ladder' men came 'The Hope'. In this case under Lieutenants Mackie in the 3rd Division and Gurwood in the Light Division. These men were closely followed by the storming party, a much larger force than 'The Hope' – several hundred men, usually under a major with three or four junior officers as well. The 'stormers' were often a mixed body, with men from each battalion in the assault, and this was so at Ciudad Rodrigo. Major Manners of the 74th led the 'stormers' in the rush for the rubble at the main breach, and Major George Napier at the smaller one. Finally, the infantry battalions advanced in column behind to give the necessary weight to push through the breaches into the city. The breaches at Ciudad Rodrigo were 100 feet and 30 feet wide. Hundreds of men might be sacrificed to get a handful through such gaps.

That was the theory. In the event it was invariably a blood-bath if the breaches were resolutely defended. It was normal for the ditch to be choked with dead and dying, and the pouring of more and more troops into the meat-grinder was merely a murderous exercise in reinforcing failure. This was to happen at Badajoz where, at the foot of the three breaches, in an area the size of two football pitches, there were over 3000 bodies. It was the most blood-soaked ground in the Peninsula.

Wellington's orders at Ciudad Rodrigo were (MAP 17) that the 3rd Division (Picton) would attack the Great Breach in the north-west corner of the ramparts at 7 p.m., on the nineteenth, advancing from a forming-up place behind the Little Teson. The Light Division (Crauford) would at the same time assault the Little Breach, starting from the Convent of San Francisco. Three diversions would start ten minutes earlier. First, Colonel O'Toole, with the 2nd Cacadores and the Light Company of the 2/83rd, was to advance from the south, cross the river by the Roman bridge, and silence two cannons which enfiladed the defences. Second, Campbell's Brigade was to advance from the Convent of Santa Cruz in the west, scale the walls and take the main breaches in flank from the south. A final diversion was that Brigadier-General Pack's Portuguese Brigade would attack the San Pelayo Gate from the east. A signal rocket would launch the assault.

Although his battalion was not taking part, the commanding officer of the *S. Essex*, *Lieutenant-Colonel Lawford*, Sharpe's old company officer from his Indian days, came to watch events. It was not until after dark, with the temperature dropping and frost beginning to appear, that the assault troops got word that the rumours were true – the storming was on. Sharpe and *Lawford* would probably have seen Picton ride up and announce to the 1/88th, 'Rangers of Connaught, it is not my intention to expend any powder this evening. We will do the business with cold iron.'

The attacks by O'Toole and Campbell's brigade met with startling success from the outset. O'Toole's mad dash over the bridge silenced the two guns under the castle, and the leading elements of the 2/5th, after a brief fight to get their ladders up, scrambled over the wall just north of the castle. Nearer the main breach the 94th were equally successful in climbing the walls virtually undetected. Both these battalions turned left towards where the main assault was having difficulties.

Sharpe and *Harper* had watched as the mass of men floundered across the ditch and began the ascent of the rubble under a hailstorm of fire. As the leading elements of the attackers gained the summit of the breach, they were confronted with a sheer drop of about sixteen feet down into the city. As they hesitated a blast of grapeshot slammed into them from both sides. The French had prepared two 24-pounder cannons to take the stormers in flank at just such a moment, and these two guns shattered the assault. According to Lieutenant Grattan of the 1/88th, 'The head of the column had scarcely gained the top when a discharge of grape

Wives and camp-followers

WHEN SHARPE lost his company and was put in charge of the battalion's wives, he had a task that was daunting and – to some – demeaning. Many of the women who followed the army, enduring the hardships, sickness, wounds and fatigue, were, or soon became, callous, cunning and even murderous. They were, with some exceptions, a rum-swilling, foul-mouthed crew. When fighting stopped, they were frequently first on the battlefield, searching for their men, but often they turned aside to strip the dead – friend or foe. In their dirty skirts and flapping cloaks, they have been likened to a flock of hungry vultures as they flitted from corpse to corpse. Many carried wickedly sharp knives, and were not averse to slitting the throat of a wounded Frenchman before fumbling for his money belt. They were a continuing problem for the high command. Major George Napier, who had some sympathy for Sharpe, felt there was only one way of controlling camp-followers: 'to have plenty of provosts, to hang and flog them without mercy, the devils incarnate'. Women were indeed flogged; Wellington was adamant that it was necessary.

The *S. Essex* was officially permitted sixty wives 'on strength' although 300, including all the 'unofficials', was a more realistic figure for many regiments. The selection procedure before leaving for Portugal involved parading the families and '. . . it was ordered that wives should draw lots to see who should remain. The proportionate number of tickets were made with "To go" or "Not to go" written on them. They were then placed in a hat, and the women called by their seniority to draw their ticket. The sergeant stood in the middle with his hat in his hand . . .'

In the Peninsula some 4500 British wives were acknowledged as 'legally' accompanying the army. To this must be added the thousands of Portuguese and Spanish women who joined the throngs of camp-followers, prostitutes, children, sutlers, wagons, carts and mules that clogged the roads for miles at the rear of every division on the march. The French were even more lavish. There were so many women with the army of Napoleon's brother, Joseph, that an officer described it as '*un bordel ambulant*' (a mobile brothel).

Most of the women were fiercely loyal to their men and their regiment; they washed, cooked, sewed, nursed, scrounged, stole and occasionally fought for their menfolk. Often a soldier's wife would do an officer's washing. A Mrs Skiddy of the 34th Regiment, whose favourite expression was, 'The curse of the crows be on the French', did Ensign Bell's laundry. A strong, square woman who, on the retreat from Burgos, when her husband fell out exhausted, picked him up and carried him, with musket and knapsack, for three miles.

cleared the ranks of the three leading battalions and caused a momentary wavering...' A matter of seconds later the mine (barrels of powder) set under the breach detonated. The timing was exact: rocks, rubble and men were flung into the air, including the brigade commander, McKinnon, and his young ADC, Lieutenant Beresford of the 88th.

This was when Sharpe and *Harper* decided to go forward, leaving *Lawford* on the edge of the glacis. What Sharpe saw was a stalled – perhaps failed – attack. He could not yet know of the successes on either flank (the Light Division eventually also got through the smaller breach). His objective was the guns flanking the breach. With them destroyed, the reserves would pour through, the log-jam would rupture, the city would fall. That was his reasoning, and it was correct. The guns were silenced; in reality by Sergeant Brasil and Privates Kelly and Swan of the 1/88th, and Ciudad Rodrigo fell. Sharpe did not know that *Lawford* had followed him into the breach and was severely, almost mortally, wounded in the final minutes of the attack. 'Black Bob' Crauford had been shot through the spine in the Little Breach. Both ended up in the same hospital; *Lawford* survived, Crauford did not.

Wellington now turned on Badajoz (MAP 16). On 28 January he signalled (by semaphore) for the 16 new 24-pounders which had arrived by sea, together with 20 18-pounders scrounged from the navy, to be sent to Elvas. These cannon would be the basis of his new siege train and Elvas the centre of his assembly area for opening up the southern route into Spain. From the ramparts of Elvas a watcher with a telescope could see the walls of Badajoz only eleven miles away. Meanwhile the army marched the familiar roads to the south. The *S. Essex*, now a part of the 4th Division under Major-General Colville, was on the road by mid February.

Major Forrest was acting as commanding officer: the battalion was rife with rumours as to who would be the new colonel; Sharpe was worried that, as only a substantive lieutenant, he might lose the Light Company. There was a three-day halt at Portalegre, then on to Elvas. The battalion,

GENERAL CRAUFORD'S BURIAL

A martinet with a quick temper and caustic tongue (which earned him the nickname 'Black Bob'), Crauford was highly respected by the Light Division. He was buried in the small breach at Ciudad Rodrigo where he had fallen. Wellington and his staff watched as his coffin was carried by sergeant-majors from his division.

Soldiers hate wet feet, but Crauford had always insisted his troops march through water not around it. Returning from the burial, the leading company of the Light Division passed an excavation half-filled with mud and icy water. They wheeled and marched straight through it, the entire division following as a mark of respect.

Reinforcement drafts

THE S. *ESSEX*, like any other regiment in the Peninsula, depended on a regular supply of men from its depot (or home battalion) to replace the wastage of campaigning. Convoys sailing from Spithead always contained scores of small detachments varying in size from a few dozen to over a hundred. They were normally in the charge of officers returning from sick leave or, like *Matthews*, newly gazetted ensigns. The voyage was often hellish, particularly through the Bay of Biscay. When they were not prostrated by sea-sickness, quarrelling and fights were commonplace among the men, and squabbling over seniority occupied many of the inexperienced junior officers. A commission dated one day before another was sufficient to give the holder the best berth.

When his ship docked at Lisbon, the young officer had to march his detachment to his battalion, perhaps 200 miles away. Neither officers nor men could speak the language, they knew nothing of the Portuguese people, customs, manners or food. As Sir Charles Oman wrote, 'they went forward in a perpetual haze of mistakes and misunderstandings'. Every draft had its incorrigibles and its criminals, and the young subaltern was constantly embroiled in disciplinary difficulties, disputes with local villagers, and in trying to prevent drunkenness, straggling and outright absence. Unfortunate indeed was the ensign entrusted with forty men who delivered only thirty-five.

The key figure was the senior NCO. If he was a wastrel or a drunk, or both, then God help the young officer. It was equally bad if the sergeant was harsh and vindictive (like *Hakeswill*). A minority were dishonest, turning a blind eye to their men's thievery provided they got their share. *Sergeant Harper* was broken and flogged for having an item of officer's property (albeit planted) in his pack. In Wellington's army, a common cause of reduction to the ranks, with or without flogging, was an NCO being found with stolen property.

including over 300 hard-bitten, squabbling wives and children, had been on the march for over two weeks, covering the 200 miles by rough road and track at a steady 15–20 miles a day. By the end of the first week in March, Wellington, who had received an earldom for the capture of Ciudad Rodrigo, had almost 60,000 troops assembled – his numbers augmented by additional regular Portuguese units and new recruits from England. Among these was a nervous sixteen-year-old ensign, *William Matthews*, the unfortunate draft conducting officer bringing reinforcements to the S. *Essex*.

His senior NCO was Sharpe's old enemy, *Sergeant Hakeswill.*

Badajoz was a much tougher proposition than Ciudad Rodrigo: bigger, with better defences, a stronger garrison and, by then, alert to what was coming. Badajoz has grown considerably since then, but many of its fortifications remain, including the walls and the old Moorish castle. It has a sullen aspect for those who know its history. For one visiting author (Jac Weller) it is a sad city, with memories of awful tragedies lingering in the old streets. As recently as 1936, hundreds of the inhabitants were rounded up in the bullring and gunned down after the city had fallen to General Franco's troops in the Civil War.

As with virtually all fortresses, the original choice of site was a compromise between strategic and tactical consider- ations. Strategy said it must block a particular crossing place, pass or route, while tactics demanded it be built on dominant ground with natural obstacles to hamper attackers. Badajoz's site was strategically sound but had serious tactical flaws: it was overlooked, and guns on a number of hills could fire directly at the walls. This weakness was partially alleviated by building small, but strong, forts on the offending high ground. These were San Cristobal, Picurina and Pardaleras. Wellington decided to breach the walls on, and between, the Trinidad and Santa María Bastions (MAP 18).

The spade and the pick replaced the musket and bayonet as the infantry's weapons. The *S. Essex* took their turns in the trenches. On 19 March their Light Company under *Cap- tain Rymer* was working on the 2nd parallel when the French launched a sortie. Some 1500 infantry charged the trenches, inspired by the offer of a Spanish silver dollar for every entrenching tool brought back. As they had only spades, *Rymer's* men withdrew and the French destroyed much of the trench before the rest of the *S. Essex* were able to drive them out after a ferocious hand-to-hand fight. In reality, the French had attacked the 1/88th and been beaten back by other elements of the 3rd Division. They left richer by 548 dollars but poorer by 200 casualties. The British paid for being caught unawares with a damaged trench, the removal of

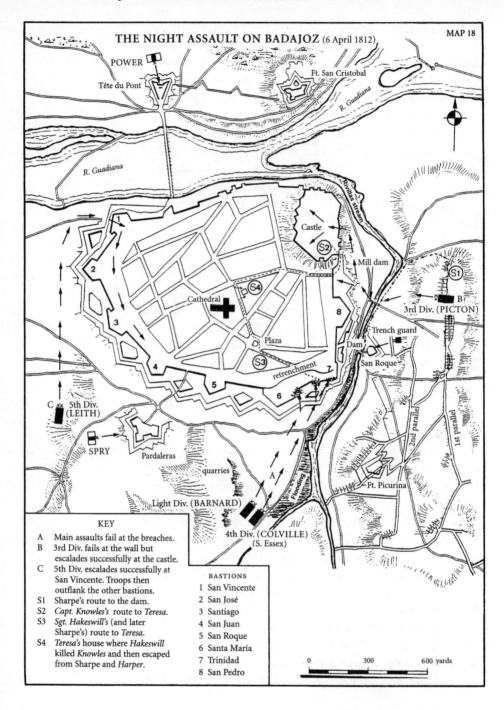

THE NIGHT ASSAULT ON BADAJOZ (6 April 1812)   MAP 18

POWER

Tête du Pont

Ft. San Cristobal

R. Guadiana

R. Guadiana

Castle

S2

Mill dam

S1

B

3rd Div. (PICTON)

Cathedral

S4

8

Trench guard

Plaza

Dam

San Roque

S3

retrenchment

7

C   5th Div. (LEITH)

6

5

4

3

2

1

SPRY

Pardaleras

quarries

A

Light Div. (BARNARD)

4th Div. (COLVILLE) (S. Essex)

Ft. Picurina

Rivillas stream

2nd parallel

1st parallel

Flooding

KEY

A   Main assaults fail at the breaches.
B   3rd Div. fails at the wall but escalades successfully at the castle.
C   5th Div. escalades successfully at San Vincente. Troops then outflank the other bastions.
S1 Sharpe's route to the dam.
S2 *Capt. Knowles's* route to *Teresa*.
S3 *Sgt. Hakeswill's* (and later Sharpe's) route to *Teresa*.
S4 *Teresa's* house where *Hakeswill* killed *Knowles* and then escaped from Sharpe and *Harper*.

BASTIONS
1 San Vincente
2 San José
3 Santiago
4 San Juan
5 San Roque
6 Santa María
7 Trinidad
8 San Pedro

0   300   600 yards

the digging tools and 150 casualties. It was a minor triumph for the French. Among the British wounded was Colonel Fletcher: he was hit in the groin, but the ball struck his purse, driving a coin an inch into his flesh. It was said that it was the most painful of injuries for a Scot to be hit in the purse! He continued to co-ordinate operations from his bed.

A more unusual preliminary operation, however, was the attempt to blow the dam by the Light Company of the *S. Essex* in which Sharpe, although no longer the company commander, participated and was wounded. There was no need to capture the San Roque Fort: all that was required was to place sufficient explosives against the wall of the dam, blow a hole and watch the flooding recede, easing the approach of the troops attacking the breaches. Darkness, stealth and silence were the ingredients of success. The *S. Essex*, under their new commander, *Lieutenant-Colonel Windham*, launched a diversionary night attack on San Roque. This is fiction, but the attempt to blow the dam is fact.

The operation took place on the night of 2 April under the command of Lieutenant Stanway, with Lieutenant Barney as his second-in-command – both engineers. They took 20 sappers to carry the powder and 30 soldiers as an escort (*S. Essex*). About 450 lbs of powder were put into two wooden cases which would be placed at the foot of the dam on the northern (dry) side (SKETCH 5); 20 sacks of earth were also carried for packing against the cases to channel the blast at the dam. The party set off at 9 p.m. from the northern end of the second parallel, creeping carefully along the Rivillas, following the route shown on MAP 18. They reached the vicinity of the dam undiscovered, despite the French sentries patrolling the walls of San Roque only fifty yards away. Silently the covering party deployed while the engineer officers and sappers crawled with the powder and sacks to the base of the dam.

Two problems then became apparent (SKETCH 5). First, the recent rains had caused water to cascade over the top of the dam; second, a large bank of compacted earth and clay had been built at the foot of the wall to reinforce it, so that

THE PORTUGUESE ALLIES

Some siege batteries at Badajoz were supplied with ammunition by the Portuguese militia. They manhandled it the eleven miles from Elvas, each man carrying a 24-pound shot, 'cursing all the way and back again'. Kincaid watched a Portuguese battery in action. One man was posted to shout a warning as to whether a 'shot' or a 'shell' was on its way from the French guns. Accordingly, he would yell, '*Bomba, balla, balla, bomba*' and the gunners ducked. Sometimes he would notice a general discharge of all arms, and threw himself down screaming, '*Jesu, todos, todos!*', meaning 'everything'.

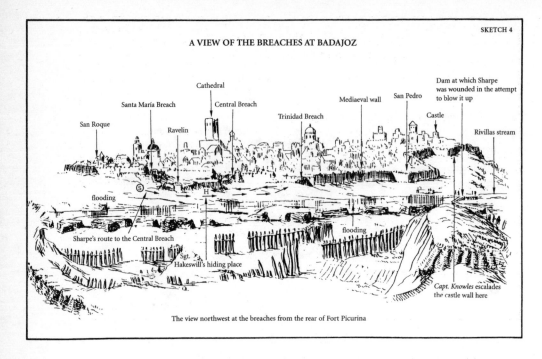

SKETCH 4

A VIEW OF THE BREACHES AT BADAJOZ

Cathedral

Santa María Breach　　　　Central Breach

San Roque　　　Ravelin

Mediaeval wall　San Pedro

Dam at which Sharpe
was wounded in the attempt
to blow it up

Trinidad Breach

Castle

Rivillas stream

flooding

Sharpe's route to the Central Breach

Sgt.
Hakeswill's hiding place

flooding

Capt. Knowles escalades
the castle wall here

The view northwest at the breaches from the rear of Fort Picurina

it was impossible to place the powder against the base. Stanway put the two cases (not barrels) as close as possible, lit the slow match and retired hastily, allowing about thirty seconds for his party to get clear. No attempt was made to use the sacks of earth. The darkness and the noise of the falling water had concealed their activities from the enemy only a few yards away, but all this had taken longer than anticipated (it was about then that Sharpe was sent to find out what was happening). The whole group waited, the sappers shivering and wet, for an explosion that never came.

It was the moment any officer in charge of a demolition dreads. Have I miscalculated? Do I wait a little longer? Do I go back and check; if I do will it explode as I get close? Stanway went back. The falling water had dampened the slow match which Stanway relit and retired again. This time he was rewarded with a monumental crash, but no wall of water. The French in the fort opened up, and a brisk fire-fight ensued as the whole group withdrew. It transpired that the

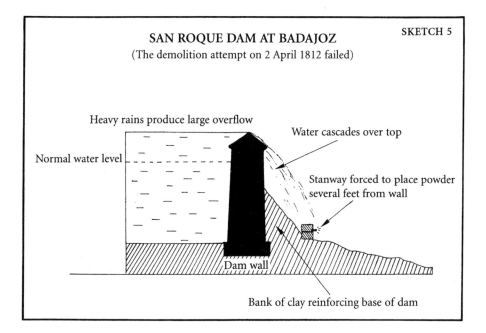

SAN ROQUE DAM AT BADAJOZ   SKETCH 5

(The demolition attempt on 2 April 1812 failed)

Heavy rains produce large overflow

Water cascades over top

Normal water level

Stanway forced to place powder several feet from wall

Dam wall

Bank of clay reinforcing base of dam

earth bank at the foot of the dam had protected it from the full force of the blast. The flooding remained to be negotiated before the final assault. (Sharpe was wounded in the leg, probably deliberately, by *Hakeswill*, and the unfortunate young ensign, *Matthews*, was killed by the explosion.)

As at Ciudad Rodrigo, the storming was to take place at night and the plan envisaged a combination of direct assault, escalading the walls and feint attacks. Except in the north along the Guadiana River, Badajoz would be under threat from all directions. By this means it was hoped to disperse the garrison, who would be expected to concentrate their efforts on defending the breaches. Five attacks and two feints were to be made (MAP 18). The Light Division was to storm the breach in the Santa María Bastion; the 4th Division (with the *S. Essex*) would do the same at Trinidad; the 3rd were to escalade the curtain wall just north of the San Pedro Bastion, with the 5th doing the same at the San Vincente Gate. The fifth attack was minor: the trench guard, under a Major Wilson, would assault San Roque. The feints were

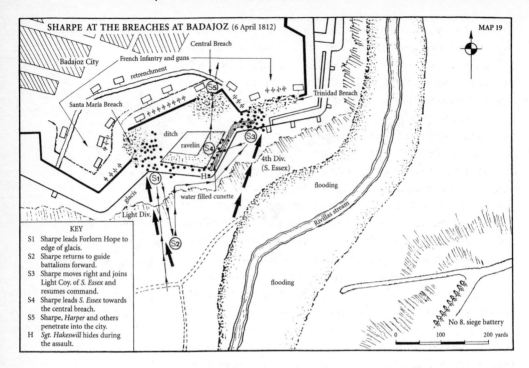

SHARPE AT THE BREACHES AT BADAJOZ (6 April 1812)   MAP 19

Central Breach

Badajoz City

French Infantry and guns

retrenchment

Santa María Breach

Trinidad Breach

ditch

ravelin

S5

S4

S3

4th Div.
(S. Essex)

S1

H

water filled cunette

flooding

glacis

Light Div.

S2

Rivillas stream

flooding

flooding

No 8. siege battery

0   100   200 yards

KEY
S1 Sharpe leads Forlorn Hope to
    edge of glacis.
S2 Sharpe returns to guide
    battalions forward.
S3 Sharpe moves right and joins
    Light Coy. of *S. Essex* and
    resumes command.
S4 Sharpe leads *S. Essex* towards
    the central breach.
S5 Sharpe, *Harper* and others
    penetrate into the city.
H   *Sgt. Hakeswill* hides during
    the assault.

demonstrations by two Portuguese brigades against the Pardaleras and Tête du Pont Forts.

Thirty-eight guns hammered the Trinidad and Santa María
Bastions. There were worrying reports that Marmont was
gathering his forces, possibly to move on Ciudad Rodrigo,
where the Spanish commandant was whining for more British
masons to repair the walls and more supplies to feed his
men. Soult was reported to be approaching the city, and
Wellington was not sure Hill's division could hold him. The
pressure to attack Badajoz, even at a heavy price in lives,
was intense. On the morning of 5 April Fletcher reported to
Wellington that another day's pounding might be enough,
and at noon Wellington inspected the breaches in person.
He made his decision: the assault would be that night.
Detailed orders were given and written down. Nevertheless,
his engineers were dubious and urged a delay of twenty-four
hours to allow the guns to open up a third breach at the
eastern end of the curtain wall between the other two

(DIAGRAM 3). With reluctance, Wellington concurred. Throughout the morning of the sixth, fourteen cannons attacked that part of the wall which quickly crumbled under the concentrated onslaught. The attackers had another breach (the one Sharpe would get through, MAP 19 and SKETCH 4).

To General Phillipon, the French garrison commander, this sudden new threat was disconcerting, and he was forced to rush 250 Hessians (Germans) from the castle to defend this breach. This was to be fortuitous for *Captain Knowles* when he led an escalade on the castle. However, as the orders for the storming had been made on the fifth, before there was a third breach, a hurried note was sent to Colville to allot troops to this task. Because Sharpe had been on a close reconnaissance of the approaches to the glacis, and two divisions were to use approximately the same route forward, he was detailed as one of the Light Division guides to get the battalions up the glacis to the edge of the ditch (MAP 19). The attacking divisions adopted the usual formation of covering troops, 'sack and ladder' men, forlorn hope, stormers, the main body, and reserves left in the quarry area. Sharpe was later to be involved with his own Regiment, and took command of his old company as *Rymer* was killed in front of the Trinidad breach. In reality, all the assaults on the breaches failed and there is little, if any, evidence that the new central breach was attacked because it was well protected by a deep, water-filled cunette (ditch within a ditch).

The assault was one of the most murderous ventures British infantry have ever been called upon to undertake. Costello, who like Sharpe was to rise through the ranks to become an officer, had this to say of his experiences as a 'sack and ladder' man at Badajoz:

Word was now given for the ladder party to move forward. We were accompanied on each side by two men with hatchets to cut down any obstacle that might oppose them ... There were six of us supporting the ladder allotted to me, and I contrived to carry my grass-bag before me ... A fireball was thrown out, which threw a bright red glare around us, and

BADAJOZ STATISTICS

The total allied casualties during the siege of Badajoz was almost exactly 5000 (4924): 72 officers and 963 other ranks were killed, and 306 officers and 3583 men were wounded or missing; 74 per cent of all casualties occurred on 6 April, when the city was stormed. Expenditure of roundshot to breach the walls was staggering: The 24-pounders fired 18,832 shots and the 18-pounders 13,029. Some 32,000 cannon balls slammed into the same tiny area of the walls – and it was still not enough to get the men through the holes.

UNUSUAL WOUNDS

Kincaid has described how, at Badajoz, Lieutenant Worsley was shot in the neck under one ear and the ball was extracted on the opposite side. This wound turned his head permanently to the right. He was adjutant of the 3/95th at Waterloo when a wound under the other ear turned his head back to normal.

DESERTERS

Eleven deserters were found hiding in Badajoz after its capture. They were sentenced to be shot. Wellington pardoned five who had good records prior to deserting (one of whom went mad with the relief and shock), and the remainder were ordered to be shot three times over an open grave. One demanded his arrears of pay before he was killed.

instantly a volley of grapeshot, canister, and small arms poured in among us as we stood on the glacis, at a distance of about thirty yards from the walls.

Three of the men carrying the ladder with me were shot dead, and its weight falling on me, I fell backwards with my grass-bag on my breast. The remainder of the stormers rushed up ... Many in passing were shot and fell upon me, so that I was actually drenched in blood. The weight I had to sustain became intolerable, and had it not been for the grass-bag, I must have been suffocated. At length, by a strong effort, I managed to extricate myself, in doing which I left my rifle behind me, and drawing my sword rushed towards the breach. There I found four men putting a ladder down the ditch [Costello had only reached the edge of the glacis]; and not daring to pause ... I slid quickly down the ladder, but before I could recover my footing, I was knocked down again by the bodies of men shot in attempting the descent. I, however, succeeded in extricating myself from underneath the dead, and rushing forward to my right, to my surprise and fear found myself immersed to my neck in water [by going right instead of straight on he had fallen in the cunette]. Being a good swimmer [I] gained the other side, but lost my sword; I now attempted to make to the breach [unarmed] ... but just before reaching it I received a stroke on the breast ... down I rolled senseless, and drenched with water and human gore ... I had now lost all the frenzy of courage that had first possessed me, and actually felt all weakness and prostration of spirit, while I endeavoured, among the dead and wounded bodies around me, to screen myself from the enemies shot [the cowardly *Sergeant Hakeswill* was doing the same thing behind the ravelin at about this time] ... accompanied by screams, groans, and shouts and the crashing of stones and falling timbers, I now, for the first time in many years uttered something like a prayer.

By midnight, the end had come at the breaches. Both attacking divisions were inextricably mixed, the floor of the ditch was carpeted with dead and dying, piles of corpses lay beneath the breaches. There was no control because most officers were down as the last of the sporadic attacks faded. Wellington, waiting in the quarry, was visibly pale. Messenger after

messenger reported failure and horrendous losses. Wellington was reported to have mumbled something about Picton
having to succeed at the castle. Within minutes, almost as
though answering a prayer, Captain Tyler, one of Picton's
ADCs, galloped up with the news that the castle had fallen.
Wellington was visibly relieved; his staff responded with a
cheer. Next, reports arrived that the 5th Division were in the
city as well. That was when Sharpe took the *S. Essex* into the
central breach, and when *Hakeswill* crawled from under a
heap of corpses and hurried into the city on his murderous
mission (MAPS 18 and 19).

The 3rd Division had been guided forward in complete
silence by an acting engineer officer, a Captain McCarthy of
the 50th, but before they had passed the first parallel the
firing from San Roque led Picton to believe he was being led
astray. In his anger he drew his sword and was, with difficulty,
restrained from cutting down the unfortunate McCarthy.
Many in the column had to cross the Rivillas in single file,
knee deep in water, on a narrow mill-dam. The defenders
were alerted, heavy firing developed, and the laddermen and
stormers surged forward to the wall north of the San Pedro
Bastion. Picton was hit in the groin, but was saved from an
agonising end by a thick bundle of papers stuffed in his
pocket. This assault failed. Caught in a crossfire and, as the
British Army historian Fortescue wrote, 'overwhelmed by a
deluge of shells, logs, heavy stones, cold shot [cannon balls]
and other missiles from the top of the wall, the men were
swept away as fast as they came to the ladders.'

Captain Knowles was then a company commander in the
2/5th (later to become The Royal Northumberland Fusiliers
– The Fighting Fifth). Earlier, he had been one of Sharpe's
company officers who had obtained promotion by purchas-
ing into a vacancy in another regiment. It was the 5th that
led the escalade on the walls of the castle, defended by the
now seriously depleted Hessians (MAP 18). *Knowles* did in
the story what Lieutenant-Colonel Ridge did in reality, with
the assistance of Ensign Canch of the Grenadier Company.
They moved two ladders to the right, to a spot where the

LIEUTENANT
HARRY SMITH AT
BADAJOZ

Sharpe and *Harper*
saved a young woman
from a dreadful death
during the sacking of
Badajoz. The most
famous real example
of this was Lieutenant
Harry Smith in the
Light Division who
rescued a Spanish
beauty of fourteen.
Later, Smith married
her and ended his
career as Sir Harry
Smith, governor of the
Cape of Good Hope.
The South African
town of Ladysmith
was named after his
wife.

wall was only twenty feet high instead of thirty, as it had not been fully repaired from its previous battering almost a year earlier. Ridge (*Knowles*) and Canch fought their way up the ladders, secured a foothold on the wall, gathered together a group of followers (among whom was Lieutenant Mackie who had led 'The Hope' at Ciudad Rodrigo), and took the castle. The French counter-attacked with their 88th Regiment but were beaten off. Ridge lost his life, as did *Knowles* a little later at the hands of *Hakeswill*.

Wellington had Badajoz – but the cost was excessive. He wept when he saw the carnage in daylight. Of the officers of the *S. Essex*, *Major Collett*, the second-in-command, and *Captains Sterritt* and *Rymer*, both company commanders, and *Ensign Matthews* had died. Dead men's shoes have to be filled, so Sharpe got his captaincy, his company, his wife and his daughter back, and *Harper* sewed on his stripes again.

The sacking of the city is better remembered than the assault. It was a Spanish town, with a populace supposedly allies of Wellington's army, but they suffered most. Some Spaniards undoubtedly fought with the French, but revenge was indiscriminate. The women, the children, the aged and the defenceless – all were terrified victims of a brutalised and drunken soldiery. The orgy of murder, rape and wanton destruction by thousands of the victorious troops following their entry into the city has left an indelible stain on the reputation of the Peninsular Army. Hundreds of *Hakeswills* roamed the streets. *Teresa* was fortunate that men like *Knowles* and Sharpe were around.

9

Sharpe's Sword

Captain Sharpe is still commanding the Light Company of the *S. Essex*, involved in a bitter vendetta with *Colonel Leroux*, a sadistic Imperial Guard chasseur officer tasked with uncovering and eliminating a British (Irish) spy code-named *El Mirador*. *El Mirador* was the Reverend Doctor Patrick Curtis, who supplied Wellington with a mass of critical intelligence from the Irish College in Salamanca. The backdrop is Wellington's brilliant victory at the Battle of Salamanca on 22 July 1812. Sharpe's hunt for *Leroux* involved him in the assault on the Salamanca forts in June, being shot in the stomach by *Leroux* at the Irish College, fighting in the battle and finally charging with the King's German Legion at García Hernandez and killing *Leroux* inside a broken French infantry square.

REVD DR PATRICK CURTIS

A priest well known to Sharpe. He was rector of the Irish College and professor of Natural History and Astronomy at Salamanca University, having entered it in the year of Wellington's birth. Although seventy-two, he ran a spy network extending throughout French-held Spain and north of the Pyrenees. His cover was 'blown' after the Battle of Salamanca so he fled to the British for protection. In 1819 he received a British pension and later left Spain to become archbishop of Armagh and Primate of All Ireland. He died of cholera aged ninety-two.

SALAMANCA was Wellington's favourite victory, surpassing even Waterloo; he regarded it as a tactical triumph of a high order. He saw and seized a brief opportunity to launch a decisive offensive stroke which rolled the French to ruin. 'I never saw an army receive such a beating,' was his comment afterwards. Had it not been for the Spanish failure to block a vital bridge on the enemy's line of retreat, Marmont's army might have been utterly destroyed. Invited by the allied sovereigns after Waterloo to demonstrate how he handled an army, Wellington chose Salamanca for repetition. The battle was refought as a field day with blank cartridges under the eyes of the foremost soldiers in Europe.

With the fall of Badajoz in April 1812, the French had lost

PAROLE

When officers (of either side) were captured, it was the custom to ask them to give their word of honour that they would not attempt to escape. If they refused, they were treated roughly, kept under guard, given poor rations and no more consideration than ordinary soldier prisoners. If they gave their parole, they were treated as officers, dined with the officers of the unit, kept their swords, generally had a comfortable life and might be exchanged for enemy officer prisoners in due course. *Leroux* gave his parole when captured by Sharpe prior to Salamanca, but broke it when he dashed over the bridge and killed the commanding officer of the S. *Essex*. This was a heinous, dishonourable crime. Colquhoun Grant broke his parole to escape, but only after the French had broken their part of the agreement.

the second of the great gateways to Spain. To Marmont an allied march on Madrid had become not just possible, but probable. Fearing for his communications if Wellington turned north from Badajoz, Marmont hastily retired from the Ciudad Rodrigo area to Salamanca. Despite 230,000 French soldiers in five armies in Spain, nothing could seemingly be done to prevent an allied advance. Marshal Jourdan, the chief of staff to the newly appointed commander-in-chief, King Joseph, summed up the French situation when he wrote (in May 1812):

> All offensive operations are impossible as long as the imperial armies have to hold down the entirety of the occupied provinces. If Wellington concentrates all his forces, he can march with 60,000 men [actually nearer 50,000] against either the Army of Portugal [Marmont] or the Army of the South [Soult]. Neither of them can assemble a sufficient force to resist him, unless they abandon whole provinces . . . The lines of communication between them are long and circuitous. It is easily conceivable that one of them may be attacked and beaten before the other is even aware of the danger.

When the S. *Essex* marched off to destroy the French fort guarding the ford over the Tormes near Ledesma (MAP 20) and Sharpe unwittingly captured *Leroux*, they were undertaking a small but significant operation on which Wellington's strategy depended. He sought to keep his opponents separated. Large armies needed to march on roads; roads crossed rivers at bridges or fords, so the control of these crossing places was critical. In May Wellington had sent Hill on a larger scale operation to capture and destroy the bridge over the Tagus at Almarez, the main French crossing place west of Toledo. To improve his lateral links he had the Roman bridge at Alcántara made serviceable.

Although the military situation was favourable to Wellington, he and his soldiers had other worries. Sharpe's men, the S. *Essex*, indeed the entire army, had not been paid for five months. The Spanish muleteers, upon whom the entire organisation of transport depended, had received nothing for

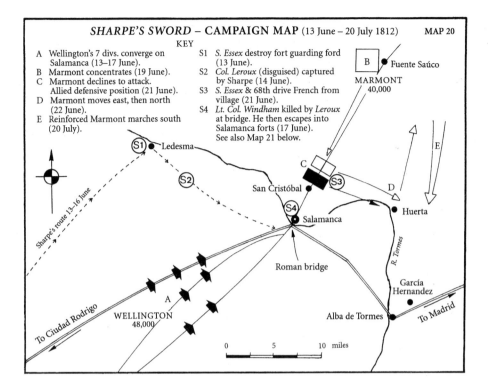

SHARPE'S SWORD – CAMPAIGN MAP (13 June – 20 July 1812)   MAP 20

KEY

A Wellington's 7 divs. converge on Salamanca (13–17 June).
B Marmont concentrates (19 June).
C Marmont declines to attack. Allied defensive position (21 June).
D Marmont moves east, then north (22 June).
E Reinforced Marmont marches south (20 July).

S1 S. Essex destroy fort guarding ford (13 June).
S2 Col. Leroux (disguised) captured by Sharpe (14 June).
S3 S. Essex & 68th drive French from village (21 June).
S4 Lt. Col. Windham killed by Leroux at bridge. He then escapes into Salamanca forts (17 June). See also Map 21 below.

a year. Outstanding meat bills alone were $500,000. Welling-ton wrote home in an explosion of frustration, 'We are abso-lutely bankrupt ... we are in debt in all parts of the country . . .' Despite this, he gathered together 28,000 British, 17,000 Portuguese, 3000 Spaniards and 54 guns. On 13 June he left his base at Ciudad Rodrigo and marched east for four days to Salamanca. Although none in his army knew it, it was the beginning of the end of the French occupation of Spain.

Salamanca was – and still is – an ancient and beautiful univer-sity city. It was an important town as early as 222 B.C. Hanni-bal took it from the Vettones; the Romans built its splendid 500-foot long bridge of 15 arches (increased to 26 in the sixteenth century); Goths and Moors came and went as the centuries unravelled; Columbus lectured on his discoveries.

CODES

Captured French despatches were usually encoded. They had learnt a lesson when a solitary ADC, carrying uncoded letters, was murdered by peasants who sold the contents of his pouch for $20 to Moore's headquarters, thus providing him with the locations of the entire French army. Initially, deciphering caused difficulties, particularly if the Great Paris Cipher was used. Luckily, the French seldom encoded the entire despatch and a Captain Scovell (57th) showed a flair for the work. It earned him exceptionally rapid promotion to brevet lieutenant-colonel within two years. He became the source of much of *Hogan*'s information with which he briefed Sharpe. Scovell was later in charge of the Corps of Staff Guides and devised a cavalry forge for carriage by mules. He was eventually promoted general and governor of the RMC Sandhurst.

There are 25 parishes, 25 colleges and the magnificent Plaza Mayor, which can hold 20,000 people. Among its most illustrious buildings are the cathedral, the university and the Irish College. On the ancient bridge *Leroux* cut down *Windham*, the commanding officer of the *S. Essex*; in the Plaza Sharpe watched as Wellington reviewed the 6th Division shortly after entering the city; in the Irish College Sharpe met Doctor Curtis, one of Wellington's most prodigious suppliers of intelligence during the war. Here also Sharpe was nearly killed by a bullet from *Leroux*'s pistol.

The *S. Essex* had rejoined the 4th Division, under Major-General Lowry Cole, on 17 June in time to march into Salamanca and sample the joyous welcome of the inhabitants. Sharpe seemed certain the householders and storekeepers would be pleased to have so many British troops billeted on them. He should have known better. His own men's pay was far in arrears and payment to the Spaniards would surely be with hastily scribbled scraps of paper rather than silver dollars. Although Sharpe lingered in the city that night, the bulk of the army marched through and out to bivouac in the open on the slopes of San Cristóbal ridge some six miles north-east of Salamanca. Only the 6th Division stayed behind. The next day Sharpe took his men to rejoin his battalion.

Marmont had left 800 soldiers and thirty guns in the city. They were divided between three forts on high ground in the south-west corner of the city (MAP 21). Originally convents, the buildings had been well prepared for defence, with the surrounding houses flattened to provide fields of fire. The forts were called, in descending order of size, San Vincente, Cayetano and La Merced. The latter overlooked the Roman bridge, and gunfire and troops from this fort assisted *Leroux* in his dash across the bridge to escape Sharpe and his riflemen. He sought sanctuary in one of these forts. The 6th Division was inexperienced in siegecraft and initially Wellington had only four 18-pounders with 100 rounds apiece. Nevertheless, work began after dark on the seventeenth, and in the days that followed 300 riflemen of the KGL were ensconced

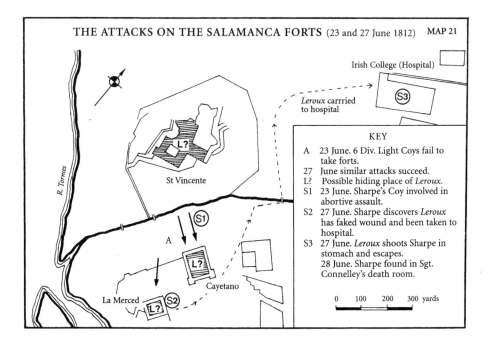

THE ATTACKS ON THE SALAMANCA FORTS (23 and 27 June 1812) MAP 21

Irish College (Hospital)

Leroux carrried to hospital

St Vincente

R. Tormes

La Merced

Cayetano

KEY
A   23 June. 6 Div. Light Coys fail to take forts.
27 June similar attacks succeed.
L? Possible hiding place of *Leroux*.
S1 23 June. Sharpe's Coy involved in abortive assault.
S2 27 June. Sharpe discovers *Leroux* has faked wound and been taken to hospital.
S3 27 June. *Leroux* shoots Sharpe in stomach and escapes.
28 June. Sharpe found in Sgt. Connelley's death room.

0   100   200   300 yards

in the nearby rubble as sharpshooters to keep the French artillerymen occupied.

On 20 June Marmont marched up to the San Cristóbal position and the two armies eyed each other suspiciously. Wellington wanted the French to attack his well-defended ridge. Marmont, on the advice of his senior generals, did no such thing. On the evening of the twenty-first Wellington sent the 68th (Durhams) and the *S. Essex* to take a small hamlet on the right of his position (MAP 20). Sharpe led his company in a brisk skirmishing action in which the battalions, in a two-deep line, reserved their volleys until within forty yards and then went in with the bayonet. It was standard Peninsular War British infantry tactics, and it succeeded. The next day the French drew off eastwards.

On 23 June Major-General Bowes, who had been wounded at Badajoz, 'drew the short straw', in that he was ordered to command a night escalade of Cayetano and La Merced with decidedly unenthusiastic soldiers (MAP 21). Although it was an assault force of some 400 light troops from six battalions, they thought it a hopeless venture. Unusually, there was no Forlorn Hope. The assault force would charge en masse, preceded by twelve ladder parties and followed by Sharpe's company, whose special mission was to capture *Leroux*. It was a disaster. The attackers came under heavy fire from their front, and even heavier from San Vincente in their rear, only two ladders reached the wall and Bowes was slightly, and then mortally, wounded. The assault collapsed with 120 casualties. The capacity of the forts to resist had been badly miscalculated, and Sharpe was no nearer to locating *Leroux*.

Despite this serious setback the siegework continued. Three days later fresh ammunition for the guns arrived and a sustained bombardment opened up a breach in Cayetano, while the red-hot shot soon had San Vincente enveloped in flames. On the twenty-seventh, just as an assault was about to be made, a white flag was waved above Cayetano. The French wanted to surrender Cayetano and La Merced but insisted on a two-hour truce to consult with San Vincente. Wellington, suspecting they merely wished to put out fires and gain a respite, gave them five minutes. Down came the white flag; in went the attack. The 6th Division stormed forward; again, Sharpe's men followed up to locate and take *Leroux*. Cayetano was carried through the breach, La Merced was escaladed and a battalion of Cacadores occupied San Vincente unopposed. Casualties were minimal, but *Leroux* was nowhere to be found. By feigning imminent death, *Leroux* had been carried to the Irish College, which was being used as a hospital. There Sharpe eventually confronted him, but *Leroux* wounded *Harper*, shot Sharpe in the stomach, and disappeared yet again.

The fall of the forts was cause for premature celebration. Illuminations were erected in the Plaza Mayor, a *Te Deum* was sung in the cathedral, the Salamanca ladies were forthcoming with their favours and the widely grinning guerrilla general, Don Julian Sanchez, rode through the streets in his huge hussar cap with its reversed French Eagle badge. The fighting thus far, however, was little better than what cricketers call 'a winning draw' for the allies. Outside the city, to the

Transport for the wounded

THAT SO MANY WOUNDED recovered verged on the miraculous. Having been hit, most soldiers had four fears: fear of not being found; fear of the journey; fear of the hospital conditions, and fear of the surgeon's saw. Finding wounded on a battlefield, particularly at night, was difficult. At Salamanca shrubs and standing corn hindered the bandsmen and buglers in their grim task. It was not uncommon for men to lie out for two or three days, then came the torture of travel to hospital. Many sat or lay in Portuguese carts, which Sergeant Donaldson (94th) has described: 'They were about five feet long and two and a half broad . . . the wheels were about two feet in diameter, rather octagonal than round; and, as they were not girt with iron, it was quite a common thing to have a piece broken out of the circumference, and, of course, every time the wheel turned the whole cart would be violently shook.' The solid wooden wheels revolved on ungreased axle-trees which produced the most ghastly squealing noise. According to the Portuguese, no grease was used as it was believed that the squeaking frightened away the devil. Drawn by a pair of bullocks, these carts travelled at about two miles an hour.

A peasant walked in front armed with a long stick with a nail on the end. Occasionally he would prod a beast to hasten it along, but all this produced was a brief zigzag trot for a few yards which increased the torment of the occupants, many of whose wounds burst open. Even the few British sprung wagons were only marginally better – no screeching and slightly less jolting; nothing could cope with the rough stony tracks. Other means of conveyance included artillery carriages (comparatively comfortable), Portuguese sedan chairs (the best, but very rare), mules harnessed with pack saddles (adjudged precarious by many), and walking. Many wounded preferred to walk if humanly possible, and would hobble as long as their legs held out, perhaps using muskets as crutches. Private Green (68th) spoke with horror of his experiences on a mule: 'It was like cutting my body to pieces. I cried, screamed, prayed, and wished to die . . .'.

north-east as far as the Duero (Douro) river, the campaign continued for four more wearisome weeks of marching and counter-marching. It was then July, with blistering days and bitterly cold nights. Even Wellington complained, 'I never suffered more from cold than during the manoeuvres of the days preceding the battle of Salamanca.' The country was virtually treeless and the troops (including the *S. Essex*) resorted to opening up coffins, scattering the contents, and

through his body and became lodged in his backbone. It was hammered out with a stone. The man recovered but was drowned while bathing in the Tormes.

Hospitals

CONDITIONS IN HOSPITALS were appalling. At Celorico in 1811, two patients per bed was normal. Sergeant Cooper (7th) later commented, 'There was not a single chamber utensil [for 12 men in one small room]. A blanket was spread on the floor instead. Some made use of the window for every purpose. I saw neither basin, soap nor towel.' At Villa Vicosa 150 men lay in the convent corridors alongside all-purpose tubs. The stench was so sickening that fir-log fires were lit at each corner of the building to disguise it. The smell was reduced, at the expense of smoke-filled rooms and burning eyes.

After Fuentes de Onoro a country house was taken over as a makeshift hospital. Lieutenant Grattan (88th) peered through the gate into the yard and saw 'about 200 soldiers waiting to have their limbs amputated . . . It would be difficult to convey an idea of the frightful appearance of these men . . . their limbs were swollen to an enormous size. Some were sitting upright against a wall . . . many of these were wounded in the head as well as limbs . . . the streams of gore that trickled down their cheeks were quite hardened in the sun, and gave their faces a glazed and copper-coloured hue – their eyes were sunk and fixed . . . there they sat, silent and statue-like, waiting for their turn to be carried to the operating tables.'

Curious cures

SICKNESS KILLED more than the sword or bullet, particularly fever. Cures for its soaring temperatures and uncontrollable shivering were varied – sometimes bizarre. Surgeon Henry prepared a glass of hot, spiced wine, mounted his horse and galloped through the night until he had lost the pursuing fever. Opium and quinine bark were often prescribed, but Major Simmons (95th) preferred to put hot stones on his chest and on the soles of his feet during the shivering phase. The cold water cure was popular with medical men but less so with patients. Bugler Green (95th), in the hospital at Elvas, took turns at taking the naked fever patients to the top of the stairs in the middle of the night and drenching them with cold water. 'They were so deranged they knew nothing about it. I put my finger into their hand, when they would jump out of bed, follow me, and sit quietly while we poured the contents of the buckets over them, and would be led by the finger back again to bed, and never utter one word.' Sergeant Donaldson swore that eating a spider's web was the answer. He had overheard General Hope suggesting this old Scottish remedy to a sceptical surgeon; impressed, he jumped out of bed, found some webs, ate them, and claimed never to have had the fever again.

Surgeons and staff

BANDSMEN, BUGLERS AND DRUM-MERS were the stretcher-bearers in Wellington's army. Their job was to find the wounded and carry them to the surgeon. Each battalion had one surgeon and two assistant-surgeons, whose competence and humanity varied considerably. In Sergeant Donaldson's opinion, many were ignorant and inexperienced and were 'thrust into the army as a huge dissecting room, where they might mangle with impunity, until they were drilled into an ordinary knowledge of their business'.

The catalogue of instruments of the medical profession in the age of amputation without anaesthetic makes frightening reading: amputating saw, knife, metacarpal saw, scalpel, a screw tourniquet, bullet forceps, curved needles, a tenaculum for lifting arteries or veins, catheters (flexible tubes), circular saw for removing part of the bone from the skull and instruments for draining fluid. Grattan gives us a graphic account of how the surgeons went to work. 'They [the surgeons] were stripped to their shirts and bloody . . . a number of doors, placed on barrels, served as temporary tables, and on these lay the different subjects upon whom the surgeons were operating; to the right and left were arms and legs, flung here and there, without distinction, and the ground was dyed with blood. Doctor Bell was going to take off the thigh of a soldier of the 50th, and he requested I would hold down the man for him. He was the best-hearted man I ever met . . . and with much composure was eating almonds out of his waist-coat pocket, which he offered to share with me . . . The operation . . . was the most shocking sight I ever witnessed; it lasted nearly half an hour, but his life was saved.'

Tough constitutions and skilful surgeons did save lives, and many men with serious or multiple injuries recovered. Examples were Corporal Buchanan (13LD) who received 13 wounds, including the loss of his nose, fighting three dragoons; an infantryman with 13 bayonet wounds collected at Badajoz; and Private Lock (Scots Greys) who was stabbed 17 times by lances at Waterloo.

using the wood for their bivouac fires. For hundreds of miles the columns of red and blue twisted and turned, often parallel, sometimes within cannon shot of each other, in an endless effort to secure strategic benefit. Wellington's advantage was that he was mostly marching on the inside of the circle (Salamanca being its centre) with the French following the outer circumference. His disadvantage was that the French marched faster, often twelve miles to the allied ten. By mid July both armies were moving south again, Marmont trying

CAPTAIN
COLQUHOUN
GRANT
Probably the greatest
of Wellington's
exploring officers. The
guerrillas were
devoted to him, calling
him '*Granto el Bueno*'
('Grant the Good') to
distinguish him from
his unpopular
namesake, John Grant
(4th), '*Granto el Malo*'.
Grant often visited
Curtis in Salamanca.
Leroux was involved in
Grant's capture in
April 1812 – he had
difficulty hiding in the
woods in his scarlet
jacket. Wellington was
depressed by the news,
telling his staff, 'He
was worth a brigade to
me; I wish he had not
given his parole.' He
offered $2000 reward
for his rescue. A series
of remarkable
adventures eventually
secured his escape
from France. He was
Wellington's chief
intelligence officer
behind French lines
during the Waterloo
campaign.

to get around Wellington's right (southern) flank, the allies
cutting corners to prevent him. By the twenty-second, the
great bend in the Tormes had been crossed as the French
moved south-west, endeavouring to threaten allied communications with Ciudad Rodrigo. Wellington, who was
quite prepared to abandon Salamanca to safeguard his life-
line, had already sent his baggage train, with its accompanying dust cloud and screeching wheels in their axles,
plodding westwards.

The Battle of Salamanca was fought on a Sunday, and thus
became a 'Red Sunday' – one of the famous Wellington
victories fought on the sabbath, the others being Vimiero,
Fuentes de Onoro, Vitória, Orthez, Toulouse and Waterloo.
It was a serious defeat for the French, who suffered 6000
casualties, including six generals (3 dead, 3 wounded) and
6000 prisoners. Among the wounded was Marmont, who
was hit by a bursting shell and carried from the field by
four grenadiers in a soldier's greatcoat, with muskets thrust
through the arms as handles for the improvised stretcher.
Eleven guns, two Eagles and six standards were among the
allied trophies. Nevertheless, it was a comparatively brief
battle. A French general later said that Wellington 'defeated
40,000 men in forty minutes': an exaggeration, but only just.
There was little serious action in the morning and not until
late afternoon was the decisive stroke made by the British
3rd Division.

Shortly after dawn Sharpe had ridden to his position of observation on the southern tip of the ridge that was part of the
allied line (MAP 22). From there a magnificent view of the
battlefield was revealed. Not far away was a small farm which
Wellington selected for his headquarters. To the east and
south undulating fields of ripening wheat dominated the
scene, except for the two steep, flat-topped hills jutting from
the corn like islands. These were the Lesser Arapile, only 400
yards from Sharpe, and the Greater Arapile, almost a mile
away. They dominated the area, and would provide perfect
gun platforms. Wellington quickly occupied the Lesser, but

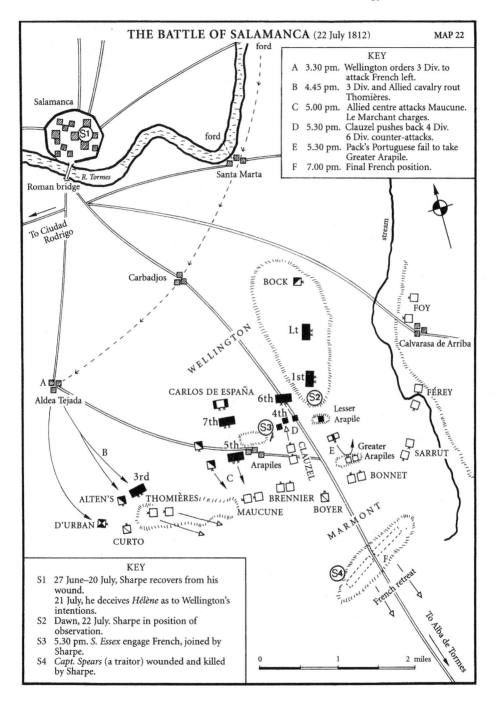

THE BATTLE OF SALAMANCA (22 July 1812)   MAP 22

KEY

A 3.30 pm. Wellington orders 3 Div. to attack French left.
B 4.45 pm. 3 Div. and Allied cavalry rout Thomières.
C 5.00 pm. Allied centre attacks Maucune. Le Marchant charges.
D 5.30 pm. Clauzel pushes back 4 Div. 6 Div. counter-attacks.
E 5.30 pm. Pack's Portuguese fail to take Greater Arapile.
F 7.00 pm. Final French position.

ford

Salamanca

S1

ford

R. Tormes

Roman bridge

Santa Marta

To Ciudad Rodrigo

stream

Carbadjos

BOCK

FOY

Lt

Calvarasa de Arriba

WELLINGTON

A

Aldea Tejada

1st

6th

S2

FÉREY

CARLOS DE ESPAÑA

Lesser Arapile

7th

4th

S3

D

Greater Arapiles

E

SARRUT

5th

CLAUZEL

BONNET

B

Arapiles

C

3rd

BRENNIER

ALTEN'S

THOMIÈRES

BOYER

D'URBAN

MAUCUNE

MARMONT

CURTO

S4

F

French retreat

To Alba de Tormes

KEY

S1 27 June–20 July, Sharpe recovers from his wound.
21 July, he deceives *Hélène* as to Wellington's intentions.
S2 Dawn, 22 July. Sharpe in position of observation.
S3 5.30 pm. *S. Essex* engage French, joined by Sharpe.
S4 *Capt. Spears* (a traitor) wounded and killed by Sharpe.

0   1   2 miles

SERGEANT
MICHAEL
CONNELLEY

The NCO in charge of
a ward in the hospital
in the Irish College
after the Battle of
Salamanca, where he
had been slightly
wounded; a real
drunken rogue,
Costello claims he was,
when sober, attentive
to the sick. His
obsession was that
British soldiers should
die nicely, quietly and
uncomplainingly.
Costello gives an
example of his
entreaties: 'Hold your
tongue, ye blathering
devil, and don't be
disgracing your
country in the teeth of
these ere furriners ...
Ye'll have the drums
beating and the guns
firing over ye, won't
ye? [totally untrue]
Marciful God! What
more do you want? ...
For God's sake die like
a man before these 'ere
Frenchers.'

He literally 'drank
himself out of this
world'. At his funeral
a cockney ventriloquist
scraped the coffin and
imitated Connelley's
voice, 'Let me out
won't you? Oh,
merciful Jesus I'm
smothered.' The
cortege halted and the
lid was prised off.
While a doctor was
fetched, the mourners
tried to force some
wine down his throat.
However, 'his teeth

Marmont beat back the 7th Cacadores from the 4th Division for possession of the Greater Arapile; thus the French gained the bigger and higher hill. Cannons were dismounted and carried laboriously to the top. Gunners sweated, panted and cursed as they toiled up the slopes but once up they felt secure.

Most of the morning was spent by both armies adjusting their positions. The French continued their general shift to the south-west; the Allies matched each move. As part of this manoeuvring the British 3rd Division was strung out in a two-mile column from Santa Marta en route for Aldea Tejada, but hidden from the telescopes of the French on the Greater Arapile, and were dispirited at the start of what they thought was yet another retreat. Sharpe met briefly with *Major Hogan* at the nearby farm, then dozed in the sunshine.

Wellington had spent much of the morning peering at the enemy from the top of the Lesser Arapile, but by the afternoon was back at the farm eating a late lunch when reports of French movements en masse arrived. Sharpe, now wide awake and nibbling cold chicken, listened with mounting excitement to what happened next. Wellington, after throwing away his chicken bone, took a long look at the enemy, exclaimed, 'By God! That will do!', dug in his spurs and rode up the slippery shale of the Lesser Arapile for a closer view. After a brief pause, he snapped shut his telescope and remarked to his Spanish liaison officer, '*Mon cher Alava, Marmont est perdu!*' The French were extending and opening up a gap between their left and centre. While Sharpe watched in awe as the divisions of Thomières and Maucune plodded west through the wheat, Wellington galloped off to give his orders personally to his divisional commanders. First he headed for Aldea Tejada and the 3rd Division, temporarily commanded by his brother-in-law and assistant adjutant-general, Sir Edward (Ned) Pakenham, arriving around 3.30 p.m. His instructions were short but clear, 'Ned, move on with the 3rd Division; take the heights on your front; and drive everything before you.' To which Pakenham responded, 'I will, my lord, if you will give me your hand.' Gravely the

Intelligence sources

ALL PLANS, military or not, depend on intelligence: raw information needs sifting, sorting and assessing before conversion into intelligence. Wellington needed topographical and operational (secret) intelligence, and the former was the responsibility of the quartermaster-general's department. He needed to know the conditions of roads, the depths of rivers, the location of fords, the state of bridges, and so on, information that would tell him what was possible in terms of movement for his (and enemy) forces. Thousands of reports and sketches were received and up to eleven officers were employed on obtaining or collating. *Major Hogan* was involved with this and with operational intelligence. For secret, or operational, intelligence on the enemy's locations, movements and intentions, Wellington exercised personal control, seeing (and keeping) every report himself. This worked well except for a week in May 1811, when he lost the keys to his boxes. Sources were:

1. Cavalry or Light Division patrols and pickets when screening the army.
2. Guerrilla bands and local population.
3. Spies, persons employed as 'correspondents' – men who reported enemy movement, counted files and identified regiments. The Revd Dr Curtis at the Irish College ran a network of such informers.
4. Captured despatches, deserters and prisoners.
5. Scouting (or 'exploring' or 'observing') officers. Men such as Captain Colquhoun Grant or *Major Kearsey*. They moved deep into enemy territory, with a handful of Spaniards and often in full uniform, seeking information on the enemy.

two shook hands. The Battle of Salamanca or, as the French and Spanish call it, the Battle of the Arapiles was about to start in earnest.

A little over an hour later, Pakenham's seven battalions crashed into the head of Thomières' division, routed them and won the battle in a matter of minutes. Despite Clausel's counter-attack pushing back the 4th Division for a while (in which the *S. Essex* and Sharpe participated with some credit), the issue was never in doubt. Marmont had been caught disastrously off balance, and by 7 p.m. had fallen back towards Alba de Tormes bridge behind a rearguard under Foy. Wellington followed up with the 1st and Light Divisions plus Anson's cavalry but could make little impression on the

obstinately opposed the draught, so that poor Mike was already pronounced "not himself" when the doctor arrived.'

French on their ridge. It was here, in the woods, that *Captain Spears* was first wounded, then finished off at his request by Sharpe. With the Alba de Tormes bridge safely in Spanish hands Wellington was confident that pursuit the next day would gather a huge harvest of prisoners and annihilate the Army of Portugal. He was to be disappointed.

The Spanish had abandoned the vital bridge three days earlier so the French, in considerable disarray, poured over the Tormes protected by Foy's bayonets. Wellington's cavalry advance guard caught them up just west of the small village of García Hernandez. These were the horsemen of Anson's brigade: three regiments of light dragoons, and two of heavy dragoons of the KGL under Bock. However, the first allied troops to sight the French were Sharpe and *Lossow*'s troop of the KGL, who had chased *Leroux* through Alba de Tormes until he found refuge with Foy's infantry. From the top of a hill they watched as Anson's men came trotting up the road from the bridge to face the French chasseurs drawn up ahead of them (MAP 23). Within minutes Bock's Germans came down the track from the fords and Huerta. As Foy's battalions saw the cavalry they formed squares. Inside one was *Leroux*. Sharpe was about to participate in a rare moment in military history when charging cavalry actually broke and destroyed infantry in square.

First Anson's brigade dispersed the chasseurs; next, Haltorf's squadron of Germans advanced on the French cavalry opposite, but failed to see the infantry square in a small re-entrant to the north. Volleys of musketry emptied numerous saddles and forced the horsemen to retire. Then Deken's squadron turned on the 1/76th Ligne. Although Deken died in the charge, a mortally wounded horse fell into the square, crushing several soldiers and creating a hole through which a number of Germans forced their mounts. A combat between a cavalryman and an infantryman is normally unequal, the horseman gaining from his greater height and the weight of his horse. The square was quickly destroyed, with the fugitives dashing for shelter in the nearby square of the 1/6 Léger. The arrival masked its fire just as Reitzenstein's

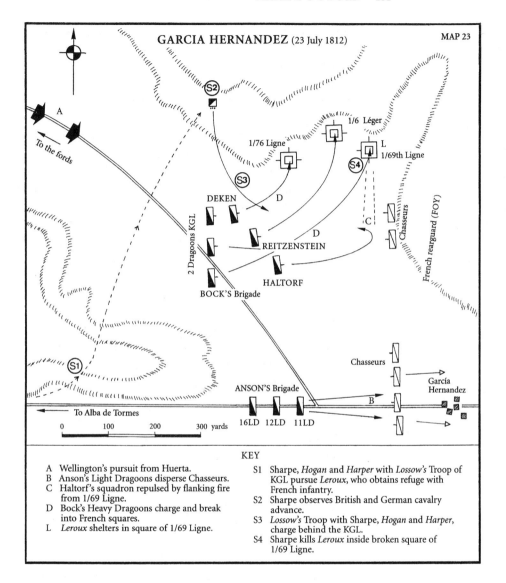

GARCIA HERNANDEZ (23 July 1812)   MAP 23

A
To the fords

S2

1/6 Léger

1/76 Ligne

L
1/69th Ligne

S3

S4

DEKEN   D

2 Dragoons KGL

Chasseurs

D

REITZENSTEIN

C

HALTORF

French rearguard (FOY)

BOCK'S Brigade

S1

Chasseurs

García
Hernandez

ANSON'S Brigade

B

To Alba de Tormes

0   100   200   300 yards

16LD 12LD 11LD

KEY

A Wellington's pursuit from Huerta.
B Anson's Light Dragoons disperse Chasseurs.
C Haltorf's squadron repulsed by flanking fire
   from 1/69 Ligne.
D Bock's Heavy Dragoons charge and break
   into French squares.
L *Leroux* shelters in square of 1/69 Ligne.

S1 Sharpe, *Hogan* and *Harper* with *Lossow's* Troop of
    KGL pursue *Leroux*, who obtains refuge with
    French infantry.
S2 Sharpe observes British and German cavalry
    advance.
S3 *Lossow's* Troop with Sharpe, *Hogan* and *Harper*,
    charge behind the KGL.
S4 Sharpe kills *Leroux* inside broken square of
    1/69 Ligne.

men came cantering up. Once more horses broke through
and another desperate mêlée resulted in another broken
square. The 2nd Dragoons then came forward and hit the
1/69 Ligne. Inside was *Leroux*. It did not take long to dissolve
the demoralised infantrymen who had witnessed their comrades being put to the sword; a third square collapsed. Sharpe,

KLIGENTHAL
SWORDS

Reputedly the best
swords in Europe at
that time. Made by a
master German
swordmaker,
hand-forged with the
blade and basket
guard both coming
from the same steel.
Leroux's sword was
some six inches longer
than the normal blade
and could thus be
worn only by a tall
man. Sharpe was the
object of curious
glances in Salamanca
when he wore his own
and the Kligenthal
swords, but he did not
keep the Kligenthal for
long. It was tainted
with innocent blood,
Leroux had killed
Windham and used it
to skin his victims
alive. Sharpe threw it
into the Tormes off the
Roman bridge.

who had followed up the Dragoons with *Lossow*, had his
final deadly duel with *Leroux*, winning *Leroux*'s beautiful
Kligenthal sword.

Wellington was impressed with his Germans, and the
Heavy Brigade of the Legion was given the privilege of providing him with a personal escort. Three weeks later, on Wellington's recommendation, an order was received from Horse
Guards: 'In consideration of the King's German Legion having so frequently distinguished themselves against the enemy,
and particularly upon the occasion of the late victory
obtained near Salamanca, His Royal Highness the Prince
Regent is pleased, in the name and on behalf of His Majesty,
to command that the officers who are now serving with
temporary rank in the several regiments of that corps, shall
have permanent rank in the British army from the date of
their respective commissions.' Sharpe could have done with
that.

British head-dress
LEFT: *Feather bonnet, Highland Regiment*
RIGHT: *Bicorne cocked hat worn by some heavy cavalry
and abolished in 1812*

————··◦◦◦··——————

10

Sharpe's Enemy

This book tells of Major Sharpe's battle over Christmas 1812 in and around the isolated Spanish village of *Adrados*, just east of the northern Portuguese border, when he was sent to rescue the 'wife' (*Josefina*) of the arrogant *Colonel Sir Augustus Farthingdale*. She had been taken hostage by a band of deserters of all nationalities, led by a former French sergeant and cook nicknamed Pot-au-Feu (Stewpot). His number two was Sharpe's old enemy *ex-Sergeant Hakeswill*, masquerading as a colonel. Sharpe ended up with an independent command of his own men, two companies of the 60th (Royal American) Rifles, a battalion of fusiliers and a rocket troop. He rescued the hostages, fought some bitter battles against massive French assaults, made devastating use of the rockets and lost his wife to the murderous attack of *Hakeswill*, before giving him the *coup de grâce* when a firing squad failed to kill him. Sharpe had at last rid the world of his enemy.

THE FIRST EIGHT MONTHS OF 1812 had been good for the allies. The great gates to Spain – Ciudad Rodrigo and Badajoz – had been prised open (at no small cost) early in the year, the French Army of Portugal had been tumbled, almost to ruin, at Salamanca and on 12 August Wellington had marched into Madrid. But the next four months developed into disaster, with the allies back where they started – on the Portuguese frontier.

Sharpe and the *S. Essex*, who had enjoyed to the full the delights of a month billeted on the outskirts of the Spanish

NEW RANKS IN THE
BRITISH ARMY

1813 saw the
introduction of two
new ranks for NCOs.
One sergeant in every
cavalry troop received
higher pay and the title
of troop sergeant-
major (TSM). Shortly
afterwards a sergeant
in all infantry
companies was
promoted to
colour-sergeant and
wore the Regimental
Colours embroidered
as a badge of honour
above his chevron. In
course of time, he
assumed the duties
of company
quartermaster-sergeant
(CQMS), which he
retains to this day.

FRENCH RANK
EQUIVALENTS

There is confusion
about *Colonel
Dubreton*'s rank and
appointment. He
introduced himself as
'*Chef du Battalion*'
and commander of a
battalion of the 54th
Ligne. This rank was
the equivalent of a
British major, not a
colonel. Sharpe clearly
regarded *Dubreton* as
his senior and as a full
colonel, which meant
he would command a
French regiment of
three battalions.

capital, were fortunate they were not among those of the investment force bogged down under the walls of Burgos castle during September and October. Their division, the 4th, was not committed to that unsuccessful and costly siege. A private of the 24th (2nd Warwickshires) complained with commendable accuracy, 'It was as foolish a piece of work as ever I saw Wellington encounter.' Short of engineers, short of heavy guns and short of time, Wellington, although he captured an outwork at the start, launched four major assaults in as many weeks, all of which failed. He had found himself against a competent enemy – General Jean Louis Dubreton. Dubreton (who may have been the elder brother of *Colonel Michel Dubreton* whose wife Sharpe rescued at *Adrados*) inflicted over 2000 casualties (many during two daring sorties), receiving only 300 killed. With other French armies closing in, Wellington abandoned Burgos on the night of 21–2 October (Trafalgar Day), and the allied army slipped south with its wagon wheels wrapped in straw.

To understand why Sharpe's action at *Adrados* was the only clash between Wellington's command and the French, apart from pickets and patrols, for the six months from November 1812 to May 1813, it is necessary to look briefly at its headlong retreat from Burgos. By November the army was unfit to fight a major action; most units, the *S. Essex* included, were demoralised and seriously depleted in numbers. Exhaustion, the weather, the winter and disease ensured the minimum of military activity for many months. Napoleon began his ruinous retreat from Moscow a mere two days before Wellington turned his back on Burgos. Although the scale was vastly different, there were the same scenes of a hungry, sometimes drunken army, losing more men to exhaustion than to the enemy, losing its discipline, morale and, with certain exceptions, the will to fight. It was ironic that the two great commanders of the day should experience their worst disasters simultaneously, thousands of miles apart.

The *S. Essex*, like the other infantry battalions, had marched and fought for 300 miles to reach Burgos, and had been within 150 miles of the French frontier. They were angry and frustrated by their comrades' recent failure, but they saw no need to retreat. It was in this mood of sullen discontent that the drudging columns plunged into the wine-growing region between Burgos and Salamanca. Twelve thousand soldiers got drunk in Torquemada and hundreds sprawled senseless in the streets. In one cellar, a pistol shot into a huge vat had a group up to their knees in wine and 'fighting like tigers'. Straggling and looting were added to drunkenness, and draconian punishments failed to eliminate them. By mid November, on the last lap, the weather broke. Roads became a foot deep in mud and most men lost their shoes. Costello described the depression and desolation of halting for the night, 'Wet to the skin – without fire or shelter – and at the same time possessed of a ravenous appetite, with nothing to satisfy it ... it was these sufferings ... that rendered some men, from the privations they endured, wish to be shot and exposed themselves in action purposely.'

It was at this stage that a blunder by the quartermaster-general, Colonel James Gordon, pushed hunger to the edge of starvation. He misdirected the supply wagons by twenty miles, and for four days the troops did not receive any rations at all. At night, those in the infantry fortunate enough to kindle a fire from drenched branches huddled for hours in the smoke trying to roast acorns. During darkness on 17 November the S. Essex (together with Wellington) were disturbed by a sudden fusillade of musket shots and shouts from the direction of the 3rd Division. The 'enemy' turned out to be a herd of hundreds of black pigs rushing through their lines. Chaos reigned. The ravenous soldiers scattered in a wild chase in which two dragoons were killed and horses wounded; a number of men were captured after blundering into French patrols pursuing the pigs. The *real* enemy did indeed press hard. In one unfortunate skirmish they seized the commander of the 1st Division, Sir Edward Paget, who was handicapped by having lost an arm at Oporto.

Another night-time alarm was caused by the 1/95th who raided some Spanish wagons laden with biscuits and liquor.

SPANIARDS
ENLISTED

During the winter of 1812–13, authorisation was given to recruit Spaniards into British battalions, and the S. Essex would have received some. The 1/95th mustered 10–12 per company, many of whom made excellent riflemen, although their propensity for murdering and mutilating wounded Frenchmen was a disagreeable characteristic. Some made corporal. All could claim discharge when their battalion passed the Spanish frontier at the end of 1813.

His officers usually
referred to him as 'the
Peer', or 'the Beau'; to
most soldiers he was
'Arty' (Arthur) or
'Nosey' (his prominent
nose); the Portuguese
would cry 'Douro
Douro' (after his
brilliant crossing of
that river at Oporto in
1809) when they saw
him; the Spaniards
called him 'the Eagle'.

ARMY CHAPLAINS

Sharpe makes no
mention of a priest at
Hakeswill's execution,
although the divisional
chaplain would
normally have been
on duty. Perhaps
Hakeswill's
blasphemous cursing
drove him away.
Lieutenant Gleig of the
85th (who later
became chaplain-
general) claimed that
Mr Briscall, the
chaplain at
Wellington's
headquarters had
'. . . a constitutional
shrinking from any
encounter with pain
and sickness kept the
reverend gentleman
from visiting the
hospitals'. This did not
prevent Wellington
reporting favourably
on him, '. . . especially
on the ground that he
kept down
Methodism in the
Army'.

A brisk fight ensued between the guards and the raiders, which continued for much of the night. Several Spaniards were shot during the 'liberation' of these supplies. Costello claimed that he '. . . would have expired, but for the liquor I had drunk'. By 20 November, Wellington's unhappy army had assembled around Ciudad Rodrigo, and a week later had dispersed to winter quarters. The last month had cost the allies almost 5000 men (the *S. Essex* were down to under 400), of whom barely 1200 had fallen in action. Behind a screen formed by the Light Division along the Agueda, the bulk of the infantry (including the *S. Essex*) were billeted along the Douro valley with supplies brought up by boat. Recuperation, re-formation and reinforcement were the priorities. Part of this process was an overhaul of disciplinary procedures.

Wellington was appalled at his army's recent behaviour. He sent a vitriolic, and not entirely justified, memorandum to officers commanding divisions and brigades, in which he blamed them and the regimental officers for slackness and incompetence. '. . . the officers lost all command over their men. Irregularities and outrages of all descriptions were committed with impunity . . . I have no hesitation in attributing these evils to the habitual inattention of the Officers of the regiments to their duties.' He even complained that the French were more able to light fires and cook quickly than his regiments. He had apparently forgotten that he had men flogged for breaking doors for firewood, whereas this was normal procedure for their enemy. He was also unaware, as it had been kept from him, of Gordon's blunder, which meant many units being without food for four days. It was a blanket condemnation, taking no account of the units, such as the 95th, which had behaved well.

Mr Francis Seymour Larpent arrived at headquarters in the bleak little village of Frenada (MAP 24) in November 1812. He was the newly appointed Judge-Advocate-General. Thirty-two general courts-martial were pending and Larpent set to work with vigour, although hampered by sickness – as fast as one prisoner or witness recovered another fell ill. With

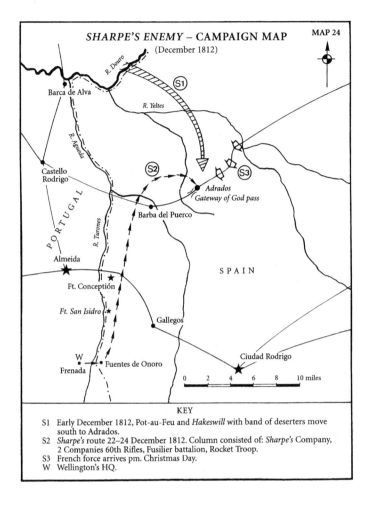

SHARPE'S ENEMY – CAMPAIGN MAP   MAP 24
(December 1812)

R. Douro

Barca de Alva

S1

R. Yeltes

R. Agueda

Castello
Rodrigo

S2   S3

Adrados
Gateway of God pass

Barba del Puerco

PORTUGAL

R. Turones

Almeida

Ft. Conceptión

SPAIN

Ft. San Isidro

Gallegos

W
Frenada   Fuentes de Onoro

Ciudad Rodrigo

0   2   4   6   8   10 miles

KEY
S1   Early December 1812, Pot-au-Feu and *Hakeswill* with band of deserters move
       south to Adrados.
S2   *Sharpe's* route 22–24 December 1812. Column consisted of: *Sharpe's* Company,
       2 Companies 60th Rifles, Fusilier battalion, Rocket Troop.
S3   French force arrives pm. Christmas Day.
W   Wellington's HQ.

Wellington's uncompromising backing, by March 1813 eight
men had been hanged, sixty flogged severely and a number
of officers broken (it is not known if any culprits belonged
to the *S. Essex* apart from *Hakeswill*). The number of officers
constituting a general court-martial was reduced from nine
to seven. According to the British army's historian, Sir John
Fortescue, this measure, '. . . was held to be a terror to evil
doers [in] that the agreement of seven officers was now sufficient to hang them [or shoot them as with *Hakeswill*] and
that courts were held ready in every division for the purpose'.

Executions

HAKESWILL HAD DESERTED to the enemy, he was tried by a general court-martial of seven officers, found guilty and sentenced to be shot. Had he committed any other capital crime, he would have been hanged. He was held in the custody of the provost-marshal while awaiting execution, and the sentence was carried out in front his Regiment (the *S. Essex* having marched to Frenada for the occasion).

All executions were grim affairs designed to deter; the maximum number of witnesses was assembled, normally at least a brigade, sometimes an entire division, particularly if several prisoners were to be shot. The condemned men, with hands tied, headed by a band playing the Dead March, were escorted in slow time along the front ranks of their comrades formed in hollow square. With a division, this could be an agonisingly slow procedure. Sometimes the prisoners walked firmly, at others men cried, pleaded and had to be half dragged to the freshly dug trench in the centre of the open side of the square. The provost blindfolded the prisoners before pinning a white paper aiming mark above their hearts. The brigade-major read the sentence, the chaplain said a prayer, the provost motioned with his cane and the firing party fired a volley. Often a second firing party would be available to despatch those not killed outright. The troops were then marched past the bodies.

Costello's first execution was a gruesome affair. One man remained untouched after the first volley and thought for a moment he had been reprieved, but '. . . two men of the reserve came up and fired their pieces into his bosom, when, giving a loud scream, that had a very horrible effect on those near, he sprang forward into his grave. To prevent unnecessary suffering, a reserve firing party was brought up, who continued to fire wherever the slightest sign of life exhibited itself . . . the provost himself winding up the tragedy by discharging a pistol shot through the head of each corpse.' This was the privilege Sharpe reserved for himself in *Hakeswill*'s case.

PROVISION OF TENTS

On 1 March 1813, bell tents became general issue for all British and German infantry. The scale was one for each field officer (majors and above), one for the company officers (up to three), one each for the adjutant,

But the winter was not all doom and gloom. Fresh drafts brought the *S. Essex* back to over 600 men, as reinforcements poured into Lisbon and tramped north. The medical services were overhauled, serious efforts were made to pay troops their arrears and several popular improvements made to conditions of service. From 1813 onwards the *S. Essex*, like the rest of the army, were issued with tents and light-weight camp kettles (stew pots), one for every six men, instead of the heavy iron pot which fed sixteen and had to be carried

Bell tent

quartermaster, paymaster, and the medical staff. NCOs and men got three per company. This meant forty-seven tents for a full-strength battalion, which was insufficient for all the soldiers at twenty per tent. The troops slept with their feet in the centre, but were so jammed together that turning had to be simultaneous on the agreed command of 'turn'! They were carried by the mules which previously carried the large camp kettles.

on a mule (as often as not the mule became separated from the men). Finally, one sergeant per company was given the rank, and extra pay, of colour-sergeant.

Wellington was an accomplished horseman. He thought nothing of riding fifty miles a day visiting divisions or, particularly during this winter, of indulging his passion for

The 60th (Royal American) Rifles

IN 1756 Parliament had authorised the formation of up to four battalions of foreign nationals for service in America. Further battalions were permitted in 1797, and in December of that year the 5/60th formed on the Isle of Wight (two years before the 95th) as a Jäger (rifle) unit. It was mainly composed of Germans and was unique in the British army in wearing green jackets and being armed with rifles, as distinct from muskets. The first four battalions served in the West Indies, but the 5th served with distinction in virtually every battle in the Peninsula, usually split up into semi-independent companies attached to divisions to boost their skirmishing capacity. The 5/60th had an enviable reputation as cooks. Each man in their mess (group) was expected to acquire and carry something extra such as cheese, onions, garlic, lard, pepper, salt, sugar, coffee, and so on, by which the evening stew was much improved. Three more battalions were formed subsequently, but none served with Wellington. By 1819 all eight had been disbanded in the nineteenth-century's equivalent of the recent British army cutback, euphemistically called 'options for change'.

Pastimes

THE WINTER OF 1812–13 was a good one for many in Wellington's army, including the *S. Essex*. Sharpe's expedition to *Adrados* was exceptional, particularly as it coincided with Christmas. Like off-duty soldiers everywhere, Wellington's officers and men devised an intriguing variety of amusements. They smoked heavily – officers 'segars', soldiers pipes; they wrote letters, read books and newspapers, gambled at cards or horse (and sometimes donkey) racing; they went for walks, rides, sightseeing, played football and cricket. They devised a variety of hunting games, one of which involved turning loose a pig with its tail greased. The first man to catch it (no easy matter) kept – and more importantly ate – the pig. More conventional methods of catching animals were also popular. Mr Larpent described three 'odd sorts of packs of hounds' at Frenada including 'the Peer's' foxhounds, greyhounds run by the commissary-general, and a certain Captain Mor with 'terriers, mongrels and ferrets ... to get rabbits'. Apart from foxes, wild boar and wolves provided additional zest and danger to the chase.

Amateur dramatics became the rage, particularly in the Light Division. An old house at Gallegos was converted for the purpose. On Thursday, 4 February 1813, Wellington and his staff rode over to watch Sheridan's *The Rivals*. One wonders if Sharpe was there! Almost certainly he was not invited to the grand dinner and ball given at Ciudad Rodrigo when General Lowry Cole received the Order of the Bath, and forty ladies and 150 senior officers attended. The food was half cooked at Frenada and carried over on military wagons and mules; the only drawback was that the roof had gaping holes and it was midwinter. It was an occasion when Wellington's stamina was well illustrated: he worked at Frenada until 3.30 p.m., rode the seventeen miles to the dinner in two hours, changed into full uniform with all his orders, dined and danced until 3.30 a.m., rode back to headquarters by 6 a.m. and was back in business by midday.

ROYAL ACADEMY
OF EQUITATION,
ANGERS

At nineteen, Arthur Wellesley had attended this academy in the Province of Anjou at the same time as the future *Colonel Dubreton*. It was not a military school like Brienne which the young Bonaparte was

fox-hunting. While Sharpe was embroiled over Christmas in defending *Adrados*, Wellington was enjoying the festivities in Cadiz. Untypically, he had covered the 300 miles in a landau (carriage) to confer with the Cortés about his new duties as commander-in-chief of all the Spanish armies. They were surprisingly conciliatory. He secured authority to approve senior appointments, control military expenditure, dismiss incompetent officers, and select a Spanish chief-of-staff to be attached to his headquarters. On his return, however, his mind was more occupied with plans for the coming spring – a renewed thrust into Spain.

Previously allied advances had been towards Talavera or Salamanca, south of the Douro River. During the winter months the French had been consolidating much of their strength north of that river. If Wellington pushed east the French threatened his left flank; the farther he marched, the longer and more exposed were his communications. With the crossing places in enemy hands, his advance would be under continual threat. If, however, he could turn the line of the Douro at the outset with a left hook from northern Portugal, the strategic advantages would be with him. Of even greater importance, he would be able, with the help of the navy, to shorten his lines of communications by hundreds of miles by switching his main supply base to the north coast. Wellington looked long and hard at the wild, mountainous region of the Traz os Montes region of northern Portugal. His staff, including Sharpe's friend *Major Hogan*, pored over maps, and exploring officers rode hundreds of miles, testing bridges, reporting on roads and contacting guerrilla leaders.

The French, meanwhile, had also been endeavouring to regroup and reorganise. A major constraint was the constant drain of anti-guerrilla operations. A predominant characteristic of the war was its squalid cruelty; to lose a hundred men a day to the bullets and knives of partisans was to die the death of a thousand cuts. To a Frenchman everyone was an enemy, be he in British, Portuguese or Spanish uniform, but the man most dreaded was the guerrilla, who wore no uniform at all. To straggle from a column was to die unpleasantly. At the start of 1813 the great road from Burgos to Madrid was cut for five consecutive weeks. Despatches from Paris arrived in Madrid six weeks after being issued, an example being Napoleon's celebrated 29th Bulletin with its first veiled account of the Russian disaster.

The Frenchman's answer to terror was more terror, and reprisals were the name of the game, which have often been the regular military's answer to partisan attack. (The Germans in Russia and Europe during World War II and the Serbs in Bosnia even more recently are obvious examples.) The 15th

attending at much the same time; it was rather a place which had trained the sons of Europe's nobility for 200 years in horsemanship, fencing, mathematics and the humanities. Wellesley left with not much more than a good French accent.

WELLINGTON'S CHARGER

At about this time a mare which had been on the Copenhagen expedition produced a foal, which was named 'Copenhagen'. It was given to Wellington, who rode it during the 1814 campaign, and at Waterloo. Copenhagen was a renowned kicker and soldiers learnt to stay clear of his hindquarters. He lived to be thirty, and in old age was said still to neigh at the sight of a red jacket.

Chasseurs à Cheval once lost thirty prisoners to a regular Spanish unit and listened powerless to their shrieks and pleas as all were burnt alive on a huge bonfire. The 15th never took a Spanish prisoner again; they claimed to have once sabred 1500 as they begged for mercy. General François Roguet shot 600 partisan prisoners, using the local cemetery for convenience. General Bigarre, ADC to King Joseph, considered that guerrillas caused more casualties during the entire war than regular troops. Costello recalls a guerrilla leader emptying the contents of his purse into his girlfriend's lap and seeing '. . . a number of human ears and fingers, which glistened with the golden ornaments they still retained'.

The evidence of unspeakable torture seen by Sharpe throughout his service in the Peninsula, including that in the dungeons of Pot-au-Feu's castle, were all too typical of what went on. The average Spaniard had an all-consuming passion for revenge. Some of its more devilish forms included burying a Frenchman alive with his head above ground and using it as a pin in a bowling match; sawing him in half between two planks; skinning alive (also favoured by Sharpe's old enemy *Colonel Leroux*); boiling alive; impaling and grilling over a fire, or crucifixion upside down. The guerrilla bands were a variable lot, an inflammable mix of fugitives from broken Spanish armies, smugglers, vagabonds, escaped prisoners of war, angry patriots, and criminals, with a surprising number of monks and priests. Of these, some were resentful of Joseph's suppression of the monasteries, others were outraged by the French looting of churches. Their exhortations that to kill a Frenchman was a certain way to God's blessing must have added to the savagery of their flock's activities. A few became leaders, none more dedicated to the Holy War than Cura Merino ('the most savage'), who specialised in castrating French officers.

A number of bands were bandits first and patriots second. They terrorised large areas of countryside, looting and murdering – preferably Frenchmen, but anybody would do. One bandit leader claimed to have committed 210 robberies and 75 assassinations of French and Spanish alike. Another villain was betrayed by his men to fellow compatriots, who got rid

Espoz y Mina

ONE OF THE MORE FAMOUS guerrilla chiefs who operated in Navarre. By 1813 he had the rank of general and commanded 14,000 men around Pamplona. The only such leader to write his memoirs, Mina had a typically cruel and colourful career. At times operating with 3000 followers and at others hiding in mountain caves with half a dozen comrades, he attacked convoys, overran isolated outposts, intercepted despatches and forwarded them to the Spanish Junta or Wellington. In late 1811 the governor of Navarre, General Abbe, ordered the execution of 'hostages' from the guerrillas' families and villages that sheltered partisans. Mina responded by executing four Frenchmen for every Spaniard killed; the proclamation was soon lifted. It was Mina's boast that in 1812 six French commanders (Dorsenne, Réille, Caffarelli, Roguet, D'Agoult and Suchet), deploying 18,000 troops, were separately hunting him.

One of his greatest successes was in April 1812, when he waylaid a huge convoy of prisoners, wounded, stores and food near Vitória. Despite an escort of 2000, including a Polish Regiment, Mina captured the convoy, killing 500 Poles in the process. Among the booty were letters from King Joseph to his wife and Napoleon. Later Mina was betrayed by a minor chief called (appropriately) Tris el Malcarado ('the False-faced'), but escaped after killing the French hussar who was beating in his door with a crowbar. Mina returned to the village after the French departure to shoot Tris for his treachery. After the war, he spent time exiled in France and England.

of him in traditional Spanish style – torn into quarters by four horses in Valladolid's market place. It was not unknown for Spanish villagers under attack by such a band to combine with French forces to drive them off.

Sharpe was involved with the last category of these gangs – dealing with army deserters. The former French army sergeant, Déron, self-styled 'marshal', collected together several hundred deserters of all nationalities. Normally, their objective was a comparatively quiet life hidden in the hills away from military operations, robbing and killing to survive, taking care to avoid unnecessary attention. Déron, whose nickname of Pot-au-Feu referred to his previous military calling, had been disturbed by the intense anti-guerrilla operations in Galicia and northern León in late 1812, and had moved south and east to find a less troublesome area. He found the ideal spot at *Adrados*: there was even a ruined castle and watchtower to fortify and a village to provide the necessities of life – food, drink and women. In reality, Pot-au-Feu was hunted down by the French under a Colonel de Marbot rather than the British. The allied deserters caught with him were handed back (as *Hakeswill* was handed to Sharpe by the French) to face almost certain execution.

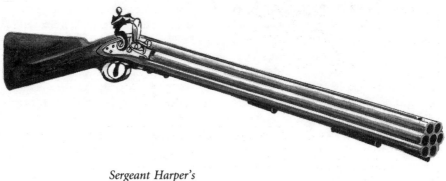

Sergeant Harper's
seven-barrelled Nock gun

The action at *Adrados* (MAPS 25a–25d) is noteworthy for Sharpe's effective employment of rockets at close range. Sir William Congreve's rockets were one of the British 'secret' weapons of the war (another being Major Shrapnell's airburst shell). A rocket troop did join the Army in 1813 (not in 1812) and had the enthusiastic patronage of the Prince of Wales (but not of Wellington). There was a remarkable variety of rockets available including shells, solid shot, canister, incendiary rockets and illuminating parachute flares. Their advantages were impressive – in theory. They could fire up to 3700 yards, were cheap to make, could be fired far faster than any gun, could go where any infantryman could go, and made a fearful noise in flight. These impressive assets, however, were almost always negated by their infuriating inaccuracy. Even more disconcerting was a tendency for some to boomerang. Against raw troops, horses or as a total surprise at short range, they could produce spectacular results.

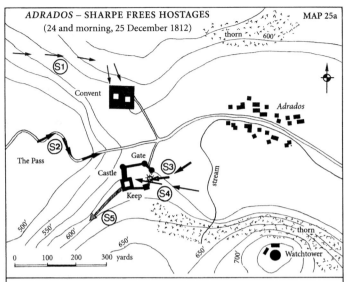

ADRADOS – SHARPE FREES HOSTAGES
(24 and morning, 25 December 1812)
MAP 25a

KEY S1 Christmas Eve. Sharpe rescued hostages and secures Convent.
S2 am. Christmas Day. Fusilier battalion arrives,
S3 am. Christmas Day. Fusilier assault defeated by mine in broken wall.
S4 am. Christmas day. 2nd Fusilier attack takes Castle.
S5 *Hakeswill* and deserters escape.

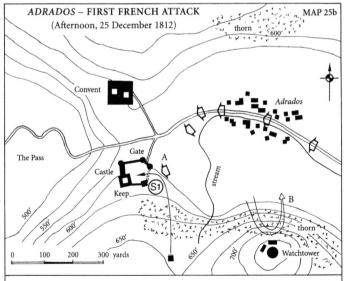

ADRADOS – FIRST FRENCH ATTACK
(Afternoon, 25 December 1812)
MAP 25b

KEY S1 Rocket Troop charges French with 'lances'. French form square and retire.
A Single battalion attack on Castle fails.
B Voltigeur advance on Watchtower driven off.

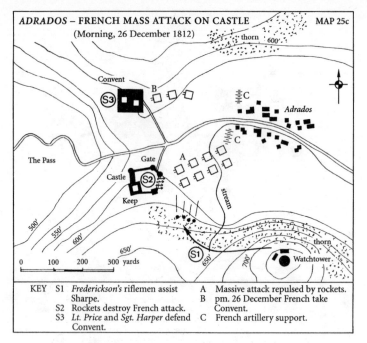

ADRADOS – FRENCH MASS ATTACK ON CASTLE
(Morning, 26 December 1812)   MAP 25c

Convent

thorn   600'

B

S3   C

Adrados

C

The Pass   Gate   A

Castle

S2

Keep

500'   stream

550'

600'   thorn

650'

0   100   200   300 yards   S1   650'   700'   Watchtower

KEY   S1 *Frederickson's* riflemen assist   A   Massive attack repulsed by rockets.
          Sharpe.   B   pm. 26 December French take
      S2 Rockets destroy French attack.   Convent.
      S3 *Lt. Price* and *Sgt. Harper* defend   C   French artillery support.
          Convent.

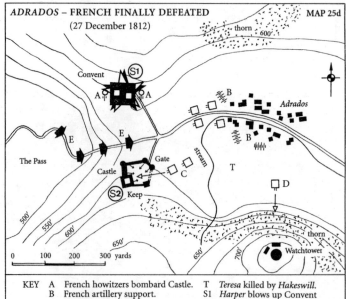

ADRADOS – FRENCH FINALLY DEFEATED
(27 December 1812)   MAP 25d

thorn   600'

Convent   S1

A   A

B

Adrados

B

E   E

The Pass   Gate

Castle   C   T

S2   Keep   D

500'

550'   thorn

600'

650'

0   100   200   300 yards   650'   700'   Watchtower

KEY   A   French howitzers bombard Castle.   T   *Teresa* killed by *Hakeswill*.
      B   French artillery support.   S1   *Harper* blows up Convent
      C   French enter Castle.   S2   *Sharpe* destroys French in yard.
      D   Battalion attack driven off.
      E   British reinforcements arive.

CONGREVE
ROCKETS

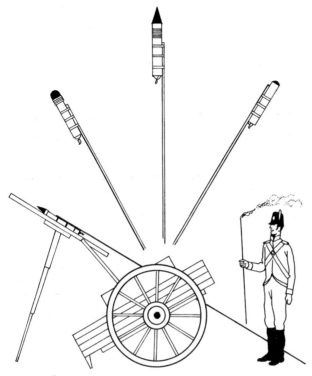

Congreve rockets:
Rockets fired from rocket cart

The rumours of the existence of rockets for use as artillery were true: they were the invention of William (later Sir William) Congreve, a British artillerist and inventor. The rockets were mounted on long sticks with the explosive head at one end, closely resembling present-day firework rockets. They were fired in salvoes. First used from specially constructed boats at Boulogne in 1806, they were also successfully used on land and afloat at the siege of Copenhagen in 1807–9. The Rocket Troop of the RA was formed in 1813 and fought at Waterloo. Wellington was initially sceptical of their lethality and accuracy.

   Congreve's heavy naval rockets were more potent, particularly if fired en masse against a large target, such as a coastal town, where accuracy was not crucial. Launching rockets from specially equipped warships, the British burnt down Boulogne in 1806 (they had been aiming at the ships in the harbour). A year later, they reduced much of Copenhagen to ashes, and at Danzig in 1813 a rocket bombardment set fire to the supply warehouses and caused the garrison, which had held out for a year, to capitulate. On land, Sharpe was to see them in action again at Quatre Bras and Waterloo.

11

Sharpe's Honour

SPANISH GIRLS
CONFINED TO
CONVENTS

Hélène's enforced confinement in the convent of *Santa Monica* was a common punishment of the Inquisition or Catholic Church for young ladies who were less than chaste. A lesser punishment was to 'be given back to her mother'. In fact, the Cortés had recently suppressed the Inquisition which must have saved hundreds of Spanish girls from this fate.

WELLINGTON'S
ARMY AT VITÓRIA

In round figures the allied army had 79,000 men deployed. Of these 36,000 were British, 28,000 Portuguese and 15,000 Spanish.

Major Sharpe, the only major with the S. Essex and therefore its second-in-command, is transformed from an impoverished officer unable to pay his mess bills into a hugely rich man. On the late afternoon of 21 June 1813 his friend *Sergeant Harper* stuffed enough of King Joseph's treasure into two haversacks to set them both up for life.

The months of May and June had been grim for Sharpe. As Wellington prepared to launch the campaign that would all but sweep the French from Spain in six weeks, Sharpe, after a successful little action on the Agueda River, was forced into a duel, arrested for murder, sentenced, and publicly 'hung' – all within two days. Another man was executed in his place and Sharpe spent two weeks in hiding at *Adrados*. June saw Sharpe rescuing *Hélène*, the *Marquesa de Casares el Grande y Melida Sadaba*, from life in a convent; being tortured by *Major Ducos*; surviving the blowing up of Burgos Castle, and finally fighting a duel with, and slitting the throat of the guerrilla leader *El Matarife* (The Slaughterman). By mid month Sharpe was walking to war, trying to catch up with the army (which believed him dead). He arrived at Vitória in time to take command of the S. Essex, who had just lost their colonel, and lead them in a crucial assault on the village and bridge of Gammora Mayor.

THE FRENCH HAD a bad winter and early spring. Following Napoleon's disastrous march on Moscow, he recalled thousands of veterans from Spain to help rebuild the Grande

Armée. These included cavalry (the loss of trained horses in Russia was as serious as the loss of men), battalions of the Imperial Guard and large drafts of experienced NCOs from all units, upon which to build the raw regiments forming in France. Throughout February and March, northern Spain had seethed with insurrection as the guerrillas redoubled their forays. Mina harried the French in Navarre; Longa operated between Burgos and the sea; Porlier was active in the Asturias; and El Pastor fought around Biscay. It was not, therefore, surprising to find Sharpe's activities from December 1812 onwards centred around rogue guerrilla leaders such as Pot-au-Feu and *El Matarife*.

King Joseph, although nominally in command, was subject to constant instructions from the Emperor, most of which were weeks out of date when they reached Madrid. In January and February Napoleon wrote directing his brother to leave Madrid with a garrison of one division and make his head-quarters in Valladolid, concentrating his forces for the paci-fication of the northern provinces. To Joseph's repeated supplications for money, the Emperor advised him to restore order in the rich and fertile provinces of which he was king, and they would be able amply to sustain the troops quartered in them. At the end of February, Napoleon replaced Caffarelli with Clausel in the Army of the North, recalled Soult to Paris and appointed General Gazan to the Army of the South, while General Réille took over the by now hopelessly mis-named Army of Portugal. Jourdan remained to guide King Joseph in his military judgements.

Few in the allied army at the end of April 1813 would have foretold that the campaign about to begin would see Wellington's 100,000 men march 600 miles, cross 6 great rivers, win a decisive victory, capture untold treasures, including the entire French army pay chest, and reach the frontiers of France – all within 6 weeks. The campaign was intended to start at the beginning of May, but three problems delayed it: rain, pontoons and rum. For several days the rain lashed down, swelling rivers, turning streams to torrents and tracks to quagmires. Mud slowed marching men, but stopped

FRENCH CASUALTIES IN RUSSIA

Napoleon's losses were staggering even by twentieth-century standards. Some 655,000 troops crossed the Vistula in the summer of 1812; only 95,000 remained by January 1813. In round figures the French lost 560,000 men, 360,000 of whom had died on the battlefield, of sick-ness or exposure to the Russian winter. The remainder, including 48 generals, were captured. Of the 1300 guns taken to Moscow only 250 came back.

THE BLOWING UP OF BURGOS CASTLE

General Aboville, who commanded the garrison, knew that it would be impossible to take all the heavy ammunition when the French abandoned Burgos. Fearful that the British might use this in a future siege of Bayonne, he had 6000 shells lined up in such a way that the firing of a mine under the wall would explode them. By negligence or accident, the mine was fired at 7 a.m. on 13 June before all troops had got clear. A passing regiment of dragoons lost 120 men and numerous horses from flying stones and debris.

PONTOONS

The building of
pontoon bridges and
their transport
overland on wagons
(drawn by horses or
oxen) was the
responsibility of the
engineers in the
British army, and the
artillery in the French.
The pontoons were
shallow, boxlike boats
over twenty feet long,
made of wood or tin,
which could be lashed
together across a river
and overlaid by
planking. Such a
bridge could support
5000 lbs but wagons
usually crossed singly
and cavalry led their
horses. Improvised
pontoons could
sometimes be made
using any small boats
or even wine casks.
Their construction
over a wide or
fast-flowing river was
a difficult and often
dangerous task.

heavy wagons. The poor weather underlined the need for pontoon bridges, which in turn travelled on wagons. With the Douro River separating the two wings of Wellington's army, it was vital to have the means of crossing the river – it gave flexibility and independence of action. Wellington personally inspected the pontoons: one was rotten, and more wagons, more oxen and more horses were needed. The pontoon train would move on 15 May, the day Sharpe's 'hanging' was watched by Wellington from his headquarters at Frenada.

The third problem was far from frivolous. Each soldier was entitled to a pint of wine or a third of a pint of rum a day. That amounted to a lot of booze, which cost a lot of money. The Portuguese government was objecting to the British practice of importing colonial rum instead of buying local wine; the rum was cheaper, of higher quality and far less bulky to move. Wellington wrote on 3 May, 'When we purchase wine or Portuguese brandy in this country we are obliged to pay for it at enormous price, all in specie [cash]. When we purchase colonial rum, we pay for it by bills drawn upon England; and I believe that we are enabled to deliver the ration to the soldier at one third of the price at which we could procure wine or Portuguese brandy . . . and we give him an wholesome, instead of an unwholesome spirit.'

Despite the difficulties, Wellington foresaw success. By 10

Pontoon Bridge

Duelling

SHARPE WAS LIABLE to be sentenced to death for duelling. That was the law, but the extreme penalty was rarely exacted. One example was in 1808 when a Major Campbell was executed for killing a Captain Boyd. In 1813 a Lieutenant Blundell was killed in a duel, and his opponent and seconds were sentenced to death but pardoned – and cashiered. The law regarded such killing as murder. Nevertheless duelling continued in Britain from the sixteenth to the nineteenth centuries as a way of settling matters of honour. It was less common in the Peninsula than in Ireland or India, as commanders actively discouraged it.

The man challenged had the choice of weapons, so when Sharpe chose swords rather than pistols, he was ensuring a proper contest: with pistols it is possible to miss deliberately. Not all participants fought honourably. In Paris, after Waterloo, a French count quarrelled with a Cossack officer and decided to settle the matter with pistols. It was agreed that the two should stand back-to-back, take six paces before turning and firing simultaneously. As soon as the Frenchman started his first step the Cossack turned and fired into the back of his opponent's head shouting, 'I've been shot at enough by your cursed countrymen; now for my turn.'

May, the rain had abated, the vines had begun to shoot, the wheat was ankle deep: the time was approaching for British drums and bugles to 'sound a long farewell to Portugal'. On that date (the day following *General Preston*'s and Sharpe's small success on the Agueda) Wellington felt able to write, 'I shall never be stronger … or more efficient than I am now; and the enemy will not be weaker. I cannot have a better opportunity for trying the fate of a battle, which, if the enemy be unsuccessful, must oblige him to withdraw entirely.'

At this time the commander-in-chief had no inkling of the intrigues and machinations of *Major Ducos* in Burgos Castle, which would ultimately lead to the signing, on 11 December 1813, of the Treaty of Valençay between Prince Ferdinand (imprisoned in Valençay Castle) and Napoleon. The idea that if the French lost another major battle they could remove British troops from the country by political means had already germinated.

SHARPE'S ACTION
ON THE AGUEDA

The book *Sharpe's Honour* records the action when *General Preston* detached Sharpe to cut off a French detachment on the Tormes River. In fact, his action took place on the Agueda River on 10 May 1813, not the Tormes. Wellington did not advance to Salamanca until the end of May so it would have been impossible for Sharpe to have done what he did after this action (including two weeks hiding at *Adrados*) had it been on the Tormes. This minor inconsistency should be put down to a memory lapse.

PORTUGUESE
GAMBLERS

Kincaid's opinion of the Portuguese was not high: '. . . The middling and lower orders are extremely filthy both in their persons and in their houses and they all have an intolerable itch for gambling. The soldiers . . . invariably group themselves into card parties when allowed a few minutes halt . . . an NCO and half a dozen men on any duty or fatigue are generally to be seen as follows, viz. one man as a sentry, to watch the approach of the superintending

The *S. Essex* had spent the winter billeted at Lamego on the Douro River (MAP 26). *Lieutenant-Colonel Leroy's* battalion was, by April, in Major-General Robinson's brigade. This brigade was part of the 5th Division commanded, during the absence on leave of Leith, by Lieutenant-General Oswald. Brigaded with them were the 1/4th (King's Own), 2/47th (Lancashires), 2/59th (Nottinghamshires) and a provisional battalion of 400 men of the 30th (Cambridgeshires) and 44th (East Essex). The division's skirmishing capacity was enhanced by one independent company of the Brunswick-Oels. The battalion had been moved to the frontier in late April and Sharpe had taken half for the operation on the Agueda on 10 May (MAP 27). On the same date, at Lamego, the provisional battalion was ordered home. The *S. Essex* were instructed to replace it by marching north to rejoin their old brigade at Outeiro. They arrived on 22 May, a week's hard marching doing little to lift the depression over the battalion since the humiliation and execution of their major.

The *S. Essex* had joined a huge force of 58 infantry battalions and 10 cavalry regiments. Six out of eight British infantry divisions were tasked with the great strategic left hook that would outflank the French north of the Douro (MAP 26). This heavy left wing was commanded by the victor of Barosa two years earlier outside Cádiz, sixty-six-year-old General Sir Thomas Graham, who had become a soldier at forty-four (like Caesar and Cromwell). At the critical moment in that battle Graham 'led the centre of his own left brigade like a general of the Middle Ages, riding ten yards ahead of the line with his plumed hat waving in his right hand, and his white hair streaming in the wind'. Wellington had moved him from Cádiz to the main army in 1811, but he had been on long sick leave, due to failing eyesight. Now, with his eyesight improved, Wellington had selected him for this crucial command, although the scope for blunders was limited by the proximity of the commander-in-chief.

Sharpe's enforced hiding at *Adrados* from the sixteenth to the thirtieth of May saw Graham's force over the Douro into Spain and in the process of crossing the Esla, with

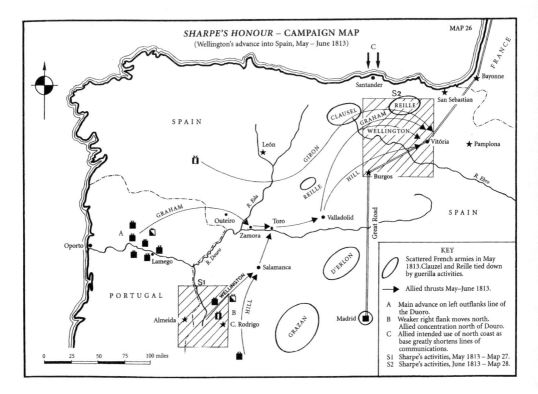

SHARPE'S HONOUR – CAMPAIGN MAP
(Wellington's advance into Spain, May – June 1813)

MAP 26

KEY

Scattered French armies in May 1813. Clauzel and Reille tied down by guerilla activities.

Allied thrusts May–June 1813.

A Main advance on left outflanks line of the Duoro.
B Weaker right flank moves north. Allied concentration north of Douro.
C Allied intended use of north coast as base greatly shortens lines of communications.
S1 Sharpe's activities, May 1813 – Map 27.
S2 Sharpe's activities, June 1813 – Map 28.

Wellington's right wing under 'Daddy' Hill approaching Toro from the south (MAP 26). The army was about to be reunited, albeit temporarily. The French had been surprised and sought desperately to concentrate their divisions and pull back at the same time. They were to keep running for another 150 miles – until they reached Vitória.

Deception was an important element in Wellington's plan. The French had to believe that the main thrust would be from around Ciudad Rodrigo (where the Light Division had spent the winter) to Madrid, via Salamanca, the traditional and easy route, which followed the better roads. To foster this belief Wellington deployed a dense cavalry screen of three brigades in the south, did not move from his headquarters at Frenada until 22 May and when he did so he accompanied Hill's right wing as it moved on Salamanca. There was also the successful little deception with Sharpe. When Wellington

officer, one man at work, and the NCO, with the other four, at cards.' Perhaps not an unusual division of duties in many armies.

SPANISH
IRREGULAR
TROOPS SERVING
FRANCE

SPANISH
IRREGULAR
TROOPS SERVING
FRANCE

Spanish irregular,
anti-guerrilla units
were not uncommon
in Spain. The leader of
one such band, Poujol,
had fought for four
years against France,
fallen out with the
Spanish authorities
and gone over to the
French. His men
received double
rations, a peseta a day,
were encouraged to
loot and took no
prisoners. In 1813 there
was also a woman
leader, La Collegiana,
said to be of noble
birth and beautiful,
who led a band of
mounted followers
and who hid her
gender by wearing a
hussar's jacket and
baggy Mameluke
trousers.

rode to join his great enterprise, he had every reason to feel confident of the outcome. He had more men under his direct command than ever before, his intelligence on the enemy was excellent, the French had been weakened during the winter by demands from Paris, and dispersed and frustrated by intense and widespread guerrilla activity. He was the acknowledged Generalissimo of all Spanish armies, he had been made Colonel of the Blues and had received the Garter (although he had been uncertain whether the ribbon should be worn over the left or right shoulder). According to Picton, as he crossed the border, Wellington, in an uncharacteristically dramatic gesture, turned his horse towards Portugal, raised his hat and cried, 'Farewell Portugal! I shall never see you again.'

Salamanca fell on 26 May (MAP 26), and Hill halted for six days to allow Graham to catch up. Graham's 40,000 were marching in three columns through country thought by the French to be impractical for a large force, and were converging on the Esla River, near its junction with the Duero (Douro). It was a critical crossing: a wild river full of melted snow and as wide as the Thames at Windsor; the possibility of opposition; the imperative need to reunite the two wings, and the need to get the pontoon bridge in place. On the twenty-ninth Wellington rode fifty miles to Miranda and was swung across the Duero gorge suspended in a wicker basket – it must have reminded him of India. He had joined the left wing. *Hogan* was, at the same time, nearing *Adrados*, and Sharpe began his ride to the vicinity of Burgos as Graham's divisions tramped across the pontoon bridge headed for Zamora (MAP 26). The Esla crossing had not been without loss. A difficult ford was found and hussars, with infantry from the 51st (Yorkshire, West Riding) and Brunswick-Oels clinging to their stirrups, struggled over, but not before some twenty men and horses had been swept away. The pontoons were lashed in position. Hill was marching on Toro.

By 3 June the first stage of the campaign was complete, with Wellington and his entire army concentrated north of the Duero. The French had been surprised, masterfully outmanoeuvred, and were streaming north in disarray. Madrid had been abandoned on 27 May; Joseph had ordered a concentration at Valladolid but fell back towards Burgos (watched by Sharpe from a position west of the city). The allied army followed in three columns, continuing their tactic of using a left hook to outflank a series of possible French defensive positions. Hill pushed up the Great Road, and Wellington and Graham moved on minor roads ten or twenty miles to the north-west. Beyond them Giron's Spaniards from Galicia swept east. The only problem was a shortage of bread and some looting of the wine vaults, which the newly formed Staff Corps (provosts) had a hard time controlling. The *S. Essex*, together with the rest of the 5th Division, suffered the

---

Spanish regular troops in French service

SPANISH AND (PORTUGUESE) UNITS fought for France in many parts of the empire, including Spain. Sometimes they clashed with their compatriots – as at Durana village during the Battle of Vitória. In 1807–8 General Romana's Spanish Corps of 9000 served in Denmark as part of Napoleon's army of occupation. John Elting, in his book *Swords Around A Throne*, described these men as, '. . . small but well built for their size . . . They moved lightly, with much talk, laughter and gesticulation followed by a long gaggle of women (described as scarcely seductive), children, horses, asses and mules. A good many of them carried guitars, and they all were readier to dance than drill.' In mid 1808 they mutinied and the majority were secretly evacuated (after killing their horses) by the Royal Navy and delivered to Wellington in the Peninsula. In 1809, those who remained were reformed into the 'Joseph–Napoleon'

Regiment of four line and one depôt battalions. All commands were in Spanish except '*Qui vive?*' (the sentry's challenge); their uniform was white, faced with bright green. The Regiment's depôt at Avignon, so close to the Spanish border, tempted would-be deserters.

Battalions were scattered in May 1810, and saw service in Flushing, Alexandria, Venice, Maastricht, Germany and Russia, where they fought well but were decimated in the retreat from Moscow. The remnants formed the grenadier and voltigeur companies of a new 1st battalion which saw action at Lutzen, Bauzen and Leipzig. In 1814 Ferdinand forbade the repatriation of any Spaniard who had held a rank higher than lieutenant, and the thousands of soldiers who returned were forbidden ever to serve in the Spanish army – no hardship for men who had had their fill of war.

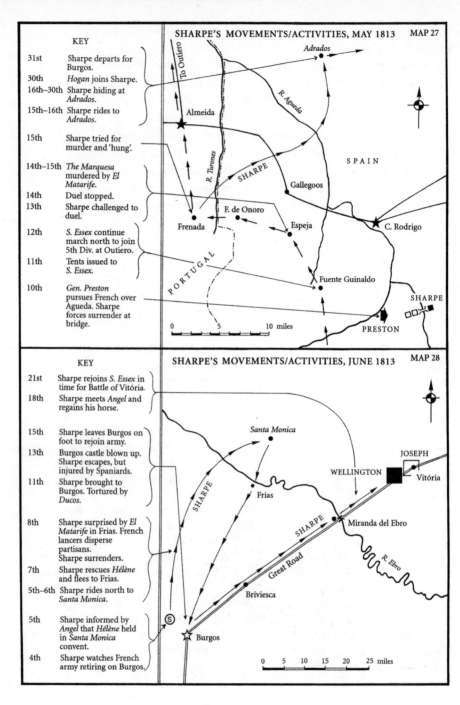

SHARPE'S MOVEMENTS/ACTIVITIES, MAY 1813   MAP 27

KEY

31st — Sharpe departs for Burgos.

30th — *Hogan* joins Sharpe.

16th–30th — Sharpe hiding at *Adrados*.

15th–16th — Sharpe rides to *Adrados*.

15th — Sharpe tried for murder and 'hung'.

14th–15th — *The Marquesa* murdered by *El Matarife*.

14th — Duel stopped.

13th — Sharpe challenged to duel.

12th — *S. Essex* continue march north to join 5th Div. at Outiero.

11th — Tents issued to *S. Essex*.

10th — *Gen. Preston* pursues French over Agueda. Sharpe forces surrender at bridge.

SHARPE'S MOVEMENTS/ACTIVITIES, JUNE 1813   MAP 28

KEY

21st — Sharpe rejoins *S. Essex* in time for Battle of Vitória.

18th — Sharpe meets *Angel* and regains his horse.

15th — Sharpe leaves Burgos on foot to rejoin army.

13th — Burgos castle blown up. Sharpe escapes, but injured by Spaniards.

11th — Sharpe brought to Burgos. Tortured by *Ducos*.

8th — Sharpe surprised by *El Matarife* in Frias. French lancers disperse partisans. Sharpe surrenders.

7th — Sharpe rescues *Hélène* and flees to Frias.

5th–6th — Sharpe rides north to *Santa Monica*.

5th — Sharpe informed by *Angel* that *Hélène* held in *Santa Monica* convent.

4th — Sharpe watches French army retiring on Burgos.

pangs of hunger more than most, although there was always some beef on the hoof.

An interesting incident occurred on 18 June during a clash between a troop of German Hussars at the head of the Light Division commanded by a sergeant, and some German cavalry in the French service. It showed that Sharpe was not the only NCO promoted on the battlefield by Wellington. The skirmish took place at San Millan village. There was a brisk mêlée with vigorous sabre work on both sides. Afterwards, one German hussar came in with a wounded prisoner, exclaiming in broken English, '*Mein Gott! Mein Gott!* He is mine own broder!' Wellington arrived and was so pleased with the troop that he promised the sergeant he would receive a commission – which he did a few days later.

When Sharpe rescued *Hélène* from the clutches of the convent and *El Matarife* at *Santa Monica* on 7 June, Wellington was still sixty miles west of Burgos; when Sharpe was being tortured by *Ducos* in Burgos Castle the allies were only twenty-five miles away; and when the French prematurely blew up the castle walls, elements of Hill's force could see the city. But Sharpe was unable to rejoin the army in Burgos because Wellington embarked on yet another huge left hook which took him fifty miles to the north, passing close to

Spanish
guerrillas

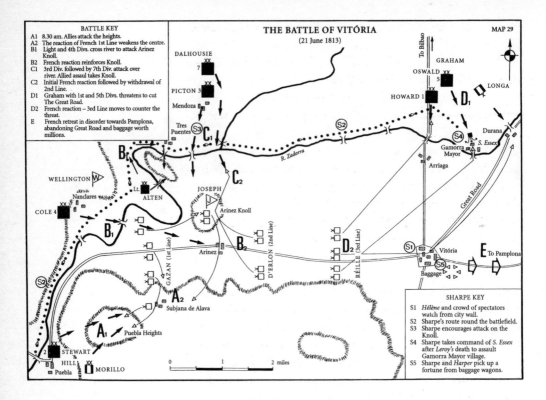

THE BATTLE OF VITÓRIA
(21 June 1813)

MAP 29

BATTLE KEY
A1 8.30 am. Allies attack the heights.
A2 The reaction of French 1st Line weakens the centre.
B1 Light and 4th Divs. cross river to attack Arinez Knoll.
B2 French reaction reinforces Knoll.
C1 3rd Div. followed by 7th Div. attack over river. Allied assault takes Knoll.
C2 Initial French reaction followed by withdrawal of 2nd Line.
D1 Graham with 1st and 5th Divs. threatens to cut The Great Road.
D2 French reaction – 3rd Line moves to counter the threat.
E   French retreat in disorder towards Pamplona, abandoning Great Road and baggage worth millions.

SHARPE KEY
S1 *Hélène* and crowd of spectators watch from city wall.
S2 Sharpe's route round the battlefield.
S3 Sharpe encourages attack on the Knoll.
S4 Sharpe takes command of *S. Essex* after *Leroy's* death to assault Gamorra Mayor village.
S5 Sharpe and *Harper* pick up a fortune from baggage wagons.

Frias and *Santa Monica* before swinging south-east to Vitória. There, on 21 June, Wellington and Sharpe would get the battle they sought.

The Battle of Vitória was Wellington's crowning triumph in the Peninsula. It threw the French out of Spain and it made thousands of troops, like Sharpe and *Harper*, rich beyond their dreams. It was a victory that generals and soldiers alike pray for, giving glory and gold in abundance. The French were evacuating the country en masse, taking with them the proceeds of five years' plundering. Never before in modern times had such a prodigious accumulation of military stores and private wealth fallen to a victorious army. Marshal Jourdan's baton, Joseph's private carriages and sword of state, 151 cannons, 415 *caissons* of ammunition, 40,000 pounds of gunpowder, exquisite jewellery, church treasures, priceless paintings, ornate furniture and rich tapestries were abandoned. But perhaps the biggest prize, for those who could get to it, was the French military chest; over five million dollars had been brought to Vitória – two years' arrears of pay – and was now strewn on the ground like silver leaves.

Vitória rewarded a masterful strategy with a tactical triumph. Before dawn the allies had stood to arms. The battalions were marshalled by torchlight in a light rain, mist hung in the hollows, and soldiers shivered at the dingy start of a midsummer day. The dampness precluded loading, so the S. Essex kept their flintlocks covered and corks in their barrels. Wellington wore a tightly buttoned grey topcoat, only his plumed hat denoting his rank. He had reconnoitred the ground the day before and intended to take position on the steep slope north of the village of Nanclares (MAP 29). It was a good vantage point. When the mist burned off, he could see through his glass the glittering French staff fluttering like a host of gaudy butterflies on the Arinez Knoll directly opposite. (On this hill in the fourteenth century, the Black Prince had lost a hundred knights.) Beyond, eight miles off, the walls and spires of Vitória were just visible through the haze. Here *Hélène* and *Captain Saumier*, with the other privileged spectators, were gathering to watch the show. Several miles to the west, Sharpe was cantering along the verge of the Great Road.

The French had drawn up their three armies of about 60,000 men in three lines, facing west. They hoped – no, believed – that their enemy would keep pushing frontally up the road to Vitória. Their left was guarded by the Puebla Heights, their front and right by the Zadorra River. They were resigned to battle, anxious to hang on until reinforced by Clausel who was hurrying from Pamplona. When he arrived, Wellington's numerical advantage would be negated, and Joseph's chances of getting his convoy of booty over the border into France greatly improved. The French high command, however, had made an inexcusable tactical blunder that morning, so elementary that a corporal of average ability could have spotted it: not one of the ten bridges over the Zadorra had been blown or effectively barricaded.

Wellington's plan was simple, and was based on the manoeuvre that had served him so well over the past month – the left hook. He had no intention of obliging the French with a head-on attack, although he intended to reinforce their belief that he would. The allied army of 79,000 men and 90 guns was split into four columns. On the right was Hill's corps of the 2nd Division (Stewart – 'an officer who never could obey an order') and a Spanish division (Morillo), which was to open the battle by attacking the Puebla Heights. This was important dominating ground on the French left flank, and such an assault would encourage the belief that he was advancing through the Puebla gorge north of that village. In the centre, Wellington took personal command of two columns. That on the right was composed of the Light Division (Alten) and the 4th Division (Cole) with four cavalry brigades. This force would advance through Nanclares as though heading straight for the French first line (Gazan). In reality, these divisions did not attack until Gazan's flanks had both been hit hard.

The left centre column was composed of the 3rd Division (Picton) and the 7th Division (Dalhousie). Its task was to approach unseen from the north, heading for Mendoza village and from there assault across the river towards Arinez Knoll and Gazan's right flank. This would be the short left hook. The fourth column of the 1st Division (Howard), the 5th Division (Oswald) and a Spanish brigade (Longa) under Graham provided the long left hook, marching unseen beyond the hills north of the Zadorra aiming first for the Vitória–Bilbao road, and then south for the bridges at Arriaga, Gamorra Mayor and Durana. Its primary task was to cut the Great Road, Joseph's umbilical cord with France.

At nine o'clock Sharpe was still an hour's ride from Puebla so he did not hear the popping of muskets which heralded the start of the action. Half an hour earlier Morillo's Spaniards had begun to scramble up the almost sheer slopes of the Puebla Heights. An observer commented, 'The ascent was so steep that while moving up it they looked as if they were lying on their faces and crawling.' The French pickets fell back but Gazan rushed a brigade up the hill from Subijana to hold the Spaniards. Fighting became intense. Morillo was hit but refused to leave the field, and Colonel Cadogan (a close personal friend of Wellington), whose 1/71st (Highland) had been sent to assist Morillo, was mortally wounded. He insisted on being carried forward so that he could watch the battle as he lay dying. As the morning progressed, more troops from each side were committed to the struggle for the Heights and Subijana village. At one point the 1/71st were forced to flee, but French reinforcements were sucked into the struggle from Gazan's centre to contain Hill's progress.

Sharpe arrived at Puebla sometime after 10 a.m. He was delayed by the crush of troops in the gorge and his enquiries as to the whereabouts of the 5th Division. He followed the river north and became entangled with battalions of the Light Division waiting to cross the river. Wellington had been forced to hold back his centre as the short left hook (Picton and Dalhousie) was late. However, a Spanish peasant brought to him insisted the bridge at Tres Puentes was unguarded and that he would lead the British to it. Wellington sent Kempt's brigade. The 1/95th, led by Colonel Barnard, followed the panting Spaniard at the double along the river bank, hidden from the French by the clifflike hill on the other side. They raced around the hairpin river bend and dashed over the bridge. The only casualty was the helpful peasant, who was decapitated by a roundshot. The fight for Arinez Knoll had started.

By the time Sharpe had got past Kempt's brigade, asked repeatedly for the 5th Division and been recognised as the man supposedly hanged five weeks earlier, it was after midday. As he cleared Tres Puentes village, he met the leading elements of Picton's 3rd Division in the process of assaulting over the Mendoza bridge. He took it on himself to encourage a hesitant brigade to join in. Shortly before Sharpe appeared, Picton, in blue coat and top-hat, whose temper was notoriously short-fused, had been cursing and slapping his horse's mane with his cane – a certain sign of an imminent explosion. 'Damn it! Lord Wellington must have forgotten us.' At last an ADC galloped up.

'Have you seen Lord Dalhousie?'

COLONEL HENRY CADOGAN

His death was a severe blow to Wellington, who wrote, 'My grief for the loss of Cadogan takes away all my satisfaction at our success.' Cadogan's sister was married to Henry Wellesley (Wellington's younger brother). In 1809 she was seduced by, and ran off with, Lord Henry Paget (he later commanded the cavalry at Waterloo). Cadogan tried desperately to stop this, even going to the extent of duelling with Paget on Wimbledon Common, with pistols. Cadogan missed, and Paget refused to fire back.

'No, sir! I have not seen his Lordship; but have you any orders for me?'

'None.'

'Then pray, sir, what orders do you bring?'

'Why, that as soon as Lord Dalhousie with the 7th Division shall commence an attack on that bridge [Mendoza bridge] the Fourth and Light are to support him.'

Picton exploded. His face red with rage he yelled at the flabbergasted ADC, 'You may tell Lord Wellington from me, sir, that the 3rd Division under my command shall in less than ten minutes attack the bridge and carry it, and the Fourth and Light may support if they choose.'

He kept his word. Gazan's line was outflanked, the assault on Arinez Hill could not be repelled, and with the launching of Cole's 4th Division over the Nanclares bridge the whole French 1st line was rolled back.

When Sharpe at last crossed the Vitória–Bilbao road, it was mid afternoon and the *S. Essex* had led the first unsuccessful assault on the village of Gamorra Mayor. *Lieutenant-Colonel Leroy* was dead and the battalion, seriously shaken, was falling back. Graham has been accused of holding back, of not attacking earlier (he had reached the area in the morning), thus allowing the French to move two of Réille's divisions across the bridges and form strong bridgeheads north of the river. Picton would probably not have waited, but Graham followed instructions. He was not to attack until he received a specific order; that order was timed at 2 p.m. and took an hour to reach him. Wellington wanted to be certain that the fighting in the centre was successful before committing the long left hook. By two o'clock Joseph had abandoned Arinez Hill and his first and second lines had merged under enormous pressure. His third line was no longer west of Vitória but north of the river facing the menace of Graham's thrust at the Great Road. Some of Graham's command had been spotted arriving during the morning and Réille had rushed two divisions across the Zadorra at Arriaga and Gamorra Mayor to block him. Spanish regiments loyal to France were positioned at the Durana bridge.

Sharpe rallied his battalion, assumed command and led it forward in company columns in a second assault on Gamorra Mayor. It was supported by the remainder of Robinson's brigade, also now in column. The *S. Essex* secured the houses, but could not cross the bridge. Some of the most ferocious fighting of the battle raged for three hours around the bridges and villages of Arriaga and Gamorra Mayor. The bridge at Gamorra was taken and retaken by the French several times during the afternoon. Meanwhile Longa's Spaniards had clashed with their compatriots for the crossing at Durana. After a brief but bloody battle, Longa was over the river and astride the Great Road. Joseph, whose main position was now not more than a mile west of Vitória and crumbling fast, ordered a withdrawal along the Pamplona road, climbed into his carriage and headed east. For the French it became a '*sauve qui peut*' situation. For the Allies the cry was, metaphorically, '*vive le pillage*', provoking Wellington into his oft-quoted description of his soldiers as 'the scum of the earth'. The cavalry, however, got the pickings.

Captain Wyndham of the 14th Light Dragoons and

Joseph's narrow escape

HAVING GIVEN the order to retreat, Joseph clambered into his carriage and, with a mounted escort, forced his way through the congestion to the road east of Vitória. Here his progress was handicapped by the seething crush of animals, wagons and humanity which barred the way. No amount of lashing and cursing, jolting and jarring could clear the royal route. The carriage, its doors boldly emblazoned with the royal arms of Spain and the Napoleonic Eagle, was overtaken by Captain Wyndham of the 14th Light Dragoons, who drew level with the carriage and fired a pistol through the near window. The opposite door flew open and Joseph made a dash towards his escort, who were ahead trying to force a passage. He was hauled up onto a riderless horse and disappeared in the confusion. His carriage was captured: inside was his ornate silver 'pot de chambre'. It was christened 'The Emperor', and the successors of the 14th Light Dragoons still use it for champagne toasts at mess dinners, after which the pot is placed ceremoniously on the head of the officer who finishes the drink. Another carriage yielded up the King's sword of state.

Marshal Jourdan's baton

AMONG THE FINEST TROPHIES seized at Vitória was Marshal Jourdan's baton. Only one other baton of a Napoleonic marshal was ever taken by the enemy, that of Marshal Davout, found by a Cossack in his carriage amid the snows of the Moscow retreat. Jourdan, who had been sick during the day, abandoned his carriage and fled on horseback, leaving behind his baton. It was over a foot long, covered in blue velvet embroidered with 32 Eagles, and in a red morocco case with silver eagles and clasps. At each end, in gold characters, was written, 'Le Marechal Jean-Baptiste Jourdan'. The finder had wrenched off the gold bands that tipped it before handing it to Colonel Gough who commanded the 87th (Prince of Wales' Irish) at Vitória. Wellington sent it to the Prince Regent who had him promoted field-marshal and given a British baton. He became the first British general to attain that rank; all subsequent field-marshals have received identical batons.

ARMY AUCTIONS

It was the normal custom for personal effects in the baggage of officers (and sometimes men) who had died on campaign to be sold by auction among their comrades. The amateur auctioneer displayed his grim humour with cries of, 'Shirt with nine tails!' or 'Trousers with holes to cool the blood.' Captured French baggage was sometimes auctioned off and the proceeds distributed among the soldiers who had seized it. This depended on the generosity of the commander, and happened during the advance to Vitória when General Alten arranged a sale of

Lieutenant Lord Worcester of the 10th Hussars were among the first to arrive at the city's eastern gate, where an incredible scene confronted them. As far as one could see, the ground was choked with carriages 'filled with imploring ladies', wagons with coin and ammunition, droves of cattle, sheep, goats and mules. At one point, heavy wagons lettered 'Domaine Extérieure de S. M. l'Empereur' blocked the way; at another was a string of Spanish court conveyances and a huddled mass of commissariat wagons, rows of powder and baggage wagons, carts laden with provisions and wine-casks, ox-carts heaped with furniture and booty from every part of Spain. All around carriages carried the wives, mistresses (plus *Hélène* and *Captain Saumier*) and children of high-ranking officers or civil officials (many of whom had been with *Hélène* watching events from the west wall). Some of these women had abandoned their carriages out of sheer fright and were 'scuttling about with tucked up petticoats', frantically seeking assistance, some of them holding shrieking infants in their arms, others carrying lap-dogs, parrots in cages and even monkeys. Everywhere was terror; everywhere was panic.

Infantry looters had problems with their booty – carrying it and keeping it secure during the weeks ahead. Sharpe and

The Treaty of Valençay

Towards the end of 1813, when Napoleon's empire was tottering, attempts were made by diplomatic methods to redeem the military situation. The offer to Prince Ferdinand, who had been held in France since 1808, was restoration of his Spanish kingdom; French forces would be withdrawn from Catalonia, and the thousands of Spanish prisoners in France would be repatriated. In return, Ferdinand had to marry an imperial nominee, end hostilities, terminate the alliance with Britain (this was the clause that *Ducos* rightly regarded as crucial), and grant an amnesty to all *afrancesados* (Spanish collaborators).

The possibility of such a deal being struck and his army being compelled to leave the Peninsula certainly worried Wellington, and he expressed his concern in his despatches. Ferdinand signed in December 1813, and was repatriated, but he had done so only in order to get back to Spain. The Cortés refused to ratify the treaty, claiming Ferdinand had no legal authority to sign it and that it was void. For a while the French endeavoured to keep their side of the deal, but by March 1814 they too realised that the treaty was worthless.

Harper were lucky to be able to stuff jewels and coins into haversacks, but many items were bulky – or even alive. Sergeant Costello of the 95th has left an account of how these difficulties could be overcome:

> The next morning the sale of the spoils which fell into our hands took place ... The Spaniards were in general the purchasers, and property such as ... uniforms, horses, camp equipage etc. was sold in abundance at about one-tenth of its value. Mules worth thirty or forty dollars brought on average three. As I had no means of conveyance for the spoil I had obtained, I set about disposing it where I thought it would be safe. Three hundred pounds I entrusted to our quartermaster, and several sums to other officers of the battalion, distributing ... about one hundred pounds among the men of my own squad; very little of the latter, however, I ever received back.

baggage taken during a skirmish at San Millan. A variety of loot was auctioned, including horses, mules, carts, even feminine underwear belonging to Spanish women married to French officers taken prisoner. The money was distributed to 2/95th, who had captured the wagons.

Wellington had won a great victory. Sharpe and some of his men picked up fortunes. France had lost it all, including Spain.

12

Sharpe's Regiment

THE ESSEX REGT.

At the time of the Peninsular War, the 44th and 56th Foot were the East and West Essex Regiments respectively. Both had two battalions. The 44th, like the S. Essex, had yellow facings. The 1/44th served in Sicily in 1809, then Naples, then the east coast of Spain in 1813–14, and finally in America. The 2/44th served in the 5th Division in 1811, 1812 and 1813. The battalion was at Badajoz and captured the Eagle of the French 62nd Ligne at Salamanca. By 1813 it was so reduced in numbers (with both battalions overseas) that it was amalgamated with the 2/30th (Cambridgeshire) to form the 4th Provisional Battalion. Reinforced, it fought at Quatre Bras and Waterloo. The 1/56th (West Essex) served in India during this period. The 2/56th were in Africa and India.

This book covers the period from July to October 1813, from the Battle of Vitória to the Battle of the Nivelle. Sharpe and *Harper* spent these months in England trying to raise recruits for the *1st Battalion S. Essex*, which needed urgent reinforcement if it was to avoid being broken up. They discovered that *Lord Fenner, Colonel Simmerson* and the commanding officer at the Chelmsford depôt, *Lieutenant-Colonel Girdwood,* had been making a fortune by 'selling' recruits to other regiments. This 'crimping' within the army was illegal; Sharpe and *Harper* had to enlist under false names to expose what was happening. After some extraordinary scrapes at Chelmsford, and in his childhood haunts in London, Sharpe was able to muster several companies of the *S. Essex,* parade them at a Hyde Park Review in front of the Prince Regent, and return to Spain with them in time to fight at the Nivelle crossing.

THE ALLIED PURSUIT after Vitória was not pressed with vigour; too many units were preoccupied gathering plunder, and the victory had temporarily demoralised the army. Major Harry Smith of the Light Division wrote that the soldiery, '. . . after many days of privation, had so gorged themselves and loaded their haversacks that they were hardly able to move . . . the soldiers have got among them about a million in sterling.' Detachments left in the city to preserve order and collect the wounded behaved outrageously. The S. Essex were one of these units, although there is no evidence as to how they conducted themselves. Their battle casualties had been severe – death and wounds at the Gamorra Mayor bridge had crippled the battalion. Sharpe reported to *Major-General Nairn* that he had 234 effectives on parade at the end of June – no wonder they were employed on fatigues and guard duties around the docks at Pasajes.

A battalion of under 300 was doomed to disbandment unless reinforced substantially. They had been expecting drafts for some weeks from the *2nd Battalion* recruiting in Essex. The infantry regiments serving in the Peninsula were composed of either one or two battalions, the theory being that the 1st Battalion served overseas while the second, based at home, provided regular drafts of trained men to replace wastage in the field. With single-battalion regiments reliance had to be placed on the depôt to supply reinforcements. The *S. Essex* had been authorised to form a *2nd Battalion* at the start of 1813, so drafts were now overdue. After its disastrous encounter at *Valdelacasa* three years previously, Wellington had made the *S. Essex* a battalion of detachments. Its fate was now again uncertain.

There were several possibilities. If the *2nd Battalion* sent

Temporary rank

IN THE PENINSULA, as in most wars, dead men's shoes were the easiest and quickest means of climbing (albeit temporarily) the promotion ladder. Sharpe was temporary commanding officer of the S. Essex at Vitória and the Nivelle due to the death or illness of the substantive commander. Temporary rank was the norm throughout the war. After the Battle of Bussaco in 1810 the records show 2 units (both Guards) commanded by colonels, 30 by lieutenant-colonels, 16 by majors and 1 by a captain. The situation within a brigade of the 2nd Division after the Battle of Albuera (1811), was unique: it

went into the action 1651 strong and suffered 1054 casualties – a bigger butcher's bill than the breach at Badajoz or the ridge at Waterloo. The acting brigade commander the next day was a French emigré captain called Cimitière who paraded an ad hoc battalion of under 600.

It was possible for a lieutenant-colonel to command a division. The best example was Lieutenant-Colonel Andrew Barnard who commanded the Light Division for five months, and led it at the storming of Badajoz after Craufurd was killed. The only other general in the division (Vandeleur) had been wounded at Ciudad Rodrigo.

at least 400 men the *S. Essex* could function as a combat unit again. If not, it might be amalgamated with another in similar circumstances to form a Provisional Battalion, which had been in existence since the previous year and had worked reasonably well. The sister battalion of the *S. Essex*, the 2/44th (Essex), had recently combined successfully with the 2/30th (Cambridgeshire). This system was favoured by Wellington, who preferred to keep his veterans in Spain – rightly so: four companies of experienced, hardened, acclimatised troops were worth double the number of inexperienced recruits arriving as a battalion of novices. This was why Sharpe was allowed to spend three months drumming up reinforcements. If he failed, the remnants of the battalion would be dispersed to other units, the Colours hung up in a Chelmsford church, and the regimental history of the *S. Essex* would not be worth writing.

The system of commanding, financing, recruiting and administering the British army in 1813 was complicated and, in many respects, corrupt. As Sharpe quickly discovered in England, many men became rich by 'ripping off' the military. A substantial number of politicians, officers (both senior and junior), civil servants and contractors worked the system for financial gain. It was a venal age. The salaries of office-holders, and the rewards given to senior military and naval officers, were extremely high, perhaps ten times that of their modern counterparts (Wellington became the equivalent of a multi-millionaire through his military service). Some of the practices legally engaged in by officials would today be considered outright theft. But then, when miscreants were exposed they were rarely punished, so abuses abounded.

The complexity of the system encouraged waste and bred corruption. In constitutional theory the monarch was head of the army, but in practice could do nothing without Parliament's passing the annual Mutiny Act which provided the money to keep the army in being. However, it was the sovereign's commission that appointed officers and he or she was the colonel-in-chief of numerous regiments (these royal

The Duke of York's resignation

IN 1809 the duke was charged in the House of Commons with the corrupt employment of his patronage in the granting of military appointments, commissions and promotions. The charge was investigated by a committee of the whole House. The duke had kept a mistress, Mrs Mary Ann Clarke, for a number of years. She was a beautiful, charming but expensive luxury. As Fortescue puts it, '. . . she was an unmitigated rogue [and] her extravagance was unspeakable.' In three years the duke had parted with £16,000, but despite his generosity she was always heavily in debt. In 1806 he tried to buy her off with a £400 a year pension. This was soon withdrawn and, in 1808, Mrs Clarke resorted to blackmail, threatening to publish all his letters and reveal everything that had come to her knowledge during her intimacy with him. The duke defied her.

The inquiry showed that she had received hundreds of letters and bribes from people anxious to promote their interests in the army, and public service, through her influence. She had not been above forging the Duke's handwriting, but it was shown conclusively that the duke had no knowledge of what was happening. The House overwhelmingly acquitted him, but he resigned as commander-in-chief. His absence for two years was a heavy blow to the army.

prerogatives remain today). When Sharpe arrived in England, King George III had been declared insane, so the Prince of Wales was Prince Regent. He was eventually able to confirm Sharpe as a major, endow the *S. Essex* with royal patronage and change their title to *The Prince of Wales' Own Volunteers (PWOV)*. Once this happened, their future was more secure, despite the Prince Regent's being a total ignoramus regarding serious soldiering and continually at loggerheads with his brother, the Duke of York, the commander-in-chief of the army in England.

Although Sharpe cleverly secured the support of the Prince Regent in his efforts to rescue his Regiment, he was able to do so only after outmanoeuvring the dishonest and unscrupulous politician, *Lord Fenner*, who held the powerful post of Secretary at War. Although not in the Cabinet, and nominally under the Secretary for War and the Colonies, *Fenner* was responsible to Parliament for the financial affairs of the army. He had formerly been the king's personal

CARLTON HOUSE,
PALL MALL

Built in the early
eighteenth century.
When Sharpe visited it
was the residence of
the Prince Regent – a
luxurious palace with
Corinthian columns,
hall, octagonal double
staircase, dining room,
bedrooms, and
elaborate Chinese
drawing room
(admired by Sharpe),
agents having travelled
to China for the
furniture. The huge
extensions and
decorations
continued
intermittently for
thirty years, at
enormous cost, and it
was the scene of many
grand receptions. A
fête for Wellington in
1814 had 2000 guests.
When he became
King George IV, the
former Prince of
Wales thought it
unworthy of his new
status so the building,
described by Horace
Walpole as 'the most
perfect palace in
Europe', was
demolished. Its
columns were used for
the portico of the
National Gallery,
several fireplaces,
furniture and doors
went to Buckingham
Palace and Windsor
Castle.

secretary for military matters and retained the right of direct
access to the sovereign 'in his closet'. He supervised the War
Office, whose main functions were fiscal: it paid the army
(with the co-operation of the Paymaster-General), audited
regimental accounts, approved movements of units and negotiated the passage of the Mutiny Act through Parliament. It
also defended the annual military budget in the House of
Commons. Such a position offered enormous scope for personal enrichment which *Fenner* exploited to the full. It is
strange that he was involved in the comparatively minor
transgression of crimping with the *S. Essex*, but his friendship
with (and possible indebtedness to) *Colonel Simmerson* was
surely part of the explanation.

Sharpe had experience of *Fenner*'s bureaucracy when he
had dealt with the clerk responsible for the muddle over the
records of his commissioning. These individuals had almost
unlimited opportunities for wielding their petty powers and
making money: they attended the office for only five hours
daily, received extra pay for work taken home and, additionally, many were entitled to sinecure allowances. One example
was the clerk permitted to supply coal to the garrison at
Gibraltar for a profit; another, the chief messenger who
charged exorbitant fees for the delivery of messages, thus
securing an annual income of £500 sterling – 25 per cent
more than a full colonel. According to Fortescue, '. . . the
whole place [War Office] was a sink of jobbery and extortion,
the more repulsive since there were hundreds of deserving
officers, crippled by long service and wounds, who were starv-
ing on a pittance of half-pay.'

The offices of the commander-in-chief were at Horse
Guards, in Whitehall. Despite his grand title, his authority
was limited to the infantry and cavalry Regiments of the Line.
He had no control over the Foot Guards and Life Guards
(except through the king and their colonels), nor could he
issue orders to the artillery, the engineers, the militia,
the volunteers, the yeomanry or the supply services. The
Duke of York was, however, a professional soldier and
proved an able military administrator and reformer. His

ABOVE The assault on the 'Great Breach' at Ciudad Rodrigo on 19 January 1812 by Lt-General Picton's 3rd Division. The French have just exploded a mine that severely wounded *Lt-Col. Lawford* of the *S. Essex* as he watched the assault.

RIGHT The Forlorn Hope of the 4th Division. A young subaltern moves forward under cover to rush the righthand breach at Badajoz on 6 April 1812.

BELOW RIGHT The escalade of the walls at Badajoz on 6 April 1812 by General Picton's 3rd Division. The drawing shows the assault on the castle wall which succeeded, whereas the attacks on the breaches did not. In *Sharpe's Company, Captain Knowles* was the first man up the ladders.

The bridge and cathedral at Salamanca. It was in the foreground that *Lt-Col. Windham*, the commanding officer of the *S. Essex*, was killed by *Col. Leroux* before he made his escape across the bridge in to the city on 17 June 1812.

Inside the Irish College at Salamanca today. In this passage way *Colonel Leroux* fought with Sharpe. The door on the left leads to Father Curtis's room.

The Battle of Vitoria, 21 June 1813. A scene towards the end of the battle as the Allies close in on the city. At this stage, the chaotic exodus from the other side of the city would have begun.

RIGHT King George IV when Prince of Wales (and Prince Regent). Sharpe secured his patronage for the *S. Essex* and the title *The Prince of Wales' Own Volunteers*. Note the Prince of Wales' feathers above his head which were incorporated into the badge of the PWOV.

BELOW A cartoon of the period showing the Duke of York as Commander-in-Chief of the British Army, agreeing to promote his mistress' friends. Although exonerated of the charges, he voluntarily resigned but was reappointed within two years as the only man competent to fill the post.

BELOW RIGHT 'Slender Billy', the Prince of Orange, later King William II of Holland. He was Sharpe's corps commander at the Battle of Quatre Bras and Waterloo. Sharpe became so exasperated with his stupidity that he deliberately shot him in the shoulder at Waterloo.

OPPOSITE ABOVE British cavalry get in amongst the French baggage carts at the end of the Battle of Vitoria. It was the cavalry that got the first pickings of the plunder and almost captured Joseph Bonaparte, Napoleon's brother.

BELOW The crush of carriages (which included *Hélène*'s) struggling to leave Vitoria as the French accept defeat on 21 June 1813. It was in these circumstances that Sharpe and *Harper* (and hundreds of other Allied troops) picked up a fortune in jewels and coins.

LEFT Sergeant Ewart of the Scots Greys captures the Eagle Standard of the French 45th Regiment at the Battle of Waterloo.

BELOW The French Eagle Standard of the 45th Regiment captured by Sergeant Ewart.

OPPOSITE ABOVE The Battle of Waterloo. A Highland regiment in a square repulses French cuirassiers during one of the numerous cavalry charges launched by Marshal Ney during the battle. Sharpe and *Harper* took shelter first inside a Guards' square and later inside that of the *PWOV* (*S. Essex*).

BELOW The scene at the north gate of Hougoumont as Capt. and Lt-Col. James MacDonnell (the officer with the sword) and others struggle to close the gates after Sous-Lieut. Legros and his men have burst through. Sharpe and *Harper* were fighting at this moment with Legros in the yard.

The Allied Union Brigade (heavy cavalry) capturing some of the guns of the French 'Grand Battery' at Waterloo. They had in fact over-reached themselves and were soon driven off with heavy losses by a French cavalry counter-attack. *Lord John Rossendale* was severely wounded and later murdered by a looter nearby.

The end of Waterloo and the remains of a French rearguard of the Imperial Guard in the late evening of 18 June 1815.

performance as a field commander was less successful. As a young soldier of sixteen in the 33rd Foot (1st West Riding), Sharpe had experienced the shambles of the Flanders expedition in 1794; the duke's role is recalled for posterity in the nursery rhyme about marching 10,000 men up and down hills to no purpose. His dealings with his brother (the Prince Regent, who had a grossly inflated opinion of his military abilities) ranged from frigid tolerance to absolute rejection. When Sharpe arrived in England in July 1813, the duke had been back in his post for two years. Although appointed in 1795, he had resigned in 1809 because of financial double-dealing and blackmail by his mistress, Mrs Anne Clarke. Within two years he was reappointed as the only person capable of sorting out the mess his senile successor (Lord Dundas) was making.

Yet another person of exalted rank had authority over vital elements of the country's armed services – the Master-General of the Ordnance. He was usually a soldier, always in the Cabinet and was regarded by the government as their principal military adviser. His command was limited to the artillery, the engineers and their supporting services; he also had responsibility for the manufacture of cannons and sup-plying them, as well as arms, ammunition, greatcoats, maps and assorted military stores to the troops. In 1811, Lord Mul-grove was appointed; he was 'too old and ill' to remain at the Admiralty. None of these office-holders could achieve anything of consequence without the co-operation of the Treasury, which provided food, forage and fuel. In the Penin-sula this necessitated setting up a commissariat, so a massively cumbersome civilian army of commissariat officers, contrac-tors, local merchants, drivers, wagons, carts, mules, horses and oxen was improvised.

During the early years of the nineteenth century, ordinary recruiting (the likes of *Sergeant Havercamp* persuading or tricking volunteers to enlist) could not keep pace with losses. The annual loss from all causes (death, discharge and deser-tion) never fell below 16,000 (in 1806) and climbed as high as 25,500 in 1812. Recruiting brought in 15,000 in a good year

BOUNTY-JUMPER
EXECUTED

Rifleman Harris (95th) was a member of the firing party that shot a man who had enlisted sixteen times. There were sixteen in the squad. The prisoner, arms bound, was blindfolded and made to kneel behind a coffin. Then, '... the drum-major giving us an expressive glance, we commenced loading ... There was then a dreadful pause ... the drum-major, again looking towards us, gave the signal before agreed (a flourish of his cane) and we levelled and fired.' The victim fell back and Harris observed that, 'his hands wavered for a few moments like the fins of a fish in his death agonies'. The drum-major signalled four men forward who fired point-blank into his head. Companies were marched past in slow time, marking time when close to the mangled remains, so that all had a good look.

BREAKING
TRIGGER-FINGERS

Joining the army was, for most, to be avoided. The ballot, which took place in every parish, was in effect a draft that the able-bodied and poor

(1807) and only a little over 7000 in a poor one (1810). The reason for this shortfall, at a time when the army was desperately looking to expand, was the militia. It was composed of men compelled to serve (by the ballot) but who could not be sent overseas, and in 1808 its strength was nearly 87,000 men. If a militiamen joined the regular army, he could be imprisoned for six months.

By 1813, when Sharpe went hunting overdue reinforcements, this obstacle had been removed. Soldiers in the militia could now volunteer for a lifetime of regular service, or for a seven-year engagement, and bounties to do so were high. Given the choice, few would have joined the military, but if a person was caught by the ballot (virtually a draft) there was the possibility of paying a substitute 20–25 guineas to serve for you, which secured exemption for life. If no substitute could be found, the payment of fifteen guineas postponed enlistment for five years. Once in, militia service was limited to twenty-eight days of training annually and the recruit could not be sent to dangerous stations such as the Peninsula or the 'Sugar Islands' (Caribbean), where disease took a notoriously high toll. Once the militia was open to regular recruiting, regiments concentrated their efforts on it, because they got a better class of man than the rogues, criminals, drunks and down-and-outs who enlisted directly. Above all they would get partially trained soldiers, men who were disciplined, could drill and load their muskets. This is why *Simmerson* and *Girdwood* were doing so well out of 'selling' the trained soldiers of the *2nd Battalion* of the *S. Essex* for £50 a head. They were of even greater value than militiamen, so it was a huge success. Between January and September 1809 almost 50 per cent of 112,000 recruits were ex-militiamen.

The only way Sharpe and *Harper* could find out quickly what was happening at Chelmsford was by enlisting with the nearest *S. Essex* recruiting sergeant (*Havercamp*). The men who joined with them were a not untypical bunch of 'King's hard bargains'. A similar group of ordinary volunteers has been described by Oman as '... the usual raw stuff swept up by the recruiting sergeant – all those restless spirits caught

Enlistment for life – or not?

AFTER 1808, a man joining the regular army had a choice of signing on for life or seven years (with the option of renewing his engagement). There was an extra five guineas if he did the former. It might be supposed that prudence would have persuaded most recruits taking their first step into the military to err on the side of caution. Statistics prove otherwise: the meagre extra bounty, plus undoubted assistance from the bottle, was enough to get 75 per cent to sign their lives away. Of 3143 who enlisted in 1814, only 772 took the seven-year option. While 29 per cent of English recruits and 25 per cent of Scots showed circumspection, only one out of 566 Irishmen limited his service. Why did they join at all? A survey done in 1840 is perhaps relevant for the earlier years of that century. The reasons given (out of 120 men):

– Unemployed seeking work (regular meals)	80
– Respectable persons induced by misfortune or imprudence	2
– Idle; those who think army life easy	16
– Bad characters/criminals	9
– Perverse sons who sought to grieve their parents	2
– Discontented and restless	8
– Ambitious	1
– Others	2

by the attraction of the red coat, country lads tired of the plough or town lads who lived on the edge of unemployment, and to whom a full stomach had been for sometime a rarity ... sons of hard fathers and stepsons of intolerable stepmothers ... rowdy spirits who were wanted by the constable ... Not only were there poachers [who, like *Dan Hagman*, usually made excellent infantrymen], smugglers and streetcorner roughs, but pickpockets, coiners and footpads.'

A disproportionate number were Irishmen. Some joined with the intention of becoming 'bounty jumpers', men who enlisted one day and deserted as soon as possible, only to re-enlist under a different name in a different regiment for another bounty. For a few this became a way of life. The penalty if caught was death. The record was a man in Ipswich who was hanged in 1787 after confessing to bounty jumping 49 times, thus 'earning' 397 guineas.

As Sharpe discovered at Chelmsford and Foulness, *Fenner, Simmerson, Girdwood* and the junior officers were all

could not avoid without considerable expense. Farmers who needed their sons to work for them sometimes deliberately broke their child's forefinger, in the hope that a deformed trigger-finger would bar them from military service. Rifleman Harris's father had done this, but it did not deter the recruiting sergeant.

FOULNESS ISLAND

All traces of the secret camp of the *S. Essex* have long since disappeared from the island. It is possible that *Simmerson*'s house was located north of the village of Great Wakering. The bridge in the south connecting the island to the mainland is still used, and the island remains much as it did in Sharpe's day: a complex and confusing maze of channels, creeks and streams, many of them tidal. It is possible to locate the approximate spot where the unfortunate *Marriott* was shot. The remote village of Churchend is approached from the south across flat, marshy ground which is now a military live firing area. Access is still restricted.

implicated in 'crimping'. A crimp was a person who, for a fee, undertook to produce recruits for the army, selling men for profit. This was not illegal if carried on by civilians, but was not permitted by serving officers or high officials such as *Fenner*. There was more to it than just crimping. The *2nd Battalion* of 700 men was in camp at Foulness, from where it was being sold off as it completed training to unpopular regiments in desperate need of recruits. It should have been at the Chelmsford depôt sending drafts to Spain. The pay for 700 soldiers was going to the corrupt officers involved, with the knowledge of *Fenner* at the War Office. Indeed it was his department which was charged with auditing regimental accounts. There was now no *2nd Battalion*, merely a holding unit for a handful of sick or time-expired men awaiting discharge; no recruits went to Chelmsford for training. Instead, as happened to Sharpe and *Harper*, they were marched to the secret, isolated camp at Foulness for training and sale. These were the rackets that Sharpe exposed.

Sharpe's visits to London took him back to St Giles Rookery where he had spent so much of his boyhood (MAP 30). Rookeries were the worst slums in London: narrow alleys full of garbage, open drains, gambling dens, brothels, decrepit boarding houses, taverns and gin-shops. They were places of poverty, filth, decay, drunkenness and disease, and the refuge of the most vicious gangs who wielded the knife and the cudgel with impunity. They were places of maimings and murders. To reach the age of thirty in a rookery was to be old.

Of these, St Giles was perhaps the most infamous. It was bounded by Great Russell Street, Bloomsbury Street, Broad Street and St Giles's High Street. Today's Tottenham Court Road tube station marks its centre. The area has a long history, growing around a leper hospital founded in 1101. In 1417 Sir John Oldcastle was hanged in chains over a slow fire for having plotted a *coup d'état* in St Giles; it was not a regular place of execution, although tradition says condemned criminals were offered a final drink at the Bowl Tavern – invariably gin.

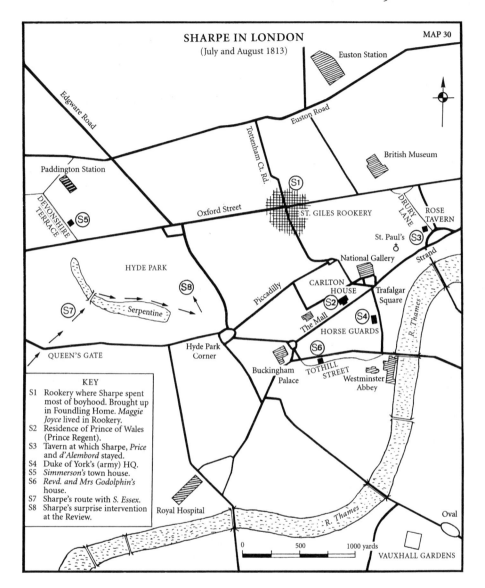

SHARPE IN LONDON
(July and August 1813)

MAP 30

KEY
S1 Rookery where Sharpe spent most of boyhood. Brought up in Foundling Home. *Maggie Joyce* lived in Rookery.
S2 Residence of Prince of Wales (Prince Regent).
S3 Tavern at which Sharpe, *Price* and *d'Alembord* stayed.
S4 Duke of York's (army) HQ.
S5 *Simmerson's* town house.
S6 *Revd. and Mrs Godolphin's* house.
S7 Sharpe's route with *S. Essex.*
S8 Sharpe's surprise intervention at the Review.

The eighteenth century was, in London in particular, the great gin-drinking period. Over 90 per cent of the country's gin was distilled (and probably drunk) in London at the time of Sharpe's boyhood. Gin-drinking was a disease of poverty: it was cheap, warming and brought forgetfulness. It also

IRISH ENLISTMENT

Wherever there was action in the Napoleonic Wars, there was an Irishman. This is no exaggeration. They fought for France, for Spain, for Portugal and for the United States as well as for England. London was awash with poor Irish (mostly living in the rookeries) in search of work. The army offered food, money, drink and the chance of a scrap, and the British army had 13 battalions almost wholly recruited in Ireland. Virtually every other regiment had a strong Irish contingent, and in some battalions the proportion was extraordinarily high. In 1809 the 57th (West Middlesex) had 34 per cent Irish; in the 29th (Worcestershire) it rose from 19 to 37 per cent. Scottish regiments, however, were more clannish – the Gordon Highlanders had only 6 per cent Irish in 1813 and a mere 3 per cent English.

INSURANCE AGAINST THE BALLOT

One popular way of avoiding enlistment, even if balloted to do so, was insurance to pay for a substitute or the exemption fee, and insurance

brought death. In 1750, out of 2000 dwelling houses 506 were gin-shops. *Maggie Joyce*, Sharpe's rescuer when he absconded from the foundling home and a life climbing chimneys, ran one such – part gin-shop, part 'two-penny house', part brothel. A two-penny house was a lodging house where the cost of a bed in a tiny, stinking room with four other beds was two pennies. A Mrs Farrel, whose death in St Giles was recorded in 1765, owned twenty such houses and had amassed a fortune of £6000. Like many such landladies, she was Irish.

A report in the mid-nineteenth century about St Giles Rookery contains this passage:

> But nine-tenths of the inhabitants are Irish ... the Irish coming to London seem to regard it as a heathen city and to give themselves up at once to a course of recklessness and crime ... The misery, filth and crowded condition of the Irish cabin is realised in St Giles ... in the very densest part of which the wretchedness of London takes shelter ... In one house a hundred persons have been known to sleep on one

The Rose Tavern

night . . . In these rooms are piled the wares by which some of the inhabitants gain their precarious living – oranges, herrings, water-cresses, onions . . .

The Rose Tavern in Drury Lane where Sharpe, *D'Alembord* and *Price* stayed in 1813 was more up-market, located on the present site of the Drury Lane theatre. It was a famous tavern of its period, fashionable but often the scene of brawls. It was frequented by young gentlemen and men of letters, such as Samuel Pepys. Early in the eighteenth century, a Lord Gerard of Bromley died during a drinking bout at the Rose – possibly the victim of a gang known as the Hectors, who were notorious for picking fights – and here in 1712 the seconds arranged the duel between the Duke of Hamilton and Lord Mohun.

In less than three weeks between the fourth of August, when Sharpe and *Harper* enlisted, and the twenty-first, when they paraded the *S. Essex* in Hyde Park, they achieved all their objectives and saved the Regiment from extinction. The Prince Regent was particularly fond of military reviews, the pomp and circumstance of marching bands, the immaculate lines of scarlet and gold, the flash of sunlight on cuirass or sabre – all excited his military instincts. Hyde Park was the usual location, with space for thousands of troops as well as thousands of spectators. It was a shrewd move by Sharpe to provide the highlight of such an occasion, but he only escaped a punishment posting to Australia when documentary proof of the happenings at Chelmsford was produced at the last moment.

The West Indies, Africa and Australia were postings to be avoided. With the first two it was the awful climate, and the frightening illnesses which filled the cemeteries with graves of British soldiers. If you survived, promotion could be rapid because you stepped from dead men's shoes to dead men's shoes. Many officers who received such a posting sold up cheaply to impoverished comrades desperate for promotion. With Australia, it was the remoteness, the fact that it was a

societies or clubs did a brisk trade in the early years of the century. Premiums varied from five shillings a year in Lichfield to one pound in Blackburn. The societies did good business: the substitutes were highly paid and the draftee escaped at a moderate cost. The only loser was the army.

SICKNESS STATISTICS

For soldiers throughout the world sickness and disease were far more prolific killers than the enemy. In 1811, a year with bloody battles at Albuera and Fuentes de Onoro, the British army lost almost 23,000 men from all causes worldwide. Of these 2000 were killed in action or died of wounds in the Peninsula and another 100 died in the fighting in Java. Over 4000 died of disease in the Peninsula, and over 16,000 elsewhere. Put another way, these figures indicate that each year a soldier had a one in 11 risk of dying of disease, but only one in 100 of being killed in battle.

Re-enlistment of an officer

JOHN SHIPP first joined the army as a boy in 1795, the year Private Sharpe sailed for India with the 33rd Foot. Like Sharpe, he also served under Wellington there. Shipp ended up as a lieutenant in the 87th (Prince of Wales' Irish Fusiliers) after selling his commission and re-enlisting as a private. Here is his account of this episode: 'The routine of dissipation . . . was not to be sustained by me without expense . . . This extravagance – with the loss of fifty pounds, of which I was robbed by my servant, and the assistance of a designing sergeant who took advantage of my youth and inexperience – soon involved me in debts, to liquidate which I was obliged . . . to sell my commission. With the residue of the money I repaired to London where, in about six months, I found myself without a shilling, without a home and without a friend. Thus circumstances, my fondness of the profession induced me to turn my thoughts to the army again . . . Accordingly I enlisted at Westminster in his majesty's 24th Dragoons.'

He was recognised by an officer who had served with him in India and within a week was made a sergeant (he later regained a commission through gallantry).

WELLINGTON MINTS COINS

During the winter of 1813–14 Wellington became exasperated by the French peasants' refusal to accept dollars or guineas as payment for food or forage. He turned to the former criminal element in his army, and colonels were asked to identify professional coiners (forgers). About forty coiners were assembled at St Jean de Luz, tasked with melting down Portuguese and Spanish silver and minting five-franc pieces. It was a successful venture.

convict station and that to be sent there was to be forgotten by the army. It was a sentence to endless years of boredom, to lack of promotion, lack of prospects and probably signalled the end of a military career – if not life itself.

By mid October Sharpe was back in Spain and the *S. Essex* were up to strength. He arrived in time to participate in the Battle of the Nivelle as the senior major under his old enemy from Chelmsford, *Lieutenant-Colonel Girdwood*. But he had missed several battles during the four months since Vitória. In July, Soult had launched a brilliant counter-offensive across the Pyrenees, timed when Wellington had paused to catch his breath after a 400-mile advance in forty days, and had his 60,000 men strung out south of the mountains from the coast to Pamplona. On 25 July divisional actions were fought at the Passes of Maya and Roncesvalles to hold dangerous French thrusts. On the same day the 5th Division (without the remnants of the *S. Essex*) assaulted San Sebastian. It failed, and among those killed was Lieutenant-Colonel Fletcher, Wellington's chief engineer who had overseen the construction of the Lines of Torres Vedras. The second

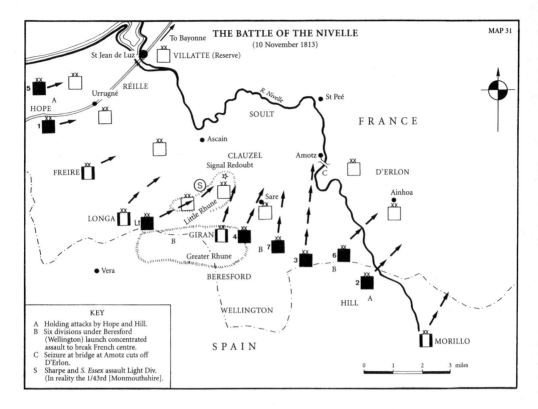

THE BATTLE OF THE NIVELLE
(10 November 1813)

MAP 31

To Bayonne

St Jean de Luz — VILLATTE (Reserve)

RÉILLE

Urrugné

HOPE

5

A

1

R. Nivelle

St Peé

SOULT

FRANCE

Ascain

CLAUZEL

Amotz

D'ERLON

Signal Redoubt

C

FREIRE

Ainhoa

S

LONGA

Lt

Little Rhune

Sare

GIRAN

B

4

B 7

Greater Rhune

3

6

B

2

Vera

BERESFORD

HILL A

WELLINGTON

SPAIN

MORILLO

KEY

A Holding attacks by Hope and Hill.
B Six divisions under Beresford
   (Wellington) launch concentrated
   assault to break French centre.
C Seizure at bridge at Amotz cuts off
   D'Erlon.
S Sharpe and S. *Essex* assault Light Div.
   (In reality the 1/43rd [Monmouthshire].

0   1   2   3 miles

assault, again by the 5th Division, took place five weeks later. The Forlorn Hope was swept away and, after an hour of murderous fighting, General Graham ordered Colonel Dickson, his artillery chief, to cover another attack by firing over the heads of the assaulting troops. The range was 1200 yards, the clearance 40 feet. It was probably the first time such close covering fire had been used by the British on a battlefield. The Gunners succeeded: French casualties were high and the town taken, although the castle held out for another nine days. The troops went on the rampage (as usual) and the town was burnt down, much to the fury of the Spanish government who thought Wellington had done it deliberately.

On 28 July Wellington blocked Soult's offensive at the Battle of Sorauren, outside Pamplona, and further actions at

San Marcial and Vera on the Bidassoa River were fought to push back fresh French attacks. A vital bridge at Vera was held by eighty men of the 95th under a Captain Cadoux. An entire French division was desperate to escape back over this bridge, having been stranded on the allied side, but Cadoux held out for two hours, inflicting 200 casualties including killing the enemy divisional commander (General Vander-maesen). His repeated requests to the acting divisional commander of the Light Division, General Skerrett, were unavailing and he was eventually overwhelmed and killed. Such was the resentment against Skerrett that he was sent home and left the army.

In early October the Allies crossed the Bidassoa into France. The plan was brilliantly conceived and executed by the *S. Essex*'s former comrades in the 5th Division wading across the estuary guided by local shrimpers. In late October the *S. Essex* were posted not back to the 5th Division but to the élite Light Division. They marched up to reinforce Kempt's brigade and fight alongside the 1/95th, 3/95th and 1st Cacadores. MAP 31 illustrates the Battle of the Nivelle in which the *S. Essex* (in reality the 1/43rd (Monmouthshire)) assaulted the Little Rhune and captured a strongpoint on the top. In this action, *Girdwood* went mad and command devolved to Sharpe yet again.

British head-dress
LEFT: *Leather helmet, Royal Horse Artillery*
RIGHT: *Light Dragoon's Shako, adopted 1812*

13

Sharpe's Siege

In February 1814 Wellington's army had secured a toehold in southern France. Sharpe was a major, but no longer serving with the *PWOV*. He was given the task of capturing a small, coastal fort at Teste de Buch (about thirty-five miles south-west of Bordeaux) with two companies of the 60th Rifles under *Captain Frederickson ('Sweet William')*. They were assisted by three companies of Royal Marines; the whole force were taken by sea to within a few miles of the fort.

The main objective was to capture a number of small coastal luggers/fishing vessels – *chasse-marées* – which Wellington needed urgently to build a bridge of boats across the Adour River. Sharpe secured the fort by ruse but was abandoned by the navy (under *Captain Bampfylde*) and had to fight desperately to hold Teste de Buch. He was finally evacuated by sea on an American privateer schooner under *Captain Killick*.

NAVAL EXPENDITURE

The Royal Navy cost more than the army. In 1800, at £12.6 million, it represented some 47 per cent of the entire war chest. By 1814 it had peaked at £22 million, of which £6.5 million was spent on victualling. It was money well spent. The navy defended the trade routes, escorted convoys of merchantmen, blockaded ports, prevented invasion, attacked enemy ports, ships and sea lanes. Occasionally, it fought major battles at sea. By the end of the Revolutionary and Napoleonic Wars, the navy had sunk or captured 1209 French vessels for the loss of 166. Britain lost only one warship of over 50 guns, whereas the French navy lost 90.

IN EARLY 1814 the allied armies were on French soil. After six years of largely defensive warfare in the Peninsula, British, German, Portuguese and Spanish soldiers were at last the invaders. The French under Soult had pulled back behind the Adour River and its smaller tributaries, the Bidouse and the Grave de Pau (MAP 32). The riverline was well defended and solidly anchored near the mouth by the fortress of Bayonne, into whose defences some 7000 Frenchmen had been crammed. Wellington paused to take stock.

During this period he was urged by various French royalists

CANNING FOOD

When Sharpe captured some tinned food in February 1814, it was unknown to the British army. In 1795 the French government had offered a reward of 12,000 francs for the discovery of a practical method of preserving food for the army and the navy. In 1809, François Appert, a Parisian confectioner, succeeded in preserving foods in glass bottles kept in boiling water for varying lengths of time. His work was published in 1810; from there it was a short step to keeping food in hermetically sealed tins.

PRIZE MONEY

Soldiers sought loot from towns they sacked or the battlefield, as did Sharpe and *Harper* from the pickings at Vitória. Sailors looked to capture ships and take them home as 'prizes', of which they got a share according to their rank (rate). A captain's share was the largest; seamen made do with a pound or so. *Bampfylde*'s eagerness to capture the *Thuella* was typical of most captains; it was not unknown for naval operations to take

to raise the standard of the lilies and declare for the Bourbons. It was claimed that this would lead to a formidable royalist uprising throughout France. Southern France, and the Bordeaux region in particular, was said to be hostile to the Emperor. Wellington listened to these exhortations with considerable reserve. Sharpe was specifically ordered before proceeding on his mission to take the fort at Teste de Buch not to march on Bordeaux. Any stories of the inhabitants declaring for the king or the allies after the fort fell were to be discounted. The traitorous *Comte de Maquerre* tried to persuade him otherwise.

Nevertheless, in general the French peasantry and middle class proved very ready to co-operate with the British and supply Wellington with whatever he required – for cash. Soult's army, on the contrary, received little assistance from their own people. The French troops resented this attitude and were the more willing to take by force what they wanted, a habit deeply ingrained from their years in Spain. During this period fraternisation developed on a large scale. Sentries and pickets seldom molested each other although posted only a few yards apart. Cavalry horses of both armies would water alternatively from the same stream by mutual arrangement. The story was told of an Irish sentry who was found one night with a British musket on one shoulder and a French one on the other, doing guard duty for both armies, the French picket having gone to buy brandy for them both.

Wellington was ruthlessly determined that his troops would behave well towards the French people. Several soldiers were hanged for theft, *pour encourager les autres*. He was particularly firm with the Spaniards, many of whom relished the prospect of revenge for the years under French occupation. Army orders insisted that all transactions must be paid for. The problem was that the French would not accept the Spanish dollar – no matter how shiny the silver. The solution was to make French five-franc pieces at a secret mint near St Jean de Luz, operated by professional coiners within the ranks of Wellington's army. Spanish coins were melted down. Strict supervision was necessary at the mint to prevent the

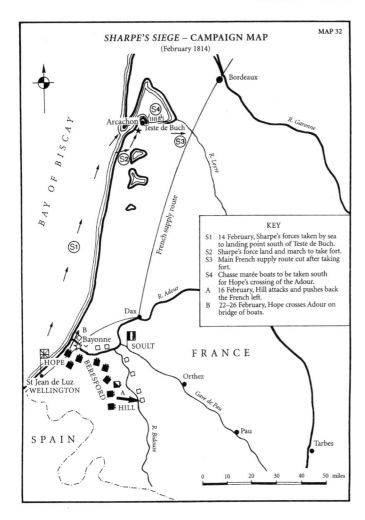

SHARPE'S SIEGE – CAMPAIGN MAP
(February 1814)

MAP 32

BAY OF BISCAY

Bordeaux

R. Garonne

Arcachon
Teste de Buch
S4
S3
S2

R. Leyre

French supply route

S1

KEY
S1 14 February, Sharpe's forces taken by sea
    to landing point south of Teste de Buch.
S2 Sharpe's force land and march to take fort.
S3 Main French supply route cut after taking
    fort.
S4 Chasse marée boats to be taken south
    for Hope's crossing of the Adour.
A   16 February, Hill attacks and pushes back
    the French left.
B   22–26 February, Hope crosses Adour on
    bridge of boats.

R. Adour

Dax

B
Bayonne   SOULT
HOPE
St Jean de Luz
WELLINGTON
BERESFORD
A
HILL

FRANCE

Orthez

Gave de Pau

R. Bidouse

SPAIN

Pau

Tarbes

0   10   20   30   40   50 miles

official 'forgers' from introducing lead or pewter and pocketing the silver thus saved. In the event the finished product was well-nigh perfect. Sharpe used these coins to pay for supplies when he was preparing for the siege of Teste de Buch.

Soult had a thankless task. To be successful in halting the invasion he had to hold the line of the Adour. His chief concerns were lack of sufficient troops – and the Royal Navy. He had 60,000 men and 77 guns locked into Bayonne and

second place to prize-hunting, and captains were occasionally punished for this offence.

JUNIOR NAVAL OFFICERS

Junior commissioned officers were lieutenants of varying degrees of seniority. They could either serve on a rated ship or command a small unrated vessel. On a large 1st- or 2nd-rated warship (84–100 guns), there was a complement of six lieutenants numbered from 1st to 6th in seniority, although Nelson's flagship HMS *Victory* had nine at the Battle of Trafalgar. A small frigate or sloop would have only one to assist the captain. A naval lieutenant was the equivalent of an army captain, which remains so to this day. Young lieutenants got their command experience in cutters or brigs where they might be the only commissioned officer on board. In some larger sloops the 'captain' might have the rank of 'commander' with a 1st lieutenant as his second-in-command; a lonely life, compared with an army captain's.

Because there were so
many specialists on a
large warship, the rank
structure below
commissioned rank
was complex. The
most senior WO
(virtually equal to a
lieutenant) was the
master, with his own
instruments and
charts, responsible for
navigation. The others
were boatswain
(rigging, sails, tackle,
anchors, ropes);
gunner (guns, powder,
ammo); surgeon,
carpenter
(maintenance of hull,
masts, spars); purser
(victualling). Below
these were a host of
senior and junior POs,
including the
chaplain, midshipmen,
and various 'mates'
(e.g. master's mate,
gunner's mate and so
on), cook, armourer,
quartermaster,
sailmaker and
schoolmaster. *Harper*,
as a senior sergeant,
very roughly equated
to a 'mate'; as an RSM,
to a gunner.

strung out along forty-five miles of riverline (the Adour and
Bidouse Rivers). But French borders everywhere were under
threat. Napoleon faced the Prussians, Austrians and Russians
and was clinging to the belief that the Spanish would ratify
the Treaty of Valençay (see Chapter 12) and thus neutralise
Spain and possibly Wellington's army. In anticipation, he
had ordered Soult to send 14,000 men north. While a river
offers an effective barrier to an attacker, the defender suffers
from not knowing where the blow will fall and has to be
strong everywhere, which is impossible. The attacker can
choose his time and place: he can concentrate and bring
decisive strength against a thinly held part of the line and
force a quick crossing. In short, he has the initiative.

Soult's second worry was even more acute. Wellington
could outflank the Adour in the west by sea. The single most
crucial element in Wellington's success in the Peninsula had
been the support of the Royal Navy. Without control of the
sea, his army would have been unable to land in the first
place. Having come ashore, it could not have survived without the ceaseless stream of supply ships bringing food, arms,
munitions, guns, horses and men – every convoy guarded by
warships. Britain was a world power because she projected
her authority, protected her trade and defeated her enemies
on the sea. The 'wooden walls' as the ships were known, were
Britain's first line of defence; one-fifth of the nation's annual
budget went on the Royal Navy.

Wellington had made full use of the strategic flexibility
this naval power gave him. Admiral Sir Home Popeham's
raiding squadron sailing out of Corunna had been so successful along the north coast of Spain in 1812 that the French
Army of the North had been unable to send a single soldier
as reinforcement in the Salamanca campaign. It was the Royal
Navy which enabled Wellington to open a new supply base
at Santander as an alternative to Lisbon, and now, in 1814,
it allowed him to land troops behind the enemy defences.
The French high command feared this option would be used.
The French spymaster, *Major Ducos*, desperately wanted to
know: would Wellington land a force on the coast behind

the Adour and march inland to sever the main French supply route? Would he mount a shorter left hook to isolate Bayonne or seize Dax where the French had a large forward base? Or would he do one of these in conjunction with a river crossing?

Wellington opted to cross the Adour, but at a place where the French would least expect it – near the mouth, where the river was wide and close to the Bayonne garrison. This could not be done until the French reserves had been lured away to the east, towards Orthez, and enough suitable boats collected to build a huge pontoon bridge. This was the task of the navy – assisted by Sharpe. Admiral Penrose was given overall responsibility for assembling the boats, presently located in the Arcachon Basin (MAP 33). Penrose delegated the task of bringing the thirty-six *chasse-marées* to St Jean de Luz to *Captain Horace Bampfylde RN*, a twenty-eight-year-

SENIOR NAVAL
OFFICERS

As an army major, Sharpe was the approximate equivalent of a junior post captain in the RN. He might therefore have got command of a small frigate – a 6th-rater with perhaps 24 guns. A few more years and a successful mission at Teste de Buch would have put *Bampfylde* in the running for a flag. Admirals were allowed to fly their own flags and were thus 'flag officers'. They were promoted through three grades (rear-admiral, vice-admiral and admiral) of the fleet's three squadrons. The squadrons were blue (the most junior), white and red (the senior). Ranks were given as Rear-Admiral of the Blue, Admiral of the White, and so on.

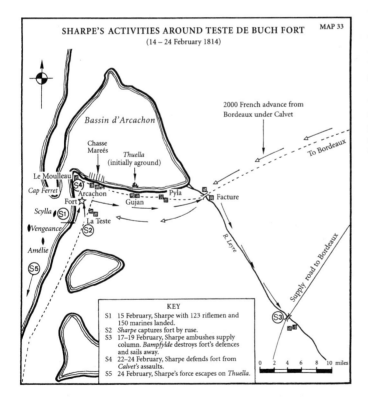

SHARPE'S ACTIVITIES AROUND TESTE DE BUCH FORT   MAP 33
(14 – 24 February 1814)

2000 French advance from
Bordeaux under Calvet

To Bordeaux

Bassin d'Arcachon

Chasse
Mareés

Thuella
(initially aground)

Le Moulleau

Cap Ferret

Arcachon
Fort

Gujan

Pyla

Facture

Scylla (S1)

Vengeance

La Teste (S2)

Amélie

(S5)

R. Leyre

Supply road to Bordeaux

(S3)

KEY
S1   15 February, Sharpe with 123 riflemen and
       150 marines landed.
S2   *Sharpe* captures fort by ruse.
S3   17–19 February, Sharpe ambushes supply
       column. *Bampfylde* destroys fort's defences
       and sails away.
S4   22–24 February, Sharpe defends fort from
       Calvet's assaults.
S5   24 February, Sharpe's force escapes on *Thuella*.

0   2   4   6   8   10 miles

Royal Marine

old post captain in command of the 74-gun warship HMS *Vengeance*.

Bampfylde's command consisted of the *Vengeance*, the 36-gun frigate HMS *Scylla* under *Captain Grant RN* and, being used to transport Sharpe and his men, the grimy former collier, the *Amélie*, whose master was *Captain Tremgor*. When afloat *Bampfylde* would command; land operations would be Sharpe's responsibility. Sharpe had 123 men of two companies of the 60th Rifles under *Captain Frederickson*; the warships had their full complement of marines under *Captain Neil Palmer*: ninety plus on the *Vengeance*, and another forty on the *Scylla*, though extra marines may have been taken on this occasion.

The operation planned was perfectly feasible and similar to previous raids on the north coast of Spain where troops and marines had landed to attack isolated garrisons, cut supply routes and provide the guerrillas with stocks of arms and

HMS *Vengeance*

THE *VENGEANCE* was a 3rd-rate, two-deck, 74-gun, line of battle ship. It had a complement of 650–700 (all ranks including marines). As with all warships, there were only enough gun crews (15 men per gun) to man half the 32-pounder guns simultaneously. It was sometimes a difficult judgement whether to man all on one side, half on each, or cut the crews in two and reduce the rate of fire. *Bampfylde* had only four commissioned officers (lieutenants) under him. Additionally, there were six sea warrant officers (master, boatswain, gunner, carpenter, surgeon and purser); nine inferior warrant officers (chaplain, cook, schoolmaster, sailmaker, armourer, three surgeon's mates, and master-at-arms); and 65 petty officers

including 16 midshipmen, 6 quarter-masters, and 18 quarter gunners.

Interesting is the high status given the chief carpenter, which reflects the importance of maintenance and repair in wooden ships. Oak was the timber used in the hull. The *Vengeance* would have required 2000 full-grown trees – about 50 acres of oak forest. Her mainmast was over 100 feet tall. She carried 150 tons of guns, 50 tons of ammunition, 30 tons each of cable and rigging, 12 tons of sail and almost 8 tons of paint and tar. Her marine contingent (under *Captain Palmer*) consisted of one lieutenant, one 2nd lieutenant, three sergeants, two corporals, one drummer and about 90 marines.

*74-gun
warship*

Warship's 'ratings'

A SHIP'S 'RATE' was a method of classi-fying its size/class in terms of the number of gun ports through which a gun could be fired. The actual number of guns on a ship could exceed its rating if it carried carronades for close-range fire. There were six 'rates' which categorised all ships of the line (battleships) and frigates. Ships of the line were the three- or two-deckers rated from 1st–4th. Frigates were rated 5th or 6th, and smaller vessels such as brigs or sloops were unrated. Generally, the larger the ship the higher the rate, the more senior its captain, the more guns, crew and marines it carried. Marines were allocated approximately on the basis of one per gun, with a captain and three lieutenants on a 1st-rate ship and a sergeant commanding the twenty or so marines on a sloop. Post captains commanded rated ships.

Rate	Guns	Seamen
1st	100	875 (HMS *Victory* had 104 guns)
2nd	98	750
3rd	70–84	650 (*Vengeance* with 74 guns was the most common)
4th	50	420 (a weak line of battle ship)
5th	32–44	300 (A frigate such as *Scylla*)
6th	24–28	300 (A small frigate)
Corvette	20–22	250
Sloop	14–18	125
Brig	10–14	100
Cutter	4–10	30–75

Naval officers

CAPTAIN BAMPFYLDE RN was a post captain commanding a 74-gun (3rd rate) ship at twenty-eight. He was the equivalent of a colonel. There was no purchase system in the RN. Gentleman or no, all naval recruits in the early nineteenth century began their careers as ratings (ordinary crew members). Candidates for commissions had to pass an oral seamanship exam, to have served six years at sea, two of which had been in the Royal Navy in the rating (rank) of master's mate or midshipman.

There were three main routes to a naval commission as a lieutenant. First, to go to sea as a boy (usually aged 10–14) as an officer's servant and, under his patronage, gain the sea time required and pass the exam. This was the normal route for the sons of better-off families. The second way was to join as a boy and gain petty officer

(PO) rating. Any PO who had been a midshipman or master's mate for two years could try the lieutenant's exam. Third, a man who rose to be a mate in the merchant service could join the RN as a PO and hope to qualify for a commission. Sharpe might have found this system more to his liking and would probably have climbed higher more quickly. Merit was the main requirement. An outstanding example was John Perkins, a mulatto and possibly a former slave, who joined the Jamaica squadron in 1775 as a pilot extra from the merchant service. Within a year or so, he was in command of the schooner *Punch*; by 1782, he was a lieutenant commanding the brig *Endeavour*; and in 1800 he was promoted post captain to command the frigates *Arab* and *Tartar*.

WOMEN IN THE RN

Unlike the army, where 60 wives were permitted to accompany a battalion on campaign, the RN did not officially sanction women aboard a ship at sea. In harbour, they swarmed aboard, usually without check. Nevertheless, a substantial number went to sea, often the wives of POs, who in action helped the surgeon. Children were occasionally

ammunition. The *chasse-marées* were under the guns of the Teste de Buch fort, so it had to be taken first. The use of the *Scylla*'s guns to bombard the fort from the sea while the troops assaulted (by escalade) was a sound tactical plan. Sharpe's encounter with *Captain Cornelius Killick*, commanding the privateer schooner *Thuella*, could not have been foreseen. However, Britain was at war with America, *ergo* the Americans were allies of the French.

On 14 February *Bampfylde*'s small flotilla sailed from St Jean de Luz. At dusk on the fifteenth, Sharpe took the fort by a ruse; the co-operation of the *chasse-marée* crews was purchased with counterfeit coins, and they prepared to sail south. On 16 February, General Hill launched an attack on the French extreme left along the Bidouse, and for the next week Soult's left was forced farther and farther east towards Orthez. Wellington's plan was working: Soult was heavily committed in the east while Penrose was assembling the boats for the Adour crossing. The time was ripe to cross the river and launch the battle for Bayonne.

General Sir John Hope's corps was responsible for the river crossing, which was to be followed by the investment of the city. Design of the floating bridge was entrusted to Major Sturgeon, with supervision of the construction to a Captain Todd – both of the Staff Corps. The site of the crossing was about two miles below the fortifications of Bayonne, where the Adour narrowed to 300 yards and was deeper and more rapid flowing than at other points. The floating bridge had to be of considerable strength to withstand the current; upriver, above the site, a boom would be positioned to protect it

born aboard ship. A woman gave birth on HMS *Tremendous* during the Battle of the Glorious First of June. He was named Daniel Tremendous McKenzie. Some years later he had the gall to apply for the Naval General Service Medal; it was refused.

Royal Marines

THE CORPS OF MARINES, which originated in 1664, as the Duke of York and Albany's Maritime Regiment, was given the title Royal in 1802. Prior to this, infantry regiments had served at sea as required. By 1814 the corps numbered over 31,000. Their first duty was as soldiers who manned the sides with muskets during close action, formed boarding parties or fought ashore with landing parties (such as that with Sharpe at Teste de Buch). Although they were not seamen, and never worked aloft in the rigging, they were required to perform some of the ship's chores, such as pulling and hauling, raising the anchor and cleaning. Some learnt seamanship and transferred into the navy, which marginally improved their pay and status.

The corps was organised admini-stratively into four 'divisions' based at Chatham, Portsmouth, Plymouth and Woolwich. Each had up to forty-eight companies of marines and an artillery company. In practice, virtually all personnel were scattered in detachments throughout the ships of the fleet. The number of ships' guns was approximately equal to the number of marines on board. In 1808 the 1st Marine Battalion was formed; it garrisoned Lisbon and took part in the landings along the north coast of Spain, including Santander. A 2nd Battalion was formed in 1812 and in early 1813 both were detailed for service in North America, as was a third created that year. The detachments fighting with Sharpe at Teste de Buch were from the normal ships' complement of the *Vengeance* and *Scylla*.

PRIVATEERS

These were fast raiding vessels, often sloops with 14–18 guns, which had been given 'Letters of Marque' by their governments. The Letters authorised the crew in time of war to attack merchant ships for profit. The crews received no pay and the cost of their food and medical treatment was deducted from their share of prize money. The *Thuella* was an American privateer, one of many that caused serious losses to British merchantmen during the war of 1812.

French 12-pounder cannon

from floating masses the enemy might send downstream. The intention was for the navy to bring the flotilla to the mouth of the river on the twenty-third and get it over the sand bar at high tide. Shore batteries and gunboats guarded the boom, but the weather was foul. Although Penrose put to sea, the bar proved impassable. At the river Hope ordered a battalion of Guards to cross in small boats and rafts. This was achieved on the twenty-third when the small force was weakly attacked by a French column, driven off by a flight of Congreve rockets which, fired as Sharpe used them at close range, burst over the head of the column. The following day, Sharpe left the fort to the French and slipped away with his men on the *Thuella*; the *chasse-marées* negotiated the bar. The event is described by Fortescue:

SEA SERVICE MUSKETS

These weapons were based on the army's Brown Bess but were cheaper to make and had wooden ramrods because iron rusted at sea. They were divided into two categories, 'black' or 'bright'. The former had blackened barrels to prevent corrosion, the others did not and were possibly for use by the marines. A 74-gun ship like the *Vengeance* carried about 150 blackened muskets for the sailors' use; they were wildly inaccurate.

> On the 24th a favourable breeze brought the flotilla off the mouth of the Adour by daybreak. The surf on the bar was very formidable but Captain Reilly RN nevertheless essayed to pass it; and though his boat was upset, a few of his men drowned, and himself seriously injured, he launched it again into the river ... A six-oared cutter followed Reilly without mishap, and then with the fall of the tide the bar became impractical ... The tide turned ... the wind freshened and blew almost with the force of a gale. Admiral Penrose therefore ordered the flotilla to attempt the passage of the bar again.

The leading boat – the barge of the Lyra – capsized, and every soul in her perished, but the second boat found the right line of entry. The rest then followed in succession; and though several of them were overset and many brave officers and men were drowned yet . . . the great majority entered the river in safety.

On the afternoon of the twenty-sixth the bridge was finished and 8000 men crossed the river. Twenty-six *chasse-marées* were positioned at forty-foot intervals, anchored bow and stern. The troops and guns marched on a roadway of oak planking held in position by five cables controlled by capstans. On this bridge, in the early evening, Sharpe confronted *Bampfylde* with his cowardice, and a few minutes later he executed the traitor *de Maquerre* with his sword and tumbled his body into the muddy waters of the Adour. The next day, fifty miles to the south-east, Wellington won another battle – at Orthez.

Chasseurs Britanniques officer

Sharpe's Revenge

In 1814, Sharpe was given a staff appointment as brigade-major to *Major-General Nairn*'s brigade – part of Lieutenant-General Clinton's 6th Division – and took part in the assault by that division at the Battle of Toulouse on 10 April. His horse was decapitated under him just before he led the final assault on the Mâs des Augustins redoubt, which changed hands a number of times before the 6th Division finally captured it.

The French spymaster, *Major Ducos*, forged a letter which implicated Sharpe and *Captain Frederickson* (60th Rifles) in stealing Napoleon's treasure from the Teste de Buch fort. They were arrested, but escaped to track down *Ducos*. The trail led them to Normandy, where Sharpe was badly wounded by former *Commandant Lassan*'s sister, *Lucille*, but later fell in love with her. Sharpe, *Frederickson* and *Harper* located *Ducos* in Naples, where he was in hiding with a dozen dragoons and Napoleon's treasure. They allied themselves with *General Calvet*, who was sent by Napoleon from Elba to recover the lost fortune. Their combined attack succeeded, *Ducos* was captured (and later executed for treason) with the jewels and the gold, most of which was taken to Elba by *Calvet*. Sharpe returned to Normandy and *Lucille*.

BY MARCH 1814 the allies were in France to stay. But to Napoleon, Wellington's successes in the south were of secondary importance as he fought with consummate skill to defend France to the north. At the beginning of the year

Napoleon was facing three enemies apart from Wellington: Bernadotte with 60,000 men was advancing west through the Low Countries; Blucher with 75,000 Prussians was moving up the Moselle valley into Lorraine; Schwarzenburg and 210,000 Austrians were marching through Switzerland towards the Belfort Gap. Their joint objective was Paris.

During January and February, as Sharpe defended the fort at Teste de Buch, Napoleon was conducting one of his most brilliant campaigns. Despite recurring bouts of illness, despite the poor quality of his troops (when Marmont asked a young soldier at the Battle of Champaubert why he did not fire his musket, the boy replied that he would fire if only he knew how to load!), Napoleon defended his capital in a series of manoeuvres and battles which compelled the admiration of his opponents. By the end of March, however, it was over. With Austrian artillery able to shell Montmartre, Marmont surrendered the city.

Southern France had many royalists and the idea that Sharpe might have been persuaded to enter Bordeaux after the capture of Teste de Buch was not a far-fetched notion. Bordeaux was a hot-bed of Bourbon support. On 4 March, Wellington received an agent from the mayor informing him of the weakness of the garrison (*General Calvet*'s victory over Sharpe at Teste de Buch with 2000 recruits from Bordeaux had been an exceedingly costly affair), and promising to hand over the city to the British. On the day that Sharpe made *Bampfylde* 'eat grass for breakfast', Beresford led the 7th Division and the cavalry into Bordeaux. The mayor and the majority of the populace came out to greet them. French officials tore the tricolour from their hats and wore the white cockade of the Bourbons. The imperial flag was hauled down and the royal standard hoisted in its place. A *Te Deum* was sung in the great cathedral in honour of the restoration of King Louis XVIII – perhaps a trifle premature.

After his defeat at Orthez at the end of February, Soult had no option but to retreat yet again: north towards Bordeaux or east towards Toulouse? He chose the east because the country in that direction was better able to supply food and forage,

ARMY OF KINGDOM OF NAPLES

Sharpe's low opinion of Neapolitan troops was justified. Created by Joseph Bonaparte and organised on French lines, the battalions were crammed with impressed peasants and criminals, many of whom deserted at the first opportunity. French and German officers had little hope of moulding them into an effective force. The 9th Regiment was formed entirely from captured deserters and the sweepings of the jails. The 10th mutinied in 1815. Twelve regiments were raised, plus a Royal Guard and cavalry. In Spain they were useless – of 1000 convicts marching to the Peninsula as reinforcements in 1810, half had gone before they reached the Pyrenees. The battalion facing Sharpe and *Calvet* was from the 11th Regiment, raised only three months earlier; it was still in pristine white uniforms with scarlet facings.

King Louis XVIII

BORN IN 1755, he escaped the fate of his brother (Louis XVI), whose dripping head tumbled into the basket after being 'kissed' by 'Madame Guillotine', by fleeing the country during the Revolution. He was regarded as regent-in-exile for the ten-year-old Louis XVII, who died in jail of ill-treatment. Spent much of his exile in England before returning to France to assume the throne in April 1814. Bourbons called him 'Louis the yearned for', which changed to 'Louis the unloved' and, with his second restoration after Waterloo, 'Louis the unavoidable'. At sixty he was physically decrepit – short-winded, bloated, gouty, barely able to stand unaided, let alone mount a horse. Wellington described him as, 'A perfect walking sore, not a part of his body sound, even his head let out a sort of humour [unwholesome discharge]'. He turned a blind eye to the White Terror – revenge for the Red Terror which had decimated many aristocratic families (including his own) over twenty years earlier.

During the White Terror, Marshal Brune, who had kept the tricolour flying over Toulon until late July 1814, was lynched at Avignon. Local authorities afterwards reported he had killed himself. Brune's body floated in the Rhone for two days. Women, children and disabled veterans went under the knife and the club, some crying 'Vive l'Empereur' as they died. Surprisingly, Louis lasted another nine years. The 'new' royalist army consisted mainly of former Bonapartist soldiers, most of whom boasted of their service under the Eagles. They spoke of Louis XVIII as 'le cochon' and, when playing cards, referred to the 'pig' of spades or hearts instead of the king.

the people were less obviously hostile and having an intact army hovering on his flank might deter Wellington from pushing too far north. Wellington went no farther than Bordeaux. Then he followed Soult, and there was a clash with the French rearguard at Tarbes on 20 March: the Light and 6th Divisions fought a brisk action, but were checked by the French whose main force retired unmolested into Toulouse. Sharpe, struggling to cope with unfamiliar staff duties, was present with *Nairn's brigade* in the 6th Division but was apparently not engaged in the fighting.

Afterwards, it was apparent that Toulouse had been an unnecessary battle. Those who died, on both sides, did so pointlessly – the Emperor had signed an unconditional abdication four days earlier. Not until 12 April did the news reach Wellington, and Soult did not know until the next day. At the Battle of Toulouse (MAP 34), Wellington was compelled to expose his long lines of communications stretching 150 miles to the Atlantic (he could spare only a single battalion to guard them); he had to divide his army, with the 500-foot-wide Garonne between the two parts, and he opted for a long outflanking move in full view and under gunfire before frontally attacking entrenched troops up a steep slope. It was all a recipe for disaster; that it did not turn into one was due to the gallantry and guts of Cole's 4th and Clinton's 6th Divisions. Not surprisingly, the allies paid a higher price than the French – 4568 to 3236.

Soult had 42,000 men, 100 guns, and a strong defensive position. The city was well fortified and protected by the Garonne to the west, a broad canal to the north and the Ers River in the east. The key, however, was the 600-foot Calvinet Ridge which ran for four miles north–south within a mile of the eastern walls, completely dominating the city defences and the positions lining the canal. Soult concentrated half his force on this ridge, his men sheltered in a series of entrenchments and small redoubts. Wellington had 49,000 men and 50 guns. After two abortive attempts to cross the Garonne south of the city – one of which failed because the pontoon bridge was too short, the other because the roads were impassable for guns on the east bank – his engineers got a bridge across fifteen miles to the north.

At 5 a.m. on Easter Sunday, 10 April, Hill's troops west of the city opened fire. The plan was for his division, assisted by Morillo's Spaniards and Picton's and Alten's divisions in the north, to mount diversionary attacks: the main assault would be made against the Calvinet Ridge. Four infantry divisions were committed to this attack, two Spanish and two British. Freire's Spaniards had the key role of advancing, under covering fire from Portuguese artillery, from La Pujade onto the northern end of the ridge and, ultimately, of taking the Great Redoubt. It speaks highly of the quality of these troops that Wellington had the confidence to give them such

THE GRASSHOPPER GUN

This was a three-pounder cannon developed around 1770 by General Pattison RA, but by 1814 was seldom used. The British had at one time supplied Naples with arms and it was one of these pieces that *Ducos* obtained. It could be carried by using four handspikes, one at each corner of the carriage, from which it got the name 'grasshopper'. Normally mounted on a wheeled carriage, it did not fire on 'legs', and although it could fire a ball, it was primarily a canister cannon which could accompany the infantry. It saw good service in the American War of Independence.

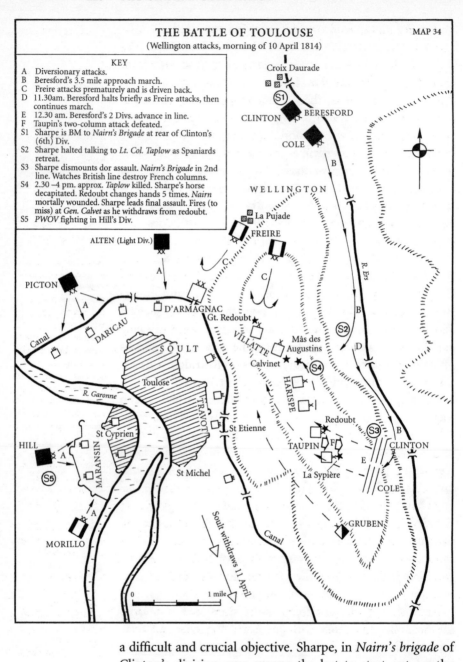

THE BATTLE OF TOULOUSE
(Wellington attacks, morning of 10 April 1814)

MAP 34

KEY

A   Diversionary attacks.
B   Beresford's 3.5 mile approach march.
C   Freire attacks prematurely and is driven back.
D   11.30am. Beresford halts briefly as Freire attacks, then continues march.
E   12.30 am. Beresford's 2 Divs. advance in line.
F   Taupin's two-column attack defeated.
S1 Sharpe is BM to *Nairn's Brigade* at rear of Clinton's (6th) Div.
S2 Sharpe halted talking to *Lt. Col. Taplow* as Spaniards retreat.
S3 Sharpe dismounts dor assault. *Nairn's Brigade* in 2nd line. Watches British line destroy French columns.
S4 2.30 –4 pm. approx. *Taplow* killed. Sharpe's horse decapitated. Redoubt changes hands 5 times. *Nairn* mortally wounded. Sharpe leads final assault. Fires (to miss) at *Gen. Calvet* as he withdraws from redoubt.
S5 *PWOV* fighting in Hill's Div.

a difficult and crucial objective. Sharpe, in *Nairn's brigade* of Clinton's division, was among the last to start out on the four-mile approach march along the west bank of the Ers.

Beresford commanded Cole's and Clinton's divisions and had the task of taking the southern end of the ridge. The plan was that these assaults, from the north and the south, should take place simultaneously; timing was of the essence. But as so often happens in military operations, the plans became unglued early on. Beresford found the clay by the river deep and sticky from recent rains; his guns bogged down frequently and the infantry pace slowed. The French were watching every move from their positions on the ridge and after about two miles, their gunners could resist the target no longer. At extreme range they opened up on the slow-moving snake below. Beresford's reaction was to push on with the infantry, but stop moving his guns and deploy them to return fire. The noise of this gunfire (French and British) was heard by Freire. He assumed Beresford had started his attack and launched his own – much too early.

At about 11.30 a.m. Sharpe got the order to halt his brigade and face right. By then the Spanish attack was in full swing and Beresford's force was opposite the Mâs des Augustins redoubt, one of the strongest positions on the ridge. If Beresford were to co-operate with and support Freire, he had to attack at once. However, the prospect of clambering up 600 feet of steep, bare hillside to assault a redoubt frontally did not appeal to Sharpe or anyone else in the column. There was a pause, hasty consultations among senior officers, a surfeit of derogatory remarks about the Spaniards and a good deal of fearful gazing at the hill. *Lieutenant-Colonel Taplow* of the fusilier battalion in *Nairn's brigade* talked to Sharpe and, as the Spanish attack began to stall, summed up the (totally unjustified) feelings of many with the remark, 'All priming and no charge, that's the Dagoes' problem.' Fortunately, Beresford decided to push on with the original plan and head for the gentler slopes of the ridge farther south.

After about a mile and a half Cole's division was ordered to wheel right and deploy into line. It took another half-hour before Sharpe's brigade, with the three Portuguese battalions behind, could get into position. The two divisions would advance abreast, each in three lines, one brigade in each line.

LIEUTENANT-COLONEL MACARA'S MANOEUVRE

The 1/42nd lost heavily at Toulouse. Twenty-six officers and 386 men were killed or wounded, the majority in the struggle for the Mâs des Augustins redoubt. Infantry battalions were divided into two wings, right and left. The right wing was the senior, with the grenadier company forming on the extreme right – the position of honour. This was how a battalion always paraded for drill. When Macara got the order to assault the redoubt, his left wing was facing the objective and ready to assault immediately. Not so the right. The colonel decided to carry out a manoeuvre to get this wing in its drill-book position. First he turned it right, counter-marched it past the rear of the left wing and round its left flank, and then counter-marched it across its front. By the time it reached its 'correct' position it had virtually completed a circle, much of it under heavy fire and suffering severely. Macara then led a successful charge. He was killed at Quatre Bras.

MURAT, MARSHAL
JOACHIM

Born 1767, the son of
an innkeeper. He
joined the cavalry as a
trooper to avoid
creditors. Personal
aide to Bonaparte in
Italy, and made a
shrewd career move
by marrying Caroline
Bonaparte (one of
Napoleon's sisters).
Commanded the
cavalry reserve in
campaigns across
Europe, earning praise
at Austerlitz. Fought at
Jena, and saved the
day at Eylau by
leading a cavalry
charge. Sent to
Madrid in 1808, where
he suppressed the
May uprising. In
August he was
proclaimed King of
Naples, replacing
Joseph Bonaparte, but
left to lead the cavalry
in 1812 in the Russian
invasion, and
commanded the
remnants of the
Grande Armée in
retreat. He then
returned to Naples.
A fiery, ostentatious
character of whom
Napoleon wrote, 'You
are a good soldier on
the field of battle, but
beyond that you have
neither vigour nor
character.' After
Waterloo he fled to
Corsica; shot by firing
squad after failed
attempt to regain his
Neapolitan throne.

In terms of battalions there were seven in the first line, seven in the second and six in the third, which was composed of all the Portuguese battalions from both divisions. *Nairn's brigade* formed the second line of Clinton's division (on the right) with the company of the 5/60th (*Frederickson*) deployed forward as skirmishers. It took a long time for 10,000 men to shake out into the required formation. When all was ready, it was a splendid sight: two long lines of scarlet backed by one of blue and brown with some 3500 bayonets in each of the first and second lines and 3000 in the third. The attack covered a frontage of almost a mile. Sharpe had never seen a British formation like it in all his years in the Peninsula.

The advance got under way around 12.30 p.m. Slowly, steadily the divisions climbed the slope. When they were about halfway up, Soult sent General Taupin to counter-attack with two columns. As they came forward they masked the fire from the La Sypière Redoubt. Then, instead of charging downhill, they halted and were blown away by an endless, rolling blast of musketry. Taupin fell, mortally wounded. His men turned to run, the battalion in La Sypière followed. It was a classic example of a line defeating a column.

There was a lengthy pause after the crest was taken: not until after 2.30 did the assault on the Mâs des Augustins and Calvinet Redoubts begin. After some pedantic drill-book manoeuvres under fire by the commanding officer (Colonel Macara) of the 1/42nd (Black Watch), they charged and took Mâs des Augustins, as did the 1/79th (Cameron Highlanders) at Calvinet. However, neither could hold against counter-attacks. Mâs des Augustins changed hands five times before Sharpe led the last assault. During this vicious and bloody fighting *Nairn* was mortally wounded, *Taplow* killed and Sharpe's horse decapitated with him in the saddle.

To be accurate, Napoleon abdicated twice in April 1814. On the third, he had 60,000 troops at Fontainebleau but 145,000 allies were in Paris. He reviewed his beloved soldiers and was greeted with spontaneous shouts of, 'Vive l'Empereur! À Paris! À Paris!' The next day, however, when he summoned

The final shots

EIGHT DAYS after Napoleon abdicated, the Peninsular War was still not quite over. On the night of 14 April General Thouvenot, the garrison commander of Bayonne, launched a major sortie against the siege lines of the British 5th Division. From loyalty to the Emperor, defiance, honour, or sheer bloody mindedness, Thouvenot cost 1743 needless casualties (French 905, Allies 838). Despite a warning from a deserter, the British were caught unawares as Thouvenot, at the head of 5000 troops, charged through the village of St Etienne in pitch darkness. The British broke in confusion, General Lord Hay was killed and Sir John Hope captured when his dying horse fell, trapping him. The fighting was mostly hand to hand, the bayonet being more useful in the dark than the bullet. Eventually, a reserve brigade of Foot Guards counter-attacked and pushed the French back. These were the final shots of the Peninsular War, although Thouvenot did not surrender the city until 27 April 1814.

Napoleon's farewell to the Guard

THIS TOOK PLACE at Fontainebleau on 20 April – about the same time Sharpe escaped from Bordeaux to begin his search for *Lassan*. Napoleon reviewed the Old Guard for the last time at an emotional parade where the men who were to accompany him to Elba were selected. As their Emperor appeared on the stairs the Guard's commander, General Petit, ordered 'Present Arms'. Drummers beat 'Aux Champs' (a general salute or music played at the start of the march to a battle-field) followed by trumpeters sounding the fanfare, 'To the Emperor'.

Napoleon addressed his beloved 'Grumblers': 'Officers, non-commissioned officers and soldiers of my Old Guard, I bid you farewell. For twenty years I have been pleased with you. I have always found you on the path to glory ... Never abandon this dear country that has suffered so long ... Now I shall write the story of what we have done ...' After embracing General Petit he said, 'Let the eagle be brought.' He kissed it three times, saying, 'Dear Eagle, let my embrace echo in the hearts of these brave men! Farewell, my children!' As his carriage pulled away, his soldiers were stunned into silence, but tears flowed openly.

his marshals for their orders, Ney declared, 'The army will not march', and news from Paris told of Marmont deserting with his troops. This was the final blow; Napoleon signed a

Gendarmerie élite

NAPOLEON'S
POISON

Opium, belladonna
and white hellebore
were an unpleasant
cocktail of plants.
Opium comes from
the poppy, belladonna
from deadly
nightshade and white,
or false, hellebore
from the flowering
plant of that name
poisonous to animals.
Of these, the most
toxic is the deadly
nightshade whose
black, shiny berries can
be tempting to
unsuspecting children
– although the entire
plant is poisonous. It
contains atropine,
which is a valuable
medical drug, but in
uncontrolled doses
causes death from
cardiac and
respiratory failure.

conditional abdication – the main proviso being that his son
would succeed him. Understandably, this was unacceptable
to the allies, and on the sixth of April Napoleon gave in. In
a burst of exasperated rage, he yelled at his marshals, 'You
want a rest – go and take it!' He wrote and signed his second,
definitive and unconditional abdication.

Several days of distasteful wrangling over details ensued.
The allies felt they were being magnanimous to the man
whom they saw as the scourge of Europe for so long. He was
to be Emperor of the tiny island of Elba, and would receive
two million francs a year; the Empress was to receive the
Duchy of Parma with reversion to her son; other relatives
were given pensions. Finally, he was to be allowed to take a
battalion of infantry, a squadron of cavalry and 120 gunners
as his personal guard. Napoleon called for volunteers from
the grenadiers, chasseurs, marine artillery and cavalry of the
Imperial Guard, and was swamped with requests. Many
officers begged to go as simple soldiers. Only the cream of
bemedalled veterans were selected, among them Sharpe's old
enemy from Teste de Buch, *General de Brigade Calvet*.

On 12 April, as Sharpe celebrated victory and survival in
a Toulouse tavern, the Emperor gave way to despair 350 miles
away. Fearful for his future, frightened that the Empress and
his son might not be allowed to join him, Napoleon attempted suicide. Ever since he had nearly been captured by
Cossacks in Russia, he had carried a small, black bag containing opium, belladonna and white hellebore around his neck.
He swallowed this concoction and called for his master-of-
the-horse, Armand Caulaincourt, to take his dying depo-
sition. Caulaincourt later wrote in his memoirs, 'The voice
was barely audible; the closing sentence, like those before it,
had been interrupted by recurrent hiccups and violent
nausea. His skin was parched and chill; all of a sudden it was
covered with an icy sweat; I thought he was about to expire
in my arms.' But the poison had been so long in the bag, it
had lost much of its potency. The attempt was hushed up,
and speculation continued until Caulaincourt's memoirs
were found in the 1930s.

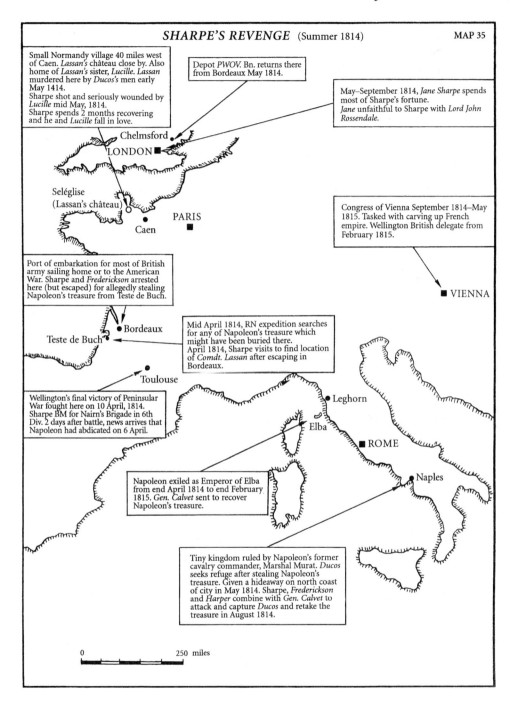

SHARPE'S REVENGE (Summer 1814)   MAP 35

Small Normandy village 40 miles west of Caen. *Lassan's* château close by. Also home of *Lassan's* sister, *Lucille*. *Lassan* murdered here by *Ducos's* men early May 1414.
Sharpe shot and seriously wounded by *Lucille* mid May, 1814. Sharpe spends 2 months recovering and he and *Lucille* fall in love.

Depot *PWOV.* Bn. returns there from Bordeaux May 1814.

May–September 1814, *Jane Sharpe* spends most of Sharpe's fortune. *Jane* unfaithful to Sharpe with *Lord John Rossendale*.

Chelmsford

LONDON

Séléglise (Lassan's château)

PARIS

Caen

Congress of Vienna September 1814–May 1815. Tasked with carving up French empire. Wellington British delegate from February 1815.

Port of embarkation for most of British army sailing home or to the American War. Sharpe and *Frederickson* arrested here (but escaped) for allegedly stealing Napoleon's treasure from Teste de Buch.

VIENNA

Bordeaux

Teste de Buch

Mid April 1814, RN expedition searches for any of Napoleon's treasure which might have been buried there.
April 1814, Sharpe visits to find location of *Comdt. Lassan* after escaping in Bordeaux.

Toulouse

Wellington's final victory of Peninsular War fought here on 10 April, 1814. Sharpe BM for Nairn's Brigade in 6th Div. 2 days after battle, news arrives that Napoleon had abdicated on 6 April.

Leghorn

Elba

ROME

Napoleon exiled as Emperor of Elba from end April 1814 to end February 1815. *Gen. Calvet* sent to recover Napoleon's treasure.

Naples

Tiny kingdom ruled by Napoleon's former cavalry commander, Marshal Murat. *Ducos* seeks refuge after stealing Napoleon's treasure. Given a hideaway on north coast of city in May 1814. Sharpe, *Frederickson* and *Harper* combine with *Gen. Calvet* to attack and capture *Ducos* and retake the treasure in August 1814.

0   250 miles

French Mameluke

MAMELUKES

Since the thirteenth century the Mameluke beys, warriors originating from the Caucasus, had ruled Egypt. Bonaparte was given a Mameluke (Raza Roustam) as a personal bodyguard after his conquest of the country. He admired their fighting qualities, so formed a squadron of 150 in 1801. They retained their oriental dress, even after Frenchmen were drafted in to keep up numbers, but they were always commanded by French officers. Later they were grouped with the Chasseurs à Cheval of the Imperial Guard, forming part of Napoleon's escort. Disbanded in 1814.

GENDARMERIE D'ÉLITE

A detachment escorted the bulk of Napoleon's treasure from Orléans to Paris in April 1814. They were the military police of the Imperial Guard, raised in 1802 from the gendarmeries of all departments of France. Apart from military police duties, they provided the Emperor's personal security, plus ceremonial guards at palaces. Uniform: blue coat, red facings, buff-coloured

The whole object of Sharpe's efforts throughout the summer of 1814 was to locate *Ducos* and Napoleon's missing millions, so as to disprove the charge that Sharpe had stolen the fortune (MAP 35). No treasure was concealed in the fort at Teste de Buch, but the Emperor had a vast horde of wealth, much of which went missing in those desperate days of April. One of the first acts of the provisional Bourbon government had been to order commissioners to seize Napoleon's treasure. The attorney-general, Dudon (a former officer cashiered for deserting his post in Spain), with an escort of eighty élite gendarmes, was sent to find it. On 11 April they rode to Orléans where the Empress was on her way to join Napoleon. Also riding to the same city for the same purpose was Napoleon's paymaster, Baron (Inspector) Peyrusse. He carried a letter authorising Napoleon's treasurer-general, de la Bouillerie, to send the funds with Peyrusse to Briare (a village

The Elba garrison

NAPOLEON sailed to Elba; his soldiers marched. After a 750-mile trek via Lyons, through the Mont Cénis pass and on to Savona, his personal guard arrived on the island on 26 May (when Sharpe was lying seriously wounded in *Lassan*'s château in Normandy). They had marched through scores of villages with drums beating, shouldered muskets and tricolour cockades in their bearskins. 'Where are you going?' the people asked. 'To join the Emperor.'

Napoleon met them on the quayside, and that night the Guard officers dined with their Emperor. The infantry battalion under Major Malet consisted of a small staff and six companies totalling 607 grenadiers and foot chasseurs. Its standard was white with a diagonal red stripe emblazoned with three gold bees on one side, the other had a crowned 'N'. The cavalry was under Major Roul, who had first fought for the Revolution in 1793. There were five chasseurs and Mamelukes, two NCOs and a lieutenant; the rest of the squadron were Polish lancers. Twenty-two were mounted, ninety-six dismounted. Like the infantry they had a white standard but with 'Polish Light Horse, Napoleon Squadron', embroidered on it in crimson. There was a detachment of gunners plus twenty-one marines attached to the Elba navy – one brig, three small boats and three gigs.

forty miles south-east of Orléans). Later that same day the Emperor despatched an escort of Polish cavalry and grenadiers of the Elba battalion to give his paymaster more muscle in case of an argument over ownership. The rest of the battalion marched at dawn the next day. Dudon arrived first. Waving his piece of paper, he demanded custody of the treasure, but de la Bouillerie refused to hand it over. There was a great deal at stake. The wagons and court carriages carrying the treasure were parked in the courtyard of the town hall. They contained twenty-three million francs in gold and over four million francs in presents, portraits encrusted with diamonds, gold and silver services, and boxes of jewels. Soldiers of the Imperial Guard protected it.

Peyrusse had a difficult journey. He had left Fontainebleau for Orléans with his servant and one guide, and had been compelled to make many detours. At one point he ran into a party of Cossacks and was forced to hide in a forest, then he lost his way. It was not until noon on 12 April that a

breeches, black boots and black bearskin with a red plume. Recognisable in inclement weather by their blue cloaks faced with red. They were armed with a heavy cavalry sabre and carbine, although not normally employed in combat. A squadron was present at Waterloo.

nervous and exhausted paymaster reached his destination only to find he was too late. De la Bouillerie had, after heated and protracted arguments, surrendered the Emperor's fortune to Dudon. The wagons were on their way to Paris.

But not quite all the loot had gone. Six million francs had been secretly 'withdrawn' from the coffers before they departed from the Place de la Cathedrale. From these Peyrusse succeeded in salvaging 2.6 million francs in gold which he packed into eight boxes and hid under a pile of manure in the cathedral stables. All the next day he waited anxiously in the stable loft, having sent his servant and guide back to Fontainebleau for help. Towards evening he was found by Captain Laborde, who commanded the escort Napoleon had sent to help him. The cases were loaded into a wagon, concealed under a torn canvas and taken to an inn on the suburbs of the city guarded by a sergeant and eight grenadiers.

This money went with Napoleon to Elba, as did Peyrusse, who remained paymaster on the island, but it was only a small fraction of the whole. *Ducos* got his hands on either the remainder of the six million francs that 'dropped off the back of the wagons' by the cathedral, or a sizeable slice of the main treasure that went to Paris. It is impossible to be certain which.

French head-dress
LEFT: *Hussar's forage cap*
RIGHT: *Trumpeter of the 16th Dragoons*

15

Sharpe's Waterloo

Sharpe was a lieutenant-colonel in the Dutch army, serving on the staff of the Prince of Orange, the enthusiastic, but worthless, twenty-three-year-old son of the Dutch king, who, for diplomatic reasons, had command of the 1st Corps of Wellington's army. *Harper*, although a civilian, contrived to accompany his friend into one of the most illustrious and bloody battlefields of history – Waterloo.

The story begins on the Sambre River as Napoleon launched his One Hundred Days' campaign. Sharpe observed the French as they streamed north from Charleroi on 15 June 1815. He contrived to be in Brussels that evening at the Duchess of Richmond's ball, reporting to Wellington and having an ugly confrontation with *Lord John Rossendale*, who had stolen both Sharpe's wife (*Jane*) and his fortune. At the battle of Quatre Bras he disobeyed a direct (but catastrophic) order from the Prince of Orange but saved the *Prince of Wales' Own Volunteers* from being shredded by cavalry. On Sunday, 18 June at Mont St Jean (Waterloo) Sharpe helped the Guards to close the gates of Hougoumont Farm; joined the *PWOV* in square to receive the flood of horsemen flung at the allied centre; deliberately shot the Prince of Orange in the shoulder; led the *PWOV* in a bayonet charge into the flank of an Imperial Guard column in the final, decisive minutes of the battle.

THE WATERLOO BRIDGE

On the second anniversary of the battle, Waterloo Bridge was opened over the Thames in London. At 3 p.m. a signal gun fired and the flags on the bridge unfurled. Shortly afterwards the procession of barges arrived, bringing the Lord Mayor, the Prince Regent, the Duke of York and Wellington. As they came under the central arch, guns were firing a 202-gun salute (one for each cannon captured at the battle). They landed on the south side and, after going through a toll-paying ceremony, the Prince Regent, accompanied by the Dukes of York and Wellington, walked across the bridge.

BY THE END OF FEBRUARY 1815, Napoleon had had enough of being 'Emperor' of Elba, the 140-square-mile island off the north-western Italian coast. On the night of the twenty-sixth he boarded the brigantine *L'Inconstant* and, with

NAPOLEON'S
ORDERLIES

Two personal
orderlies who always
rode close to the
Emperor were the
Mameluke (Raza
Roustam) and a page
(Louis Saint-Denis).
Roustam carried a flask
of brandy on a
shoulder strap and
had Napoleon's cloak
and spare coat in a
bundle across his
saddle; Saint-Denis
carried his telescope
and paper, pens, ink,
pencils, sealing wax
and dividers in his
saddle bags.

three generals, 1100 soldiers in six small boats, and watched by an excited crowd of loyal Elbans, he sailed for France. As the little ships got under-way, the singing died down and a solemn silence enveloped the lantern swinging well-wishers. The Emperor was resolved to take back his empire. The hugeness of his gamble was apparent to all.

On 1 March, when Napoleon stepped onto French soil, Sharpe and *Harper* were both civilians. Sharpe was living with *Lucille* on her family farm near Caen in Normandy, while *Harper* had used the loot from Vitória to buy a tavern in Ireland, also a convenient cover for a profitable horse-stealing business. Neither wanted to take up arms again. Not that Napoleon wanted to fight to regain (or indeed to hold) France. He offered himself to the people as a target or as an emperor – they had to choose. He ordered his tiny force never to open fire; when soldiers opposed them, they marched with arms reversed, Napoleon at their head. On 7 March, the first serious confrontation took place at the small town of Grenoble. Napoleon's force paraded outside the garrison gates; inside Colonel de la Bedoyère had drawn up the 7th Regiment with loaded muskets. An angry mob of anti-Bourbon peasants battered down the gates and surged forward to be greeted by defenders who rushed towards them, not with bayonets but with open arms, to embrace them. It was the turning point. As Napoleon was fond of saying in later years on his other island, St Helena, 'Before Grenoble I was an adventurer. At Grenoble I was a reigning prince.'

It was a week before the news of his escape reached the gross, gout-ridden Louis XVIII. Marshal Ney, now serving the king, vowed he would bring Napoleon to Paris in an iron cage. He rode south to take command of 30,000 men and keep his promise, but he found the troops disaffected. When Napoleon sent a message saying he would greet Ney as he had on the day of the Battle of Moscow, the emotional Marshal announced he would take his troops over to the Emperor. The more soldiers sent to oppose Napoleon, the greater became his following. At the Place Vendôme, a wag posted a notice, 'FROM NAPOLEON TO LOUIS XVIII. MY GOOD

BROTHER THERE IS NO NEED TO SEND ANY MORE TROOPS, I HAVE ENOUGH.' One shot was all it needed to defeat Napoleon, but nobody fired, so on 20 March he was carried shoulder-high into the Tuileries with his arms outstretched, eyes shut and a trancelike smile on his face. The Hundred Day clock had started.

In March 1815, the Congress of Vienna was in session, debating precisely how to rearrange the boundaries of Europe now that Napoleon's empire was restricted to an insignificant island. His arrival in Paris jolted the representatives (which included Wellington) into forming the Seventh Coalition. War was declared, not against France but against the person of Napoleon as, 'an enemy, and disturber of the world'. His emissaries of peace were rebuffed at every border, and an invasion of France was agreed which would stretch from the Channel to the Alps and involved over 600,000 men converging on Paris. The plan envisaged an Anglo–Dutch force of 150,000, a Prussian army of 120,000, with 150,000 Russians and 200,000 Austrians being in position on the French frontiers by June. Wellington arrived in Brussels on 5 April to take command of the Anglo–Dutch element of this military alliance.

One of the most intractable problems confronting Wellington was the unreliability of the Dutch and Belgian soldiers who made up a third of his army. Only a year before, many had been serving under the Eagles, as Belgium had been part of France and still wore French uniforms, although the eagle badge had been removed from their shakos. Wellington sought to stiffen their resolve by putting Dutch and Belgian units into British divisions, which had worked well with Portuguese battalions in the Peninsula. The young Prince of Orange, or 'Slender Billy' as he was known in the Peninsula because of his gangling body and elongated neck, was part of the problem. Because of the size of the Netherlands' troop contribution, because he was King William's son, and because he had visions of military glory, he had to be appointed to a very senior command. He got the 1st Corps. When Sharpe offered his services, Wellington had no hesitation in offering

NAPOLEON'S MAMELUKE

Raza Roustam was Napoleon's personal orderly and valet, dressed always in Mameluke clothes. He was originally a slave, given to Napoleon in 1799 by the Egyptian ruler. He made a fortune selling favours but deserted in April 1814 and married a Frenchwoman, ran a state lottery and wrote some colourful memoirs. Later he lived in England, returning to France for the state burial of Napoleon in Paris in 1840. He died in 1845, aged 65.

NAPOLEON'S
'GRUMBLERS' FADE
AWAY

For fifteen years the
Imperial Guard had
been masters of
Europe. Disbanded
and disgruntled, they
were scattered
throughout France
and beyond. Some
had no talents beyond
the manual of arms,
but all belonged to an
élite company. Most
found a home,
however humble,
where they could put
away their uniform
and hang their medals
under a portrait of
their Emperor. Old
men sat to tell tales, to
relive their glories.
Toasts were drunk to
'the other one' or 'his
Guard'. They never
forgot 'him' and when
he died on St Helena
many refused to
believe it. A rumour
said he had landed at
Ostend. 'Where are
you going?' asked the
wife of a Belgian
veteran when he
pulled on his
grenadier's greatcoat.
'To him!' In 1845 there
was a dinner for
former officers; fifteen
years later (the year
Sharpe died)
survivors received
from 'his' nephew the
St Helena Medal while
trumpeters of the old
horse chasseurs
saluted with the
fanfare, 'To the
Emperor' at the foot of
'his' column.

him a staff job at the prince's headquarters; some of his experience and military common sense would surely rub off. As an inducement, Sharpe was made an acting lieutenant-colonel – in the Dutch Army (although he stubbornly resisted efforts to get him to wear Dutch uniform). The 'Young Frog' (another nickname, King William being the 'Old Frog') was quite flattered to have him.

Although protesting peaceful intentions on the political front, Napoleon was in desperate haste to mobilise for war. His experience in 1814 had been that the vast coalition armies arraigned against him were cumbersome and slow. Their efforts were often uncoordinated, and they were vulnerable to surprise, speed and defeat in detail. To wait until all the allies were ready to crush him would be the ultimate folly (a mistake Saddam Hussein made in 1990): to survive he had to attack and defeat them one by one. In modern jargon, he had to make a pre-emptive strike.

The instrument for such an undertaking had to be created within weeks. The Army of the North would be created from the dismembered and dispersed remains of the old Grande Armée. Every ruse to raise troops was employed: sailors were withdrawn from the redundant fleet, six foreign regiments were recruited and old soldiers were persuaded to rejoin the Eagles by all means, short of conscription. By early June about 124,000 fully equipped men had been assembled as the field army – the strike force. Workshops in Paris had worked day and night turning out 1250 uniforms a day; the daily production of muskets had risen to 2000, and 12 million cartridges had been manufactured in two months. It was a stupendous effort.

The Emperor had his sword; now he had to use it before the Austrians and Russians could launch an offensive along the Rhine. His intention was to attack north-east to crush the Anglo–Dutch and Prussians, who had conveniently spread themselves out from Ostend to Liège (MAP 36). It would take allied units up to a week to march from one extremity of their deployment area to another; even to complete a

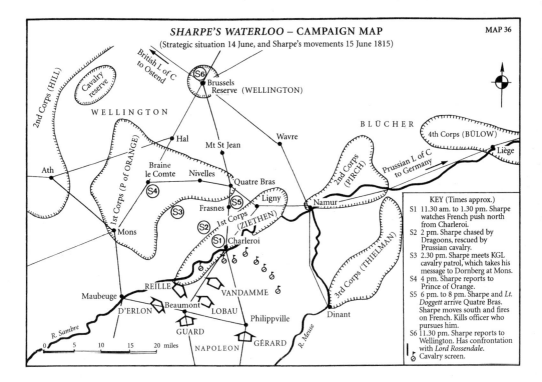

SHARPE'S WATERLOO – CAMPAIGN MAP

(Strategic situation 14 June, and Sharpe's movements 15 June 1815)

MAP 36

KEY (Times approx.)

S1 11.30 am. to 1.30 pm. Sharpe watches French push north from Charleroi.

S2 2 pm. Sharpe chased by Dragoons, rescued by Prussian cavalry.

S3 2.30 pm. Sharpe meets KGL cavalry patrol, which takes his message to Dornberg at Mons.

S4 4 pm. Sharpe reports to Prince of Orange.

S5 6 pm. to 8 pm. Sharpe and *Lt. Doggett* arrive Quatre Bras. Sharpe moves south and fires on French. Kills officer who pursues him.

S6 11.30 pm. Sharpe reports to Wellington. Has confrontation with *Lord Rossendale*.

Cavalry screen.

concentration on the centre would require forty-eight hours. Another key factor was that the supply bases of Wellington and Blücher (the Prussian commander) were located in opposite directions: one on the coast at Ostend, the other over the Rhine in Germany. Armies which were forced to retreat or were defeated invariably fell back towards their base, towards supplies and reinforcements. In this case it would mean the allies splitting farther and farther apart. Together they outnumbered Napoleon almost two to one; separately he was as strong, or stronger, than each. To succeed he had to deceive them and strike them before they could combine; next, he had to defeat one or other army, ensuring it retired towards its base, away from its ally; finally, he would turn on his second adversary. To overthrow a superior enemy in detail was a strategy of which Napoleon, with nineteen years as commander-in-chief behind him, was an acknowledged master.

One veteran lived in three centuries: Lieutenant Markiewicz (Polish Lancers) was born in Cracow in 1794, fought in the Russian campaign, charged at Waterloo, and was still alive in 1902.

Napoleon and his soldiers

THE EMPEROR had a tremendous rapport with his soldiers: he believed that a general must love his soldiers to understand them, and understand them to lead them. He had been a soldier all his life, climbing from sous-lieutenant to emperor, and the professional bond was profound. To his *grognards* (veterans), 'emperor' was a military rank above 'general' or 'marshal'. Soldiers never addressed him as 'Your Majesty' or 'Sire' but always 'Mon Empereur'. He seldom forgot a face, never a kindness.

At a review in 1809, he recognised a grenadier who had risked his life to save his hat at the Siege of Acre nine years earlier. Napoleon demanded why he was still a grenadier. The man replied that he could not write, and gestured that he was something of a drunkard. His Emperor gave him fifty francs. After Austerlitz, he adopted all the children of soldiers killed in the battle: the boys would be brought up at the Imperial palace at Rambouillet and the girls at Sainte Germaine. All could add 'Napoleon' to their names.

RED LANCERS

Those spotted by Sharpe near the Sambre belonged to the 2nd Lancers of the Guard, part of Pajol's cavalry screen. They were raised in 1810 by the incorporation of the Dutch Royal Guard into the Imperial Guard as cuirassiers. However, their horses were too small so they converted to lancers with square, Polish-style caps and brilliant scarlet uniforms. Even in 1815 most were still Dutchmen. Their old second-in-command, General van Merlen, died at the head of a Netherlands cavalry brigade fighting for the allies.

On 7 June the French frontiers along the Sambre, Rhine and Moselle were sealed. There must be no whisper (apart from false information) as to where or when he would strike. He had assembled his army, in total secrecy, just south of the Sambre around the town of Beaumont. By the fourteenth, the Armée du Nord, with 124,000 men and 370 guns, was encamped in that precise area. It was the anniversary of his great victory at Marengo. His Order of the Day, to be read to every regiment the next morning, proclaimed this auspicious fact. From Beaumont he would advance north, cross the river at and near Charleroi before pushing up the highway to Brussels. Such a route would place him between the allied armies. The Prussians (Ziethen's 1st Corps) would be hit first, and could be expected to withdraw, covering the concentration of the Prussian army somewhere around Ligny or Namur. Knowing the impetuous character of Blücher, he expected and hoped for a forward concentration, which would give him the early battle he sought. The scattered Anglo–Dutch forces could be held at arm's length by a strong detachment if necessary. A glance at Map 36 makes the strategy clear. The Philippeville–Charleroi–Brussels road runs north, cutting the allied cantonments at their junction; for the Allies to combine they had to march along the Liege–Namur–Ligny–Nivelles–Braine-le-Comte road which runs east–west. The two highways cross at the hamlet of Quatre Bras. Whoever held that crossroads held the key to the development – if not the outcome – of the campaign.

When Sharpe rode along the north bank of the Sambre on the morning of 15 June, he had strayed (deliberately) into a Prussian area of responsibility. Ziethen guarded the Sambre crossings in this area, and his advanced patrols had already clashed with the French cavalry inside Belgium, south of the river. Sharpe could not know that twelve regiments of cavalry were screening the invasion of Belgium. Close behind came engineer detachments with pontoons, clattering cannons (Napoleon's beloved 12-pounders), followed by endless dark-blue columns of marching infantry. The majority headed for the Charleroi bridge. Between about 11.30 a.m. and 1.30 p.m., Sharpe watched as cavalry, guns and infantry streamed north up the Quatre Bras road.

There had been a serious delay at the bridge: the hussars of the French 4th Cavalry Division had arrived to find it intact but barricaded and defended by infantry. A hastily organised charge proved futile, so the horsemen waited for infantry. These were supposed to be Vandamme's 3rd Corps, but the messenger with his movement order had fallen from his horse so Vandamme was late starting. The first infantry to arrive around noon was a battalion of the Young Guard with Napoleon himself, and the bridge was quickly taken. While Sharpe peered through his telescope and counted the units and guns, Napoleon sat in a chair outside the Belle Vue tavern receiving the acclamations of his troops, some of whom kissed his nearby horse. After a while he dozed.

By half past one Sharpe had seen enough, having been sufficiently close to General Excelman's dragoons to spot their pigtails. His task was to inform his headquarters with the utmost urgency of what was happening. He had a twenty-mile (two-hour) ride to Braine-le-Comte, during which he was

CAPTAIN JOHN MCCULLOCK, 2/95TH

An officer known to Sharpe. Lost the use of one arm in the Peninsula in 1811, and the other at Waterloo. Told the Duke he was still anxious to serve and was promoted major in the 2nd Garrison Battalion. He died in 1818.

LIEUTENANT-COLONEL HAMILTON, 2/30TH (CAMBRIDGESHIRE)

Commanding officer of 2/30th (nicknamed 'The Three Tens') which fought beside the PWOV at Quatre Bras and Waterloo. He was severely wounded at Quatre Bras: three times a tourniquet was tied round his leg prior to amputation, three times the surgeon was called away. His leg was saved.

Napoleon and his horses

NAPOLEON KEPT a stable of a hundred for riding and carriage horses. His carriage had light draught animals from Normandy, which had speed and stamina. For the saddle he used mares or stallions, preferably white, grey or chestnut. He liked Arab breeds as well as Spanish and Russian, and his finest animals were gifts from the Emperor of Morocco and the Sultan of Turkey. He worked them hard, liking nothing better than to dash off at a gallop (in his carriage or the saddle) from a standing start – much to the exasperation of his staff.

A good horse was invariably pensioned off to green grass and a warm stable. All were painstakingly trained by one of his equerries, Auguste Jardin, being taught to ignore blows to the body, the noise of guns and muskets, the smell of blood and flags waved over their heads. On campaign there was a pool of 130 horses for himself and his household staff, divided into ten teams of thirteen. Three were for Napoleon and one each for his master-of-horse, an equerry, a page, an outrider, his Mameluke (not after 1814), a guide, his surgeon and three grooms. Horses for his use had a pair of pistols in the holsters which had to be unloaded at night and reloaded every morning by one of his Mamelukes, supervised by the duty equerry.

TROOP SERGEANT-MAJOR MATTHEW MARSHALL, 6TH DRAGOONS

Marshall charged with the Inniskillings as far as the French Grand Battery. While cutting at a cuirassier on his right, his bridle arm was broken by a sword cut on his left. More enemy closed in, unhorsing him with a lance through his side. He lost consciousness for a while then, as he dragged himself towards a riderless horse, another trooper cut him several times with his sword. A French

chased by dragoons (the only dragoon unit in this area could have been General Guyot's Dragoons of the Guard). A lucky encounter with some KGL cavalry saved him and shortly afterwards he found another KGL unit to take his information to Major-General Dornberg at Mons. Dornberg commanded Wellington's cavalry screen south of Mons – the 1st and 2nd Light Dragoons of the KGL plus the 23rd Light Dragoons. Until 1813, when he switched sides, Dornberg had been a colonel fighting for the French. Despite his rapid promotion, he was a disgruntled officer: Sharpe's message was torn up and he also rejected a similar report from Lieutenant-Colonel Colquhoun Grant, operating inside France as Wellington's chief of intelligence. He did eventually report that the French were not advancing via Mons, but this did not reach Brussels until around ten o'clock that night.

When Sharpe reached the Prince of Orange's headquarters, the prince had left for Brussels to lunch with the duke and attend the Duchess of Richmond's ball that evening. At almost the same moment, Marshal Ney was reporting to Napoleon at Charleroi. He was given command of the left wing of the French army, which was pushing due north up the road towards Quatre Bras; almost 50,000 men, although they were strung out over twenty miles of road, with much of d'Erlon's Corps still south of the Sambre. Ney had the four infantry divisions of Lieutenant-General Count d'Erlon's 1st Corps (Allix, Donzelot, Marcognet and Durutte) and the chasseurs, hussars and lancers of Jacquinot's cavalry division. Ahead of them were three infantry divisions of Lieutenant-General Count Réille (Bachelu, a battalion of whose men was the leading infantry unit, Prince Jerome, and Foy) plus the light cavalry of Piré's division. Out in front were the cream of the French light cavalry – Lieutenant-General Lefebvre-Desnöettes' Lancers and Chasseurs à Cheval of the Imperial Guard. Ney also had over 80 cannons. Accompanied by a solitary staff officer, he cantered up to Gosselies, about eight miles south of Quatre Bras. The road north was open. At 4 p.m. the key crossroads were there for the taking.

Shortly after Sharpe's arrival at Braine-le Comte his chief-of-staff, Major-General Constant de Rébecque, another old Etonian but a more competent soldier than his commander, made a crucial decision. He authorised Perponcher, commanding the 2nd Netherlands Division, to send a brigade to Quatre Bras. Sharpe took this message. In fact Prince Bernard of Saxe-Weimar's 2nd Brigade was already billeted in the area, and had one of his five Nassau battalions and a solitary battery of horse artillery close to the crossroads. While Sharpe was at 1st Corps headquarters, these troops had seen off the probings of Ney's advancing squadrons clattering north from Frasnes. When Sharpe returned, he was in time to clash (at around 6.30 p.m.) with the leading battalion of Bachelu's division on the outskirts of the village. With dusk only an hour or two away, Ney had no wish to become embroiled in a serious fight so a halt was called. The road south from Frasnes to the Sambre and beyond was soon lit by thousands of bivouac fires as 45,000 Frenchmen camped by the roadside. As they cooked and slept Sharpe hurried north for

artilleryman rested his foot on his body while he rammed his gun. For two days and three nights he lay on the field with nineteen wounds. He lived in Belfast for another seven years, on a pension of two shillings a day.

CAPTAIN KENNEDY CLARK, 1ST (ROYAL) DRAGOONS

This officer, a Peninsula veteran, captured the Eagle of the 105th Ligne, a Regiment in Marcognet's division, after a desperate fight in which he was wounded. He handed the Eagle to Corporal Stiles to carry to the rear. Stiles was promoted sergeant and then ensign in the West India Regiment for assisting Clark. Clark attended the last Waterloo banquet as Colonel Clark-Kennedy, ultimately becoming a lieutenant-general. He was from a family that produced sons for the cavalry for many generations to come – the writer's company commander at Sandhurst in the 1950s was Major Clark-Kennedy (9th Lancers) who had fought in World War II.

Brussels, the ball, and his confrontation with *Lord Rossendale*.

In Brussels Wellington had still not left for the ball at 10 p.m. News of French activity around Charleroi had reached him by mid afternoon from several sources, so by early evening orders had gone out to his divisions to concentrate – but not move. He was uncertain that the Charleroi attack was the main thrust, and worried that the real route might still be through Mons. Within the space of a few minutes, two messages arrived. One from the Prussians and, equally important, Dornberg's confirmation that Mons was clear. Wellington ordered a concentration forward at Mont St Jean–Nivelles–Braine-le Comte, and left for the ball. He had not appreciated the significance of Quatre Bras.

Shortly before a late dinner, Lieutenant Harry Webster, an ADC on the Young Frog's staff, appeared with a message indicating the Prussians had been pushed back from Fleurus (only eight miles from Quatre Bras). The duke spoke brusquely to the ADC, 'Webster! Four horses instantly for the Prince of Orange's carriage.' Within a few minutes of the meal starting, Slender Billy was back, whispering anxiously in Wellington's ear. Another message had arrived from de Rébecque, timed at 10.30 p.m., which indicated the French had pushed up the road towards Quatre Bras. De Rébecque's message said he had ordered all of Perponcher's division to the crossroads – this was Sharpe's message. Wellington realised he had been 'humbugged'. The race for reinforcements, to assemble the entire Anglo–Dutch Army around that cluster of farm buildings, was now on.

Controversy has raged over Ney's dilatoriness on the morning of 16 June. Had Napoleon made it clear that Ney had to take the crossroads as a matter of urgency – or not? The Prussians had concentrated forward on Sombreffe, thus playing into the Emperor's hands by giving him his early battle against one opponent. So what was Ney's role? Was he to push up the road to Brussels as far as Quatre Bras, thus severing the direct road link between the two allies? Was he merely to keep Wellington occupied while Napoleon crushed the Prussians?

From his actions that day, one thing is clear: either Ney was a grossly incompetent commander or Napoleon had failed to brief him properly – possibly some of both. At dawn that morning, indeed until long after, Ney had Réille's 20,000 men and 60 guns to confront Slender Billy's 7000 men and eight guns. Ney did not know the exact number of his enemy, who used the ground skilfully to conceal their weakness, but it is not good military practice to sit on one's hands, as the 'bravest of the brave' did that morning.

Wellington had less than two hours' sleep after leaving the ball. He was up at 5 a.m., dictating orders at 5.30, and on the road two hours later: there was considerable catching up to be done. He arrived at Quatre Bras around 10 o'clock, shortly after Sharpe and *Harper*. They all had a long look at Frasnes. The French were there, but there was no obvious preparation for an advance – no cavalry probing the flanks, no voltigeurs fanning out into the fields of rye, no guns being positioned, no bands playing, no marching men. Within a matter of minutes the duke had seen enough; his troops were

Napoleon's command post

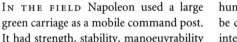

IN THE FIELD Napoleon used a large green carriage as a mobile command post. It had strength, stability, manoeuvrability and was weather-proofed. Inside, considerable ingenuity had ensured that the needs of a commander on campaign were met. One seat across the back was partially partitioned so that two persons could work without being thrown around. Opposite this, was a lockable cabinet with a leaf which could be pulled out to make a writing desk, and contained several drawers for files, despatches, and a map case. Other cupboards contained writing materials, books, telescopes, food, drinks and toilet necessities; a silver chronometer hung on one wall. Napoleon's seat could be converted into a bed, and at night the interior was lit by a large suspended lantern. His camp bed was under the driver's seat, and spare clothes and bedding were in the boot. The carriage was designed so that the Emperor and his chief-of-staff (usually Berthier, but Soult at Waterloo) could travel and work on the move. Riding outside would be a duty equerry on the right and a senior officer of the Guard cavalry on the left. Messages could be handed through the window, maps consulted, orders written and ADCs summoned to deliver them – all without stopping.

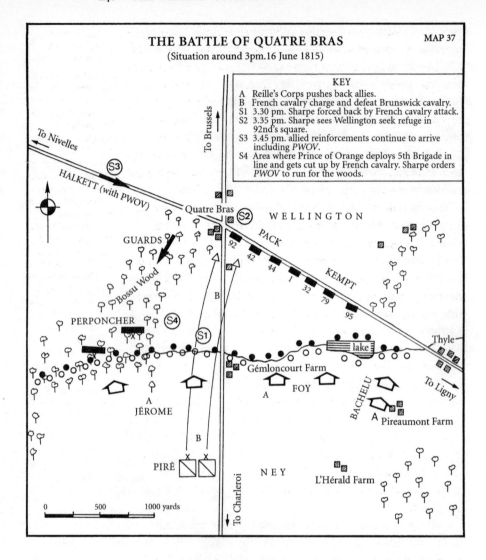

THE BATTLE OF QUATRE BRAS
(Situation around 3pm.16 June 1815)

MAP 37

KEY
A Reille's Corps pushes back allies.
B French cavalry charge and defeat Brunswick cavalry.
S1 3.30 pm. Sharpe forced back by French cavalry attack.
S2 3.35 pm. Sharpe sees Wellington seek refuge in
    92nd's square.
S3 3.45 pm. allied reinforcements continue to arrive
    including PWOV.
S4 Area where Prince of Orange deploys 5th Brigade in
    line and gets cut up by French cavalry. Sharpe orders
    PWOV to run for the woods.

To Nivelles

To Brussels

HALKETT (with PWOV)

Quatre Bras

WELLINGTON

GUARDS

PACK

Bossu Wood

92

42

44

KEMPT

1

32

79

95

PERPONCHER

B

Thyle

lake

Gémloncourt Farm

To Ligny

FOY

A

BACHELU

A Pireaumont Farm

A
JÉROME

B

PIRÉ

NEY

L'Hérald Farm

0   500   1000 yards

To Charleroi

converging on the crossroads from the north and west, and
with every passing minute his position would strengthen. He
would do nothing to stir up the French. Instead he turned
his horse's head east, and cantered away, trailing a gaggle of
staff officers, to meet Blücher near Ligny.

The Battle of Quatre Bras did not start until after 2 p.m.
Réille personally supervised the attack of his leading brigade

(MAP 37). Wellington returned by three o'clock, in time to organise a counter-attack on Gémioncourt and Piraumont. The battle swung backwards and forwards, temporary success going to the side able to rush reinforcements into the fight. Brigade after brigade of Réille's corps marched up to be deployed left and right of the road in the struggle for the farms and Bossu Wood until Bachelu, Foy and Napoleon's brother Jérome, had committed all their men. Piré's green-jacketed lancers and chasseurs were thrown in. Ney now needed d'Erlon's corps to tip the scales in his favour.

On the allied side, Picton's division came up, then the Guards, then Alten's division and the *PWOV* marching in Halkett's brigade, the troops tired and sweating from their forced march. As the afternoon wore on the Duke of Brunswick was killed, 'Slender Billy' made his blunders, Wellington narrowly escaped Piré's lance points by leaping Copenhagen into the square of the 1/92nd (Gordon Highlanders), Ensign Christie saved the Colours of the 2/44th (East Essex), and Sharpe took command of the *PWOV* from the bumbling, half-blind *Colonel Ford*. They, like the rest of the brigade, had been ordered into line by the Prince of Orange and then caught by cavalry. Sharpe led them in a rush for shelter in Bossu Wood; the 2/69th (South Lincolnshire) were cut to pieces, losing a Colour, and the 33rd (Sharpe's old Regiment) reached the trees only after serious loss. By evening, however, the French had exhausted themselves. Réille could not succeed without more men against the ever more numerous allied army.

During the afternoon there occurred one of the most infamous misunderstandings in military history, an event which probably more than any other cost Napoleon the campaign. Over 21,000 men (d'Erlon's corps) marched to and fro between the battlefields of Quatre Bras and Ligny without firing a shot. When, by late afternoon, Ney sent for d'Erlon he discovered to his fury that the entire corps was marching to Ligny, having been ordered there by an ADC from the Emperor. Almost incoherent with rage, Ney sent a galloper with a peremptory order of recall, though a moment's

2/44TH (EAST ESSEX) BATTLE HONOUR

This battalion lost many men at Quatre Bras and Waterloo and was awarded the battle honour Waterloo to be borne on its Colours. However, because it had been so reduced in numbers, the survivors were posted to the 1st battalion and the 2/44th ceased to exist. On 26 July 1815, the Prince Regent agreed that this battle honour could be transferred to the Essex Regiment, which amalgamated with the 16th Foot (Bedfordshire and Hertfordshire Regiment) in 1958 and is now a part of the Royal Anglian Regiment. Its soldiers still wear on their sleeves cloth replicas of the Eagle captured at Salamanca.

thought would have told him that d'Erlon could never return in time. D'Erlon dutifully turned round. That corps at Ligny could have fallen on the Prussian right flank and crushed them completely. That corps at Quatre Bras could have taken the cross-roads. It did neither. Napoleon was compelled to use the Imperial Guard at Ligny to pierce the Prussian centre. The enemy fell back, but were allowed to retire north instead of east; they arrived on Napoleon's right flank at Waterloo two days later – with fatal consequences.

On 17 June, Napoleon's basic strategy was still intact despite the d'Erlon fiasco. His right wing (Grouchy) and his reserve had hit the Prussians hard; they could be discounted for up to two days no matter what direction they took. He was free to turn on Wellington, who was grouped forward at Quatre Bras, a mere three hours' march away. Grouchy with 33,000 men could pursue the Prussians, keep them moving away from Wellington, while Napoleon swung his reserve west to strike the duke's left flank at Quatre Bras. The campaign could have been concluded in the Emperor's favour on the Saturday. The window of opportunity was open throughout the morning of the seventeenth; by midday it was closing as Wellington withdrew north, in the afternoon it slammed shut as thunderstorms and torrential rain turned the ground into a quagmire, slowing pursuit to a miserable crawl.

The key had been to keep Wellington at Quatre Bras during the morning while Napoleon came up against his exposed flank. This meant Ney had to hold him, attack him, and prevent withdrawal. He did no such thing, nor did Napoleon send him urgent orders to do so. A blanket of lethargy enveloped the French until 11 a.m. when a report from Ney arrived and cavalry patrols said that Wellington was still in position. Napoleon's mind cleared. But by the time Sharpe spotted him through his telescope at around one o'clock, only the allied rearguard was still at the crossroads, and storm clouds were piling up in the west.

The French pursuit became a nightmare in the lashing rain and deep Brabant mud. Drenched to the bone, exhausted and hungry, the infantry were forced to leave the roads to the cannons and wagons. Men sank to their knees, lost their shoes, cursed and got lost in the darkness and downpour. Sleep was an impossibility. Discipline slipped. At the village of Glabais, about four miles north of Quatre Bras, some of the Old Guard invaded the local houses, burnt the furniture, demanded food and remained absent from their units until daybreak. Company officers condoned the lapses. Unable to maintain discipline, the Imperial Guard's provost marshal resigned. By early morning the rain had stopped but the soldiers of both armies were wet, weary and ravenous. Few Frenchmen got breakfast: most supply *caissons* were still stuck in the mud near Charleroi.

A bird flying south over Mont St Jean Farm at around 10 a.m. on Sunday, 18 June 1815 would have seen a sight similar to that in SKETCH 6. The battlefield was small, with the opposing armies each occupying a low ridge separated by 1500 yards of undulating valley, filled with high-standing rye and corn. From Hougoumont Farm in the west to Papelotte village in the east was only 5000 yards; it was possible to walk around the circumference in a few hours. Within these three square miles, 140,000 men with 400 guns were preparing to fight. The bird, wheeling over the farm, would see that the French were drawn up equally on either side of the Brussels–Charleroi highway, straight as a lance through the centre of each army, leaving the Anglo–Dutch position close to a solitary elm tree, passing La Haye Sainte Farm and entering the French lines at La Belle Alliance. Several hours were needed to deploy 72,000 Frenchmen and 246 guns and, anyway, the ground needed time to dry out. Napoleon's force was set out with beautiful symmetry in three huge lines on either side of the road. From Sharpe's vantage point on the right of the allied ridge, only a fraction of the enemy was visible: dark masses were marching; distance dulled the colours; the dirty uniforms, rust-streaked helmets and cuirasses, the haggard, bearded faces were invisible. Perhaps occasionally, very faintly, cheering was audible as a battalion passed its Emperor, or the drums rolled, or

THE WATERLOO MEDAL

This was the first medal issued by the British government to both officers and other ranks. It set the pattern for the scores of campaign medals and hundreds of bars and clasps awarded since, and any soldier present at the Battles of Ligny, Quatre Bras or Waterloo was entitled to it. The medal was silver, with the Prince Regent's head on the obverse. The reverse had the word 'Wellington' over the seated winged figure of Victory, underneath were the words 'Waterloo June 18 1815'. Sharpe and *Harper* both received it.

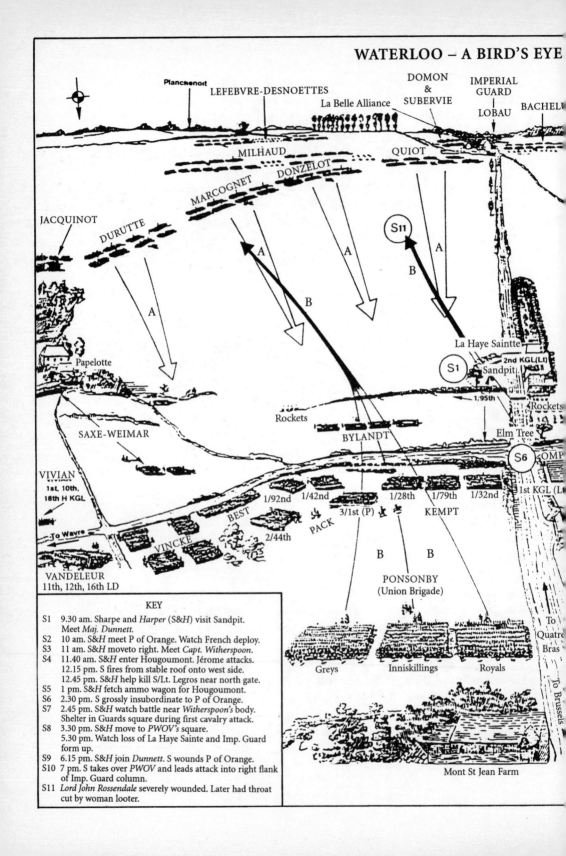

WATERLOO – A BIRD'S EYE

KEY

S1 9.30 am. Sharpe and *Harper* (*S&H*) visit Sandpit.
Meet *Maj. Dunnett*.

S2 10 am. *S&H* meet P of Orange. Watch French deploy.

S3 11 am. *S&H* move to right. Meet *Capt. Witherspoon*.

S4 11.40 am. *S&H* enter Hougoumont. Jérome attacks.
12.15 pm. S fires from stable roof onto west side.
12.45 pm. *S&H* help kill S/Lt. Legros near north gate.

S5 1 pm. *S&H* fetch ammo wagon for Hougoumont.

S6 2.30 pm. S grossly insubordinate to P of Orange.

S7 2.45 pm. *S&H* watch battle near *Witherspoon's* body.
Shelter in Guards square during first cavalry attack.

S8 3.30 pm. *S&H* move to *PWOV's* square.
5.30 pm. Watch loss of La Haye Sainte and Imp. Guard
form up.

S9 6.15 pm. *S&H* join *Dunnett*. S wounds P of Orange.

S10 7 pm. S takes over *PWOV* and leads attack into right flank
of Imp. Guard column.

S11 *Lord John Rossendale* severely wounded. Later had throat
cut by woman looter.

FOY

KELLERMAN

GUYOT

JÉROME

PIRÉ

Guards Light Companies

Hougoumont

15th H

S4

BYNG

2/3rd G

2nd CG

S3

1/23rd

7th H

DU PLAT

1st KGL

MAITLAND

S7

S2

3rd KGL

4th KGL

C

C

D

C

C

C

D

C

C

S10

2/1st G

3/1st G

Artillery limbers

15th H

13th LD

GRANT

DORNBERG

2nd KGL

1/71st

ADAM

1/52nd

S9

C

HALKETT

KIELMANSEGGE

PWOV
(S. Essex)

2/30th

23rd LD

1st & 2nd LD KGL

2/95th

h KGL HANOVERIAN

S8

1/33rd

2/69th

h KGL

HANOVERIAN

NASSAU

CUMBERLAND H

8th KGL

NASSAU

B

B

SOMERSET
(Household Brigade)

3rd H KGL

MERLEN

BRUNSWICKERS

2nd LG

1st LG

1st DG

Blues

TRIPP

S5

KEY

A French attack with D'Erlon's 4 divisions.
B 2–2.30 pm. Union and Household Brigades charge
   retreating French but pursue too far, and are scattered
   and destroyed.
C 3.45–5 pm. Continuous, but fruitless, cavalry atacks by
   Milhaud, Lefebvre-Desnöettes, Kellerman and Guyot.
   Involved cuirassiers, lancers, hussars, dragoons,
   chasseurs and horse grenadiers.
D 7 pm. Final assault by Imperial Guard also fails.

snatches of a band played 'Let Us Watch Over the Empire'.

Wellington's army of 68,000 men and 156 guns was a patchwork of units – British, German, Dutch and Belgian. They were drawn up along the line of the east–west sunken road which cut the main Brussels road at the elm tree. All of them, except Bylandt's Dutch-Belgians, were kept below the crest, so little could be seen from the French lines. Saxe-Weimar's men, who had frustrated Ney at Quatre Bras, held the important outpost of Papelotte on the left; the KGL were in La Haye Sainte, and alongside them in the sandpit were the 1/95th, with *Major Dunnett* desperate to avenge himself for five lost years as a French prisoner. On the right were the wood, orchard and buildings of Hougoumont: three strongpoints in advance of the allied line.

As at Quatre Bras, not much happened in the morning. Sharpe had time to renew acquaintanceship with *Major Dunnett* and the 95th in the sandpit next to La Haye Sainte, move to the right flank, meet with 'Slender Billy', watch the French deploy and position their 'Grand Battery', chat with *Captain Witherspoon* of the 15th Hussars (who had been at Eton with the Prince of Orange), and then join the light companies of the Guards in Hougoumont, all before the French moved.

Napoleon's plan lacked subtlety. He intended to smash his way through, up the road to Brussels. No manoeuvring, no outflanking, just a massive frontal attack preceded by a pounding from 80 guns (the Grand Battery) which included three 12-pounder batteries ('beautiful daughters') from the reserve artillery. At about 11.30 a single cannon fired the three shots that signalled the start of the Emperor's battles. It was the last time they were heard. On the left Jérome's division from Réille's corps rushed forward to storm the woods of Hougoumont in a diversionary attack to draw Wellington's reserves from his centre. The struggle for this farm lasted all day and sucked in Foy and Bachelu – it became a battle within the battle. The French succeeded only once in getting inside the farmyard, when Sous-Lieutenant Legros, a huge man with an axe, nicknamed 'The Enforcer', smashed his way through the north gate followed by 20–30 men. Sharpe and

Harper were involved in the frantic fight to close the gate and kill the Frenchmen trapped inside. Sharpe almost lost his own life in helping to kill Legros before spending some time sniping through a barn roof at Jérome's men west of the farm.

The next phase was intended to deliver the battle-winning blow. After half an hour's pounding by the Grand Battery the four divisions of d'Erlon's corps (yet to fire a shot) were to advance through the rye east of the Brussels road. Napoleon, having announced his general intentions, handed over the conduct of the assault to Ney – a decision he would regret. With the exception of Durutte, the divisions (Quiot, Donzelot and Marcognet) adopted totally unsuitable formations, advancing on a deployed battalion frontage of some 180 men, inviting massive loss from gun and musket fire. Behind came seven or eight battalions in the same formation, forming solid blocks 180 men wide and 24–27 men deep. Captain Duthilt, in Marcognet's division, was appalled, 'My regiment had to advance like the others in deployed battalions, with only four paces between one and the next . . . [it] cost us dear . . . the enemy's artillery could plough through our formations to a depth of twenty ranks.' Ney also failed to ensure sufficient cavalry or artillery support; the attack was decimated by gunfire and blown away by a long line of muskets at close range. Among the few British losses was Sir Thomas Picton (5th Division commander), killed instantly by a musket ball through his top-hat.

The rout was completed by headlong charges of the two British heavy cavalry brigades. Galloping with the Household Brigade was *Captain Lord John Rossendale*, the man who had stolen Sharpe's wife and fortune. These were big men on big horses who, after smashing through the fleeing infantry, careered out of control up to the Grand Battery and sabred a number of gunners. At this point, French lancer squadrons spurred into the disorganised British cavalry and exacted a heavy price for their impetuous behaviour. Sir William Ponsonby, the Union Brigade commander, died when his blown horse was slowed by mud; *Lord Rossendale* was skewered by lance thrusts and lay in agony for hours. His throat

BRITISH HEAVY CAVALRY

The two brigades that charged d'Erlon's divisions consisted of the 1st (Household) Brigade under Major-General Lord Somerset (1st and 2nd Life Guards plus the Blues) and the 2nd (Union) Brigade under Major-General Sir William Ponsonby (1st Royal Dragoons, 2nd Dragoons (Greys)), and 6th Dragoons (Inniskillings). It was the 'Union' Brigade because it consisted of Regiments from England, Scotland and Ireland.

THE HORSES

Injuries to horses were as horrendous as those inflicted on their riders. Crippled animals would crop the grass around themselves, twisting so that they surrounded themselves with a circle of bare earth. Riderless mounts would graze despite the awful noise of battle then, as a squadron charged past, their instinctive training took over and they would gallop along in the rear.

'WATERLOO
TEETH'

Making false teeth
from whalebone was
an expensive business.
Nineteenth-century
dentists often used
natural teeth instead,
collected from a
mortuary or a
battlefield. Especially
prized were the teeth
of healthy young men,
so the scavengers at
Waterloo had rich
picking. For a number
of years after the
battle, it was
fashionable to claim a
mouthful of 'Waterloo
teeth'. During the
American Civil War
tooth-drawers
followed the armies,
shipping teeth to
Europe by the barrel.

was slit by a peasant woman after the battle because he moaned as she stripped his body. D'Erlon had been routed, but the cost to Wellington was seven regiments of heavy cavalry severely mauled.

By this time (around 2 p.m.) Napoleon had been forced to acknowledge the presence of the Prussians (Bülow's 4th Corps) pushing towards Plancenoit on his right. Domon's chasseurs were sent east, to be followed by Lobau's infantry divisions. Blücher had kept his promise to support Wellington and had abandoned his communications to do so. Grouchy had failed to hold them off. In time the strength of the allies would be more than doubled.

Sharpe had watched the 'heavies' smash d'Erlon from near the elm tree. A little later, close to the same spot, he was threatened with arrest by the Prince of Orange for insulting remarks. Throughout the afternoon Sharpe and *Harper* were dumbfounded spectators to the greatest and most sustained cavalry charges in history. They sheltered first in a Guard's square, then in that of the *PWOV* who had combined with the 2/30th. Between about 3.30 and 5 p.m., a boiling sea of up to 10,000 horsemen ebbed and flowed around tiny islands of red.

This was another of Ney's blunders. As with d'Erlon, little attempt was made to co-ordinate the assaults with other arms. Between twelve and sixteen attacks were made and thrown back as more and more fresh units were flung in. It was a perfect example of trying to succeed by reinforcing failure. By 5 p.m. Napoleon's magnificent cavalry had disintegrated. Milhaud, Lefebvre-Desnöettes, Kellerman and Guyot had led their formations, at the trot, up the slope to oblivion. The broken bodies of horses and men – cuirassier, chasseur, dragoon, carabinier and grenadier à cheval – were heaped in hundreds along a front of 600 yards.

Late in the afternoon La Haye Sainte fell to some of d'Erlon's battalions, the only French success on the ridge. Voltigeurs pressed up to the allied line near the elm tree. Alten suggested that Ompteda deploy his KGL battalions to drive them away but he declined because French cavalry were close behind the skirmishers. At that moment 'Slender Billy' rode up and, dismissing Ompteda's protestations, peremptorily ordered him to deploy. He did so, losing his own life and most of the 5th KGL. This so enraged Sharpe that he crept forward with Harper, joined *Major Dunnett* and some 1/95th, and deliberately shot 'Slender Billy' (he was indeed wounded at about this time).

After the endless cavalry attacks the finale was almost an anti-climax. At 7.30 p.m. Napoleon personally led the advance of six battalions of the Imperial Guard. At the start of the battle he had twenty-four Guard battalions in reserve. It is a reflection of the intensity of the Prussian pressure on his right flank that only six battalions were left for his last gamble. These last battalions were from the Middle Guard. Each led by a colonel, they were formed in individual squares on a two company frontage in three ranks, Eagles and drummers in the centre. This meant a frontage per battalion of about forty men with eighty muskets able to fire to the front.

Spongeman　　*Ventsman*　*Loader*　　　　*Firer*　　　*NCO in charge of gun*

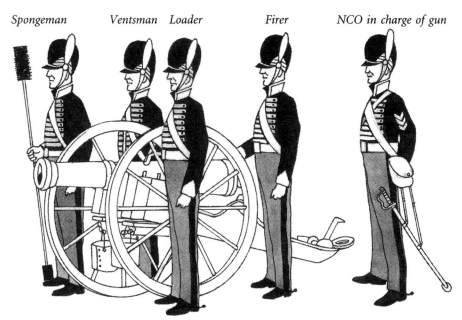

Gun detachment, Royal Horse Artillery

Advancing in the gaps between each battalion were two cannons of the horse artillery of the Guard. From Sharpe's viewpoint, the squares gave the appearance of a huge column.

If the Guard failed, the emperor had lost the battle, the campaign and his throne. But the Guard had never been beaten, there was a shining aura of victory around their burnished Eagles. They epitomised the adage, 'There is no temple without a god, no throne without a Guard.' They came in on echelon from the right with repeated shouts of, '*Vive l'Empereur!*', while dozens of drummers beat a frantic *pas de charge*. About 600 metres from the allied line, Napoleon handed over command to Ney.

As they approached and came under a crippling fire from cannons along the allied ridge they seemed to divide into

Waterloo awards

THE BRITISH GOVERNMENT was lavish in bestowing honours and awards on those who fought at Waterloo. The thanks of both Houses of Parliament were given to Wellington and to the officers and men; a national monument was to be erected in honour of the victory. Memorials to Sir Thomas Picton and Sir William Ponsonby were to be placed in St Paul's Cathedral. All general officers were decorated; no less than 121 lieutenant-colonels and majors were made Companions of the Military Order of the Bath (CB); 52 majors were promoted to lieutenant-colonel, and 37 captains to major, within eleven days (Sharpe missed out; he had been put under arrest by the Prince of Orange).

All Regiments which took part were given the battle honour Waterloo. Ensigns in the Foot Guards would be ranked as 'Ensigns and Lieutenants' and the 1st Foot Guards was renamed the Grenadier Guards. Disability pensions for officers would increase with promotions and not be tied to the rank held at the time of injury. Subaltern officers who participated were granted two years' extra seniority and an extra shilling a day after five years' service. Every NCO, trumpeter, drummer and private was to be shown on muster rolls and pay lists as a 'Waterloo Man' and could count an extra two years' service towards pay and pension. A Waterloo Medal was awarded and the Prince Regent instructed that the ribbon should never be worn without the medal. Two years later prize money was paid to all participants: commander-in-chief £61,000; generals £1275; colonels and field officers £433; captains £90; subalterns £35; sergeants £19; and corporals, drummers and privates £2 11s 4d.

two columns, the whole led by a marshal of the empire (Ney) and five generals (Friant, Cambrone, Christiani, Roguet and Harlet). The left-hand column could see nothing of the British Guards lying below the crest. With the enemy a mere thirty yards from the top of the slope, Wellington shouted, 'Now, Maitland! Now's your time!' Four ranks of 250 men stood up. The crashing volleys were more than even the Imperial Guard could withstand. They shrank in on themselves and recoiled. For this action the British 1st Guards Regiment was awarded the title 'Grenadier' Guards in the mistaken belief that they had destroyed the grenadiers of Napoleon's Guard (it was the chasseurs).

Waterloo medal

Sharpe and *Harper* had returned to the front line a few yards to the left of the *PWOV* who were lying down in four

The Last Waterloo banquet

THIS WAS HELD on 18 June 1852, at Apsley House, Wellington's London residence. He had only three months to live. These banquets (for surviving officers) had been a regular anniversary feature since the battle, and were sumptuous occasions, attracting large crowds to applaud the arriving guests. Prince Albert attended, together with eighty-four veterans from the military aristocracy: men who had fought as fit young captains came as decrepit generals. The lowest rank of officers attending was colonel. Present were General Maitland, whose Guards had thrown back the Imperial Guard; General Halkett, in whose brigade the *PWOV* had served; Lieutenant-General Scovell, Wellington's decoder from those distant days in the Peninsula, and Major-General Sir Harry Smith (95th), whose wife had been the girl he rescued at Badajoz forty years before.

Because of the special relationship between the duke and Sharpe, going back to India, Sharpe had often been invited but had declined. Almost seventy-five and still in France, the journey bothered him and he would have felt uncomfortable in such exalted company. The Guards band played as the duke, walking with Prince Albert, led the way into the Waterloo Gallery: a dazzling display of gleaming gold and silver, highlighted by huge vases of fresh flowers, awaited. Dinner was served on Dresden china, the dessert on dishes of solid gold. It was interspersed with countless toasts, martial music, and a series of ancient generals staggering to their feet to propose yet another toast – that to the Duke was drunk three times as the band played, 'See the conquering hero comes'.

ranks. As the left column topped the slope the battalion stood and fired, as did the 2/30th on its right. But then there was hesitation, an inching back. Somebody was thought to have given an order to retire; *Colonel Ford* had dropped his glasses and could not see and *Major d'Alembord* was wounded. As the battalion began to pull back Sharpe yelled, '*South Essex! Halt!*' The *PWOV* responded, fired twice and charged with the bayonet into the flank of the second column, rolling it to ruin. 'Le Garde recule!' was the cry. Wellington stood in his stirrups, waved his hat to signal a general advance. The Battle of Waterloo had been won.

French head-dress
TOP LEFT: *Dragoon of the Guard*
TOP RIGHT: *Caporal d'Infanterie de Ligne*
BELOW: *Carabinier's helmet*

16

Sharpe's Devil

Sharpe and *Harper* have been civilians for over four years. Sharpe stayed lean and fit working the farm in Normandy; *Harper* became slow and fat running a hostelry in Dublin. Sharpe accepted a commission from the *Countess of Mouromorto* to find out what had happened to her husband, *Blas Vivar*, Sharpe's old comrade who had disappeared while acting as Spanish Captain-General in Chile, where a rebellion against Spanish colonial rule was succeeding.

On the voyage to Chile, Sharpe and *Harper* stopped at St Helena to visit Napoleon. He gave Sharpe a portrait of himself to take to Chile, in which he concealed a secret message to the rebels. On arrival Sharpe came up against the new and sadistic *Captain-General Bautista*, who had the pair arrested and expelled. The ship that transported them was captured by Admiral Lord Cochrane, an Englishman fighting for the rebels. Sharpe joined forces with Cochrane and they succeeded in storming the last Spanish stronghold at Valdivia. *Vivar* was discovered to be alive and imprisoned on the Juan Fernandez Islands. A plot to bring Napoleon to South America came to nothing when he died on St Helena in May 1820.

AFTER WATERLOO and Napoleon's final abdication, Sharpe, *Harper* and tens of thousands of other soldiers were united in their clamour to go home. It had been a long, long war. For *Harper* it was easy; he was a civilian at the battle. Sharpe, however, was still a serving soldier and intended to live in Normandy with Lucille. Napoleon's situation was infinitely more complex: he had the option of surrendering to his enemies and relying on their magnanimity, or trying to escape. The idea of sanctuary in America did more than cross his mind. Within a week of Waterloo, Fouché, the Emperor's Minister of Police, wrote to Wellington and the British Foreign Minister asking for passports to enable Napoleon to reach America. They were not forthcoming.

Could he slip away by sea? For almost a month after his ultimate defeat, and despite the close blockade of French ports by over thirty British warships, strenuous efforts were made to get him away. Two French frigates at Rochefort were alerted for the purpose. On 29 June Napoleon left Paris for Rochefort, narrowly avoiding a Prussian detachment which Blücher had sent to capture him. When he arrived at the port, it became obvious that the obstacles to French ships breaking the blockade were numerous. Several wild propositions were mooted, including Napoleon's being shut in a barrel, with holes for breathing, and placed in a neutral ship. The Emperor would have none of it; he had a horror of being taken captive by his enemies. He much preferred to surrender with honour, to place himself under the protection of his adversaries. In truth, he could not relinquish being Emperor, and life as an ordinary citizen in America had little appeal. When his brother Joseph arrived at Rochefort, Napoleon was on the islet of Aix in the centre of the Basque Roads. Joseph nobly offered to remain on Aix and impersonate Napoleon while he attempted to make a break, but Napoleon declined this sacrifice. His brother left and got away to America on a ship he had prepared.

On 15 July 1815, Napoleon surrendered to Captain Maitland on board the 74-gun warship HMS *Bellerophon*, saying, 'I come to throw myself on the protection of your Prince and your laws.' English breakfast was served, which Napoleon did not enjoy, but from that time until his death six years later, he regarded himself not as a prisoner of England but as a guest. Although the *Bellerophon* sailed for England, Napoleon was not allowed ashore. The British Prime Minister, Lord

Liverpool, had proposed St Helena as his only possible destination.

In Torbay, and then in Portsmouth harbour, his close proximity caused great excitement. Crowds of sightseers clambered into small boats to catch a glimpse of the man who had straddled Europe for a generation, and Napoleon encouraged them by appearing on deck frequently and doffing his hat to any well-dressed woman he saw. At Plymouth frigates positioned themselves on either side of the *Bellerophon*, and put out guard boats which rammed the tourist craft, capsizing one and drowning an occupant. Volleys were fired in the air, but the crush grew worse. On 30 July, about a thousand craft bobbed and jostled around the warships. Seamen on the *Bellerophon* erected a large blackboard on which Napoleon's activities were chalked up: 'At breakfast', 'In his cabin', 'Dictating to his officers' or 'Coming on deck' were some of the brief but informative bulletins posted.

When the mules carrying Sharpe, *Harper* and the Spanish

St Helena

AN ISOLATED VOLCANIC ISLAND in the South Atlantic, 1800 miles from S. America, 1750 from Capetown. Viewed from the sea, it appears as a huge barren rock, rising sheer from the water. Discovered (uninhabited) by a Portuguese sailor in 1502. The British East India Company appropriated the island after the Dutch abandoned it in 1651, keeping it until it passed to the British crown in 1834.

While Napoleon was exiled there, its garrison was supplemented by regular British troops and the governor was Sir Hudson Lowe. The capital, Jamestown, lies in a narrow valley between two masses of rock (Ladder Hill and Rupert's Hill).

Wellington (who stayed for two weeks in 1805 on his way back from India) remarked, 'The interior of the island is beautiful, and the climate apparently the most healthy that I have ever lived in.' The civil population in 1815 was 2871 (whites 776, slaves 1353, freed slaves 447, Chinese 280, Lascars 15); the local garrison of about 1,000 soldiers, doubled during Napoleon's residence.

It was used to accommodate Boer prisoners during the South African War (1899–02), exiled black chiefs and an ex-Sultan of Zanzibar. It is still a British dependency.

Napoleon had a
personal
(non-British)
household of
twenty-seven. There
were six officers, two
with their wives, four
officers' children and
fifteen domestic
servants including
valets, cooks, grooms
and coachmen. One
of the oldest serving
was his second *valet
de chambre*, Louis
Saint-Denis, who had
joined the imperial
household when he
was eighteen, as an
under-groom. He
accompanied the
Emperor to Spain,
Germany and
Holland, after which
he was promoted to
2nd Mameluke (under
Roustam) and given
the name Ali. He was
at Napoleon's side in
Russia in 1812 and at
Ligny and Waterloo.
On Elba he became a
copyist and had charge
of the library.

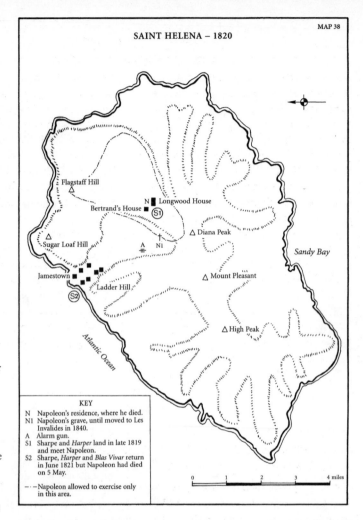

MAP 38

SAINT HELENA – 1820

Flagstaff Hill

N Longwood House

Bertrand's House S1

Sugar Loaf Hill

△ Diana Peak

A N1

Sandy Bay

Jamestown

△ Mount Pleasant

Ladder Hill

S2

△ High Peak

Atlantic Ocean

KEY
N   Napoleon's residence, where he died.
N1 Napoleon's grave, until moved to Les
    Invalides in 1840.
A   Alarm gun.
S1 Sharpe and *Harper* land in late 1819
    and meet Napoleon.
S2 Sharpe, *Harper* and *Blas Vivar* return
    in June 1821 but Napoleon had died
    on 5 May.

--- Napoleon allowed to exercise only
     in this area.

0   1   2   3   4 miles

NAPOLEON'S TABLE
MANNERS

The officers on HMS
Northumberland, the
warship that took
Napoleon to
St Helena, were
startled by his eating
habits, which, coupled
with his sedentary life
on the island, may
have hastened his end.
He '. . . ate every dish
using his fingers

officers on St Helena struggled up the steep, twisting four-mile incline from Jamestown harbour to Longwood in November 1819 (MAP 38), 'General Bonaparte', as the British insisted on calling him, was a sick man, although the cause was a matter of dispute among the medical men who attended him. His illness was plain: his features pale and sweaty, with a huge belly resting on fat thighs. He did virtually no exercise, ate fast and masticated little, indulging freely in rich meat dishes with few vegetables. Creamy pastries were never

Napoleon's grievances

NAPOLEON'S STAY on St Helena was unhappy. Apart from illness, he was at loggerheads with the governor, Hudson Lowe, who arrived in April 1816. After a meeting at which Napoleon lost his temper, the two did not meet again (on Napoleon's insistence) in his remaining years of life. Napoleon enunciated ten grievances against the British government:

1 His detention – he objected to being treated as a prisoner of war.

2 The place of detention – he objected to the isolation.

3 The climate – he claimed it was unhealthy.

4 Longwood House – he claimed it was inadequate (Sharpe seemed to agree).

5 Sir Hudson Lowe – the two were incompatible.

6 His title – he wished to be called the Emperor Napoleon not 'General Bonaparte'. (Sharpe was given careful instructions on how to address him.)

7 Limits – he objected to restrictions on movement beyond certain limits without British escort (MAP 38).

8 Visitors – there was conflict with the issue of passes allowing visitors to Longwood (resolved prior to Sharpe's visit).

9 Correspondence – he demanded freedom of correspondence. When not granted, he resorted to sending secret letters to Europe via obliging ships' captains. (Sharpe was used unwittingly for this purpose.)

10 Provisions – he objected to budgetary restrictions being imposed on his staff and food.

refused, and all was washed down with a half bottle of claret diluted with water. Undoubtedly Napoleon welcomed talking to an old enemy, but he had a task for Sharpe, he would not otherwise have had such a lengthy audience.

By the time Sharpe and *Harper* arrived in Chile in December 1819, the rebellion had reduced Spanish rule to a handful of ports and towns, the largest and most important of which was Valdivia. Much of the credit for the rebels' success was due to the efforts of an English admiral, Lord Thomas Cochrane, who had fallen foul of the Admiralty. To them he was an insubordinate troublemaker who was convicted of a (probably) trumped-up charge of fraud, imprisoned, escaped and was imprisoned again. By 1818, such was his fame as a fighting sailor that Chile offered him command of the rebel navy to rid the seas of the Spaniards. He accepted.

instead of a fork, seeming to prefer the rich dishes . . . and not even tasting vegetables. At dinner he ate heartily of every dish, his fork remaining useless, whilst his fingers were busily employed.'

Valdivia (MAP 39) was thought to be impregnable to attack from the sea. But to capture it would be to win the war, and this final Spanish stronghold had long been Cochrane's objective. His operation with Sharpe on 8 January 1820 (to seize *Puerto Crucero*) was a sideshow. Immediately afterwards he sailed north to Concepción to find troops for the clash at Valdivia. He obtained a Chilean schooner, the *Montezuma*, the Argentinian brig Intrépido, 250 Chileans under a French mercenary, Major Beauchof, and more than forty marines under the Chilean marine commandant, Major Miller. Sharpe and Miller were two peas from the same pod: both were born soldiers, consummate battlefield leaders, had

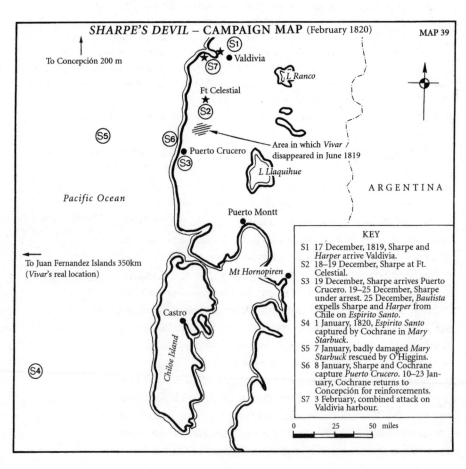

SHARPE'S DEVIL – CAMPAIGN MAP (February 1820)   MAP 39

To Concepción 200 m

S1
• Valdivia
S7

🌊 L. Ranco

Ft Celestial
★
S2

S5   S6

• Puerto Crucero
S3

Area in which *Vivar*
disappeared in June 1819

L. Llaquihue

Pacific Ocean   ARGENTINA

Puerto Montt

To Juan Fernandez Islands 350km
(*Vivar*'s real location)

Mt Hornopiren

Castro

Chiloe Island

S4

KEY
S1 17 December, 1819, Sharpe and *Harper* arrive Valdivia.
S2 18–19 December, Sharpe at Ft. Celestial.
S3 19 December, Sharpe arrives Puerto Crucero. 19–25 December, Sharpe under arrest. 25 December, *Bautista* expells Sharpe and *Harper* from Chile on *Espirito Santo*.
S4 1 January, 1820, *Espirito Santo* captured by Cochrane in *Mary Starbuck*.
S5 7 January, badly damaged *Mary Starbuck* rescued by O'Higgins.
S6 8 January, Sharpe and Cochrane capture *Puerto Crucero*. 10–23 January, Cochrane returns to Concepción for reinforcements.
S7 3 February, combined attack on Valdivia harbour.

0   25   50   miles

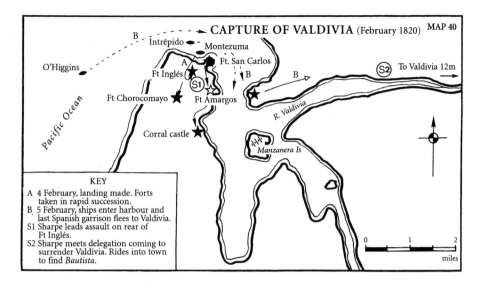

CAPTURE OF VALDIVIA (February 1820) MAP 40

B Intrépido Montezuma
O'Higgins Ft. San Carlos
A
Ft Inglés S1 B
S2 To Valdivia 12m
Ft Chorocomayo Ft Amargos
B
Pacific Ocean R. Valdivia
Corral castle
Manzanera Is

KEY
A 4 February, landing made. Forts
   taken in rapid succession.
B 5 February, ships enter harbour and
   last Spanish garrison flees to Valdivia.
S1 Sharpe leads assault on rear of
   Ft Inglés.
S2 Sharpe meets delegation coming to
   surrender Valdivia. Rides into town
   to find Bautista.

0   1   2
                miles

fought throughout the Peninsular War, and both had been
wounded countless times. Miller had been wounded in the
arm, had a ball pass through his chest and exit his back and
had a shattered left hand. During the manufacture of rockets,
an explosion had crippled his hand and so badly burned his
face that Miller retired to a dark room for six weeks, taking
his food through a plaster mask. Sharpe, Harper, Cochrane
and Miller made a formidable team.

On the night of 29 January, Cochrane's three ships were
becalmed about fifty miles from the mainland (MAP 40).
Cochrane, on The O'Higgins, had only two lieutenants – one
under arrest for insubordination, the other an incompetent
drunk. Utterly exhausted (he did virtually all duties from
ship's captain to carpenter himself), he handed over the
watch to the incompetent drunk, who delegated his duty to
a midshipman, who fell asleep on deck. Inevitably, the wind
sprang up, the midshipman awoke and in blind panic drove
the ship onto some rocks. It says much for Cochrane's skill
and character that he manned the pumps, warped the ship
off the rocks, transferred his men onto the other two vessels
(he went to the Montezuma) and continued to limp towards
Valdivia with most of his powder soaked and useless. The

GENERAL
BERNARDO
O'HIGGINS

Born 1776 (a year
before Sharpe), the
illegitimate son of an
Irish soldier in Spanish
service who rose to be
governor of Chile
(1795–1801). Educated
in England and Spain.
Joined the Chilean
nationalists at the
outbreak of the
revolution against
Spain in 1810. Became
their leader and, with
the help of
adventurers such as
Cochrane, succeeded
in overthrowing the
Spaniards, then in
liberating Peru.
Became
director-general of
Chile. Cochrane's
flagship was named
after him, as was
(later) a Chilean
province. Retired to
Peru in 1832; died 1842.

attackers would have to rely on trickery, bluff and the bayonet.

First the trickery: On 3 February, with *The O'Higgins* trailing far out of sight, Cochrane hoisted the Spanish colours on the *Intrépido* and *Montezuma* as they came in sight of the forts guarding the harbour. Cochrane had hidden his small boats on the side of the ships away from land; they were packed with Miller's marines. When close inshore they were hailed from Fort Inglés.

Next the bluff: 'We've just arrived from Cádiz. We need a pilot,' yelled Cochrane's boatswain.

'Send in a boat,' was the Spanish reply.

'We lost them all in a storm round the Horn.'

The Spaniards were doubly suspicious; only two weeks before Cochrane had pulled the same trick with *The O'Higgins* and forced the unfortunate pilot to reveal the details of the harbour defences. Infantry were seen coming down to the landing place in the bay below Fort Inglés. At this moment, one of the boats full of marines drifted out from behind the *Montezuma*. All was revealed, the fort opened fire, hitting both ships and killing two men. It was time for the bayonets.

Juan Fernandez Islands

THE CHILEAN EQUIVALENT of St Helena: three volcanic islands in the South Pacific, 350 miles west of Chile. Named after the Spanish sailor who discovered them in 1574. The main island, Más a Tierra, is half-moon shaped, with exuberant vegetation and a mountain (The Anvil) rising to over 3000 feet. Cumberland Bay provides a safe anchorage. During the sixteenth and seventeenth centuries it was a refuge and refreshing landfall to countless scurvy-ridden crews of Dutch and British buccaneers. Frequently used to maroon sailors, the most famous being Alexander Selkirk (1676–1721), whose four years on the island inspired Defoe's *Robinson Crusoe*. Más a Tierra is marked on some maps, in brackets, as Robinson Crusoe Island; it has also been used as a place of exile or imprisonment for political or military rivals of various Chilean dictators.

Bautista imprisoned *Blas Vivar* there and in 1821, shortly after Sharpe's departure, Bernardo O'Higgins peopled the place with his enemies.

Major Miller with his forty-four marines was first ashore leading a charge up the beach. Brutal work with the bayonet disposed of the opposition at the landing place – an action in which Sharpe played a prominent lead. By nightfall about 300 men had come ashore and established a beach-head. The next, and most difficult task, was to take the forts. Fort Inglés was the first: after dark the long column, in single file, crept carefully up the only approach – a narrow precipitous track. At the top the main body made a noisy demonstration, while a smaller force under Ensign Vidal (Sharpe) moved round a flank to the landward side. He was undetected and able to tear down some of the palisade to make a bridge over the ditch. Vidal led the assault, with his men screaming their battle cry, 'Cochrane!' whom the Spaniards regarded as the devil incarnate. The defenders panicked and fled helter-skelter for the next fort (San Carlos), with Miller's men, Cochrane and Sharpe on their heels, hacking and killing as they went. An unbelievable chain reaction developed. The fort opened its gate and the horde of pursued and pursuers, inextricably entangled, poured in. Minutes later, an even larger mob poured out of the rear gate. This murderous farce was played out again at Fort Amargos. It had all the ingredients of a comic film; but fact is frequently stranger than fiction.

By dawn Chorocomayo had also fallen, and the only fort of significance on the western side of the harbour still in Spanish hands was Corral Castle. This was potentially a much tougher nut, but fortune favours the brave. The garrison commander, Colonel Hoyos, distraught and humiliated, had taken to the bottle. The morale of his soldiers was abysmal: they had lost over a hundred men, were petrified of Cochrane and realised that the guns in Fort Chorocomayo overlooked Corral Castle. At daylight on 5 February, after a token resistance and the flight of many up the river in boats, Colonel Hoyos surrendered his sword. A minor military miracle had occurred: all the forts on the western side were in Chilean hands, 100 Spaniards had been killed, 100 taken prisoner and

800 had fled into the forests. All this at a cost of 7 killed and 19 wounded.

There remained Fort Niebla on the eastern bank. When the garrison saw the Chilean flag fluttering from every fort on the opposite side, followed by the arrival of *The O'Higgins* with 50 guns, they abandoned the notion of resistance and, with the gunners on Manzanera Island, hoisted the white flag. It was time to march (or sail) on Valdivia itself, about twelve miles upriver. The following day Cochrane embarked his force on the *Montezuma* and *Intrépido* to mount an attack from the river. En route, Sharpe spotted a delegation from the city with a flag of truce, and it transpired that the garrison wanted to lay down their arms. He, with Cochrane and twenty men, commandeered horses, rode into Valdivia, and had his rendezvous with *Bautista*.

Except for a few scattered outposts, such as the island of Chiloe to the south, the liberation of Chile had been achieved. But Cochrane had a more ambitious plan. A fervent admirer of Napoleon, who he thought had been shamefully treated by being exiled to St Helena, Cochrane had conceived the most extraordinary idea: rescue Napoleon, bring him to Chile or Peru, and carve out a United States of South America under his generalship. He would be an Emperor again. Part of the plot had been for Cochrane to stop briefly at St Helena on the way to Chile in late 1818 to see how Napoleon felt about the idea. Unfortunately, the captain of the *Rose* (the ship taking Cochrane and his wife to South America) was given categorical orders to sail direct to Valparaiso. Despite this setback, Cochrane had not abandoned the concept, and in 1820 he offered Sharpe promotion to marshal in the Chilean army if he would stay and fight under Napoleon. Sharpe refused and was detained in Chile until he could no longer compromise the plot. In 1821 Cochrane sent a Lieutenant-Colonel Charles, a military adviser to the Chileans, to St Helena to convey the proposal to Napoleon. As with Sharpe and *Harper* on their return voyage, the colonel arrived too late: the Emperor was dead.

*   *   *

Vivar and *Harper* made the journey up the hill to the little grove of willows where Napoleon was buried. Sharpe did not. Napoleon had died on 5 May 1821, aged fifty-one. He was only eight years older than Sharpe and had been sick for at least two years. His last seven weeks were spent suffering a painful, lingering death from what was thought until recently to have been cancer. His long illness had not been helped by a succession of incompetent doctors who diagnosed liver disease, hepatitis and various stomach disorders aggravated by the climate.

When Napoleon had requested a French doctor, priest and cook, the 'doctor' sent was a semi-qualified Corsican named Francesco Antommarchi. He had been the assistant of a prominent anatomist in Florence, in which capacity he had spent his time dissecting corpses; he did not practise on the living. Among the remedies tried on the unfortunate patient by a number of medical men were bleeding, the application of blisters and emetics. In late March 1821, Napoleon complained of a pain in the abdomen, 'like the cutting of a knife'. Antommarchi induced him to take doses of tartar emetic which caused violent vomiting. His suffering was considerable and he finally refused to continue the ordeal. The emetic was then disguised in lemonade. Napoleon viewed the glass with suspicion and demanded that Montholon (a courtier), drink it. Montholon was instantly sick, prompting Napoleon to turn furiously on Antommarchi calling him 'an assassin'. He had lost all confidence in medicines, exclaiming on one occasion, 'I do not wish to have two diseases, one due to nature and the other to medicine.'

The 1995 publication of Dr Ben Weider's and toxicologist Sten Forshufvud's book, *Assassination at St Helena Revisited*, set out to prove that Napoleon died as a result of arsenic poisoning over a long period of time, and not of cancer. Their evidence is compelling. People who die of cancer do not die fat, but Napoleon was grossly overweight at the time of his death – Sharpe commented on this when he met him on his visit to the island. When the emperor's body was exhumed seventeen years after burial it was in a remarkably

CAPTAIN GEORGE NICHOLLS

Officer of 66th Regiment, who was responsible for 14 months for sighting Napoleon twice a day on St Helena. Napoleon and his staff made his duties impossible. Nicholls, armed with a telescope, was forced to prowl around Longwood in all weathers trying to catch a glimpse of Napoleon, who would sometimes be peering at him through holes in the shutters. Napoleon and his staff enjoyed the game; Nicholls did not.

He failed to 'see' Napoleon on 134 days. He complained bitterly and petitioned his commanding officer to be allowed to resign his 'arduous duty'.

IMPERIAL GUARD
OFFICER BURIED
UPRIGHT

In 1845 the former
officers of the
Imperial Guard held a
reunion at which their
president, General
Schramm,
congratulated
Lieutenant Noisot
(formerly 1st
Grenadiers of the
Guard and the Elba
Battalion) for erecting
a monument to
Napoleon at his own
expense near Dijon.
When Noisot died, he
had himself buried
upright a few yards
away so that he could
mount guard on the
Emperor throughout
eternity.

THE WEEPING
WILLOW TREES

The original trees at
Napoleon's grave in
St Helena have long
died, but their
progeny were planted
all over the world.
Perhaps the most
notable are the willows
lining the banks of the
River Avon in
Christchurch, New
Zealand. Slips of the
original willows were
carefully propagated
by successive
guardians of the tomb,
and to be given a
cutting was
considered a great
privilege.

good state of preservation. The authors attribute this to the
arsenic in the body preserving it, explaining that biologists
have long known its preservative properties in preparing
museum specimens of bird and small animal life.

A sample of Napoleon's hair was submitted to the Federal
Bureau of Investigation's top expert for testing for arsenic.
The result was positive. Traces of arsenic, 20–30 times normal
levels, and fully consistent with poisoning were confirmed.
The authors contend that the arsenic (administered in wine)
was not intended to kill quickly but rather to break down
the Emperor's health gradually. Shortly before his death
Napoleon was given calomel to relieve his constipation and
orgeat to relieve his thirst (both symptoms of chronic arsenic
intoxication). These combined in the stomach, creating mer-
cury cyanide that caused his actual death. The authors point
the finger at Count Montholon as the assassin.

Napoleon realised he was dying. At the end he was delirious
much of the time, but in a patch of near normality he
declared, 'When I am dead each one of you will have the
sweet consolation of returning to Europe. You will see your
relations and your friends; as for me, I shall rejoin my comrades in the Elysian Fields ... [they] will all come to meet
me; they will talk of what we have done together ... We will
talk of our wars with Scipio, Hannibal, Caesar, Frederick.
There will be pleasure in that.' On the evening of 5 May,
shortly after the sunset gun had fired, his time finally came.
His mouth fell and the eyes opened; the shallow breathing
stopped. He was covered with the cloak he wore at Marengo,
a crucifix upon it; by his side they placed his sword.

Napoleon's grave on St Helena

Napoleon's post-mortem

ANTOMMARCHI WAS GIVEN the honour of cutting up Napoleon's body in front of six doctors, all agog to discover the cause of death. Lieutenant-Colonel Sir Thomas Reade recorded the proceedings: 'During the first part of the operation nothing appeared to arrest the attention of the medical gentlemen except the extraordinary quantity of fat which covered almost every part of the interior, under the chest, but particularly about the heart, which was literally enveloped in fat ... They found the stomach had adhered to the left side of the liver, in consequence of the stomach being very much diseased. The medical gentlemen immediately and unanimously expressed their conviction, "that the diseased state of the stomach was the sole cause of his death". The stomach was taken out and exhibited to me. Two thirds of it appeared in a horrible state covered with cancerous substances ...' Reade ordered Assistant-Surgeon Rutledge to remain in the room all night and not to let the body, heart or stomach (these latter having been put in a vase) out of his sight. (Antommarchi wanted to take the stomach to Europe to prove death could not be attributed to him.)

The next day a plaster cast was taken of Napoleon's head. Lieutenant Darroch of the 20th wrote to his mother, 'I went in once again when they were taking the cast of the head, but the stench was so horrible that I could not remain.'

He was buried four days later among willow trees near Hutt's Gate, in the centre of the island. He was dressed in his favourite uniform of the Chasseurs of the Guard with his decorations, white breeches, long boots and spurs. Twelve grenadiers of the 20th (East Devon) Regiment carried the coffin to the funeral carriage. The procession was one third of a mile long. Behind the carriage came his horse, 'Sheikh', then his personal household, midshipmen of the squadron, naval and army officers, members of the island council, the French commissioner, the commandant, the admiral, the governor, followed by units of the garrison, arms reversed, bands playing a funeral dirge. The troops were headed by the St Helena Volunteers followed by the St Helena Regiment, St Helena Artillery, 66th (Berkshire) Regiment, Royal Marines, the 20th (East Devon) Regiment and the Royal Artillery. Twenty-four grenadiers, from every unit present, carried the coffin to the graveside, where his Marengo cloak and sword were removed. Three volleys of musketry were fired, followed by a 33-gun salute. The noise was deafening. Then there was the booming of minute guns from the ships in the harbour. The great stone slab was let down, hot cement was poured on it and the grave was filled with earth.

Twenty-five years later Napoleon got his wish – he was taken home to France and interred at Les Invalides. On 15 December 1840, the surviving 'grumblers' of the Imperial Guard shook out their moth-eaten greatcoats and, bent and shuffling, formed behind 'his' hearse for the final parade. Veterans came from Belgium and the Rhineland, and marched again, down the Champs-Elysées, under the Tri-colour, under the Eagles. Guns crashed, crowds cheered, memories flooded back. This time Sharpe (at sixty-four) was one of the thousands lining the streets. He took *Lucille*, and he wore his Waterloo Medal. He had fought against Napo-leon, but he was also an old soldier with memories and belonged to the brotherhood. When the sixteen black horses drawing the funeral car passed by, Sharpe saluted.

Napoleon's tomb, les Invalides, Paris

ABBREVIATIONS
GLOSSARY
BIBLIOGRAPHY

Abbreviations used in text and glossary

The Sharpe Books (in historical chronological order)

ST	*Sharpe's Tiger*	AWI	American War of Inde-
STr	*Sharpe's Triumph*		pendence
SR	*Sharpe's Rifles*	b.	born
SE	*Sharpe's Eagle*	bde	brigade
SG	*Sharpe's Gold*	BM	brigade major
SB	*Sharpe's Battle*	bn	battalion
SC	*Sharpe's Company*	B. of	Battle(s) of
SS	*Sharpe's Sword*	brig-gen.	brigadier-general
SEn	*Sharpe's Enemy*	Brit.	British
SH	*Sharpe's Honour*	bty	battery
SRegt	*Sharpe's Regiment*		
SSge	*Sharpe's Siege*	capt.	captain
SRev	*Sharpe's Revenge*	capt-gen.	captain-general
SW	*Sharpe's Waterloo*	cav.	cavalry
SD	*Sharpe's Devil*	C-in-C	commander-in-chief
		CO	commanding officer
AAG	assistant adjutant-general	C-of-S	chief-of-staff
ACW	American Civil War	col.	colonel
ADC	aide-de-camp	comdt	commandant
adjt	adjutant	coy.	company
adm.	admiral	cpl	corporal
AG	adjutant-general	C. Rodrigo	Ciudad Rodrigo
ammo.	ammunition	c/sgt	colour sergeant
AQMG	assistant quartermaster-		
	general	d.	died
arty.	artillery	div.	division
asst-comm.	assistant-commissary	dmr(s)	drummer(s)
a/surg.	assistant surgeon		

EIC	East India Company	OC	officer commanding
engr(s)	engineer(s)	offr	officer
Eng.	English		
F. de Onoro	Fuentes de Onoro	Pen.	Peninsula
f-m.	field-marshal	Pen. War	Peninsular War
fmn	formation	Pl(s).	platoon(s)
Fr.	French	P. of	Prince of Orange
ft	fort, fortress	Orange	
		P. of W.	Prince of Wales
gen.	general	Port.	Portuguese, Portugal
Ger.	German	pte	private
GOC	general officer	*PWOV*	*Prince of Wales' Own*
	commanding		*Volunteers*
govt	government		
		Q. Bras	Quatre Bras
HQ	headquarters	QM	quartermaster
		QMG	quartermaster-general
Imp. Guard	Imperial Guard		
inf.	infantry	R.	river
insp.	inspector	rds	roads
		Regt	regiment
KGL	King's German Legion	Regtl	regimental
		rflm.	rifleman
Lines of TV	Lines of Torres Vedras	RN	Royal Navy
LD	Light Dragoon	RSM	regimental sergeant-major
lt	lieutenant		
lt-col	lieutenant-colonel	sect.	section
Lt. Coy./	light company/division	*S. Essex*	*South Essex Regiment*
Div.		sgt	sergeant
lt-gen.	lieutenant-general	sgt-maj.	sergeant-major
		s/lt	sous-lieutenant
maj.	major	Span.	Spanish
maj-gen.	major-general	sqn	squadron
mts	mountains	sub.	subaltern
		surg.	surgeon
Nap. Wars	Napoleonic Wars		
NCO	non-commissioned officer	2IC	second in command

Glossary

Abrantes (MAPS 4, 11) Port. city on hill overlooking Tagus R. 75 miles NE of Lisbon. Key road and river junction. Linked to Lisbon by main road or small river boats. Important supply depot. Described as 'The mirror in which the commissariat department may be seen'.

Adour River (MAP 32) R. in SW France 200 miles long, flowing into Bay of Biscay. Near mouth is fortress city of Bayonne. Soult took up defensive position behind this river in 1814. Wellington crossed on large bridge of boats on 24–6 Feb., thus surrounding Bayonne and outflanking Soult. Sharpe was involved in securing the boats from Teste de Buch in SSge.

Adrados (MAP 1, 24, 25A, B, C, D) Span. village in mts. 15 miles N. of C. Rodrigo. Guarded *Gateway of God Pass*, used as a refuge by deserters led by Pot-au-Feu and *ex-Sergeant Hakeswill* in late 1812. Scene of Sharpe's rescue of hostages, use of Congreve rockets, murder of Sharpe's wife Teresa and capture of *Hakeswill* (*SEn*). Sharpe hid there for 2 weeks after being 'hung' on 15 May 1813.

Ahmednuggur Indian town stormed by Brit. under Wellesley on 11 Aug. 1803. Sharpe present as sgt.

Aix Tiny islet in Basque Roads near port of Rochefort, France. From there Napoleon hoped to escape, perhaps to America, in Jul. 1815. Gave himself up to Capt. Maitland RN on HMS Bellerophon on 15 Jul.

Alba de Tormes (MAP 20) Span. village on Tormes R. 12 miles SE of Salamanca. Failure of Span. to hold the bridge was main reason Fr. army was not destroyed after the B. of Salamanca 22 Jul. 1812. Sharpe pursued *Col. Leroux* across this bridge in SS.

Alcántara (MAPS 5, 16) Important fortified Span. town guarding key crossing place over Tagus close to border with Port. Possession of the bridge crucial for communications between armies south of Tagus and in the C. Rodrigo and Salamanca areas. With this Roman bridge destroyed (by Span. Gen. Cuesta in 1808), Fr. had to rely on crossing at Almaraz, 60 miles E. Wellington had 100-foot suspension bridge constructed to repair the central arch of Alcántara bridge in May 1812.

Allen, Maj. Officer in 12th Foot in India in 1798 who shot and mortally wounded his former CO, Col. Ashton, in a duel. This led to Wellesley receiving Ashton's horse, Diomed, and task of preparing Army of Madras for 4th Mysore War against Tippoo Sultan.

Almante, Mr Chilean midshipman aged thirteen on *Kitty*, employed by Adm. Cochrane to send signals during attack on Valdivia, Feb. 1820. In *SD*.

Almaraz (MAPS 5, 16) Key crossing place over Tagus which, like Alcántara, had a magnificent Roman bridge. In May 1812, Wellington sent Hill to capture it, which he did in remarkable surprise attack.

Almeida (MAPS 1, 8, 11, 12, 16) Port. ft close to Span. border 20 miles from C. Rodrigo. Fell to Ney on 28 July 1810 after main magazine was exploded. Fr. garrison escaped on the night of the 10–11 May 1811, after blowing up the defences when Wellington surrounded it after victory at F. de Onoro. Sharpe responsible for detonation in Jul. 1810. In *SG*.

Alten, Lt-Gen. Charles, Count Served throughout war in KGL. Commanded Lt. Div. from 2 May 1812. At Vitória, the Bidassoa, the Nivelle, the Nive, Orthez. Commanded 3rd Div. at Waterloo.

Alzaga, Father Catholic priest; sacrist (responsible for the churches' treasures) at Santiago cathedral. Present with Sharpe and *Blas Vivar* at *Vivar*'s stronghold in the mts. prior to attack on Santiago. Hated Eng. almost as much as Fr. Was officiating priest at public garotting of collaborators in Santiago. In SR.

Andrews, Lt. Subaltern in *S. Essex*. Present at Battle of Vitória. In SH.

Anfrancesados Span. who collaborated with Fr. In territory firmly held by Fr. most of the upper and professional classes became *anfrancesados*. Span. govt. officials under King Joseph were obvious collaborators; had they not been, they would have lost their jobs and pensions.

Angel Span. boy assigned to assist Sharpe in clandestine activities prior to B. of Vitória. Fought in the Lt. Coy. of *S. Essex* at the B. of the Nivelle. In *SH*, *SRegt*.

Angel Tower Ancient tower in citadel of Valdivia, Chile, previously used for executions/imprisonment. In 1820 used by *Capt-Gen. Bautista* as secret living quarters and for homosexual activities with his ADC (*Marquinez*). In *SD*.

Angers Town in Anjou, France. Site of Royal Academy of Equitation, attended by Arthur Wesley (Wellington) and *Col. Michel Dubreton* in 1785.

Antommarchi, Prof. Francesco Semi-qualified doctor who treated Napoleon on St Helena. Corsican, dissecter of bodies by training, accused by Napoleon of being 'an assassin' when he kept prescribing a violent emetic.

Ardiles, Capt. Span. naval officer who captained the *Espiritu Santo*, ship which took Sharpe and *Harper* to Chile in 1819. In *SD*.

Arguam One of Wellesley's victories in India fought on 27th Nov. 1803. Sharpe ensign in 74th Foot.

Assaye Wellesley's victory in India over greatly superior forces on 23 Sept. 1803. Sharpe, sgt. on special duties, was commissioned ensign for saving Wellesley's life.

Astorga (MAPS 5, 6) Span. town in Galicia. On line of Moore's retreat to Corunna, where he divided his army, sending the Lt. Bde and German lt. troops by the southerly route to Vigo while he marched on to Corunna.

Ayres, Lt Commanded mounted patrol of provost in village SE of Celorico in August 1810. Found *Pte Batten* of Sharpe's coy. stealing a chicken and wanted to hang him on the spot. Sharpe threatened to shoot him, but was later forced to apologise. In *SG*.

Bachelu, Lt-Gen. Commanded Fr. 5th Div. in Réille's Corps at Waterloo.

Badajoz (MAPS 1, 16, 18, 19) Large Span. ft one mile from Port. border on main road to Madrid. Guarded southern invasion route from Lisbon; of strategic importance since Roman and Moorish times. Situated on Guadiana R., it was disadvantaged by high ground within cannon range. Captured by Soult from Span. on 10 Mar. 1811, Wellington twice failed to retake it in May 1811. Allies finally took it with 5000 casualties on 6 Apr. 1812, although assaults on breaches failed. *S. Essex* were in 4th Div. tasked to storm main breach. *Sgt Harper* reduced to ranks and flogged during the siege. Sharpe tried unsuccessfully to blow the dam over the Rivillas R., then acted as guide to the Lt. Div. Later commanded the *S. Essex* Lt. Coy. and stormed central breach.

Baird, Maj-Gen. Sir David b. 1757. Captured and imprisoned for 44 months in Seringapatam by the Tippoo Sultan in 1780. Deputy to Lt-Gen. Harris at the Siege of Seringapatam in 1799, and led the storming of the breach. Was instrumental in sending *Lt Lawford* (and therefore Sharpe) on the special mission into Seringapatam in 1799; d. 1829.

Baker, Ezekiel Inventor of the rifle that bore his name and with which Sharpe and all Brit. Rifle Bns were armed during Pen. War. Had 30-inch, seven-groove, quarter-turn barrel. Accurate up to 250 yards but could only be loaded about twice a minute. Excellent for skirmishers and picking off enemy leaders or gun crews.

Balin Bullying Span. seaman on *Espírito Santo* whom Sharpe beat up when expelled from Chile in Dec. 1819. In *SD*.

Bampfylde, Capt. Horace, RN Commanded *HMS Vengeance* in 1814 based at St Jean de Luz, and combined operation with Sharpe to take ft at Teste de Buch. Abandoned Sharpe to defence of the fort against overwhelming odds.

Sharpe fought a duel with him, wounding him in the buttocks in Mar. 1814. In *SSge*, *SRev*.

banquette Ledge on which soldiers stood to fire over parapet.

Barnard, Lt-Col. Andrew Commanded the 3/95th early in Pen. War and acting commander of the Lt. Div. at Badajoz after death of Gen. Crauford and wounding of Gen. Vandeleur at C. Rodrigo in 1812. Later commanded 1/95th at Vitória. Wounded at B. of Barrosa, the Nivelle and Waterloo.

Barrett, Sgt NCO in *S. Essex*. At B. of Vitória. In *SH*.

Bascable, Ensign Officer in *S. Essex*, B. of Vitória. In *SH*.

bastion Defensive work, with two front faces forming salient from the curtain wall to allow flanking fire along wall.

battalion (bn) Tactical infantry unit varying from 500 to 1000 men (sometimes less). British bns usually divided into 10 coys. and commanded by lt-col. Fr. bns six coys. commanded by maj.

Battalion of Detachments (Bn of Dets) An innovation whereby a bn was made up of odd drafts: returning sick, detached groups or coys., often under officers from variety of units. Frequently only temporary until personnel could return to their Regts. At Talavera the 2nd Bn of Dets had coys. from 92nd, 42nd, 79th and 95th. *S. Essex* became one after its heavy losses and poor showing at *Valdelacasa*, Jul. 1809.

Batten, Pte A useless soldier in *S. Essex* Lt. Coy. Caught by provost stealing chicken. Saved from hanging by Sharpe. At attack on Cayetano Ft 1812 and B. of Salamanca Jul. 1812. In *SS*.

Bautista, Capt-Gen. Miguel Sadistic,

homosexual Span. officer who took over as Capt-Gen. in Chile when *Blas Vivar* disappeared in 1819. Had Sharpe arrested and expelled. Killed himself with *Harper's 7* barrelled Nock gun rather than face capture when Cochrane and Sharpe took Valdivia in Feb. 1820. In *SD*.

Beauchof, Maj. Fr. mercenary who commanded 250 Chileans during Cochrane's capture of Valdivia.

Bennett, Sgt S. Essex senior NCO at Foulness Camp under *Lt-Col. Girdwood* in 1814. In *SRegt*.

Beresford, Lt-Gen. William Carr b. 1764. After serving at Corunna, was entrusted with training Port. army. Became Port. marshal in 1809. Independent command ended with hard-won victory at Albuera in May 1811. Wellington entrusted him with important roles during the campaigns 1813–14. Commanded corps at Toulouse which launched main allied attack. Sharpe was BM of *Nairn's* bde in this assault. Created Lord Beresford of Albuera, governor of Jersey, served king of Portugal in Rio de Janeiro, master-general of the ordnance. d. 1854.

Berry, Lt John Overweight officer in S. Essex Lt. Coy. at *Valdelacasa*. Involved (with *Lt Gibbons*) in rape attack on *Josefina* in Plasencia in Jul. 1809. Killed by Sharpe in revenge during Fr. night attack at Talavera on 27 Jul. 1809. In *SE*.

Berthon, Maj. Fr. decoding officer for Marmont at B. of Salamanca, 22 Jul. 1812. In *SS*.

Bessières, Marshal Jean-Baptiste, Duke of Istria b. 1768. Fought in Spain in 1808 as corps commander, and in 1811 brought reinforcements to Masséna prior to B. of F. de Onoro. Commander of cavalry of Imp. Guard during Russian campaign. Commander Imp. Guard in 1813. Killed by cannonball at Lutzen, 1 May 1813.

bhinjarries Grain merchants contracted to supply Brit. army on campaign in India.

Blair, Mr George Liverpool merchant and trader in hides; Brit. consul in Chile in 1819. In *SD*.

Blasendorf, Capt. Hans Commanded sqn. of KGL cavalry. Met Sharpe who was on his way to Brain-le-Comte on 15 Jun. 1815 to report the Fr. army had crossed Sambre R. at Charleroi. Blasendorf undertook to take message to Gen. Dornberg at Mons. Dornberg disbelieved it and tore it up. In *SW*.

Blücher, F-M. von Gebhard b. 1742. Enlisted in Swedish cavalry at 14. Fought in three campaigns against Prussians under Frederick the Great. Was captured and allowed to change sides. Retired as captain. Recalled in 1786 and fought in Revolutionary Wars. Developed hatred of the Fr. Fearless and forceful character, became general in 1813 and commanded Prussian forces against Napoleon in 1813–14. Commander of Prussian Army in Waterloo campaign, aged 73. Defeated at Ligny, he nevertheless brought his army, with decisive effect, onto Napoleon's right flank at Waterloo. Nicknamed 'Papa Blücher' or 'Old Forward' for strength of character; d. 1819.

bomb-proof A shelter against shot or shell.

Bonaparte, Jérome (Prince) b. 1784. Napoleon's youngest brother, initially a naval officer. Poor performance commanding Fr. right wing of army in Russia. GOC 6 Div. in Réille's Corps at

Waterloo. Responsible for escalating the fight for Hougoumont. Exiled until 1847. Became governor of Les Invalides; marshal 1850; d. 1860.

Bonaparte, Joseph b. 1768 in Corsica. Brother of Napoleon; made king of Naples 1806; king of Spain 1808. Had no military talent but fondness for titles. Known by Span. as 'Pepé Botella' ('Uncle Bottle'). Remained titular ruler of Spain for 5 years. Heavily defeated at Vitória. Went to the USA after 1815; d. 1844.

Bonaparte, Napoleon b. 1769 in Corsica. Arty. officer who proved brilliant general in the Revolutionary Wars. Conquered Europe but invasion of Russia failed in 1812. Abdicated in 1814 and confined to Elba. Escaped and launched the Hundred Days' campaign which ended at Waterloo. Exiled to St Helena where he died in 1821; re-interred in Les Invalides in 1840.

Bordeaux (MAP 21) Fr. city and port on west bank of Garonne R., 60 miles from sea, has flourished since Roman times. Belonged to England 1154 to 1453, here the Black Prince had his court for a time. Suffered under 'Red Terror' of the Revolution; its population pro-royalist in 1814. *Gen. Calvet* marched from there to retake ft. at Teste de Buch from *Sharpe. Maj. Ducos*, the Fr. spymaster, had his base there. Gen. Beresford and allied troops welcomed on 12 Mar. 1814. Sharpe escaped from arrest there in Apr. 1814.

Borellas, Father Catholic priest who visited *Vivar*'s mtn. ft to plan attack on Santiago. In *SR*.

Bounty jumper Man who enlisted, deserted and then re-enlisted under a false name in a different regt. for bounty money. This was sometimes repeated many times – record was 49. Culprit hanged if caught.

Bounty money Sum given to encourage man to join army. In 1803, £7 12s 6d, but by 1812 had risen to £23 17s 6d for life service and £18 12s 6d for seven years. Usually spent on drink and deductions for kit issued on joining (Necessaries').

Boxtel Small Dutch town; scene of Sharpe's first action when 33rd Foot under Lt-Col. Wesley (Wellington) skilfully covered withdrawal of main Brit. force on 15 Sept. 1794.

Braine-le-Comte (MAP 36) Small Belgian town SW of Waterloo; HQ of Wellington's 1 Corps under P. of Orange at start of Waterloo campaign. Sharpe's place of duty, where he reported Fr. advance from Charleroi.

Brigade (bde) Tactical military fmn of about 3000 men containing 2 or 3 bns Until 1809, was highest (largest) formation in Wellington's army. Commanded by maj-gen. in Brit. army, a *général de brigade* in Fr.

Brigade major (BM) Staff officer attached to inf. bde.

Brightwell, RSM RSM of *S. Essex 2nd Bn* under *Lt-Col. Girdwood* at Foulness Camp in 1813. Remained as depôt RSM when Sharpe took reinforcements to Spain. In *SRegt*.

Briquet, Capt. Fr. officer killed by Sharpe during Fr. assault on ft at Teste de Buch. In *SSge*.

Bristow, Mr Butler to duke of Richmond. Responsible for preparations for ball in Brussels on eve of Waterloo.

Brooker, Capt. OC Gren. Coy. of fusilier bn at *Adrados*, Dec. 1812. In *SEn*.

Brown Bess Nickname of Brit. smoothbore musket. 'To hug Brown Bess' meant to enlist.

Bulford, Mr Civilian in Godalming, England, who expected to marry *Louisa Parker* on her return from Spain. In *SR*.

Bunbury, Lt Coy. officer in 2/95th; first Brit. soldier killed in Pen. War, near Obidos, in Aug. 1808. Sharpe promoted lt into his vacancy.

Burgos (MAPS 1, 26, 28) Span. city, formerly capital of Old Castile. Strategically located on main road to France. Successfully defended by Fr. against Wellington in 1812. Sharpe injured when castle wall prematurely blown up, 13 Jun. 1813. In Jul. 1936 became seat of govt of Franco during Span. Civil War.

Burrard, Lt-Gen. Sir Harry Appointed 2IC of Brit. expedition to Port. in Aug. 1808, arrived day after B. of Rolica and took over from Wellesley, refusing to allow him to continue advance on Lisbon. Compulsorily retired by court of inquiry investigating Convention of Cintra.

Butler, Capt. OC No. 3 Coy. *S. Essex* in Vitória campaign. Killed there. In *SH*.

Bywaters, Sgt-Maj. 33rd Foot in India. In *ST*.

Cabral, Lt 3rd Lt on *Kitty* during attack on Valdivia, Feb. 1820. Spokesman when Cochrane tried to trick Span. at harbour entrance. OC Sharpe's longboat during landing. In *SD*.

Cacadores Port. lt. inf. or rflm. Name means 'hunter'. Usually wore brown uniforms.

Cadiz (MAP 1) Naval base on tiny island off S. coast of Spain. Garrisoned by British throughout Pen. War. Although besieged and cut off from Wellington, could hold out indefinitely because supplied by sea and out of range of mainland guns. Refuge for Span. govt (Cortés). Sharpe told guerrillas their gold would be delivered to Cadiz in Aug. 1810.

Cadogan, Col Henry Friend of Wellington; killed commanding the 1/ 71st (Glasgow Highlanders) at Vitória.

caltrop A four-pointed metal spike which, thrown on the ground, always has one spike upright. Used to pierce feet of cav. horses.

Calvet, Gen. of Bde Jean-Baptiste Joined army as common soldier. Fought in most of Napoleon's campaigns, including Russia, bringing intact bde back during retreat. Commanded demi-brigade at Bordeaux which forced Sharpe to evacuate Teste de Buch. Went with Napoleon into exile on Elba; then sent to recover the treasure stolen by *Ducos*. Allied with Sharpe to capture *Ducos* and recover the treasure in Aug. 1814. After Waterloo went to Louisiana. In *SSge*, *SRev*.

Cameron, Rflm. Arrived in Pen. with Col Wade's 4 coys. With Sharpe on march to Santiago; wounded during ambush in gorge, 4 Jan. 1809. In *SR*.

Camoynes, Dowager Countess Anne Reluctant mistress of *Lord Fenner*. Assisted Sharpe in exposing crimping scandal with 2nd Bn *S. Essex* in Aug. 1813. In *SRegt*.

Canister Arty. projectile of lead balls in tin container. Resembled giant shotgun cartridge and had similar effects at short range. Also known as case-shot.

carcase Incendiary or illuminating shell of oil-soaked hay, fired from mortar or howitzer.

Carew, Sgt Ted Armourer Sgt at

Chelmsford depôt when Sharpe arrived in Jul. 1813. Had lost a leg at Talavera. In *SRegt*.

Carline, Capt. Officer on staff of Chelmsford depôt in Jul. 1813. Made coy. commander when Sharpe took over *2nd Bn S. Essex* at Foulness camp. Fought at B. of the Nivelle; killed at Q. Bras. In *SRegt*, *SW*.

carronade Large-calibre, short-range cannon commonly used on ships for firing canister. Named from place of manufacture: Carron Iron Works. Sharpe fired one on the *Espírito Santo* in fight with *Mary Starbuck*, Jan. 1820.

Casatejada (MAP 12) Small Span. village. Birthplace and home of *Teresa Moreno*, 10 miles N. of C. Rodrigo. Sharpe tasked with securing the gold here in Aug. 1810. *Teresa* buried there after being murdered by *Hakeswill*.

Castineau, Col. Xavier Fr. cav. officer, husband of *Lucille (née Lassan)*, he was killed shortly after the marriage. In *SRev*.

Castineau, Gen. Retired Fr. general, father-in-law of *Lucille Castineau*. In *SRev*.

Castineau, Madame Lucille Also entitled *Madame la Vicomtessa de Seléglise*; former wife of *Col. Xavier Castineau*. Owned château/farm near Caen in Normandy. Shot and wounded Sharpe in May 1814, thinking him responsible for her brother's murder. Became Sharpe's mistress after end of Pen. War; he lived with her in Normandy. Had a son and a daughter (*Patrick* and *Dominique*) by Sharpe, both of whom took their mother's maiden name (*Lassan*). Married Sharpe – 1844. In *SRev*, *SW*.

Castrador, El Span. guerrilla leader in F. de Onoro. Nicknamed *El Lobo*.

Sharpe used him to kill and mutilate deserters from *Real Compañía Irlandesa* as deterrent. As name implies, was competent with a knife. In *SB*.

Catolico, El Self-seeking Span. guerrilla leader, wanted to prevent Sharpe obtaining the gold from *Casatejada* in Aug. 1810. Attacked and wounded Sharpe, but was killed on night of 25–6 Aug. 1810. In *SG*.

Cavalry of St George Nickname given to Eng. gold guineas with picture of St George killing a dragon. Seen as a powerful enemy of Napoleon – Eng. guineas supported his enemies in Europe and elsewhere.

Cazadores Span. chasseurs or lt. cavalrymen.

Celorico (MAP 11) Port. town 30 miles W. of Almeida. Wellington's HQ Apr.–Aug. 1810. *S. Essex* HQ in church of São Paulo.

Challon, Sgt Fr. dragoon NCO who helped *Maj. Ducos* to steal some of Napoleon's treasure in Apr. 1814. Killed *Henri Lassan* to prevent him testifying that Sharpe had not taken the treasure. Fled with *Ducos* to Naples; captured Aug. 1814. Presumed executed. In *SRev*.

Charleroi (MAP 36) Town in southern Belgium on Sambre R., which bulk of Napoleon's Army of the North crossed at start of Waterloo campaign. Sharpe watched Fr. crossing on 15 Jun. 1815.

Charles, Lt-Col. Brit. born soldier of fortune, military adviser to Gen. O'Higgins in Chile in 1820. Sharpe was to deliver a secret message concealed in a portrait to him via the American consul (*Fielding*) in Valdivia. Cochrane sent Charles to St Helena in 1821 to liaise on possibility of Napoleon's escaping to Chile, but Napoleon was dead.

chasse-marée Small, coastal sailing lugger/fishing boat. Sharpe's capture of ft at Teste de Buch was to seize these boats for pontoon bridge over R. Adour so that Wellington could attack Bayonne.

cheval-de-frise Portable barrier of sword blades used to block breaches.

chosen man A pte soldier given responsibility; later called lance-corporal. A number of Sharpe's rflm. (e.g. *Hagman*) were 'chosen men' who wore a white stripe on the right arm.

Christie, Lt Sub. in 2/44th (East Essex) who, although grievously wounded, saved the Colours at Q. Bras, 16 Jun. 1815.

Ciudad Rodrigo (MAPS 1, 5, 8, 11, 12, 13, 16, 17, 24, 26, 27) Ancient Span. ft. city on main road from Salamanca to Port. border at F. de Onoro; guarded northern invasion route from Portugal; castle dated back to Moorish times. On Agueda but dominated by high ground within cannon range. Captured by Ney in Jul. 1810; Wellington besieged and took on 6 Jan. 1812. *S. Essex* in McKinnon's bde of 4 Div. but did not take part. Sharpe and *Harper* captured a cannon in main breach.

Clarke, Mrs Anne Beautiful but unscrupulous mistress of Duke of York, whose corrupt activities led in 1809 to his resignation as C-in-C.

Clausel, Gen. Bertrand b. 1772. Senior Fr. div. commander at B. of Salamanca who took command after Marmont wounded. Tried to counter-attack allied centre held by 4 Div., which included *S. Essex*. Commanded Army of the North 1813–14; marshal 1831; d. 1842.

Clayton, Pte Soldier in PWOV. Said to have prettiest wife (*Sally*) in bn. Fought at Toulouse and Q. Bras; killed by Imp. Guard at Waterloo. *Sally* went with *Weller* after his death. In *SW*.

Clinton, Lt-Gen. Sir Henry b. 1771. AG to Sir John Moore in Corunna campaign. Commanded 6 Div. from 1811–14. Sharpe served under him in *Nairn's bde.* at B. of Toulouse; fought at Waterloo; d. 1820.

Clissot, Cpl Terence Recruiting NCO of *S. Essex* under *Sgt Havercamp* when Sharpe enlisted in Aug. 1813.

cobbing Corporal punishment involving beating buttocks with flat piece of wood; awarded for minor offences in 95th Rifles.

Cochrane, Adm. Lord Thomas, Earl of Dundonald b. 1775; famous Brit. sailor renowned for his skill at taking prizes. As MP, spoke out against naval abuses, which made him highly unpopular with his superiors. Wrongly convicted of fraud in 1814, transferred services to Chile in 1818, and had many successes in Chilean and Peruvian battles for independence. Joined Brazilian navy in 1823 in struggle against Port., and Greek navy in 1827 in conflict with Turkey. Reinstated in RN 1832. Sharpe fought under him in capture of Valdivia in Feb. 1820. Died same year as Sharpe, 1860.

Colbert, Gen. Fr. cav. officer who commanded a lt. cav. bde against rearguard of Moore's army during retreat on Corunna; shot and killed by Rflm. Tom Plunket at Cacabelos on 3 Jan. 1808.

Cole, Lt-Gen. Sir Lowry b. 1772; commanded 4 Div. in Pen. 1809–14; governor of Mauritius and then Cape Colony; d. 1842.

Collett, Maj. Jack Joined *S. Essex* as 2IC at same time as *Lt-Col. Windham* became CO in Mar. 1812 before siege of Badajoz. Could have been *Windham*'s twin – bow-legged horseman, leathery skin, short grey hair. Killed at Badajoz. In *SC*.

Collip, Lt (QM) QM of *S. Essex* in Vitória campaign. In SH.

Colours Bn flags which represented the honour of a unit. Brit. bns had a King's and a Regtl Colour carried in battle by ensigns and protected by colour-sgts. To lose a Colour (as *S. Essex* did) meant disgrace. Fr. equivalent: an Eagle.

company (coy.) Basic inf. sub-unit of 60–120 men; usually commanded by capt.

Concepción Large port in central Chile; major nationalist base during struggle for independence from Spain, 1817–20. Adm. Cochrane received reinforcements from Concepción prior to attack on Valdivia.

Congreve Rockets Invented by Sir William Congreve; mounted on long sticks like modern fireworks. First used in action in 1805 firing from boats in salvoes. Erratic in flight; more inaccurate than guns. Limited lethality, although noise and sparks frightened horses. Sharpe made effective (if premature) use of them at *Adrados* in Dec. 1812 in *SEn*. Also used successfully in crossing of Adour, Feb. 1814. Rocket troop of RA formed in 1813, used briefly in Pen. and at Waterloo.

Connelley, Sgt Michael Ward NCO in Irish College hospital after B. of Salamanca. Good-hearted, drunken man who continually urged his patients to die quietly and with dignity in front of the Fr. Died (badly) from alcoholic poisoning. In *SS*.

Consuela Span. maid who looked after Sharpe in Burgos when mistaken for Frenchman and injured prior to B. of Vitória. In *SH*.

Cooper, Rflm. Served with Sharpe in 2/ 95th at B. of Rolica and Vimiero. In charge of QM's (Sharpe's) mule at start of Corunna retreat. Killed by Fr. Dragoons at La Bañeza on 31 Dec. 1808. In *SR*.

Copenhagen Wellington's horse, named after bombardment of the city in 1807. A chestnut, 15 hands high. Wellington's favourite, which he rode in Pen. War and all day at Waterloo. Died aged 28 in 1836.

Cork Street In expensive area of London close to New Bond Street, where *Jane Sharpe* bought house, with Sharpe's money but without his knowledge, in 1814.

corps Military formation consisting of 2 or 3 divs. commanded by gen. More often used by Fr. than Brit. in Pen. War. Also describes type of soldier, i.e. Corps of Engineers.

Corral Castle (MAP 40) Span. ft guarding W. approach to Valdivia harbour in Chile. Surrendered to Cochrane's forces 5 Feb. 1820. In *SD*.

Cortés, National Span. elected governing body, somewhat similar to Brit. Parliament. Based in Cadiz and responsible for running war from 1810.

Cotton, Maj-Gen. Sir Stapleton Wellington's mediocre cav. commander from Jun. 1810 to end of war.

Counterguard Earthwork to protect base of curtain wall.

Counterscarp Vertical face of ditch around ft on attacker's side.

Coursot, Col. Fr. inf. officer in command of Santiago garrison when Sharpe and *Maj. Vivar* attacked. His HQ was Rajoy Palace. In *SR*.

Cox, Lt-Col William Brig-gen. in Port. army who commanded Almeida garrison in August 1810. Forced to surrender after only one day of bombardment when main magazine in cathedral blew up. Cox did not want Sharpe to leave with the gold on 26 Aug.

Crapaud Fr. word meaning 'toad'; used by Brit. of Fr. in general.

Crauford, Maj-Gen. Robert b. 1762. Rigid disciplinarian; daring and competent bde and div. general. His strictness, quick temper and cruel tongue earned many enemies and the nickname 'Black Bob'. Rflm. Harris wrote, 'I do not think I ever admired any man who wore the British uniform more than I did General Crauford.' Commanded the Lt. Bde in the disastrous attack on Buenos Aires in 1807, and again from 1809 in Pen. War; commanded the Lt. Div. from 1810, died of wounds at C. Rodrigo, 1812.

Cresacre, Pte Thomas In *S. Essex* Lt. Coy. present at Talavera. Wounded at *Casatejada,* and killed in assault at Badajoz 6 Apr. 1812. In *SE, SC.*

Cross, Capt. Coy. commander in 5/60th (Royal American) Rifles. Fought with Sharpe at *Adrados* in Dec. 1812. In *SEn.*

Cuesta, Gen. Don Gregario García b. 1740. Obstinate and cantankerous. Capt-Gen. of Old Castile 1808; defeated at Medina and Medellin. Commanded Army of Estremadura in 1809. Joined Wellesley in Talavera campaign. Paralysed by stroke; d. 1812.

cunette or cuvette Deep, narrow ditch, often filled with water, in main defensive ditch of ft.

curtain wall or curtain Main wall surrounding ft.

Curtis, Revd Dr Patrick Rector of Irish College in Salamanca. Ran extensive spy system for Brit. until after B. of Salamanca; given protection and pension by Brit. Became Archbishop of Armagh and Primate of All Ireland; d. of cholera, aged 92.

cushoon Circumcised Muslim soldier in Tippoo Sultan's army

D'Alembord, Capt. Peter Nicknamed 'Dally'. OC Lt. Coy. *S. Essex* in Vitória campaign. Accompanied Sharpe to England in 1813, in search for reinforcements. Commanded Lt. Coy. at B. of Nivelle, Q. Bras and Waterloo. Promoted maj. on death of *Maj. Micklewhite* at Q. Bras. Leg amputated at Waterloo. In *SH, SRegt. SRev, SW.*

Dalrymple, Lt-Gen. Sir Hew Designated C-in-C of Brit. expedition to Portugal in Aug. 1808. Did not arrive until after Wellesley had won the victories at Rolica and Vimiero. Elderly, dithering and useless; dismissed after court of inquiry had investigated terms of Convention of Cintra.

Daria Dowlat Tippoo Sultan's summer palace in Seringapatam where British prisoners (except for *Sgt Hakeswill*) were executed by his *jettis* in 1799.

Davila, Lt Diego Span. army officer and 21C to *Maj. Blas Vivar* for the attack on Santiago on 28 Jan. 1808. In *SR.*

D'Erlon, Gen. Count Jean Baptiste Drouet b. 1765; served under Masséna in Switzerland in 1799, and at Jena and Friedland. Six years in Pen. War as 9 Corps commander. Corps commander in Waterloo campaign; famous for wandering between battlefields of Q. Bras and Ligny, taking part in neither. Commanded Fr. right at Waterloo;

created marshal shortly before his death in 1844.

Delaborde, Gen. Fr. commander at B. of Rolica Aug. 1808.

Delmas, Capt. Paul Fr. cav. officer in 5th Dragoons murdered by *Col. Leroux* to assume his identity. In *SS*.

demi-brigade Fr. fmn originally comprising 1 regular and 2 volunteer or conscript bns. Later applied to any provisional fmn. That which attacked Sharpe at Teste de Buch was 2000 strong.

Denny, Ensign 16-year-old sub. in *S. Essex* Lt. Coy. Fought at *Valdelacasa*. Killed at Talavera in action to capture Eagle. In *SE*.

Desaix, Capt. Pierre Fr. officer at action at *Adrados*, Dec. 1812. In *SEn*.

Diomed Grey, Arab charger given to Wellesley by Col. Ashton as he was dying from a duelling wound. Diomed died after B. of Assaye, 1803, wounded by pike, despite Wellesley's having pike removed to improve chance of recovery.

division (div.) Large military fmn, commanded by lt-gen., of around 4000–6000 men, usually containing 2 or 3 bdes. In the Pen., it became a miniature army with own staff, supply, and artillery and engineers under command.

Docherty, Lt Liam 2IC to *Capt. Killick* on American schooner *Thuella* in the Teste de Buch operation. In *SSge*.

Dodd, Rflm. One of Col. Wade's detachment of 2/95th which took part in the Santiago attack. In *SR*.

Doggett, Lt Simon Old Etonian officer, 1st Guards, ADC on P. of Orange's staff at Waterloo. Accompanied Sharpe on recce of Q. Bras on 15 Jun. In *SW*.

Donajou, Capt. 2IC of the *Real Compañía Irlandesa* attached to

Wellington's HQ in Apr. 1811. In *SB*.

Dooley, Pte Liam Irish soldier who was hanged instead of Sharpe. He and his younger brother had been convicted of looting a church; he agreed to impersonate Sharpe if his brother was freed. In *SH*.

Dornberg, Maj-Gen. Wilhelm von Col. in Prince Jérome's Westphalian army; deserted to allies in 1813. Commanded cav. bde in Waterloo campaign, with responsibility for Mons area. On 15 Jun. he intercepted a message from Colquhoun Grant (Wellington's intelligence chief) that Fr. were advancing on Brussels from Charleroi, not through Mons. Returned letter as being incorrect, and tore up Sharpe's message to same effect.

Douro River (MAPS 1, 5, 11, 16, 24, 26) One of 3 great rivers of Port. Of great value to Wellington as line of communication – from Oporto supplies could be transported the 45 miles upriver to Lamego during all seasons in large boats; in small ones another 40 miles and, after Brit. engrs had improved R. bed in 1812, could reach border at Barca de Alva.

Dragoons Type of cav. Originally mounted inf., but by Nap. Wars dragoons were indistinguishable from other lt. cav. Were bulk of Brit. and Fr. cav. in Pen. 'all purpose' cav. suited to terrain. Weapons included curved sabre, cav. carbine and pistols.

Dregara, Sgt Span. cavalry NCO who had orders to kill Sharpe on his way from Valdivia to *Puerto Crucero* in Dec. 1819. Sharpe killed him when attacking the citadel in Valdivia. In *SD*.

Dubreton, Col. Michel Fr. Officer of 54th Ligne whose Eng. wife was taken hostage at *Adrados* by Pot-au-Feu.

Attended the Royal Academy of Equitation in Angers in 1785 with Wellington. Possibly younger brother of Brig-Gen. Dubreton. In *SEn*.

Dubreton, Brig-Gen. Jean Louis Governor of ft. at Burgos, successfully defended against Wellington in Sept. 1812.

Ducos, Maj. Pierre b. Paris 1771; Fervent revolutionary; denounced his own family who were guillotined. Promoted maj. in 1804 and worked for army intelligence based in Strasbourg. In 1809 sent to Spain as independent agent reporting directly to Napoleon. Took part in several civilian massacres in Leon, Castile and Estramadura. Based in Burgos in 1812. Bitter enemy of Sharpe, who humiliated him by breaking his spectacles at *Adrados* in Dec. 1812. Forced to flee after the B. of Vitória, stole some of Napoleon's treasure in Apr. 1814, got Sharpe blamed for the theft, and hid in Naples. Arrested in Aug. 1814 and charged with treason. Shot by firing squad and buried in the ft. ditch at Valenciennes. In *SEn, SH, SRev*.

Dudon, Attorney-General Former Fr. officer cashiered for deserting his post, who was attorney-general of provisional government in Spain in 1814. Tasked with seizing Napoleon's treasure at Orléans; bulk was surrendered to him, but portion secretly retained by Napoleon's paymaster, Insp. Peyrusse, all taken to Elba.

Dunlop, Lt-Col. Commanded left assault column storming breach at Seringapatam on 4 May 1799.

Dunnett, Maj. Warren Officer in 2/95th who arrived in Pen. with Col. Wade's 4 companies; in command of wing of bn. on rearguard duties at start of retreat to

Corunna. Sharpe, whom he detested, was his QM. Gave order to break up square in face of cav. attack at La Baneza on 31st Dec. 1808. He was captured and Sharpe cut off with 50 survivors. They met again at Waterloo near La Haye Sainte. In *SR, SW*.

Eagle Fr. equivalent of Brit. Colours. Presented to all regts. by Emperor, it was a sacred standard representing unit's honour and glory. The capture of the Eagle from Dutch regt. at Talavera by Sharpe was a bitter disgrace.

Eagle in Chains New badge of *S. Essex* after Talavera, showing captured Dutch Eagle in chains.

East India Company Formed to exploit trade with India and Far East. Incorporated by royal charter in 1600, made immense profits from India. Under Charles II obtained rights to acquire territory, coin money, raise troops, make alliances, make war or peace, and exercise civil or criminal jurisdiction. Handed over functions to Brit. govt in 1858.

Ebro River (MAPS 1, 26) One of 5 great rivers of Iberian peninsula; rises in Cantabrian mts and flows 450 miles SE to Mediterranean. Of strategic importance, offering good defensive line barring advance from Spain to France and vice versa. Fr. forces under Joseph retired behind Ebro in 1808 to consolidate; springboard from which Napoleon marched on Madrid Nov. 1808.

l'Eclin, Col. Pierre de Fr. chasseur officer of Imp. Guard; mission to prevent *Maj. Blas Vivar* from bringing the sacred banner to Santiago. Tricked into leaving the city before Sharpe and *Vivar* attacked. Returned and counter-attacked, shot dead by *Sgt Harper* while fighting with Sharpe, who took his trousers and boots, which he wore from then on. In *SR*.

Elba (MAP 35) Small island off W. coast of Italy. Scene of Napoleon's first exile; he was ruler of its 112,000 population under supervision of allied commissioners; allowed garrison of 600 former Old Guard. Napoleon slipped away in Feb. 1815, landed in France and started the Hundred Days' campaign.

Elphinstone, Col. Engr. officer who briefed Sharpe on Teste de Buch operation, explaining why he was not to march on Bordeaux. In *SSge*.

Elvas (MAPS 1, 11, 16) Strong Port. ft close to Span. border, 11 miles from Badajoz; guarded main road to Lisbon. Used by Wellington as assembly area before besieging Badajoz. Here, in 1812, *Sgt Hakeswill* arrived with *Ensign Matthews* and reinforcements; *Col. Windham* took command of the *S. Essex*; *Hakeswill* attacked *Teresa*, and Sharpe lost command of Lt. Coy.

enfilade Adjective used to describe fire coming from flank.

Erskine, Maj-Gen. Sir William Notoriously incompetent gen. foisted on Wellington by Horse Guards; had temporary command of 5 Div. in 1811, then commanded advance guard of Lt. Div. and cav. Alcoholic, 'as blind as a beetle' and eccentric to edge of insanity. Earmarked as president of Court of Inquiry to investigate Sharpe and others after *San Isidro*; largely responsible for escape of Fr. garrison in Almeida after B. of F. de Onoro. Finally avoided the sack by throwing himself out of a window while suffering from fever. As Sir John Fortescue puts it, '. . . his death a day or two later was a happy release for himself and for the army.'

escalade Attack on walls of ft using ladders.

Espiritu Santo Span. frigate, commanded by *Capt. Ardiles*, which took Sharpe to St Helena and Chile in 1819. Captured and renamed *Kitty* by Adm. Cochrane. In *SD*.

Evora (MAP 1) City in S. Port 130 miles E. of Lisbon. In Jul. 1808, Fr. Gen. Loison sacked the city, slaughtering several thousand inhabitants, which greatly embittered Port. population against Fr. Typical of fate of many cities which fell to besiegers of either side.

Ewart, Sgt Charles Charged with Greys at Waterloo and captured Eagle of 45th Regt. Commissioned ensign in 1816.

facings Collars and cuffs of uniform jacket. Regts. had varying colours: *S. Essex*, yellow; 95th Rifles, black.

Fane, Maj-Gen. Sir Henry Sharpe's first bde commander in Pen. (Lt. Bde in Vimiero campaign). Transferred to command 2 Inf. Bde. Became surveyor-general of the ordnance in 1829. Wellington instrumental in getting him appointed C-in-C India 1835.

Farrell, Pte In Lt. Coy. of *S. Essex*. Present at Vitória. In *SH*.

Farthingdale, Col. Sir Augustus 60-year-old Brit. govt representative to Port. govt. Inexperienced chocolate soldier who had written young officers' guide to war in Spain, without fighting there. His 'wife' (mistress) *Josefina Lacosta* was held hostage by Pot-au-Feu and his deserters at *Adrados* in Dec. 1812. Sharpe's mission was to rescue her and other hostages. In *SEn*.

Farthingdale, Josefina *Josefina Lacosta*

masquerading as *Farthingdale's* wife. Taken hostage and rescued by Sharpe Christmas 1812. In *SEn*.

fascine Tightly bound bundle of sticks used for revetting or filling small ditches.

fausse-braie Earth rampart used to protect base of curtain wall. Similar to counterguard.

Favier, Col. Fr. officer working with *Ducos* against Sharpe in Teste de Buch operation. In *SSge*.

Fenner, Lord Secretary at War in 1813, involved in the illegal sale (crimping) of men from the 2 Bn. *S. Essex* to other regts. Sharpe exposed racket by enlisting as a recruit at Sleaford. In *SRegt*.

Ferdinand, Prince Successor to Span. throne in 1808. Tricked by Napoleon into abdicating and confined in Valençay in France. Restored as King Ferdinand VII in 1814.

Ferrara, Mr Manuel Span. mayor of Valdivia, who surrendered Valdivia to Adm. Cochrane on 5th Feb. 1820. In *SD*.

Fielding, Mr US consul in Valdivia in 1819; in *SD*.

Fillmore, Capt. Commanded No. 4 Coy. of 33rd Foot in India, 1799. Defended Sharpe when charged with striking *Sgt Hakeswill*. In *ST*.

Finch, Capt. On staff of Foulness camp under *Lt-Col. Girdwood*; left in charge of untrained men at depôt when Sharpe took reinforcements to Spain. In *SRegt*.

Fitchett, Lt Engr. officer in SC, tasked with blowing dam at San Roque Ft, Badajoz, in March 1812. His efforts were unsuccessful, Sharpe lit fuse for second time.

Fitzgerald, Lt Officer in 33rd Lt. Coy. in 4th Mysore War, 1799. Severely

wounded by rocket in night attack on Sultanpetah; later that night mortally wounded by bayonet thrust. In *ST*, murdered by *Sgt. Hakeswill*.

Fitz William Indiaman on which Sharpe and 33rd Foot sailed from Calcutta to Madras in 1798; went aground near mouth of Hooghy River at start of voyage.

Fletcher, Lt-Col. Richard A Scot; Wellington's senior engr officer at HQ, responsible for engr officers attached to divs., Royal Sappers and Miners, engineers' park (equipment and stores) and pontoon train. Under Wellington's instructions, designed and supervised construction of Lines of TV behind which allied army withdrew in 1810. Wounded in groin at Badajoz; killed at San Sebastian Sept. 1813. In *SC*.

Ford, Lt-Col. Joseph Took over as CO PWOV from Sharpe at end of Pen. War. Short-sighted and nervous; unfit for command; ineffective at Q. Bras; lost glasses and nerve at Waterloo. Sharpe took control as Imp. Guards attacked. *Ford* sent to Brussels in disgrace. In *SW*.

Ford, Maj. 2IC of Fusiliers bn in action at *Adrados* Dec. 1812. Shot by own troops due to his unpopularity. In *SEn*.

Ford, Lt RN One of *Capt. Bampfylde's* officers on *HMS Vengeance* in 1814. Acted as *Bampfylde's* second during his duel with Sharpe. In *SSge*.

Forlorn Hope Small group of soldiers, usually volunteers under junior officer, who led the storming party at breaches in wall of ft. to draw enemy fire. Officers and sergeants who survived were usually rewarded with promotion. Known generally as 'The Hope'.

Forrest, Maj. 2IC of *S. Essex* to *Lt-Col. Lawford*. Acted CO after *Lawford* severely wounded at C. Rodrigo. Later posted to Lisbon. In *SC*.

Ft Amargos (MAP 40) Span. ft guarding W. approach to Valdivia harbour. Surrendered to Adm. Cochrane. In *SD*.

Ft Celestial (MAP 39) Span. ft halfway between Valdivia and *Puerto Crucero* in Chile, where Sharpe spent night of 18– 19 Dec. 1819. His escort (under *Sgt Dregara*) plotted to kill him, but *Capt. Morillo* helped him to escape. In *SD*.

Ft Chorocomayo (MAP 40) Span. ft. Guarded W. approach to Valdivia harbour. Surrendered to Adm. Cochrane night 4–5 Feb. 1820. In *SD*.

Ft Concepción (MAPS 12, 13, 24) Span. ft on border between C. Rodrigo (Spain) and Almeida (Portugal). Garrisoned periodically by both sides. Defences blown up by Lt. Div., Jul. 1810.

Ft Inglés (MAP 40) Span. ft overlooking only landing place on W. approach to Valdivia harbour. Stormed by Maj. Miller and Sharpe on 4 Feb. 1820. In *SD*.

Ft Nielda (MAP 40) Span. ft guarding E. bank of Valdivia harbour.

Ft Pardaleras (MAP 18) Outwork on high ground 200 yards S. of walls of Badajoz; did not need to be stormed during 3rd siege in Apr. 1812.

Ft Picurina (MAP 18) Strong outworks on high ground SE of Badajoz. Essential for Wellington to capture to establish batteries for bombardment of fortress proper; taken by Maj-Gen. Kempt's bde of 3 Div. on 24 Mar. 1812. *S. Essex* in this bde at C. Rodrigo, but switched to the 4 Div., so took no part. Watched by Sharpe.

Ft St George HQ of Madras Presidency in late C18th.

Ft San Carlos (MAP 40) Span. ft

guarding W. approach to Valdivia harbour. Surrendered to Adm. Cochrane after capture of Ft Inglés. In *SD*.

Ft San Cristóbal (MAP 18) Substantial ft on hill N. of Guadiana R. close to main fortress at Badajoz. Commander of Fr. garrison surrendered after 3rd siege in Apr. 1812.

Ft San Isidro (MAP 13) Fictional ft on Port/Span. border. Sharpe, with *Real Compañía Irlandesa* plus bn. of Cacadores defended it against *Brig. Loup*'s *bde* in Apr. 1811, in SB. Real village of San Isidro is Palencia, scene of operations in Oct. 1812 when bridge over Pisuerga attained strategic significance.

Ft San Roque and Bastion (MAP 18) Name of small ft guarding dam over Rivillas at Badajoz. Unsuccessful attempt made to blow dam on 2 Apr. 1812, by engrs. and soldiers under Lt Stanway RE. In *SC* Sharpe makes this attempt. Also name of a main bastion on S. wall of Badajoz.

Ft William Calcutta. HQ of Brit. in India; 33rd and Sharpe based there on arrival.

Fouché, Joseph b. 1759. A religious youth, who became Minister of Police and eliminated much of the opposition to Napoleon in France. Abandoned Napoleon after Waterloo; reappointed to old post by Louis XVIII, but forced to resign. Retired to Prague and Trieste. Jealous of *Maj. Ducos*'s direct access to Emperor. d. 1820.

Foulness Island Waterlogged island on N. Essex coast; secret location of the *2nd Bn. S. Essex* in 1813 when the soldiers were being 'sold' by *Simmerson* and *Girdwood*. Still used today as firing range. In *SRegt*.

Foy, Lt-Gen. Maximilien b. 1775.

Entrusted by Masséna with special mission to Paris in 1810; returned in May 1811 with Masséna's dismissal letter. Gen. of div.; fought at Salamanca, the Pyrenees. At Waterloo GOC 9 Div. under Réille; d. 1825.

Fraser, Mr Adm. Cochrane's sailing master on O'Higgins in Chile. In *SD*.

Frederickson, Capt. William ('Sweet William') Half-English, half-German coy. commander in 5/60th (Royal American) Rifles. Villainous-looking, with patch over left eye and missing right ear; highly professional soldier. Fought under Sharpe at *Adrados* in Dec. 1812 when his coy. defended the watchtower. Commanded 2 coys. of 60th under Sharpe in Teste de Buch operation. Fought in *Nairn*'s bde with Sharpe at Toulouse in Apr. 1814. Accused, with Sharpe, of stealing Napoleon's treasure and helped him to catch *Ducos* in Naples and clear their names. Fell out with Sharpe when he found that *Lucille Castineau*, to whom he had proposed, was pregnant by Sharpe. Later served in Canada. In *SEn*, *SSge*, *SRev*.

Freire, Gen. Manuel b. 1765. Competent Span. gen. (not to be confused with Port. namesake, lynched by his troops in 1809). Fought throughout Pen. War. Commander of army of Galicia in 1813. Instrumental in winning at San Marcial in Aug. 1813. When he requested Brit. reinforcements, Wellington refused, saying, 'As he has already won his victory, he should keep the honour of it for his countrymen alone.' Attacked too early at Toulouse, causing problems for Beresford's advance, in which Sharpe was involved as a BM in Clinton's div. d. 1834.

Frenada (MAP 27) Small Port. frontier village 3 miles W. of Span. border opposite F. de Onoro. Used by Wellington as HQ from Oct. 1811 to Mar. 1812 (with intervals) and Nov. 1812 to May 1813.

Fuentes de Onoro, B. of (MAPS 1, 12, 13, 14, 15, 24, 27) Small Span. village on border between Spain and Portugal. Scene of 2-day battle between Masséna and Wellington on 3–4 May 1811. Sharpe involved in fighting in the village. Victory for Wellington led to Fr. retreat and dismissal of Masséna.

Fytch, Lt, RM 2IC to *Capt. Palmer RM* in Teste de Buch. Killed during Fr. attack on ft. In *SSge*.

gabion A cylindrical wicker basket 3' high and 2' in diameter, used to provide protection to working parties in trenches.

Galicia (MAP 6) Mountainous, semi-independent province in NW corner of Spain. Scene of Sir John Moore's retreat to Corunna in 1809 and Sharpe's attack on Santiago in same year. Renowned for guerrilla activities, it was never fully occupied by Fr.

galloper guns 6-pdr guns drawn by horses, as distinct from oxen (in India) to accompany cav.

Gammora Mayor (MAP 29) Span. village on Zadorra R. 2 miles N. of Vitória; its bridge was scene of bitter fighting during B. of Vitória between Fr. under Réille and Allied 5 Div., in which *S. Essex* played a prominent part.

García Hernandez, B. of (MAPS 1, 23) Famous as one of the rare occasions when cav. broke an inf. square. Heavy Dragoons of KGL charged and broke 3 Fr. squares on 23 July 1812 during Fr.

retreat from Salamanca. Sharpe, *Hogan* and *Harper* rode with KGL and Sharpe killed *Col. Leroux* inside the square of 1/69 Ligne.

Garrard, Pte Tom Friend of Sharpe in Lt. Coy. 33rd Foot in India. Promoted sgt, then commissioned into Port. army in Pen. War. Fought with Cacadores bn, assisting Sharpe defend *Ft San Isidro* in Apr. 1811. Died when he deliberately blew up powder reserve to destroy Fr. attackers. In *ST, SB*.

Garter, Most Noble Order of Founded by Edward III; premier Order of Britain, in personal gift of sovereign and limited to 25 knights. Wellington did not know on which shoulder he should wear the sash.

Gataker, *Rflm*. Soldier in 2/95th, participated in Sharpe's attack on Santiago in 1809. In *SR*.

Gawilghur, Siege of Indian town and ft. Brit. under Wellesley stormed and took it on 15 Dec. 1803. Sharpe ensign in Lt. Coy. of 74th Foot.

Gazan, Gen. Honoré Théodore Fr. div. commander who rose to command Army of the South in 1813. Commanded Fr. first line at B. of Vitória.

Gent, Col. William EIC engr. officer in charge of siege works at Seringapatam, 1799.

Gerard, Lt French 2IC to *Cmdt Lassan* in ft at Teste de Buch. In *SSge*.

Gibbons, Lt Christian Officer in *S. Essex* and nephew of first CO *Lt-Col. Sir Henry Simmerson*. Acted as unofficial ADC to *Simmerson*. Fought with Sharpe at Talavera, killed by *Sgt Harper* on the 30 Jul. 1809. In *SE*.

Gibbons, Miss Jane Beautiful sister of *Lt Gibbons*. Niece of *Sir Henry Simmerson*. Assisted Sharpe in exposing her uncle's illegal crimping in Aug. 1813. Married Sharpe, but deserted him and became pregnant by *Capt. Lord John Rossendale*. Disowned, but not divorced by Sharpe. d. 1844. In *SE, SRegt, SW*.

Gilliland, Capt. Arty. officer in command of Congreve Rocket Troop at *Adrados* in Dec. 1812. In *SEn*.

Girdwood, Lt-Col. Bartholomew In charge of *S. Essex* depôt at Chelmsford. Martinet who tarred his moustache, wore a stock and was petrified of dogs. Involved in crimping; exposed by Sharpe. CO *S. Essex* at B. of the Nivelle 10 Nov. 1813. Went insane during battle, so command devolved on Sharpe. In *SRegt*.

Giron, Gen. Pedro Augustin Span. gen. who fought well throughout Pen. War. Commanded Span. force which operated on Wellington's strategic left flank during 1813 advance.

glacis Open space or slope surrounding a ft.

Gneisenau, Gen. Augustus von b. 1760. Competent C-of-S to Blücher at Waterloo. d. of cholera 1831.

Godolphin, Revd and Mrs Provided accommodation in Tothill Street, London, to *Jane Gibbons*. In *SRegt*.

gonfalon Banner or standard, in this case battle flag of Span. Christians who defeated the Moors in the C9th. Was to be unfurled in Santiago to encourage population to rise against Fr. In *SR*.

Goodall, Capt. Commanded Lt. Coy. of 12th Foot at storming of Seringapatam, 1799.

Graham, Sgt. In 12th Foot. Led Forlorn Hope of left-hand assault on breach at Seringapatam, 1799. Killed as he planted the Colours and announced himself as 'Lieutenant Graham!'

Graham, Gen. Sir Thomas b. 1748; joined army at 44. ADC to Moore at Corunna. Won a victory at Barossa in 1811. Commanded left wing of allied advance on Vitória; corps included *S. Essex* in 5 Div. Besieged San Sebastian 1813. Fine fighting soldier; became Lord Lynedoch; d. at age 95.

Grant, Capt., RN Commanded frigate *HMS Scylla* in Teste de Buch operation. In *SSge*.

grapeshot Close-range arty. ammo, often confused with canister or case-shot: iron balls packed around an iron column attached to a base, the whole covered with canvas and tied with string. Used mostly at sea.

grasshopper gun Brit. 3-pdr cannon first manufactured around 1770. Manpackable inf. support gun, best used with canister. Did good service in AWI but not much in use in Nap. Wars. *Maj. Ducos* used one to defend his hide-out N. of Naples.

Great Road (MAPS 1, 29) Also known as the Royal Road. Main paved road from Bayonne to Madrid *via* Burgos. Principal line of communication for Fr. forces in Spain. Under constant guerrilla attack. Wellington cut it at B. of Vitória.

Green, Sgt NCO in Lt. Coy. 33rd Foot in India, 1799. In *ST*.

Grenadier Company (Gren. Coy.) In Brit. bn composed of best, strongest; posted on right flank of bn line on parade or in battle; élite coy. Title originated from C18th when they carried grenades.

Grenoble Small town in S. France. Scene of Napoleon's first encounter with armed opposition after escape from Elba; royalist troops went over to him without firing a shot.

Grommet wad Circle of rope rammed down gun barrel on top of shot to prevent it rolling out when gun depressed to fire downhill.

Grouchy, Marshal Emanuel b. 1766. Arty. officer who transferred to the cav. Fought throughout Nap. Wars in Europe, Spain, Russia and France. Marshal, Apr. 1815; commanded right wing of Army of the North in Waterloo campaign, fighting at Ligny and Wavre. Failed to keep the Prussians from Napoleon's right flank; later blamed by Napoleon for his defeat. d. 1847.

Gudin, Col. Jean Fr. officer commanding small unit of Europeans in Tippoo's army. Sharpe 'served' in it in Seringapatam while on mission inside the city. *Gudin* promoted him corporal for his services during the British night attack on Sultanpetah on 5 Apr. 1799. Shot in shoulder by Sharpe just before Sharpe prematurely exploded mine in city's wall. In *ST*.

Hacha, Father Senior priest and inquisitor of Spanish Inquisition. Brother of guerrilla leader *El Matarife*. Worked for *Maj. Ducos* during Vitória campaign, getting support among Span. nobility and church for Treaty of Valençay. In *SH*.

Hagman, Rflm. Daniel One of Sharpe's original rflm. who survived retreat to Corunna. Former Cheshire poacher, about 50 years old, who was nonetheless a crack shot. Made a 'chosen man'. Present at Salamanca and at *Adrados*. Wounded in skirmish in Pyrenees Jul. 1813; Fought at Q. Bras; mortally wounded at Waterloo 18 Jun. 1815.

Sharpe with him when he died. In *SE, SC, SG, SS, SEn, SRegt, SW*.

Hakeswill, Sgt Obadiah b. 1769. Evil senior NCO of *S. Essex* – Sharpe's main enemy throughout Pen. War. At 12, sentenced to be hanged by Sussex Assizes; cut down by his uncle and survived which led him to regard himself as a man who could not die. But the experience left heavy scarring, deformed neck and facial twitch. He also venerated mothers in general, and particularly his own, *'Biddy' Hakeswill*.

Joined 33rd Foot as drummer boy in 1781; took great pleasure in his flogging duties. In 1793 enlisted Sharpe (whom he called 'Sharpie'); caused him to be flogged in India. Murdered Lt Fitzgerald at Seringapatam in 1799 and *Col. Hector McCandless* at Assaye in 1803. Invalided out in 1806 but re-enlisted into newly forming *S. Essex* in 1808. Joined the bn before Badajoz, attacked *Teresa Morena* at Elvas and Badajoz. Tried to shoot Sharpe during the raid at Badajoz, and killed *Capt. Knowles* there before deserting to join brigands in N. Portugal until Dec. 1812. Captured at *Adrados* shortly after murdering *Teresa* (then Sharpe's wife). Tried and shot by firing squad, but Sharpe had to finish him off with rifle. Buried in unmarked grave in Portugal Feb. 1813. In *ST, SC, SEn*.

Halkett, Maj-Gen. Sir Colin b. 1774. Served in Dutch Foot Guards. CO 2nd Bn KGL 1805. Fought at Albuera, retreat from Burgos, Pyrenees. Commanded 5 Bde (which included *PWOV*) in Alten's div. at Q. Bras and Waterloo. Later served in India. Governor of Chelsea Hospital. d. 1856.

Hardacre, Lt Officer of 20th Foot who met Sharpe on arrival in St Helena

Nov. 1819 and Jun. 1821. In *SD*.

Hardy, Capt. Claud Cav. officer in *P. of Wales Dragoons* based at Lisbon, for whom *Josefina Lacosta* left Sharpe. Sent to *Moreno*'s guerrilla band to keep watch on gold, but killed in mysterious circumstances in 1810, probably by *El Catolico*. In *SG*.

Harper, Sgt Patrick Augustine Birth date unknown; probably 1780 in Tangaveane (which ceased to exist during potato famine of 1840) in Donegal, Ireland; fourth of 11 children. Left home after argument involving extra work because of his size (in 1809 he was 6' 4" and weighed 14 stone). Got drunk and woke up to find he was in the army. Initially a cav. regt but transferred to the 95th Rifles in 1803; almost certainly his regt used a request for drafts to offload a trouble-maker. He was a drunk, a brawler and hated the 'system' after crushing of Fr. invasion of Ireland and ensuing Irish rebellion of 1798. Fiercely proud of background and heritage, but aware of stigma of being Irish in Brit. Army; was focal point for dissenters. Took part in the disastrous expedition to S. America in 1805, fighting at Montevideo and Buenos Aires. Posted to the 2/95th in May 1805. Arrived Corunna 26 Oct. 1808 with Lt-Col. Wade's 4 companies; in *Maj. Dunnett*'s wing when Sharpe joined it as QM on 20 Dec. *Harper* mistrusted all officers, except for *Capt. Murray* his coy commander. During march to Santiago (*SR*) he fought Sharpe; they became allies and firm friends. Sharpe got him promoted sgt. *Harper* made the 7-barrelled Nock gun, a present from Sharpe, his personal weapon. In Mar. 1812, broken to pte.

and given 100 lashes, when portrait of CO's wife was found in his pack. Met his future wife, *Isabella*, during storming of Badajoz; married her after Vitória. She stayed with a cousin of his in London in 1813, and went from there to Ireland with their child. Sharpe promoted *Harper* RSM after *MacLaird*'s death in Jul. 1813. Reunited with family in 1814, having served throughout Pen. War. Loot from Vitória bought him a tavern in Ireland, where he also made good money at horse-stealing. Joined Sharpe as armed civilian at Q. Bras and used Nock gun to effect at Waterloo. Went with Sharpe to Chile in 1819, visiting Napoleon en route, who gave him thimble decorated with honey bee. Had 4 children, *Richard, Liam, Sean* and *Michael*. Died happy and prosperous as landlord of a Dublin pub with many grandchildren, in 1838. In *SR, SE, SG, SB, SC, SS, SEn, SH, SRegt, SSge, SRev, SW, SD*.

Harper, Isabella Span. girl saved by *Harper* at Badajoz. Married him in cathedral at Vitória. In *SH*.

Harris, Lt-Gen. George b. 1746. Commanded Madras army in 4th Mysore War against Tippoo Sultan; also combined force which took Seringapatam. On his orders Sharpe's flogging was stopped and he was sent on special mission. In *ST*.

Havercamp, Sgt Horatio *S. Essex* recruiting sgt who 'enlisted' Sharpe and *Harper* at Sleaford in Aug. 1813; in *S Regt*.

Helmut, Sgt KGL cav. NCO who assisted Sharpe in clash with *El Catolico* in Almeida and to lay the trail of powder to the magazine 25/26 Aug. 1810. In *SG*.

Hicks, Ensign Timothy Officer in 33rd Foot Lt. Coy. in India, 1799; at Siege of Seringapatam. In *ST*.

Hill, Lt-Gen. Rowland b. 1772; entered army as Lt in 53rd Foot in 1793. A popular, generous and humane div. commander of 2 Div, nicknamed 'Daddy'. One of few generals Wellington trusted with independent commands. Commanded right wing of army 1813–14; won hard-fought victory at St Pierre in 1813. Horse shot under him at Waterloo. Baron 1814; succeeded Wellington as C-in-C Brit. army 1825–39; d. 1842.

Hogan, Maj. Michael Middle-aged, balding, Irish engr. officer on Wellington's staff for intelligence/scouting duties. Befriended Sharpe, and looked after his interests at army HQ. Early background uncertain, but had attended Army Staff College and served in Dublin Castle where he met Wellesley. Wellington entrusted him with more secret aspects of intelligence-gathering; spoke Fr., Span. and Port. and worked to coordinate Span. guerrilla bands. Served throughout war, dying of fever in St Jean de Luz in 1813. In *SR, SB, SS, SSge*.

holding battalion Skeleton, non-operational unit used to hold personnel awaiting posting or discharge.

Hope, Gen. Sir John Brit. commander of corps responsible for crossing Adour and attacking Bayonne in Feb. 1814.

Horrell, Pte Jebediah Labourer from Midlands; served in *S. Essex* Lt. Coy. under Sharpe who thought him a good soldier who invariably had clean kit and musket. In *SE, SB*.

Horse Guards Can mean the 1st and 2nd Life Guards or Royal Horse Guards.

More commonly high command of the army in London, the C-in-C and his staff. Occasionally HQ building in Whitehall. Origin of saying, 'from the horse's mouth'.

hot shot Roundshot heated in furnace or portable oven; carried to cannon with pincers or spoon. Used to fire ships or buildings. Highly dangerous for gunners but most effective. Commonly used by shore batteries against ships.

Hougoumont (SKETCH 6) Large farm and orchard (called Gaomont by the Belgians) which formed strongpoint on right of Wellington's line at Waterloo. Garrisoned by lt. coys of Guards, Nassauers and Hanoverians. Fiercely attacked by Réille's corps throughout, but Fr. did not take buildings. Sharpe and *Harper* involved in its defence and closing north gate when Fr. gained entry.

'house-boner' C18th slang for burglar.

Howick Place The road in Westminster, London, where Sharpe b. 1777.

howitzer Short-barrelled cannon designed for high-angle fire.

Hoyos, Col Span. commander of Corral Castle guarding Valdivia harbour, Chile. Surrendered to Adm. Cochrane.

Huckfield, Pte Educated soldier of *S. Essex*; tried to stop bn parading at Oropesa in Jul. 1809 for mass flogging ordered by *Simmerson*. Sharpe overlooked this mutinous behaviour; promoted sgt; at B. of Salamanca and action at *Adrados*. Promoted to new rank of CSM before B. of the Nivelle. Fought at Toulouse, Q. Bras and Waterloo, where he lost little finger of left hand. In *SE, SS, SEn, SRegt, SW.*

Hughes, Capt. Sharpe first coy commander who asked for him in Lt. Coy.

Sharpe had been destined for the Gren. Coy. *Hughes* died of flux in Calcutta in 1798. Replaced by *Capt. Morris.* In *ST.*

Ibbotson, Pte *S. Essex* soldier shot for desertion at Oropesa on 21 Jul. 1809. In *SE.*

Imperial Guard Napoleon's élite formation of veteran troops, nicknamed 'Grumblers'; received higher pay and many privileges; consisted of inf., cav., arty., engrs, marines and gendarmerie units. At Waterloo the inf. was divided into Old Guard (1st, 2nd, Gren. Regts, 1st. 2nd Chasseur Regts), Middle Guard (3rd, 4th Gren. Regts, 3rd and 4th Chasseur Regts) and Young Guard (1st and 3rd Voltigeurs and 1st and 3rd Tirailleurs). Provided 600-man personal guard on Elba. Sharpe led the *PWOV* in Brit. repulse of Imp. Guard in final minutes at Waterloo.

Intrépido Argentine brig which took part in Adm. Cochrane's attack on Valdivia in Feb. 1820.

Invalides, Les Built in 1670 as hospital for old soldiers. In 1840 Napoleon's remains were brought from St Helena and placed in open crypt beneath dome in a sarcophagus made from single block of pink porphyry. Guarded by two large statues representing civil and military power and flanked by 12 statues of Victories; names of great battles are inscribed on walls.

Irish College University college at Salamanca, where rector, Revd Dr Patrick Curtis ran Brit. spy network. Used as hospital after B. of Salamanca; Sharpe shot here by *Col. Leroux.*

Jamestown Capital of St Helena Island.

Jefferson, Capt. Matthew OC Lt. Coy.

PWOV after *d'Alembord* wounded at Waterloo. In *SW*.

Jenkins, Rflm. Parry 2/95th, one of Sharpe's 50 cut off from Moore's army in Jan. 1809; in dawn attack on Santiago. Skilled fisherman, partner of *Isaiah Tongue*, who was killed in Aug. 1810. In *SR, SG*.

jettis Professional Indian strongmen employed by Tippoo Sultan to execute prisoners by twisting head through 180 degrees or driving 9-inch nail into skull.

Joliot, Mr One of the *Joliot* brothers, well-known spectacle makers in Paris. Made reading glasses for Napoleon and *Maj. Ducos*. Told *Capt. Frederickson* whereabouts of *Ducos* in Summer 1814. In *SRev*.

Jones, Rflm. 2/95th; one of Sharpe's 50 cut off from Moore's army in Jan. 1809; in attack on Santiago. In *SR*.

José, Lt Span. guerrilla working with *El Catolico* out of *Casatejada* in Aug. 1810. Killed by lancers. In *SG*.

Jourdan, Marshal Jean Baptiste Count b. 1762. Fought under Lafayette in the AWI. Distinguished himself in Revolutionary Wars. C-of-S to Joseph in Talavera campaign 1809 and again 1812–13. Fought at Salamanca and Vitória. After Waterloo, rallied to monarchy and presided over court which sentenced Ney to death. Later became governor of Les Invalides and foreign minister. d. 1833.

Jovellanos, Col. Span. officer known as *El Catolico*, the guerrilla leader. In *SG*.

Joyce, Maggie Owner of lodging-house-cum-brothel-cum-gin-shop in St Giles Rookery. Took Sharpe in when he ran away from foundling home. Taught him to live on his wits; first woman to bed him. Trusted by Sharpe to sell jewels gained at Vitória. In *SRegt*.

Juanita, Doña de Elia Span. *anfrancesado* (Fr. supporter); spy for Fr., lover of *Brig. Loup* and mistress of *Lord Kiely*, commander of the *Real Compañía Irlandesa*. Opened gates of *Ft San Isidro to Loup's* men 28 Apr. 1811. Attempted to kill Sharpe in *San Cristobal*, and shot him in shoulder in F. de Onoro, 5 May 1811. Killed by *Harper* with Nock gun. In *SB*.

Junot, Gen. Andache b. 1771. Fr. commander who opposed Wellesley in Vimiero campaign and secured advantageous surrender terms at Convention of Cintra. Secretary to Napoleon at Toulon and ADC during his Italian campaign. In 1807 given command of force for invasion of Port. Within a month was made Duke of Abrantes and governor of Port. Brave, truculent, dissipated and rapacious, Junot never made marshal; fought in Pen. War under Masséna (1810–11) and in Russian campaign 1812. d. Jul. 1813, when he threw himself from a window in a fit of insanity.

Kearsey, Maj. Exploring officer in *P. of Wales' Dragoons*; rode behind enemy lines in uniform, sometimes with guerrillas, seeking information/intelligence. Briefed Sharpe on gold-seeking mission at Almeida and guided him to *Casatejada* in Aug. 1810. Wounded and captured but rescued by Sharpe. In *SG*.

Kelly, Cpl James Junior NCO in *S. Essex* Lt. Coy, married to *Pru Baxter* (widow). Died of wounds in fight to rescue *Maj. Kearsey* at *Casatejada*. In *SG*.

Kemmis, Maj-Gen. Commanded bde in 4 Div. at Badajoz. In *SC*.

Kiely, Earl of CO of the *Real Compañía Irlandesa* attached to Wellington's

HQ in Apr. 1811. His mistress, *Juanita*, was Fr. spy responsible for easy access by *Loup*'s men to *Ft San Isidro* on 28 Apr. 1811. Showed cowardice during attack. Shot himself in church at Villar Formoso. In *SB*.

Killick, Capt. (US) Cornelius Master of American schooner *Thuella*, a privateer. In the action at Teste de Buch in 1814. Captured and released by Sharpe, he later rescued Sharpe and his men from the ft before it fell to Fr. In *SSge*.

King's German Legion (KGL) Formed from old Electorate of Hanover's army after Napoleon overran the country in 1803. By 1806, had 10 inf. bns and 5 cav. regts, plus arty. and engrs. Most fought well in Pen. and had excellent reputation until after 1811, when non-Germans were recruited to keep it up to strength.

Kinney, Lt-Col. Commanded bn of fusiliers at *Adrados* in Dec. 1812. Killed by mine in broken wall when attacking castle. In *SEn*.

Kirby, Pte *S. Essex* soldier who reported near-mutiny to Sharpe at Oropesa, Jul. 1809. In *SE*.

'Kitty, The' New name Adm. Cochrane gave to *Espiritu Santo* after he captured and repaired it. Used in attack and capture of Valdivia.

Kligenthal Master German swordmaker; all his weapons hand-forged from one piece of steel. Sharpe was desperate to own *Col. Leroux*'s Kligenthal but discarded it soon after killing *Leroux*.

Knowles, Capt. Robert One of Sharpe's officers in Lt. Coy. of *S. Essex*. Fought at Talavera as Lt; later purchased captaincy in the 2/5th and commanded coy at Badajoz. First to escalade the castle, but killed by *Sgt Hakeswill* when attempting to protect *Teresa*. In *SC, SG*.

Kunwar Singh Hindu commander of Appah Rao's bodyguard in Seringapatam, 1799. Fell in love with *Mary Bickerstaff*, mixed-race widow of Brit. sgt, and Sharpe's lover. In *ST*.

La Belle Alliance (SKETCH 6) Small farm building in centre of Fr. position at Waterloo, from which Napoleon watched much of battle. Wellington and Blücher met there after Fr. defeat.

Lacosta, Josefina High-class Port. whore, thought to have run away from her husband (*Duarte*, living in Brazil). Initially girlfriend to *Lt Gibbons (S. Essex)*, later ensnared Sharpe, but left him for *Capt. Hardy* after B. of Talavera. Masqueraded as wife of *Sir Augustus Farthindale* and taken hostage by Pot-au-Feu at *Adrados*. In *SE, SEn*. (See also *Farthingdale, Lady Josefina*.)

La Haye Sainte (SKETCH 6) Farm just forward of centre of allied defensive line at Waterloo. Garrisoned as outpost by KGL; close to sandpit defended by the 1/95th. Lost to Fr.

Lalor, Lt 73rd Foot; marked with flags route for assault on breach across South Cauvery R. at Siege of Seringapatam 1799. Shot and killed by Tippoo Sultan.

Lamont, Asst-Comm. In Fane's Lt. Bde. during Vimiero campaign in 1808. Was supply officer whom Sharpe dealt with at bde HQ for logistical arrangements for 2/95th.

Lassan, Comdt (Maj.) Henri Commander of Fr. garrison at Teste de Buch; Lost ft to Sharpe. Also *Comte Lassan*, with land and château near Seléglise in Normandy. Brother of *Lucille. Maj. Ducos* had him murdered by *Sgt Challon* in May 1814 to prevent his clearing Sharpe of stealing Napoleon's treasure. In *SSge, SRev*.

Lassan, Dominique b. 1818 in *Seléglise*, Normandy. Daughter of Sharpe and *Lucille Castineau née Lassan*.

Lassan, Dowager Countess Mother of *Henri* and *Lucille Lassan*. Murdered (with *Henri*) in May 1814 by *Ducos*'s men. In *SRev*.

Lassan, Patrick b. 1815 in *Seléglise*, Normandy. Named after *Sgt Patrick Harper*. Son of Sharpe and *Lucille Castineau née Lassan*. Joined Fr. Army as s/lt in Voltigeur regt; commanded cav. regt in Crimean War 1854–5; military attaché (*General de Bde*) with Federal Army in ACW 1861–5.

Latimer, Sgt In Sharpe's original coy.; in *SB*.

Lavin, Sgt Fr. NCO who tortured Sharpe on orders of *Maj. Ducos* in Burgos Castle on 11 May 1813. Sharpe crippled him with blow to groin and fought his way out. In *SRev*.

Lawford, Lt-Col. the Honourable (later Sir) William Coy. officer in India in 33rd Foot when Sharpe was pte; nephew of *Col. McCandless*, EIC intelligence officer in *ST. Lawford* and Sharpe pretended to be deserters to undertake special mission inside Seringapatam. Taught Sharpe to read and write in Tippoo Sultan's dungeon. Later staff officer at Wellington's HQ; appointed CO of *S. Essex* after *Simmerson* disgraced at Talavera. Same age as Sharpe. Severely wounded and lost an arm in Siege of C. Rodrigo; invalided home Jan. 1812. Thereafter nicknamed 'One-armed Willie'. Knighted by Prince Regent; left Army and became

MP and magistrate. In *ST, SC, SRegt*.

Legros, S/Lt Huge Fr. officer nicknamed 'The Enforcer' who broke through northern gate of Hougoumont at Waterloo with an axe. Sharpe helped to kill him and his men in fight to close the gate.

Lennox, Capt. OC Lt. Coy *S. Essex* under *Simmerson* at *Valdelacasa*. Had fought at B. of Assaye in 1803 in the 78th Foot; Sharpe sgt. at Assaye. Mortally wounded in *S. Essex* square when King's Colour lost at *Valdelacasa*. Gave his sword to Sharpe. In *SE*.

Leroux, Hélène Fr. sister of **Col. Leroux** married to Span. nobleman. Spied for Fr. in Salamanca, 1812. Seduced and deceived Sharpe about activities. In *SS*. (See also *Sabada, La Marquesa de*.)

Leroux, Col. Philippe Sadistic officer in Imp. Guard. Mission in *SS* to identify and kill Revd Dr Curtis. Murdered fellow officer (*Capt. Delmas*) and assumed his identity. As *Delmas*, captured by Sharpe, escaped by breaking parole and killing *Lt-Col. Windham*, seriously wounded Sharpe in stomach, but killed by Sharpe in broken Fr. square at García Hernández 23 Jul. 1812. In *SS*.

Leroy, Capt. Thomas Senior capt. in *S. Essex*, OC Gren. Coy. at Badajoz. Cigar-smoking American exile from family loyal to Britain after American Revolution. Wounded at *Valdelacasa*. Served with *S. Essex* in Pen. until severely wounded at Badajoz. CO of bn at Vitória as Lt-Col., but killed in assault on Gamorra Mayor on 21st Jun. 1813. Sharpe took over temporarily after his death. In *SE, SC, SH*.

Lerrana, Capt. Span. officer commanding escort when *Vivar* disappeared in

Chile early 1819. Promoted col.; close supporter of *Bautista*. In *SD*.

Letters of Marque Commission (papers) given by belligerent state to private shipowner, authorising him to arm his vessel and carry out operations of war. *Capt. Killick* had Letters of Marque for *Thuella* in SSge.

Light Company (Lt. Coy.) In Brit. bn this coy. composed agile men and good marksmen for use as skirmishers; élite coy. on left flank of bn line on parade. Towards end of Pen. War issued with muskets with rudimentary backsights.

Ligny (MAP 36) Small Belgian village 10m. NE of Charleroi, 7m. SE of Q. Bras. Scene of Prussian defeat on 16 Jun. 1815. Defeat not decisive; Prussians helped defeat Napoleon at Waterloo 2 days later.

Lippett, Jemmy A 'topper' (hit-man) hired to murder Sharpe in London, Jul. 1813. Sharpe killed him during fight. In *SRegt*.

Lisbon (MAPS 1, 4, 5, 11, 16) Wellesley's main supply base in Pen. and port at where most reinforcements disembarked. From the sea, view was a beautiful harbour with a backdrop of hills, plantations and vineyards; ashore things were different. 'The town is a dunghill from end to end', was a Scottish sgt's view. A surgeon commented, 'I dislike it more than any place I was ever in, and this is altogether from want of cleanliness of the inhabitants.' Built on hillside, streets were steep, narrow and open sewers. Filth accumulated until heavy rain washed it into the river.

Little, Mr Bandmaster of *PWOV* in Waterloo campaign. In *SW*.

Longa, Gen. Francisco b. 1770; Span. guerrilla leader who rose to be bde and div. commander in regular army. Fought well at B. of Vitória and the Nivelle; portrait in Hall of Fame in Military Museum, Madrid; d. 1831.

Longwood House (MAP 38) Napoleon's residence on St Helena. Stone cow-house and barn built in mid C18th. Extended later and during Napoleon's time; he complained of its inadequacies.

Lossow, Capt. In cav. of KGL; Met Sharpe on Coa R. in Aug. 1810, helped him to escape with the gold from *Casatejada*. In *SG*.

Loup, Brig. Guy One-eyed commander of mixed Fr. inf/cav. bde on anti-guerrilla operations E. of Almeida, April 1811. Bde. wore grey uniforms and had wolf-skin standard. Attacked *Ft San Isidro* 28 April 1811. Killed by Sharpe in F. de Onoro 5 May 1811. In *SB*.

Lowe, Maj-Gen. Sir Hudson b. 1769. Saw considerable service in Nap. Wars; present at 13 general actions when Napoleon commanded Fr. Appointed governor of St Helena during Napoleon's exile. May have met Sharpe during the Waterloo campaign where Lowe was QMG to P. of Orange until May 1815 while Sharpe was also on P's staff. d. 1844.

Lynch, Sgt John Brutal Irish NCO at Foulness Camp. Shot (murdered) new recruit *Marriott* when he tried to desert. Sharpe took Lynch to Spain with reinforcements for *S. Essex*; killed by his own men during B. of the Nivelle. In *SRegt*.

MacAuley, Surg. Irish surg. on The O'Higgins in Chile, 1820. In *SD*.

McCandless, Col. Hector 60-year-old Calvinist Scot, formerly of Scotch 'Brigade'. Senior EIC intelligence officer at

Harris's HQ in campaign against Tippoo Sultan in 1799. Captured and imprisoned in Seringapatam. *Lt Lawford* (his nephew) and Sharpe sent to contact him inside the city. Sharpe accompanied him again at the Battle of Assaye in 1803 when *McCandless* was shot by *Sgt Hakeswill*. In *ST, STr*.

McDonald, Ensign 16-year-old in *S. Essex* Lt. Coy. Killed by *Col Leroux* when breaking parole to escape. In *SS*.

McGovern, Sgt Senior NCO in *S. Essex* Lt. Coy.; at B. of Salamanca. In *SE, SG, SS*.

McInerney, RSM *PWOV* at Q. Bras and Waterloo Jun. 1815. In *SW*.

MacLaird, RSM *S. Essex* during Vitória campaign. Mortally wounded in skirmish in Pyrenees, Jul. 1813. Comforted by Sharpe as he died. In *SH, SRegt*.

Mahoney, Capt. Coy. commander in *S. Essex*, Vitória campaign. In *SH*.

Maillot, Col. Escorted 4 crates of Napoleon's treasure to Bordeaux, Apr. 1814; handed them over to *Maj. Ducos*. *Ducos* murdered him and stole treasure. In *SRev*.

Mallavelly (MAP 2) Scene of first clash between British under Lt-Gen. Harris and Tippoo's forces on 27 Mar. 1799. 33rd Foot with Pte. Sharpe in Lt. Coy led advance. Sharpe killed his first enemy (Indian officer) in close combat and looted body.

Mallinson, Pte Jed One of Sharpe's comrades in India in Lt. Coy. 33rd Foot. Killed in unsuccessful attack on Sultanpetah Tope (wood) near Seringapatam. In *ST*.

Mangalore (MAP 2) Main Mysore port on W. coast of India controlled by Tippoo Sultan in 1798. Fr. troops in

India would probably have landed here.

Manvell, Capt. Christopher Life Guards officer and friend of *Capt. Lord John Rossendale*, whom he protected from Sharpe's rage at Brussels ball on eve of Waterloo. In *SW*.

Maquerre, Comte de Traitorous officer in Chasseurs Britannique who tried to betray Sharpe in Teste de Buch operation. Sharpe killed him on bridge of boats over the Adour on 26 Feb. 1814. In *SSge*.

Marengo, B. of Between Napoleon and Austrians, 14 Jun. 1800. Napoleon's first victory as head of state, made out to be a greater triumph than it was. For his funeral, Napoleon was wrapped in the cloak he wore at the battle.

Marmont, Marshal Auguste Frédéric Louis, Duke of Ragusa b. 1774. Originally arty. officer; ADC and close friend to Bonaparte in Italy and Egypt; commanded arty. at Marengo. Disgruntled at not receiving his marshal's baton until 1809. Replaced Masséna as commander of Army of Portugal in 1812. Defeated and badly wounded at Salamanca. Defeated at B. of Laon (1814) and surrendered his corps. He was never forgiven, and was origin of Fr. word (of the time) for betrayal – *raguser*. Exiled in 1830. Spent years wandering Europe writing his memoirs; his appalling handwriting obviated need for codes; d. 1852.

Marquinez, Capt. Span. ADC to *Bautista* with whom he had homosexual relationship in Valdivia in 1819. In *SD*.

Marriott, Pte Giles Recruited to *S. Essex* at same time as Sharpe on 4 Aug. 1813 at Sleaford. Attempted to desert from Foulness Camp, shot dead by *Sgt Lynch* near the camp. In *SRegt*.

Martin, Lt Tom, RN Commanded brig-sloop *Cavalier* at Teste de Buch. In *SSge*.

Mary Starbuck American whaler used by Adm. Cochrane to fake shipwreck so as to capture *Espiritu Santo* on 1 Jan. 1820.

Mâs des Augustins (MAP 34) Important Fr. redoubt on Calvinet ridge at B. of Toulouse 10 Apr. 1814. Changed hands 5 times in bitter fighting with Brit. 6 Div. Sharpe, serving as BM in *Nairn*'s *bde*. led final assault.

Mason, Cpl Junior S. Essex NCO at Foulness Camp. In *SRegt*.

Master-General of the Ordnance Usually a soldier, always a Cabinet member, regarded as govt's principal military adviser; commanded arty., engrs. and supporting services.

Matarife, El (The Slaughterman) Ruthless Span. guerrilla leader who specialised in knife fighting against opponent chained to him. Murdered *Hélène*'s husband *Gen. Luis Casares*, for which Sharpe was 'hung'. Killed by Sharpe in knife fight on 21 Jun. 1813. In *SH*.

Matthews, Ensign William 16-year-old in *S. Essex* who brought out draft of reinforcements in Mar. 1812. His sgt was *Hakeswill*. Joined the Lt. Coy., but was killed in the explosion during attempt to blow dam near San Roque Ft at Badajoz. In *SC*.

Mattingley, Lt On staff of Foulness Camp in 1813. In *SRegt*.

Maxwell, Gen. Sir Barston Senior officer deputed to hear Sharpe's accusations of crimping against *Lord Fenner* at Horse Guards, Aug. 1813. In *SR*.

Mayeron, Capt. Fr. officer captured by Sharpe during Fr. assault at Teste de Buch. Informed Sharpe that Bordeaux had not risen against Napoleon. In *SSge*.

Medellin, B of 28 Mar. 1809 between Span. under Cuesta with 23,000, advancing on Fr. under Victor with 17,500. After initial success, Cuesta defeated, ridden over by own cav. and lost 10,000 men. Fr. losses were 1000.

Meer Allum Nizam (ruler) of Indian state of Hyderabad who led army allied to Brit. against Tippoo Sultan in 1799. Wellesley was his adviser (de facto commander) during Siege of Seringapatam.

Mendora, Maj. Miguel Span. officer, on staff of *Gen. Casares*, murdered by *El Matarife*. Sharpe 'hung' for this crime. In *SH*.

Merrill, Lt At Chelmsford depôt when Sharpe arrived in Jul. 1813. In *SRegt*.

Messines, Capt. Christopher ADC to Duke of York at Horse Guards in 1813. In *SRegt*.

Micklewhite, Maj. Second major with *PWOV* in Waterloo campaign. Killed protecting Colours at Q. Bras. *Capt. d'Alembord* filled the vacancy. In SW.

Micklewhite, Surg. 33rd Foot in India; present at Sharpe's flogging 30 Mar. 1799. In *ST*.

Military General Service Medal 1793–1814 Issued in 1848 to survivors of campaigns of Nap. War. Total of 29 bars including Pen. War, Egypt, East and West Indies, Italy and War of 1812–14 against America. The bar Fort Detroit is only American place name ever to appear on British military medal.

militia Second-line home defence force. Service was by ballot, although individuals could pay for exemption or substitute.

Miller, Maj. Cmdt. of Chilean marines

in 1820; Brit. soldier of fortune, wounded many times during Nap. Wars. Fought for Chilean nationalists under Gen. O'Higgins and Adm. Cochrane. Played prominent role in the capture of fts protecting Valdivia in Feb. 1820.

Mina Well-known Span. guerrilla leader who played key role in harassing Fr. in Navarre.

Minver, Lt 60th Rifles; 2IC to *Capt. Frederickson* in Teste de Buch operation. In *SSge*.

Mirador, El (The Watchplace) Codename of Revd Dr Patrick Curtis, rector of Irish College in Salamanca, who ran elaborate spy system for Allies. In *SS*.

Montbrun, Maj. Fr. aide to King Joseph. In SH.

Montezuma, The Chilean schooner used by Adm. Cochrane as flagship during attack on Valdivia.

Mont St Jean (SKETCH 6) Small Belgian hamlet on N. edge of battlefield of Waterloo behind Anglo–Dutch line. Fr. call the B. of Waterloo more accurately B. of Mont St Jean.

Moore, Lt-Gen. Sir John b. Glasgow in 1761. Ensign in 51st Foot at 15; served in Hamilton's Regt during AWI, briefly in 60th Rifles, then transferred back to 51st. In 1792 was in the operations in Corsica; wounded at taking of Calvi. Went as brig-gen. to West Indies where he distinguished himself at capture of St Lucia. As maj-gen., defeated Irish during 1798 rebellion at B. of Vinegar Hill. Commanded bde in 1899 expedition to Holland, where he was again wounded. Commanded reserve bde in Egypt, wounded at B. of Alexandria. Known for training of lt. troops at Shorncliffe in 1803, particularly the

43rd, 52nd and 95th (Sharpe's Regt), which became the famous Lt. Div. In 1808 sent to Sweden to help in war against Russia, France and Denmark, but forced to return after refusing to agree king's plans. Ordered to Port. where his retreat to Corunna and death after a victorious battle have become a highlight of Brit. military history.

Moore, Marine Killed defending ft at Teste de Buch. In *SSge*.

Moreno, Cesár Span. guerrilla leader, father of *Teresa*. Home village *Casatejada*. In *SG*.

Moreno, Ramón Son of *Cesár*. Tortured by Fr., Aug. 1810; rescued by Sharpe. In *SG*.

Moreno, Teresa Daughter of *Cesár Moreno*. Was to marry *El Catolico*, but fell in love with Sharpe during his mission to secure gold. Became guerrilla leader herself, with nickname 'La Aguja' ('The Needle'), around Badajoz. Married Sharpe in Apr. 1812 and had a daughter, *Antonia*. Murdered by *Hakeswill* at *Adrados* in Dec. 1812. In *SG, SEn*.

Morillo, Capt-Gen. Pablo Span. regular army div. commander. Served in Hill's corps at Vitória where he was entrusted with attack on Puebla Heights. Wounded but refused to leave field.

Morillo, Capt. Span. commander at *Ft Celestian* in Chile. Helped Sharpe escape plot to kill him, Dec. 1819. Broken to pte and sent to mines by *Bautista*. In *SD*.

Morris, Capt. Charles Lt. Coy. commander 33rd in India. Joined *Sgt Hakeswill* in goading Sharpe into striking him; Sharpe sentenced to 2000 lashes. In *ST*.

Mortier, Marshal Edouard Adolphe, Duke of Treviso b. 1768. Commanded V Corps in Spain 1808–11; fought at

Somosierra (1808), Saragossa and Ocana (wounded) (1809), Badajoz and Fuentes de Cantos (1810), Gebora and Campo Maior (1811). Recalled in 1811 to command Young Guard. Served in Russia (governor of Moscow), Germany and France 1813–14. Missed Waterloo due to illness. A friendly, popular man. Died in attempted assassination of King Louise-Philippe in 1835.

Moss, Cpl *S. Essex* NCO shot for desertion at Oropesa on 21 Jul. 1809. In *SE*.

Mouromorto, Count Tomás Brother of *Maj. Blas Vivar*, but confirmed *anfrancesado*. Worked with *Col. de l'Eclin* to prevent *Vivar* and Sharpe from getting the sacred banner to Santiago. Killed by sword thrust from his brother on 28 Jan. 1809. In *SR*.

Murray, Capt. John Coy. commander in 2/95th. Arrived in Pen. with Col. Wade's 4 coys. Had respect of *Rflm Harper*. Died of wounds received in rearguard action at La Baneza 31 Dec. 1808. Gave his cav. sword to Sharpe. The majority of rflm. in march and attack on Santiago came from his company. In *SR*.

Naig, 'Nasty' Indian 'entrepreneur' who ran officers' brothel of Brit. army during advance on, and siege of, Seringapatam, 1799. In *ST*.

Nairn, Maj-Gen. Scottish gen. in charge at Frenada during Wellington's absence in Dec. 1812. Briefed Sharpe on *Adrados* mission, and sent him to Chelmsford in 1813 to find out why recruits had not been drafted to *S. Essex*. Commanded bde in 6 Div. at B. of Toulouse, where he was mortally wounded. Sharpe was his BM. In *SEn*, *SRegt*, *SRev*.

Napier, Maj. George Thomas Entered army 1800. Served under Moore during Corunna campaign and Wellington in Spain and Port. Governor of Cape Province 1839–43. Full gen. 1854; d. 1855.

Ney, Marshal Michel 'The bravest of the brave': b. 1769 of poor parents; had little education and enlisted in hussar regt in 1788. Received commission by election in 1792, 12 years later marshal. Participated in most of Napoleon's victories in Europe, such as Jena, Eylau, and Friedland. Arrived Spain as commander of VI Corps, 1808; in Masséna's Army of Portugal in 1810, taking C. Rodrigo and Almeida. Fought at Bussaco before commanding Masséna's rearguard in retreat from Port. Relieved for insubordination. Commanded rearguard in retreat from Moscow in 1812; appointed Prince de la Moskowa. Fought in Europe throughout 1813 and 1814; following Napoleon's abdication went over to Bourbons and appointed C-in-C of Royal Cavalry Corps. In 1815 sent to arrest Napoleon on his return from Elba, vowing to bring him to Paris in 'iron cage', but changed sides again with 30,000 men. Fought at Q. Bras and Waterloo. After Napoleon's defeat was arrested, found guilty of treason on 6 Dec. 1815 and shot next day – gave the order to fire himself.

Nicholls, Capt. George Officer of 66th Foot; duty officer on St Helena charged with having to 'see' Napoleon twice daily for 14 months. Napoleon played hide and seek with him and generally made his life a misery.

Nickerson, Anne Daughter of Essex landowner to whom *Capt. d'Alembord* was engaged. In *SW*.

Nivelle, B. of (MAP 31) Allied victory; fought on 10 Nov. 1813 between Fr.

under Soult and allies under Wellington, who massed 6 divs. against weak Fr. centre. Involved capture of Little Rhune feature by the Lt. Div., in which Sharpe and *S. Essex* participated. Maj. Sharpe commanded bn after *Lt-Col Girdwood* went mad.

Nock gun 7-barrelled gun given to *Sgt Harper* as personal weapon by Sharpe, Christmas 1809. *Harper* only man strong enough to handle and fire it. Invention of Henry Nock, originally for use in RN, each barrel was 20 inches long and the kick was horrendous. Not a popular weapon for this reason and because it took ages to load and longer to clean. Devastating fired at close range.

O'Donoju, Gen. Cuesta's C-of-S during Talavera campaign. Of Irish descent. Wellesley thought him the only capable officer at Span. HQ.

O'Higgins, Gen. Bernardo b. 1776; son of Irish governor of Span. Chile; educated England and Spain. Joined Chilean nationalist revolution in 1810; his cav. charge led to decisive defeat of Span. at B. of Chacabuco in 1817. Eventually supreme director of independent Chile. Assisted in liberation of Peru. Adm. Cochrane's flagship named after him, as was a Chilean province. d. 1842.

O'Higgins, The 74-gun Chilean warship named after Gen. O'Higgins. Was Cochrane's flagship until attack on Valdivia, when he was forced to transfer to *Montezuma.*

Oliveira, Col. Commanded 400-strong Cacadores bn in defence of *Ft San Isidro* in Apr. 1811. Bn virtually destroyed: he died while being tortured to reveal location of regtl Colours. In *SB.*

Oporto (MAPS 1, 11, 16, 26) Port on N. coast of Portugal at mouth of Douro R., taken by Soult on 29 Mar. 1809 during advance into Portugal. In May Wellington drove Fr. from Portugal, a key victory being B. of Oporto (Sharpe was present), during which Wellington made famous river-crossing. Port became a major supply base and harbour for Wellington throughout Pen. War; RN landed supplies there which could be carried on boats up Douro.

Orange, Prince of b. 1792; eldest son of King William I of Holland. Educated Eton; attached to Wellington's staff during Pen. War. Nicknamed Slender Billy or Young Frog. For diplomatic reasons given command of Wellington's 1st Corps in Waterloo campaign. Fought at Q. Bras and Waterloo, where he made several blunders. Wounded at Waterloo (by Sharpe). Married a Russian princess; succeeded his father as king in 1840; d. 1849.

Oropesa (MAP 8) Span. town in New Castile 20 miles W. of Talavera. Here *S. Essex* billeted Jul. 1809; *Cpl Moss* and *Pte Ibbotson* were shot for desertion; *S. Essex* on verge of mutiny.

Orthez, B. of (MAP 32) On 17 Feb. 1814 between Wellington and Soult, who was defeated and narrowly escaped being cut off as he pulled back towards Toulouse. Wellington's casualties were 2165, Soult's 4000. Wellington slightly wounded. *Nairn's* bde of 6 Div. was present but not in serious fighting.

Oswald, Maj-Gen. Commanded 5 Div. during absence of Gen. Leith in 1813; Sharpe's and *S. Essex* div. commander at B. of Vitória.

Otero, Lt 1st Lt (21C) of Span. frigate

Espiritu Santo, on which Sharpe sailed to Chile in 1819. In *SD*.

Paddock, Pte Clerk at bn HQ of *S. Essex* in Vitória campaign. In *SH*.

Pakenham, Maj-General Hon. Sir Edward Served mainly as deputy in AG's department at HQ. Acting AG during Stewart's absences. Also fighting soldier; commanded 3 Div. at Salamanca and made decisive charge. Was president of Sharpe's court-martial for murder in May 1813; killed at B. of New Orleans Jan. 1815. In *SH*.

palanquin Royal carriage carried by servants/slaves – used by Tippoo Sultan.

Palmer, Capt. Neil, RM Commanded RM force operating with Sharpe in Teste de Buch. Posted to Australia; unable to give evidence at inquiry into Sharpe's activities at ft. In *SSge*.

Pannizi, Col. CO of Neapolitan bn. sent to arrest Sharpe and *Gen. Calvet* N of Naples in 1814. In *SRev*.

parapet Earth or masonry bank at front of trench or rampart.

Parker, Adm. Sir Hyde b. 1739. Entered RN at early age and became post captain when 24; commanded Brit. fleet at B. of Copenhagen, with Nelson as his 2IC. Indecisiveness led to his recall and to Nelson taking command. The *Parker* family were distant relatives.

Parker, Mr George Methodist missionary trying to convert Span. from Catholicism. Distant cousin of Adm. Sir Hyde Parker. In *SR*.

Parker, Mrs Mother of *Louisa*. Wife of George. In *SR*.

Parker, Louisa Beautiful young woman; first of many to infatuate Sharpe during Pen. War. She entered

Fr.-occupied Santiago and tricked *Col. de l'Eclin* into leaving the city with 1000 men before Sharpe and *Vivar* attacked. Married *Vivar* and became *Doña Louisa Vivar, Countess of Mouromorto*; lived in Orenze, Galicia. In 1819 commissioned Sharpe to find her husband, who had disappeared while acting Capt-Gen. in Chile. In *SR, SD*.

Parton, Surg. *S. Essex* doctor in Talavera campaign. In *SE*.

Paulette Real name Charlotte; P. of Orange's Belgian mistress, who befriended Sharpe. In *SW*.

Penrose, Adm. Responsible for assembling flotilla needed by Wellington to build bridge across Adour R. in Feb. 1814.

Perkins, Rflm. Youngest of Sharpe's original rflm. In *SB*.

'peter laying' C18th theft by cutting travelling cases off backs of carriages. Sharpe was an expert as a boy.

Peters, Sgt Senior NCO in *S. Essex*. Helped Sharpe deal with potential mutiny at Oropesa. In *SE*.

Peyrusse, Insp. Baron Napoleon's paymaster; entrusted with securing safety of Napoleon's treasure in Apr. 1814. Able to retrieve only portion, which was taken to Elba, by hiding boxes under heap of horse manure. Accompanied Napoleon to Elba.

Phillipon, Gen. Fr. commander of Badajoz garrison during 3rd siege in Mar–Apr. 1812. Competent officer who defended city to and in accordance with Napoleon's orders. He surrendered in Ft San Cristóbal to Lord Fitzroy Somerset, who later became Brit. C-in-C. Crimea.

picket (or picquet) Inf. outpost or sentry.

Picton, Maj. John Elder brother of Sir

Thomas Picton. Acting CO of 12th Foot in India in 1798. Challenged Col. Ashton to duel; he fired and missed; Ashton fired in the air. Had bellicose temperament similar to his brother's. Died of sickness shortly afterwards.

Picton, Lt-Gen. Sir Thomas Coarse, moody and impetuous, this former governor of Trinidad who had been investigated for permitting torture, took command of 3 Div. in 1810. Wounded at Badajoz Apr. 1812; next served at Vitória where he went into battle in a top-hat. Headstrong nature, but one of Wellington's able generals. Before going to Belgium in 1815 had a presentiment of death; jumped into a freshly dug grave, lay down and remarked, 'Why, I think this would do for me.' Wounded at Q. Bras, killed at Waterloo – shot through his top-hat.

Piellot, Lt. Fr. officer who took part in attack on ft at Teste de Buch when it was defended by Sharpe. In *SSge.*

Pierce, Lt On staff of Chelmsford depôt in Jul. 1813. In *SRegt.*

Plasencia (MAP 8) Span. city and road junction in Estremadura; occupied and used as advanced depôt by both sides. Soult's advance from N. forced Wellesley to retire after victory at Talavera. There *S. Essex* was made into bn of dets., and Sharpe promoted capt. and given Lt. Coy.

Ponsonby Maj-Gen. Sir William b. 1772. Served in Spain (1811–14), commanding cav. bde at Vitória. Led charge of Union Bde. at Waterloo, which shattered d'Erlon's attack; pursued too far and was killed by lancers when he tried to withdraw. Sharpe's enemy *Lord John Rossendale* met similar fate nearby.

Ponte Cardenal (MAP 8) Bridge over Tagus R. 20 miles S. of Plasencia. Called *Valdelacasa* in *SE*, was site of action when *S. Essex* lost their Colour on 11 Jul. 1809.

pontoon bridge Bridge of boats lashed together and covered in planks.

Popham, Adm. Sir Home Brit. adm. who commanded raiding squadron at Corunna which attacked and harassed Fr. along N. coast of Spain, and prevented Fr. troops being sent S. as reinforcements in Salamanca campaign in 1812.

Portalegre (MAPS 11, 16) Small Port. town close to Span. border NE of Lisbon. Key road junction for N–S movement, frequently used by allies as forward base. Troops of both sides were billeted there; *S. Essex* and Sharpe halted for 3 days on march from C. Rodrigo to Badajoz in Mar. 1812.

post captain RN rank above commander. Promotion to post captain meant independent command of rated ship (50–100 guns) and that officer was on list for possible promotion to admiral. *Bampfylde* was post captain in command of *Vengeance* in *SSge.*

Pot-au-Feu (Stewpot) Fr. deserter (ex-sgt and cook) and self-styled marshal, who led large band of deserters of all nationalities. Ruthless and cruel; eventually tracked down by Gen. de Marbot. When *Sgt Hakeswill* deserted he joined this band. Pot-au-Feu occupied *Adrados* late 1812; was driven out by Sharpe over Christmas. In *SEn.*

Preston, Gen. Brit. commander of force from which Sharpe was detached with half *S. Essex* to cut off Fr. rearguard near Agueda R. on 10 May 1813. In *SH.*

Price, Lt Harold In Lt. Coy. of *S. Essex*; dissolute young man, overfond of drink. 2IC of Lt. Coy. at Salamanca; in action at *Adrados* Dec. 1812. Commanded coy. at B. of the Nivelle when *Capt. Thomas* killed. OC coy in *PWOV* in Waterloo campaign. Auctioned belongings of officers killed at Q. Bras. In *SC, SS, SEn, SRegt, SW*.

Prince of Wales *See* Prince Regent.

Prince Regent Had powers of monarch if monarch incapacitated by illness or senility. In this case, P. of W., eldest son of King George III, who had been declared insane. Extravagant wastrel who loved military show, lived in Carlton House, Pall Mall. Sharpe impressed him at Hyde Park Review in Aug. 1813; *S. Essex* became *The Prince of Wales' Own Volunteers.*

Prior, Capt. Cav. militia officer who assisted in hunt for *Sgt Harper* at Foulness Camp. In *SRegt*.

Privateer Armed vessel with private owner commissioned by belligerent state to carry on operations of war, known as Letters of Marque. The *Thuella* in *SSge* was such a ship.

Provisional Battalion (Prov. Bn) Wellington formed these from two bns seriously weakened to around 250–300 men each. An expedient to prevent veteran units being sent home.

Provost Forerunners of the Military Police. Under Provost-Marshal, had responsibility for offenders to be tried by general courts-martial, and PoWs. Nicknamed 'Bloody Provost' for severity and eagerness to hang soldiers caught committing capital offence – which they had power to do. Large number deployed in Pen.

Puerto Crucero (MAP 39) Span.-held Chilean port 50 miles S. of Valdivia, where *Blas Vivar* was supposed to have been buried in 1819. Sharpe and *Harper* arrested there and expelled from Chile. Cochrane and Sharpe captured it on 1 Jan. 1820.

Quartermaster (QM) Officer responsible for supplies, rations, uniforms, stores, equipment etc. within a bn or regt. Usually a lt, often ex-ranker like Sharpe. Regarded as inferior by combatant officers.

Quatre Bras (MAP 37) Belgian hamlet S. of Waterloo; scene of indecisive battle between Fr. under Ney and Wellington on 16 Jun. 1815. Sharpe present as officer on staff P. of Orange. Temporarily took command of *PWOV* to save them being destroyed by cav.

Rao, Gen. Appah Hindu bde commander in Tippoo's army at Seringapatam in 1799. Secretly turned traitor and gave information to *Col. McCandless* on defences of city. Responsible for Mysore Gate during siege. In *ST*.

ravelin Triangular outwork built in ditch of ft to split attacking force.

Read, Sgt. QM pay sgt in Lt. Coy. of *S. Essex*. Responsible for coy. books and records. Quiet, no-drinking, no-swearing Methodist, blinded in breach at Badajoz. In *SC*.

Real Compañía Irlandesa Spanish Royal Guard Coy. attached to Wellington's HQ in F. de Onoro campaign. Sharpe responsible for training it. Defended *Ft San Isidro* in Apr. 1811. Took part in closing stages of B. of F. de Onoro by counter-attacking *Loup*'s *bde*.

Rébecque, Maj-Gen. Constant de
C-of-S to P. of Orange in Waterloo
campaign; Sharpe's immediate superior.
Competent soldier who, against
Wellington's orders, sent Saxe-Weimar's
bde to hold crossroad at Q. Bras on 15
Jun. 1815. Sharpe took the message.

Regiment (Regt) In Brit. army an
administrative military unit which
recruited soldiers and sent them to war,
usually as bns. Most Brit. regts provided
1 or 2 bns during Nap. Wars. In other
European armies, a tactical battlefield
unit of 2 or 3 bns, normally commanded
by col.

Regimiento de la Santa María Span.
inf. regt. destroyed at *Valdelacasa*. In
SE.

Réille, Gen. Honoré Charles b. 1775. Fr.
div. commander who commanded Army
of Portugal at Vitória. His troops
contested village and bridge at Gamorra
Mayor with Sharpe and *S. Essex*.
Commanded corps at Waterloo
responsible for assaulting Hougoumont.
Marshal 1847; d. 1860.

retrenchment Defensive work put up
by defenders to cut off breach.

revetting Shoring up of sides of
trenches or other works to prevent
crumbling.

Richmond, Duchess of Gave famous
ball in Brussels on night of 15–16 Jun.
1815, where Wellington received
confirmation of Napoleon's advance on
Q. Bras. Sharpe had confrontation with
Rossendale late that night.

Roach, Pte Disreputable soldier in *S.
Essex* Lt. Coy., who pimped his wife for
a shilling a time. In *SG*.

Robinson, Maj-Gen. *S. Essex* bde
commander at Vitória. At San Sebastian,
the Bidossa and the Nive.

Robinson, Marine Matthew Pardoned
by Sharpe for attempting to rape girl
during Teste de Buch operation. In
SSge.

Roche, Col. One of Wellesley's liaison
officers at Gen. Cuesta's HQ in
Talavera campaign. Reported
unfavourably on Span. army.

Roland, Mr Fr. Treasury lawyer based
in Caen, former employee of Napoleon,
but representing Louis XVIII in
enquiries into theft of Napoleon's
treasure. Initially held Sharpe
responsible; secretly kept Napoleon
informed. In *SRev*.

Rolica, B. of (MAPS 1, 4) First battle of
Pen. War. Fought in Port. 17 Aug. 1808
between Wellesley with 14,000 men and
Fr. force of 4500 under Delaborde. Fr.
forced to retire, losing 700 casualties;
Brit. lost under 500. Sharpe present as
QM of 2/95th.

Rorden, Pte *S. Essex* Lt. Coy., died of
wounds at *Casatejada*. In *SG*.

Rose Tavern Well-known tavern in
Drury Lane, on site of present Drury
Lane Theatre. Used by Sharpe in
Jul-Aug. 1813.

Rossendale, Capt. Lord John 1st Life
Guards, ADC to Prince Regent. Brought
invitation to Chelmsford for Sharpe to
meet Prince Regent in Jul. 1813. Stole
Sharpe's wife (*Jane*) and fortune.
Confrontation at the Duchess of
Richmond's ball. Charged with
Household Bde at Waterloo; badly
wounded by lancers. Throat slit by
Belgian peasant woman looting his
valuables. In *SRegt*, *SW*.

Rossner, Sgt NCO of 5/60th at
Adrados Dec. 1812; at Teste de Buch.
In *SEn*, *SSge*.

Rothier, Sgt French NCO in *Col*.

Gudin's unit with Tippoo's forces in Seringapatam. Tasked with blowing concealed mine intended to destroy assault on breach; in *ST*.

Roundshot Primary projectile of cannon; simple iron ball was 75 per cent of all arty. ammunition held in field. Highly effective against troops or obstacles. Single shot could kill file of many men. Ball bounced or grazed several times in its flight. (*See also* hot shot.)

Royal Patriotic Fund, The Public fund set up by Brit. govt to reward servicemen for outstanding acts, e.g. grant towards uniform to soldier given battlefield commission. Sharpe's ceremonial sword awarded for capture of Fr. Eagle at Talavera purchased from this fund.

Royal Staff Corps Organised as regt under QMG, originally of artificers, to give army engineering capacity apart from the engrs. Officers appointed without purchase – only 37 in 1811. Responsible for designing and constructing pontoon bridge over Adour. Disbanded 1837.

Ruiz, Col. Span. arty. officer who sailed with Sharpe and *Harper* to Chile in 1819. In *SD*.

Runciman, Col. Former Wagon-Master-General of Royal Wagon Train appointed liaison officer to *Real Compañía Irlandesa*. Fat, likeable, useless; earmarked as official scapegoat for defence of *Ft San Isidro* on 28 Apr. 1811. In *SB*.

Rymer, Capt. Aristocratic young officer who purchased captaincy in *S. Essex*, depriving Sharpe of command of Lt. Coy. in Mar. 1812. Commanded Lt. Coy. during attempt to blow dam at San Roque

Ft, Badajoz. Shot and killed in the ditch at Badajoz, 6th April 1812. Sharpe resumed command of Lt. Coy. In *SC*.

Sadaba, La Marquesa de Casares el Grande y Melida (Hélène) Col. *Leroux*'s sister and Fr. spy. Told by Napoleon to marry Span. nobleman close to royal court; successful in passing information to Fr. Tricked by Sharpe into believing allies withdrawing from Salamanca; passed to Fr. and Wellington able to exploit at B. of Salamanca. Worked for *Ducos* prior to Vitória. Rescued by Sharpe from *Santa Monica* convent and escaped with her wealth after the battle. Known as 'La Puta Dorada' – 'The Golden Whore'. In *SS, SH*.

St Giles Rookery (MAP 30) Notorious slum area of London where Sharpe lived with Maggie Joyce from age of twelve to fifteen centred on what is now Tottenham Court Road station.

St Helena (MAP 38) Brit. island in S. Atlantic off Africa, where Napoleon spent last 6 years of exile; died and was buried there in 1821. In 1840 his remains transferred to Paris and laid to rest in Les Invalides.

St Jean de Luz (MAPS 31, 32) Small Fr. port in extreme SW corner, where Wellington established HQ prior to crossing Adour. Here Sharpe was briefed and left for Teste de Buch.

Salamanca, B. of (MAP 22) Large Span. university city founded prior to 222B.C. Scene of Wellington's victory over Fr. under Marmont on 22 Jul. 1812. The Revd Dr Curtis operated Allied spy network from Irish College there. Sharpe was seriously wounded in attached hospital by *Col. Leroux*.

San Cayetano (MAP 21) Fortified convent in Salamanca. One of 3 such fts. garrisoned by Fr. when they left city in Jun. 1812. Wellington used the lt. coys. of 6 Div. in assault on 23 Jun. (failed) and 27 Jun. (successful). Sharpe's coy. deployed to locate and capture *Col. Leroux*, thought to be inside.

Sanchez, Don Julian Prominent Span. guerrilla leader, who worked with field armies (as at F. de Onoro). Old soldier who valued discipline and enjoyed ascendancy over his troops and peasantry. Produced valuable intelligence for Wellington, and many of his reports and letters have been preserved. In his opinion, *Loup*'s base in *San Cristóbal* needed 1000 men plus arty. to take it (*SB*).

San Cristobal village (MAP 13) Fictional fortified village used as base for anti-guerrilla activities by *Loup's bde* in 1811. In *SB*.

Santa Monica (MAP 28) Small village and convent in mts. 50 miles NE of Burgos. *Hélène* forcibly confined there by *El Matarife*; rescued by Sharpe on 7 May 1813. In *SH*.

Santarém (MAPS 4, 11) Important Port. city on Tagus 40 miles NE of Lisbon. Used by Masséna as base while wintering in front of Lines of TV in 1810–11.

Santiago Capital of Chile under Span. colonial rule. Captured by nationalists and became seat of rebel govt in 1817.

Santiago de Compostela (MAPS 1, 6, 7) Ancient capital of Galicia, Spain. Famous for the legend of St James being buried there; hallowed site for Catholic Christians and destination of pilgrims for centuries. Captured and looted by Marshal Ney's troops in 1808.

Sharpe and *Maj. Vivar* attacked it on 28 Jan. 1809 and held long enough to start popular insurrection. Span. Gen. Carrera retook it from Fr. in May 1809 at a cost to the Fr. of 600 lives. Today, tourist city of some 85,000 people.

sap Narrow trench designed to make progress towards ft to facilitate construction of parallel.

sapper Soldier trained in siege operations; usually working under engr officer.

Sarsfield, Father Padre of *Real Compañía Irlandesa*; also Fr. spy. Shot by Sharpe when he pointed pistol at *Capt. Hogan*. In SB. Span. guerrilla leader of same name carried out successful raid into France in Feb. 1812, returning with 2000 cattle and sheep.

Saumier, Capt. Fr. officer assigned to protect *Hélène* during B. of Vitória. Shot by *El Matarife* as he tried to take her from city on 21 Jun. 1813. In *SH*.

Saxe-Weimar, Prince Bernard of Commanded 2nd Bde, consisting of 5 Nassau bns, in 2 Netherlands Div. (Perponcher) during Waterloo campaign. Had troops billeted near Q. Bras and held crossroad with bn until reinforced. Sharpe took message to him from 1st Corps HQ to hold Q. Bras.

Scovell, Capt. George Officer in Wellington's HQ responsible for deciphering captured messages. Promoted rapidly to lt-col.; finally became general and governor of RMA Sandhurst.

scrambling Slang term for deserting, particularly applied to recruits.

Scylla Frigate used to fire on ft. at Teste de Buch while marines attacked from the land, 1814.

Sebastiani, Gen. Count Horace François b. 1772. Brig. 1803; div. gen. 1805. Commanded IV Corps at Talavera. Served in Russia, Germany and France 1812–14. Became prominent politician; marshal 1840; d. 1851.

Secretary at War A civilian, normally an MP but not in Cabinet; had responsibility for War Office; powers mainly fiscal. Theoretically under Secretary of State for War and the Colonies but had direct access to sovereign. Post held by venal *Lord Fenner* in 1813.

Secretary of State for War and the Colonies A civilian Cabinet post which combined foreign and colonial affairs; responsible for overall military strategy.

Sedaseer Indian town in Western Ghats, scene of Brit. victory (under Lt-Gen. James Stuart) over Tippoo Sultan's forces 6 Mar. 1799.

Seléglise (MAP 35) Small village in Normandy about 40 miles WNW of Caen; near home of *Lassan* family.

Seringapatam, Siege of (MAPS 2, 3) Apr.–May 1799 30,000 of Tippoo Sultan's troops were besieged in the city. 33rd played prominent part in the storming, during which Sharpe killed the Tippoo.

shako Peaked, cylindrical head-dress usually made of felt, often black; worn by all armies in Nap. Wars. Fr. had bell-topped shape easily recognisable, particularly when Brit. wore 'stovepipe' variety.

Sharpe, Richard See Chapter 1.

Sharpe, Antonia Daughter of Richard Sharpe. Born 1812, mother *Teresa Sharpe* (née *Morena*), murdered by *Hakeswill*. Brought up by relatives near Port. border. In *SEn*.

Shee, Maj. John Irish officer overfond of bottle, who became CO of 33rd after Col. Wellesley took over general officer's responsibilities in 4th Mysore War against Tippoo Sultan. As Sharpe's CO he handed down 2000 lashes for striking *Sgt Hakeswill*; in *ST*.

shell (common shell) Arty. ammo. Hollow iron sphere filled with gunpowder which exploded at predetermined moment by means of adjustable fuse lit by flash of ignition. Airburst could be achieved by reducing propellant charge; could be fired over heads of attacking troops.

Sherbrooke, Lt-Col. Commanded right assault column in storming breach at Seringapatam.

Shorncliffe Small town on the Kent coast, England; home of lt. inf. tactics, drills and doctrine. Gen. Sir John Moore trained the lt. inf. regts there in roles in war.

shrapnel (spherical case) Invented in 1784 by Henry Shrapnell; similar to ordinary shell but thinner casing filled with musket balls. Careful adjustment of fuses made shell explode over enemy, showering them with musket balls.

Simmerson, Lt-Col. Sir Henry Aristocratic, incompetent first CO of *S. Essex*. His stupidity resulted in bn losing its Colour at *Valdelacasa* in Jul. 1809. Sent home in disgrace after withdrawing bn from battle line at Talavera. Hon. colonel of *Essex Militia* cav. regt. Became involved with crimping in 1813. Exposed by Sharpe. In *SE*, *SRegt*.

Simms, Rflm. In *Capt. Murray*'s coy. of 2/95th; arrived in Pen. with Col. Wade. Wounded when Sharpe's force ambushed on way to Santiago; in attack on Santiago. In *SR*.

Smith, Capt. Hamish Adjutant at Foulness Camp under *Lt-Col. Girdwood.* Sharpe made him coy. commander of reinforcements going to Spain. Fought at B. of the Nivelle Nov. 1813. Killed at Q. Bras 16 Jun. 1815. In *SRegt, SW.*

Smithers, Pte Brit. deserter in Pot-au-Feu's band who murdered Brit. officer on *Hakeswill's* orders at *Adrados;* in *SEn.*

sortie An attack by besieged outside their own defences.

Soult, Marshal Nicolas-Jean de Dieu b. 1769. Vain and ambitious man, but competent marshal. Commanded II Corps and pursued Moore to Corunna in 1808–9. Invaded Portugal; driven back by Wellesley at Oporto. Descended on allied rear after Talavera and forced retreat to Port. Invaded and occupied S. Spain and recaptured Madrid. Recalled to France to command Imp. Guard in 1813. Returned to command against Wellington in the Pyrenees. Napoleon's C-of-S at Waterloo. Banished by Bourbons but returned in 1820. Became Minister of War (1830–4), Foreign Minister (1839) and Marshal-General of France (1847). d. 1851. Seeker of wealth; accumulated huge fortune though plunder. On his death had held marshal's baton for 43 years.

South Essex Regt Later called *Prince of Wales' Own Volunteers (PWOV).* See Chapter 2.

Spears, Capt. Lord John One of *Hogan's* exploring officers in cav. Captured by *Leroux,* turned traitor, betrayed Colquhoun Grant. Wounded after Salamanca, he confessed to Sharpe and told him he had syphilis. Persuaded Sharpe to kill him so that he could be thought a hero dying in battle and save family honour. In *SS.*

Spindacre, Lady Juliet Young society widow previously married to middle-aged gen. Befriended *Jane Sharpe* in London and persuaded her to spend much of Sharpe's money on high living. In *SRev.*

Staff Corps of Cavalry Unit of 200 formed in 1812 for police duties with the army; worked with Provost-Marshal. Not to be confused with Royal Staff Corps, who were artificers.

Stanway, Lt Engr officer in charge of unsuccessful attempt to blow dam near Ft San Roque. Stanway went back to relight, but resultant explosion failed to breach dam.

Sterritt, Capt. Coy. commander in S. Essex. Fought at *Valdelacasa,* Talavera, F. de Onoro, C. Rodrigo; killed at Badajoz 6 Apr. 1812. In *SE, SC.*

stock Hated, leather collar worn around neck under jacket collar; restricting and unhealthy. Worn by Brit. inf. for most of Pen. War; many contrived to lose them. Sharpe was popular when he used them for target practice in 1809.

Sturgeon, Maj. Staff Corps officer who designed bridge for crossing Adour.

Suarez, Maj. Span. officer on staff of *Bautista* who arrested Sharpe in *Puerto Crucero,* Chile, Dec. 1819. In *SD.*

subaltern Junior officer of ensign (2/ lieut.) or lt rank in Brit. army.

sub-unit Brit. military term usually referring to coy., platoon, or troop of men.

Sultanpetah (MAP 3) Village near Seringapatam. Scene of Wellington's only military defeat, when 33rd repulsed in night attack on nearby wood. Sharpe had 'deserted' to Tippoo's side and was shouting orders to confuse the enemy.

Sgt. Hakeswill murdered Lt Fitzgerald of 33rd in the wood.

Sycorax Sharpe's horse at B. of Toulouse. Decapitated by cannon ball while he was in saddle.

Tagus R. (MAPS 1, 4, 5, 8, 11, 16) One of 3 major rivers of Port. Lisbon, at its mouth, was Wellington's main base; river used like Douro as communication waterway; small boats could reach Abrantes, 80 miles upriver.

Talavera, B. of (MAPS, 1, 8, 9, 10) Fought on 27–28 July 1809 between Brit. under Wellesley (21,000) allied to Span. under Cuesta (35,000), and Fr. under Joseph (46,000). Repeated Fr. attacks failed to break Brit. line. Brit. losses 5000; Fr. 7000. *Simmerson* relieved of command of *S. Essex*; Sharpe captured Eagle.

Taplow, Lt-Col. Commanded fusilier bn in *Nairn's bde* at B. of Toulouse on 10 Apr. 1814. Killed attacking Mâs des Augustins Redoubt; in *SRev*.

Tarleton. Gen. Sir Banastre b. 1754; fought in AWI including White Plains, Ft Washington, Brandywine and Germantown. Formed mixed force of lt. inf. and cav. known as Tarleton's Green Horse. MP on intimate terms with P. of Wales. Dashing, brave pleasure-seeker who lived with the P. of W.'s former mistress, Mary Robinson. Instrumental in getting *Sir Henry Simmerson* to form and command *S. Essex*. d. 1833.

Taupin, Gen. Eloi Fr. commander of unsuccessful counter-attack against Beresford on ridge at B. of Toulouse; killed leading 2 columns against Brit. lines. Sharpe, as BM of *Nairn's bde*, was part of this assault.

Taylor, Rflm. Thomas American

national and soldier in 5/60th (Royal American) Rifles; at the *Adrados* action and Teste de Buch. In *SEn, SSge*.

telescope Essential for most officers. Sharpe's was gift from Wellington as reward for saving his life in India. Inscribed: IN GRATITUDE. SEPTEMBER 23RD 1803. Broken by *Maj. Ducos*, but Sharpe replaced it with one presented to King Joseph by Napoleon, from loot captured after B. of Vitória.

terre plein Flat surface behind rampart, usually with parapet, on which defenders placed cannons.

Teste de Buch (MAP 33) Small coastal village and ft about 35 miles SW of Bordeaux. In Feb. 1814 Sharpe was tasked with taking ft. in combined operation with RN and RM. In *SSge*.

Thomas, Capt. Killed commanding coy. of *S. Essex* at B of the Nivelle. In *SRegt*.

Thomières, Gen. Jean Guillaume Fr. div. gen. whose command was destroyed by Wellington's masterful counter-stroke at Salamanca, 22 Jul. 1812. Thomières killed in the battle.

Tippoo Sultan p. 1753. Became Muslim sultan of Mysore on death of father (Hyder Ali) in 1782. Fought in Mahratta and Mysore Wars against Brit. Exceedingly cruel; favoured executing prisoners by driving nails into their skulls or breaking their necks by twisting their heads. Courageous and competent soldier with fixation for tigers. Killed in Seringapatam by Sharpe on 4 May 1799.

Todd, Capt. Staff Corps officer who supervised construction of floating bridge over Adour.

Tongue, Rflm. Isaiah Educated soldier

in 2/95th, *Capt. Murray*'s coy. Took part in march and attack on Santiago; killed in skirmish with French voltigeurs, 25 Aug. 1810. In *SR, SG*.

town major Staff officer permanently posted to specific town and responsible for its military administration. ·

Trant, Col. Nicholas Irishman, b. 1769, entered 84th Foot as lt 1794. Helped form Minorca Regt. Joined Royal Staff Corps in 1803 as ensign. Sent to Port. as military agent in 1808 and rose to brig. in Port. army. Commanded the lt. troops co-operating with Wellesley in Vimiero campaign. Prevented Masséna from crossing to N. of Mondego R. in March 1811; d. 1839.

Tremgar, Master Capt. of ex-collier *Amelie* which transported Sharpe and his force to landing S of Teste de Buch. In *SSge*.

Trotter's Firm which made Brit. canvas and wood knapsacks. They split easily and straps restricted breathing; whenever possible, soldiers replaced with Fr. cowhide packs.

Trumper-Jones, Lt Michael ADC to *Gen. Preston* in Vitória campaign. Brought charge-sheet when Sharpe accused of murder in May 1813. At Vitória brought orders for *S. Essex* but fainted on seeing Sharpe whom he thought dead. In *SH*.

unit Brit. term usually referring to bn-sized body of men.

Uxbridge, Lt-Gen. Earl of b. 1786; with Sir John Moore in Corunna campaign. Commanded cav; was Wellington's 2IC at Waterloo; lost leg to a cannon ball at end of battle. Died as f-m, 1854.

Valdelacasa (MAP 8) Site of Roman bridge over Tagus, about 20 miles S of Plasencia. Real name Ponte Cardenal. *S. Essex* lost King's Colour there. In *SE*.

Valdivia (MAPS 39, 40) Chilean port. Last major stronghold of Span. in 1820 in campaign against the nationalists. Adm. Cochrane captured it for rebels, with Sharpe and *Harper* playing prominent part. In *SD*.

Valençay, Treaty of Signed by imprisoned Prince Ferdinand and Napoleon in Dec. 1813. Ferdinand was to be restored to Span. throne in return for making peace with France and forcing Brit. to leave Pen. Ferdinand restored, but Cortés declared treaty invalid.

Valverde, Gen. Span. gen., liaison officer with Wellington's HQ. In *SB*.

Vaughn, Maj. Prosecuting officer at Sharpe's trial for murder in May 1813. In *SRev*.

Venegas, Gen. Francisco Xavier Span. gen. defeated at Ucles and Amonacid. Failed to carry out his strategic role in Talavera campaign. Served in Latin America. d. 1838.

Vengeance, HMS 74-gun line-of-battle ship commanded by *Capt. Bampfylde* in combined navy–army operation to take Teste de Buch. Sharpe briefed aboard.

Ventakesh, Dr Indian doctor working for *Col. Gudin* in Seringapatam, who treated Sharpe's back after flogging. In *ST*.

Verigny, Gen. Raoul Fr. gen., *Hélène* was his mistress during Vitória campaign. Rescued Sharpe from *El Matarife* at Frias on 8 Jun. 1813; took him as prisoner to Burgos. In *SH*.

Veteran Battalion (Vet. Bn) Composed of old or semi-invalid soldiers fit only for garrison duties.

**Victor, Marshal Claude, Duke of
Bellune** b. 1764. Enlisted 1781; brig.
1795; div. gen. 1797; marshal 1807.
Commanded I Corps in Spain 1808–11.
Victorious against Span. at Espinosa and
Medellin; repulsed at Talavera and
Barossa. Served in Russia, Germany
and France, 1812–14. Tried to
organise resistance to Napoleon in
1815 – struck from the roll of marshals
and fled. Returned with Louis XVIII;
made peer and commander of Royal
Guard. Minister of War 1821–3;
d. 1841.

Vidal, Ensign One of Maj. Miller's
marine officers who led successful night
attack on Ft Inglés at Valdivia harbour.
Sharpe fulfilled this role in *SD*.

Vienna, Congress of 1 Nov. 1814–9 Jun.
1815. After Napoleon's abdication Russia,
Britain, Austria and Prussia convened
congress at Vienna to agree
post-Napoleonic Europe. Wellington
was Brit. representative when Napoleon
escaped from Elba. Diplomatic
wrangling was curtailed, and 7th
Coalition formed against Napoleon.

Vignali, Father Catholic priest who
administered to Napoleon on St Helena
and conducted his funeral.

Vigo (MAPS 1, 6) Span. port on NW
coast from which Lt. Bde embarked
after their retreat in late 1808. Sharpe
became separated and was not evacuated
from Pen.

Vimiero, Battle of (MAPS 1, 4) 21 Aug.
1808, between Brit. under Wellesley
(almost 17,000 men) and Fr. under
Junot (13,000 men). Brit. victory. Losses
Brit. 700; Fr. 2000. Sharpe present as
QM of 2/95th.

Vine, Maj. Edwin 2IC to *Lt-Col. Ford*
in *PWOV* at Waterloo. Unpopular,
spiteful 'yes' man. Killed at Waterloo, 18
Jun. 1815. In *SW*.

Vitória, B of (MAPS 26, 28, 29) Decisive
victory for Wellington over King Joseph
on 21 Jun. 1813. Huge amount of booty
taken by allies, and Fr. driven from
Spain. *S. Essex* had to take critical
bridge at Gamorra Mayor. *Lt-Col. Leroy*
killed (CO *S. Essex*); Sharpe took
command.

Vivar, Maj. Blas Span. army officer
who enlisted Sharpe's assistance in
1808 in taking banner to Santiago to
inflame populace against Fr. occupation;
planned the successful attack on
Santiago. Married *Louisa Parker* and
inherited title *Count of Mouromorto*
when he killed his elder brother, who
fought for Fr. Later appointed
Capt-Gen. in Chile but imprisoned on
Juan Fernandez Islands, in 1819. Sharpe
commissioned by his wife to find him.
In *SR, SD*.

Wade, Lt-Col. Hamlet Irishman. One
of original members of 95th rifles,
having transferred as maj. from 25th
Foot. Given command of 2/95th on
formation in 1805. Fanatical shooting
enthusiast and a crack shot (see Chapter
1 box). Commanded 2/95th in Denmark
under Wellesley in 1807; arrived in
Spain with 4 coys. (including *Capt.
Murray*'s), 26 Oct. 1808. d. 1821 after
retirement from army.

Waterloo Medal Awarded in 1816 to
participants in B. of Ligny, Quatre Bras
and Waterloo.

Webster, Lt Henry Sub. 9th LD. ADC
on P. of Orange's staff at Waterloo.
Brought key message to Wellington at
the ball that Prussians driven back from
Charleroi and only 8 miles from Q.

Bras. Killed himself in fit of insanity in 1847.

Weller, Pte Charlie Joined *S. Essex* with Sharpe (who enlisted under false name) in Aug. 1813. His dog killed by *Sgt Lynch* at Foulness Camp. Saw action at B. of the Nivelle, Toulouse, Q. Bras and Waterloo. Promoted sgt by Sharpe after Waterloo. Looked after *Sally Clayton* when husband killed. In *SRegt, SW*.

Wellesley, Arthur See Wellington.

Wellesley, Henry Youngest of three brothers; private secretary to Richard when governor-general of India 1797–1805.

Wellesley, Richard b. 1760. Elder brother of Arthur. As Lord Mornington was appointed governor-general of India in 1797. Found EIC a trading body; left it an imperial power. Ambassador to Spain 1809, Lord Lieutenant of Ireland 1821. d. 1842.

Wellington (Wesley, then Wellesley), Sir Arthur, Duke of Brit., and later allied C-in-C throughout Pen. War. Born Dublin 1769, educated Eton and Military Academy at Angers, France. Purchased rapid promotion from ensign to lt-col. in 6 years, by which time he was only 24 and had been on the strength of 4 inf. and two cav. regts. As CO of 33rd Foot (many years later called Duke of Wellington's Regt) handled his bn well at Boxtel in 1794. Sharpe fought as a young pte in the 33rd in this action. Arrived in India with 33rd (and Sharpe) in 1797. Napoleon contemptuously called him the 'Sepoy General' after his victories at Assaye (where Sharpe saved his life and received a battlefield commission), Argaum and Gawilghur. By 33,

substantive maj-gen. In Sept. 1809 created Viscount Wellington of Talavera; became Earl of Wellington Feb. 1812; marquess in Oct., promoted f-m. in Jul. 1813 after triumph at Vitória, and made Duke of Wellington in 1814. Defeated Napoleon at Waterloo in 1815. Hit by musket balls on 3 occasions (Talavera, Salamanca and Orthez) but never seriously injured. Became C-in-C of Brit. army on death of the Duke of York in 1827 and Prime Minister following year. Retired from public life in 1846. d. 1852; buried in St Paul's Cathedral.

West, Capt. Francis Commanded Gren. Coy. of 33rd at Seringapatam.

Wetherby Town in W. Yorkshire about fifteen miles west of York. Sharpe fled here from London as a young lad and took a job at a coaching tavern, but accidentally killed the landlord in a fight over a girl called *Elsie*, the incident which forced him to enlist.

Whistler, Revd Sebastian Div. padre to 5 Div. in Vitória campaign. In *SH*.

Wigram, Col. Staff officer at HQ of 1 Div. Involved in briefing Sharpe on Teste de Buch operation. Presided over the inquiry into Sharpe's alleged theft of Napoleon's treasure. In *SSge, SRev*.

Williams, Col. OC lt. coys. defending F. de Onoro on 3 May 1811. A 5/60th (Royal American) officer, he was seriously wounded. In *SB* he sent Sharpe to fetch reinforcements.

Williams, Sgt Senior NCO in 2/95th, serving in *Capt. Murray*'s coy. with *Rflm Harper* in action at La Baneza on 31 Dec. 1808. Only NCO of that rank with Sharpe on march to Santiago and condoned semi-mutiny led by *Harper* over Sharpe's decision to escape S rather than N. Shot and killed in farmhouse action in Jan. 1809. In *SR*.

Winckler, Col. Yes-man staff officer at P. of Orange's HQ Waterloo. In *SW*.

windage The gap between ball and side of barrel of firearm – difference between calibre of ball and bore of barrel. Some gap needed to allow gases caused on firing to escape, but too much adversely affected the muzzle velocity, range and accuracy of the shot.

Windham, Lt-Col. Brian Replaced *Lt-Col. Lawford* as CO of *S. Essex* at Elvas in Mar. 1812, prior to the Siege of Badajoz. Made Sharpe officer in charge of wives, had *Harper* reduced to the ranks and flogged when CO's property found in *Harper*'s pack. Commanded the bn in the (fictional) attack on San Roque. Killed by *Col. Leroux* on 17 Jun. 1812 on Roman bridge at Salamanca when *Leroux* broke parole and escaped. In *SC, SS*.

Windham, Mrs Jessica Wife of *Lt-Col. Windham*.

Wise, Lt Coy. officer in 5/60th under *Capt Frederickson*; at *Abrados* Dec. 1812. In *SEn*.

Witherspoon, Capt. Officer in 15th H. Killed at Waterloo. In *SW*.

Worcester, Lt 10th Hussars who, with Capt. Wyndham, almost captured King Joseph after B. of Vitória.

Wyndham, Capt. Henry Officer of 14th LD who, with Lt Lord Worcester, almost captured King Joseph after Vitória, but secured his silver chamber pot instead. Helped close the gate at Hougoumont Farm at Waterloo while serving with 2nd Coldstream Guards. Afterwards Gen. Sir Henry Wyndham.

York, Frederick Augustus, Duke of b. 1763; youngest son of George III. Commanded disastrous expedition to Flanders in 1794. Able military reformer and administrator who was C-in-C at Horse Guards during Pen. War, except for 2 years from 1809–11 when scandal involving his mistress became public. Only royal duke and C-in-C who became godfather to daughter of a private soldier (Peter McMullin of 27th Foot). The child was Frederica McMullin 'of Waterloo', whose father had both arms blown off (and survived) during the battle. Died 1827; buried St George's Chapel, Windsor.

Zadorra R. (MAP 29) Fr. took up defensive position behind this river at Vitória, but failed to destroy or barricade 10 bridges. *S. Essex* attacked the Gamorra Mayor bridge; suffered heavily taking the village at second attempt under Sharpe, but failed to capture the bridge.

Ziegler, Capt. Commanded sqn of Prussian cav. which rescued Sharpe NW of Charleroi on 15 Jun. 1815, when he was being chased by Fr. cav. In *SW*.

Ziethen, Lt-Gen. Graf von b. 1770; commanded Prussian 1 Corps at Waterloo. His troops guarded Sambre crossing, including bridge at Charleroi, and were first to clash with advancing Fr. d. 1848.

Bibliography

London is place of publication, unless otherwise specified.

Brett-James, Anthony, *Life in Wellington's Army*, Allen & Unwin Ltd., 1972

Chandler, David, *The Campaigns of Napoleon*, Macmillan, 1966

Cope, Sir William H., *The History of the Rifle Brigade*, Chatto and Windus, 1877

Costello, Edward, *Adventures of a Soldier*, Colburn and Company, 1852

Dalton, Charles, *The Waterloo Roll Call*, Eyre and Spottiswoode, 1904

Elting, John R., *Swords Around a Throne*, Weidenfeld & Nicolson, 1877

Fortescue, Sir John W., *A History of the British Army* (vols 5–9), Macmillan and Co., 1910–1930

Fuller, Col. J. F. C., *Sir John Moore's System of Training*, Hutchinson and Co., 1925

Gates, David, *The Spanish Ulcer*, Guild Publishing, 1986

Glover, Michael, *Wellington's Army*, David and Charles, 1977

Haythornethwaite, Philip, *Uniforms of the Peninsular War 1807–1814*, Blandford Press, Poole, 1978

—— *Weapons & Equipment of the Napoleonic Wars*, Blandford Press, Poole, 1979

Hibbert, Christopher (ed.), *The Recollections of Rifleman Harris*, Leo Cooper, 1970

James, Charles, *The Regimental Companion* (3 volumes), 1811

Kincaid, Capt. Sir John, *Adventures in the Rifle Brigade*, Maclaren and Co., 1909

Longford, Elizabeth, *Wellington, The Years of the Sword*, World Books, 1971

Lachouque, Henry, *The Anatomy of Glory*, Arms and Armour Press, 1978

MacGilchrist, John, *The Life and Exploits of Lord Dundonald*, James Blackwood, 1861

Maxwell, Herbert, *The Life of Wellington*, Sampson Low, Marston and Co., 1907

Myatt, Frederick, *The Soldier's Trade*, Macdonald and Janes, 1974

—— *British Sieges of the Peninsular War*, Spellmount, Staplehurst, 1987

Oman, Sir Charles W. C., *Wellington's Army*, Edward Arnold, 1912

—— *History of the Peninsular War* (7 vols), Oxford, 1902–1930

Paget, Julian, *Wellington's Peninsular War*, Leo Cooper, 1990

Rathbone, Julian, *Wellington's War*, Michael Joseph, 1984

Tute, Warren, *Cochrane*, Cassell, 1965

Ward, S. G. P., *Wellington's Headquarters*, Oxford University Press, Oxford, 1957

Weller, Jac, *Wellington in the Peninsula*, Nicholas Vane, 1962
—— *Wellington at Waterloo*, Longman, 1967
—— *Wellington in India*, Longman, 1972
Young, Norwood, *Napoleon in Exile at St Helena* (vols. 1 and 2), Stanley Paul and
    Co., 1915